I0735885

A Realm of Seers and Shifters

A TRIAL OF KINGDOMS BOOK 1

SHERRY LECLERC

TERNIAS PUBLISHING

Copyright © 2023 by **Sherry Leclerc**

All rights reserved. No part of this publication may be reproduced, distributed or transmitted in any form or by any means, without prior written permission.

Sherry Leclerc/Ternias Publishing

Sydney, Nova Scotia,

www.sherryleclerc.com

www.terniaspublishing.com

Publisher's Note: This is a work of fiction. Names, characters, places, and incidents are a product of the author's imagination. Locales and public names are sometimes used for atmospheric purposes. Any resemblance to actual people, living or dead, or to businesses, companies, events, institutions, or locales is completely coincidental.

A Realm of Seers and Shifters / Sherry Leclerc.

ISBN:

EBook: 978-1-989383-15-5

Paperback: 978-1-989383-14-8

Dedication

To Sylvain, Lance, and Max for being my rocks and for their
unending patience and support.

"It does no good to spend all your time worrying
about what may come and being blind to what you
have in the present." -Blaez

STERRENVAR
Northern Mountains
North
The Dark Lake
Darkwood
CF
NG
BF
Division Wood
EF
Fair Harbor
BF
WG
GG
Clearview
WF
EF
Fairwood
Sacred Forest
Hope Bay
WF
SG
DF
Dragonburn Mountains
Southwood

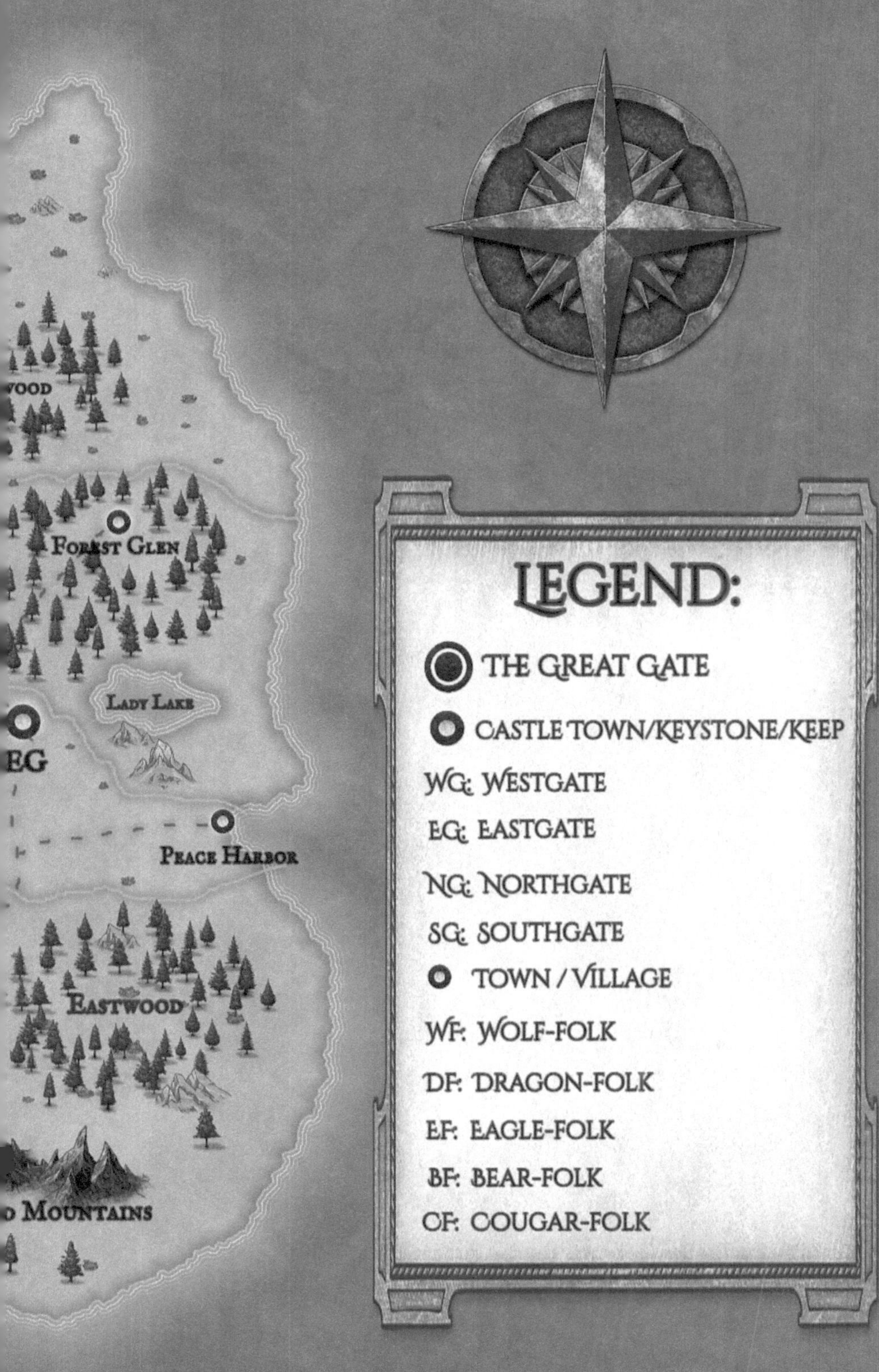

WOOD
FOREST GLEN
LADY LAKE
EG
PEACE HARBOR
EASTWOOD
MOUNTAINS
LEGEND:
THE GREAT GATE
CASTLE TOWN/KEYSTONE/KEEP
WG: WESTGATE
EG: EASTGATE
NG: NORTHGATE
SG: SOUTHGATE
TOWN / VILLAGE
WF: WOLF-FOLK
DF: DRAGON-FOLK
EF: EAGLE-FOLK
BF: BEAR-FOLK
CF: COUGAR-FOLK

Contents

CHAPTER ONE

Dark Visions

Maelona had been having more dreams than usual lately.

Not your usual kind of dreams, though. No, these were dream-visions that showed the future. That was not unusual since she was only one of an entire race of seers that regularly had dream-visions.

What was unusual was the subject—dark, violent images that tripped and looped through her mind, getting clearer each time—and the feelings of dread they left behind.

Tonight, the sounds of people screaming and the acrid stench of smoke and fire stayed with her even after she awakened.

These visions left her with the certainty that the prophecy given years ago by Sorceress Dimia was about to come to pass, no matter how much she wished to avoid it.

Keeping her eyes shut as she continued to lie on her bed, Maelona brought her hand to her sweaty brow and tried to slow her breathing and her heart rate. She could almost believe she'd been there experiencing everything herself. When she opened her eyes, however, she was greeted with the familiar sight of the small opening in the roof and just a glimpse of the stars peeking through the foliage above her hut.

"Ah, bane of my blight," she muttered to herself. "The middle of the night again." Sighing, she sat up and slung her legs over the side of her bed.

Then she froze.

All around her in the room, every small item—her wooden bowl and spoon, the knife she'd been using earlier, pieces of trimmed leather, her pants and boots; just about everything aside from the larger pieces of wooden furniture—was floating in the air.

Her eyes widened and her breaths sped up. She'd hardly had time to catch her breath from her dream, and she was already on the verge of panic again.

"Okay, calm down, calm down," she whispered to herself. She closed her eyes and inhaled deeply, holding the breath for a few beats before slowly blowing it out through her mouth. She repeated this pattern while trying to clear her mind of anything aside from the sound of her breaths and the feeling of her chest rising and falling.

When she felt calm and under control again, she opened her eyes slowly, afraid of what she'd find. Her shoulders slumped with relief when she saw everything was back where it belonged.

"Cursed magic," she swore under her breath. The stuff had ruined her life. She wished she didn't have to deal with it ever again. Yet she knew from tonight's dream-vision that her wish was pointless. She needed to come to terms with its existence in her life somehow.

Experience taught her she would not sleep again after such a vision, so she got up to prepare for the day. Staying busy would keep her mind off everything she'd just experienced, within the dream and without.

It was too early to go into the village, so she lit a candle and worked on the new outfit she was making. With her enhanced seer senses, she didn't need the extra light from the candle, but it helped her clearly distinguish the finer, more subtle details. She'd already had the valley's cobbler make her new boots in exchange for some of the leather she had collected and tanned from her hunts. Now, she spent the time until she could head to the village working on the rest of the clothing.

Seer guardians were expected to be capable of doing a lot of things independently, such as hunting, tanning, and making clothing, since they often went on long journeys. For Maelona, though, it was also a calming activity. When she was feeling stressed or upset, working with her hands gave her something to focus on so she could clear her mind.

She finished the pants just as the sun rose, and the vest about an hour later. Maelona tried them on, running her hand down over her stomach as she checked the fit of the new vest.

"Perfect. Well, I think I'm ready," she said.

Her old outfit was still usable, but she wanted to be prepared for the journey that was undoubtedly coming. Many of the villagers had recently had similar dream-visions to hers. However, she, her fellow seer champions, and their Elder always received more intense and clearer visions, because they meditated and trained their minds daily to leave themselves open to them. Not only that, but the astronomers had been watching the sky and the time of the Great Alignment was almost upon them. She needed to be prepared to leave at a moment's notice.

Maelona was happy with the fit of her new clothing; the thick leather laces up the center of her chest and along the sides of her pants currently left a small gap, which was perfect. She and the other guardians often traveled between their assigned gate towns and the seer village of Clearview in the Valley of Sight. So, they preferred to wear tough clothing that they could loosen in times of plenty and tighten in times of scarcity.

Maelona figured she would be away for longer than usual for the coming journey, so she needed two outfits that she could switch out when they needed to be cleaned. She had already packed her older clothing in her backpack, along with some other provisions, ready to go at a moment's notice. For now, she left her pack and weapons in her small wooden hut.

Like most other seers, she had built her hut around the trunk of a large tree, hidden from above by dense foliage. Unlike most of the others, however, her home was outside the village, outside the valley even, about an hour's casual walk away.

Today, she planned to visit the observatory to check in with Huet, the lead astronomer. The fastest way to get there was to descend into the valley, go through the village, cross the bridge over the river, then ascend the other side. It would allow her to check in with some people along the way.

Inside the Sacred Forest, it was sunny and warm even in the early morning, and Maelona wished it was enough to burn away the cold, foreboding feeling left behind by her dream-vision. But it clung to her, continuing to occupy a part of her mind even as she headed out.

The forest was alive as Maelona jogged along paths and through the underbrush. The canopy of the ancient trees high above shaded most of the forest floor, but there were several areas where slight breaks in the foliage allowed the sunlight to burst through. In these areas in particular, the light-loving flowers, plants, and ferns grew wild, painting the forest floor with spots of vibrant color.

The Sacred Forest was a beautiful, magically protected place where the weather was always pleasant. The trees here were ancient, tall, and strong, and life was lively and abundant. Birdsong and the buzzing of insects filled the air around her as she traveled.

The surrounding beauty and serenity stood in sharp juxtaposition to the mental images that lingered from her visions, reminding her of what the people stood to lose should she and the other three guardians fail in their missions. Not only did her people stand to lose much, but so did everyone in Sterrenvar—the humans and the magical races as well.

The trees and brush thinned only when she reached the edge of the valley and the slope became too steep to allow purchase for the larger plants. She avoided the narrow stairway that zig-zagged down the slope and made her way straight down instead, running for part of the way and sliding on the steepest parts. She had barely entered the seer village of Clearview when a small, pre-adolescent girl bound up to her, calling her name.

"Maelona! I was just coming to find you. Elder Berinon directed me to give you this."

Maelona smiled at the girl and placed a hand on her head, smoothing her light-brown hair that was a little wild from running.

"Thank you, Emm." She took the offered note from the young girl.

Emm pouted. "I really want to stay and catch up with you, but Elder Berinon warned me to go straight back to him for another errand."

When Maelona came into the village, Emm followed her around as much as possible. Even though Maelona liked her privacy, she didn't get annoyed by it. Emm was a cute, happy child, all smiles and lightness.

Maelona laughed quietly. "Well, you had best get going then. You can try to find me later when you're free."

Emm nodded, then took off at a jog. Maelona opened the note and read it. Elder Berinon Sagespirit wanted the four seer champions to meet with him at twilight. Maelona sighed and put the note in her pocket. Her journey would start even sooner than she'd feared, it seemed, and she had some things she wanted to do before she left.

She headed for the center of the village later in the day and made her way to the smithy. As she approached, a familiar face came into view and she smiled fondly.

"Aleyn," she greeted him.

One of the first people she met in the village was Aleyn Whitesteel. It was during one of her childhood visits with her father. After she came to live here a little over forty years ago, they became close. There was a time when Aleyn showed interest in exploring whether there could be more between them, but Maelona hadn't been ready to consider that kind of relationship. She probably would never be with anyone.

She had to admit, though, that Aleyn impressed her. His time spent mining and forging the raw materials he collected, painstakingly hammering metal into weapons and tools, left the tall, dark-haired man heavily muscled. Yet, he never seemed to make anyone feel uneasy or physically intimidated. His friendly smile and cheerful voice helped in that regard.

"Maelona!" he said, smiling. "I am so glad you came to see me before you leave."

"So you know then?" she questioned as she moved in for a quick embrace.

He sighed as he pulled back. "There's been no announcement yet, but I've been having strange dream-visions. And if I have been having them, then surely you and the other champions have had even more."

Maelona nodded solemnly. "You are not wrong. Emm delivered a note from Elder Berinon just as I was entering the village. We will meet with him this evening, and I have no doubt we will receive our traveling orders."

"Well, I guess it's good that I decided to give you these today, then." Aleyn's voice cracked, but he quickly cleared his throat and pasted his smile back on.

Maelona looked at her good friend and noticed the strain of emotion hiding behind his gaze. He turned and retrieved a large, long, cloth-wrapped parcel from a back table.

"I made these for your day of birth celebration, but as you won't be here, I thought it fitting to give them to you now. You will have eighty-four years behind you, right?" he asked as he turned back toward her, and she nodded in response. "Only sixteen more until you reach the century mark."

Maelona was surprised that Aleyn remembered. She was younger than most of her friends, but seers lived so long that the day of her birth usually passed without notice. It probably would have again this year if not for the dark times looming on the horizon. An uncertain future caused people to take less for granted.

Maelona carefully accepted the package and placed it on the bench before pulling back the thick fabric wrapped around it. There were a set of daggers, six throwing knives, and a short sword the likes of which she had never seen before.

Finally, there was her favorite weapon, rendered from a dark-gray metal she was not familiar with. It was a two-foot-long cylinder with a subtle oval shape about the size of the tip of her thumb at the center. This button was flush with the surrounding area, making it difficult to activate unintentionally.

She pushed her thumb in and another one-foot section extended on each side, turning it into a four-foot-long short staff. She pressed the button a second time, and another section shot out on each side, transforming it into a six-foot long staff. Now that it was at its full length, she rotated it slowly, taking in the ornate designs carved along its length.

"This is beautiful, Aleyn. You should not have gone through the trouble."

He shrugged. "It is a fitting gift from one soul friend to another. Not only is your day of birth coming up, but you are leaving on a long journey. Scholars will assuredly write the coming battles into formal accounts of Sterrenvar's history, so I thought you should have weapons fit for the occasion."

Finally, she pressed and held the button, placed the tip to the ground and put her free hand to the other end. Pushing down, she returned it to the original two-foot cylinder.

She smiled and looked at Aleyn. "You know me so well."

"Of course I do. I know the retractable staff is your favorite, and I know exactly how you like to use it. But Maelona," he said, pointing at the other weapons, "you are going into battle. Use the sharp pointy ones as well. Some enemies deserve no mercy."

Maelona nodded noncommittally. Seer history taught her he was right, but she was still not comfortable with that idea.

She placed the retractable staff back on the bench and lifted the daggers. She turned them in her hands, feeling the weight and balance of them as they glinted in the early morning light. Aleyn had intricately carved patterns into their hilts—symbols that were important to the seer people, including one that had three spiraling arms reaching out before curling back in towards the center. It was the symbol of the three-in-one—the Ternias.

Maelona quickly glanced up at her friend—all seers knew of the prophecy and the importance of the Ternias to the future of Sterrenvar, but she suddenly wondered if his including it on the daggers meant he knew its particular connection to her. She didn't see the extra signs of worry in his expression that she knew would be there if he did, however, and she let out a breath she hadn't realized she'd been holding.

She cleared her throat. "These are exquisite, Aleyn. They must have taken a long time to forge."

"I have been working on them since my return from the Dragonburn Mountains. I found the metal I used there. The nomadic tribes that sometimes stay on the eastern part of the mountain range call it galanite. It isn't as flashy as gold or silver, but it's stronger and lighter than any other metal I have worked with. I thought it would be perfect for your new weapons. I completed them last week, and it would seem the timing is just about perfect, since you now have need of them sooner than expected."

"Speaking of the Dragonburn Mountains, did you find any signs of the dragon-folk rumored to live there?"

"There are recent signs if you know what to look for. But they are just as reclusive as always. I've never seen one in the flesh—not in recent years, anyway."

Maelona shook her head, but otherwise didn't comment. She looked at the weapons again.

"Hey," Aleyn said. "What's wrong?"

She shook her head. "Nothing. I'm thinking about what I need to do to before I leave."

"Tell that to someone who doesn't know you," Aleyn said. She looked up and gave him a small smile, and he reached out and squeezed her shoulder. "I will miss you as well," he said.

Maelona pursed her lips together to hold back her emotion and focused on the gifts Aleyn had so painstakingly created for her. "These are all magnificent, my friend, but I did not wear my straps or belt today."

Aleyn gave her a big, warm smile. "Not to worry." He reached beneath the counter. "With new weapons, one should always have good, fitted holders." He plopped down a few thick strips of sturdy leather on the countertop. They were long, notched, and had decorative patterns matching those on the weapons branded into the leather and etched into the metal clasps. Maelona smiled and let out an amused huff.

"You have thought of everything, haven't you?"

Not only was Aleyn the village blacksmith, but he was recognized as the best metallurgist the people had known since the ancient forgers millennia ago. Maelona looked over each of the weapons, getting a feel for them and admiring the workmanship. She knew she would not find such high quality, reliable weapons anywhere else.

Tears burned at the back of her eyes, threatening to fall. Carrying these weapons would be like carrying a piece of her heart with her through the coming journey and struggles.

Maelona donned the straps and belt and put her new weapons in their places. Then she turned to her friend and said, "I shall carry them with me always, Aleyn, and care for them as if they were part of myself."

"I know you will," he said. Then he went quiet and looked down. "Are you going to the observatory today?"

"I am. I will go there straight from here."

"Listen, if you find out anything new. . ."

She placed a hand on his forearm. "Even if I find out nothing, I will still let you know." She gave her friend a last nod, turned, and continued on through the village.

Maelona crossed the low bridge over the narrowest part of the Forestsong river. She reached the bottom of a steep wooden stairway—a mirror of the one on the other side of the valley—and began the ascent without pause. She walked on for another ten minutes before coming to another stairway. This one climbed the side of a rocky cliff to the observatory that sat just below the top of the tree line. The designers and builders specifically positioned it here to have a good view of the stars above while also remaining hidden from any prying, unfriendly eyes. It was one of the many defenses put in place to protect the Sacred Forest from any evil forces.

"Come in, come in, Maelona," a voice greeted her the moment she opened the observatory door. The sound was a little muffled since the old astronomer didn't turn to face her as he spoke. His eyes remained fixed to the largest of the telescopes he used to track the movements of the celestial bodies; his hands, up to brace and guide the tool's movements, partially blocked his face.

"Wouldn't it be easier to see the stars at night?" she asked.

"Of course. But that doesn't mean nothing is visible during the day."

"Anything new, Huet?"

"There have been no changes in the timeline for the Great Alignment, if that is what you wish to know."

"Well, of course it is." She huffed out an amused breath through her nose.

The white-haired man pulled back from his equipment and turned to look at her. He was old, wise, and experienced enough to be an Elder alongside Berinon. However, Huet devoted his life to the art and science of tracking and predicting celestial events, leaving no extra time to give to anything else. He lived in his observatory, only leaving when he needed to go to the village for food and supplies. If someone wanted to speak with him, they usually had to come here, or speak with one of his apprentices when they made an appearance.

"You know," Huet said, "it is not very often that something changes in my observations, and when it does, I let Berinon know. But you. . ." he paused and shook his head, "you keep asking as if you hope we can change the movement of the stars themselves. We cannot."

Maelona sighed. "I know, but there is always a slight chance that something else could have moved into your field of vision, or you could have updated your equipment."

"Hmm. Right." He descended the few steps of the platform and shuffled toward her. "I know why you are worried, Maelona. It's the prophecy, isn't it?"

She hesitated, wondering if she should admit it. But he would undoubtedly see through any excuses, so she nodded.

"The prophecy is not a bad thing, Mae."

Maelona's breath caught. Huet called her Mae sometimes because he had known her father, and it was what he had called her most of the time. The little reminder momentarily gave her a sharp pang of loss and longing.

"'There is a ray of hope that can burn through the darkness.' Do not forget that line."

She took a deep breath. Remembering that line and believing in her ability to make it happen were two completely different issues.

"I know it isn't really a bad thing, Huet. But it allows for a chance of failure."

Huet walked closer until he stood only a step or two in front of her. He raised his hands to cup her face and met her eyes with his steely, sure ones. "You won't fail."

"But how can you be so certain? I can't even stomach having any magic around me, so how can I not fail?"

"You will not fail." He repeated it with such conviction that she could almost believe it was true. Almost.

Huet had been close to her parents, especially her father, when he was still alive. Therefore, he was one of the few who knew her secret, knew what her tie to the prophecy was.

She just wished she could have the same level of faith in herself that he had in her.

CHAPTER TWO

The Mission

Maelona arrived at the gathering place early. The others wouldn't arrive for another hour. But, after dropping by to update Aleyn, she'd completed her errands in the village and came here.

The gathering place was a large, thatch-roofed, wooden structure where the seers came together to discuss matters of importance. She didn't enter the open-air building right away, though. First, she walked around it, taking it in from every angle. Would it still be here after the battles to come?

She found a large boulder that sat a short way into the woods, climbed up over its cool, rough surface, found a spot that was smooth, and sat down. The only sounds she could hear were the chirping, whistling songs of local birds and the sighing of the leaves as the wind blew through them. She closed her eyes and breathed in, smelling the petrichor and the surrounding trees. The sweet scent of a flowering bush that grew all throughout the forest around the village wafted through the air, bringing a sense of familiarity and peace.

A peace that could not last. Not unless they fought for it. And not unless they won.

Maelona opened her eyes again, focusing back on the wall-less building with thick, carved wooden columns that held up the roof. Would this place still stand six moon-cycles from now?

Maelona hadn't come to live in Clearview until her adolescence—she had around forty-four years at the time—but she had visited her father often before then. He had taken her here whenever he had to take part in meetings—which was often given he'd been the only seer sorcerer.

These meetings were never taken lightly, and tonight's gathering promised to be one of the most important in centuries. That thought, and the knowledge of her part in what was to come, caused a moment of panic. She took a deep breath and went through the teachings of her father in her mind to bolster her courage.

Her father had explained the core of the seers' belief system to her when she was just a child—before she understood its importance. Because of their particular gifts, seers considered themselves the Guardians of the Realm. They believed whole-heartedly that the Universe gifted them their abilities so they could protect the realm and all the beings in it. It created and placed them here for this purpose. To do this, they watched for any new threats to the realm. As much as possible, they acted from the shadows in unobtrusive ways.

She was taught by her father that small acts of evil can ruin the world. In response to this, the solemn oath of the seers was to be the antithesis of this darkness. They influenced or cured the corrupted, bringing them back to the side of good through subtle, almost invisible actions. Only in cases of extreme threat and danger did they play a larger, more visible part in the world.

This would be one of those times.

Seers were taller and stronger than the others that they had sworn to protect. Her father told her that there was a time when humans, and even other magical beings, looked at the seers with suspicion and mistrust. The demonkin had spread rumors about them, and because of their mysterious nature, their size, strength, and ability to see the future, it had been easy for the evil beings to convince the humans that the seers were the enemy.

Some of her people pushed back when the visions concerning this situation started. It was quite ironic to her they would be the ones fighting to bring everyone together, fighting to protect the humans and the Folk, when her people had been painted in a negative light by them in the past. However, her father would never have allowed that to keep him from protecting them. He'd told her that those who had turned on the seers were also victims, this time of the demonkin's lies and manipulation.

It was her father's beliefs—and his goodness—that gave Maelona the strength to face what was to come. To do what he would have done. After all, it was her duty and responsibility to honor his memory. It was the least she could do for him.

But first, she needed to get past her greatest fear.

Maelona was still sitting on that large rock, lost in her memories, when Elder Berinon arrived with Huet at his side. She was surprised to see that the bright day had given way to a clear and vibrant sunset. How had she been stuck in her head for so long?

She jumped down from the rock and followed the older men inside.

"Maelona Mistreaver," Elder Berinon greeted with a nod of his head when she entered, as was the custom.

"Berinon Sagespirit." She nodded in return.

Huet smiled at her. "I am happy to see you again so soon."

Maelona gave him a nod, and a smile that was a little strained. She was happy to see him, but his presence at the meeting could only mean one thing. She was now certain that she and her fellow guardians would leave soon.

Berinon greeted the three other seer champions as they entered the gathering place, one after another. Maelona nodded to each of them, wishing that somehow that slight gesture could tell them how much they meant to her; to show the parts of herself that she was never brave enough to share.

Many dangers lay ahead for all of them, and the foreboding feeling from last night's dream-vision still lingered. The entire realm was in danger, and none more so than herself and her fellow champions. Since the future was uncertain, she allowed herself to really look at her friends as they entered, hoping against the odds this would not be the last time she saw them.

Maelona had become close with the others over the years and would trust them with her life. Yet, she hadn't let them in completely. There were always parts of herself she kept hidden from others. Now the time of the prophecy was near and the potential for loss was high, and she regretted the distance she always kept. But they were certain to find out more about her soon, anyway.

Maelona, Talwyn, Edun, and Ryia sat on a bench near the center of the space and Elder Berinon and Huet stood in front of them.

"We are here tonight because of the visions we've all had. The present danger affects not only our village and people: the future of our entire island realm is at stake."

Berinon turned to Maelona and said, "Would you like to be the first to share your dream-vision with the others, Maelona?"

Maelona nodded and took a deep breath. "I saw us gathered together, fighting demonkin in a town that was nothing but fire and ruin," she said. "We rescued many, but enemy demonkin injured or killed countless more. Many allies accompanied us."

"Well, that's good, right?" Edun interrupted.

"Of course, but my dream-vision didn't end there," Maelona said. "We had many allies, and we fought back the demonkin horde. Just when we were ready to cheer our victory, however, a figure stalked out from between two burned-out huts. There was smoke everywhere, and it hid him at first. As he walked forward, I still couldn't see his face. His cowl hid it, making it shadowed and unclear."

"You say 'he'," Talwyn—her tall, fiery, red-haired friend—said. "Are you certain it's a man? I haven't seen anything that would tell us."

"Not from anything I've seen either, but I have heard some demonkin call him 'Emperor' in my visions. Emperor, not Empress. I'm assuming based on that, though I've never seen this person uncloaked."

"Emperor. *Pfft.*" Edun said. "He hasn't won anything yet, and he's calling himself that? I get the feeling he's quite arrogant."

"I haven't yet seen the face of this enemy in any of my visions," Ryia said, ignoring Edun's comment. Ryia was the oldest among them, though she did not look it. She was the most petite of the four guardians and kept her hair short—though she did like to use her inner-sight to change the color often. But her youthful appearance belied her wisdom. If she hadn't seen the enemy's visage, chances are that none had.

"Nor I," Edun said, as if he'd read Maelona's thoughts.

"Do you think this could mean he is someone we're familiar with?" Talwyn asked. All four guardians looked at Berinon.

"It is possible," he said, "but I don't believe that's the reason. There's too much blurred from our Sight. Too many holes in our visions—all centered around one being. It is as if there is a powerful sorcerer blocking us."

Maelona sucked in a sharp breath.

"Is that even possible?" Talwyn asked, eyebrows lifted and eyes wide in alarm.

"If the being was powerful enough," Berinon said.

"That person would have to be immensely powerful to block visions on such a large scale," Ryia said.

"Indeed," Berinon confirmed.

"Hmm. Perhaps he has reason to be arrogant after all, Edun said. "Maybe we should stay out of this one. Stay hidden in the forest. It's not like the humans, or the Folk, have appreciated it when we've put our lives on the line for their sakes."

"I hope you're joking," Talwyn said, her voice edged with irritation.

"Of course I am," Edun responded. "About the not helping, anyway. The part about them not appreciating our sacrifices is true. Otherwise, the humans would not have turned on us 300 years ago. I am curious, though, why we fight so hard to protect people who fear and mistrust us."

Edun was large and well-muscled, with light-blond hair. Like Aleyn, though, his personality was not as intimidating as his looks. He joked a lot and was quite sarcastic, and apparently that included at times as serious as this. Maelona shook her head.

Berinon heaved a sigh and clasped his hands together behind his back. "We protect them because they are not equipped to survive in this world. They were not meant to exist in a world of magical peoples when they have no magic themselves."

What? She was not expecting their Elder to answer the question at all, let alone tell them something like this.

"What do you mean?" asked Edun. Maelona glanced around, and everyone except Huet looked just as curious as Edun.

Berinon took them all in. Edun was looking at their elder with his head tilted and eyes narrowed.

"Our people, and our Elders in particular, have been keeping histories of Sterrenvar for longer back than you can fathom. Three-thousand years ago, the Great Gate was used to bring demons across from another realm to fortify the Dark Sorcerer's army, as you already know. What you don't know, however, is that the magical stone circle existed long before, and that was not the first time it was used."

"Let me make sure I understand," Ryia said. "The humans crossed over through the Great Gate like the demons did? They don't come from Sterrenvar?"

"Yes," Berinon replied. "That is exactly what I'm saying."

"How?" Talwyn asked. "Was there another sorcerer involved?"

"The full details are not clear, but the Elders who recorded the histories had a theory, based on incomplete records from the time. They believed that a stone formation like our Great Gate also exists in the human world. Nine-thousand years ago, there was a great battle near its location. A large group of humans was targeted, and many fled. In the chaos of their escape, they discovered this formation and accidentally ended up here in our world. Since the Great Gate is close, it was our people who first discovered them. No one knew how to return them to their world, so our ancestors taught them how to survive here and helped them get settled."

Maelona shook her head. Like many, she'd assumed that the Dark Sorcerer from three-thousand years ago had created the Great Gate. She was amazed that it existed so long before that, and yet it was still standing and still powerful.

"Why weren't we told of this?" Talwyn asked. "Wouldn't it have been easier for us to do our duty as guardians if we'd had this information?"

Maelona didn't see how it could have made a difference other than in a guardian's attitude to their job, which could go either way.

"This story was recorded in a tome meant only for the eyes of future Elders. There was concern that this information could cause tension in the realm—that it could cause magical folk to look at humans as invaders who do not belong."

"If what you're saying is true, they don't, do they?" Edun asked.

Berinon looked at Edun with raised brows. "They've lived here for almost nine-thousand years. I doubt we can still say that. But I am hoping this information can at least help you understand why we continue to protect them. We have done so since they first arrived here. It was a duty we assigned ourselves and carried down through the generations."

Much that Maelona's father told her made so much more sense now. She was a little annoyed that he'd not told her, but at least she knew now, and it clarified so many of his teachings.

Huet, still standing next to Berinon, cleared his throat. "Let's get back to the topic at hand," he said.

"Of course, you are right," Berinon said, nodding. "Our time is limited." He looked at Maelona again. "Did you see anything else in your dream-vision?"

"Yes," she replied. "And it supports your theory about a powerful sorcerer. In my vision, the figure came from between two huts and, as he came closer, he raised his hand. It was glowing brightly, as if he were holding a ball of blue light. Just as he was about to throw it, I awoke."

Maelona, as one of the few who was told the full prophecy given by Dimia, had known they would face a sorcerer. However, that this sorcerer could block or blur significant details about himself from all seers was enough to make her doubt their chances of success. They would need all the help they could get.

"In my dream-visions," Ryia added, "I saw white flying beasts, but they weren't close enough to be really clear."

"Ainmith," Edun said.

Everyone was silent, no doubt considering the implications. Ainmith were large, winged creatures with bodies shaped like overgrown wolves, only their front legs were longer than the back. Most of them were completely white. If the Dark Sorcerer and his demonkin had tamed ainmith to use in battle, that means they would have an aerial advantage.

"It is clear through our visions that our hope that the current alignment would pass unnoticed, or at least not used for evil, is not the case. It is also clear that the time the prophecy spoke of is almost upon us." Berinon turned and nodded to Huet, who stepped forward to address them.

"According to my calculations, we have a little over five moon-cycles before the celestial alignment. It will happen on the twentieth Diel of the Second Moon-cycle, during the Supermoon event. The very moment that the planets Chephus and Agarus align with the Supermoon will be when the magical power at the Source will be at its highest peak, and the most stable. That will be this sorcerer's best chance to open the Great Gate."

Around five centuries ago, in anticipation of the next alignment, a keystone was put in place at each of the four axes of the ley lines in order to limit the amount of power readily accessible at any moment. Keeps, castles, and castle towns were built over the keystones to hide and protect them, and there was always a seer champion assigned as a guardian to each of the gate towns, as an extra measure of protection. When she became a guardian, Maelona was assigned to watch over Eastgate.

Talwyn, who was standing next to Maelona with her arms crossed over her chest, shook her head. "Less than five moon-cycles. I think this sorcerer must have shielded his plans from our visions for some time. It's doubtful that he only recently decided to use the Great Gate when the Great Alignment comes."

"He would only need to keep his final plans to himself until the last possible moment, and to shield himself from us," Berinon said. "As long as he didn't make his plans known, and as long as he kept himself protected, there would be no way for us to foresee what he was plotting."

"That much power is already formidable," Edun said. "I certainly hope he cannot block more than himself."

"Since they are using ainmith, chances are good that they're hiding out in the north." He turned to Ryia, who was the Guardian of Northgate. "You will need to be on your guard even more than usual, Ryia. If they don't already have a foothold in Northgate, they will at least have spies. We can only pray they won't have accessed the keystone by the time you get there."

Berinon swept his eyes across them. "I think we all can agree that with such an obviously powerful foe, one who has the potential to travel and attack by air, we need to gather as many powerful allies as we can." He looked at Talwyn. "The last time Aleyn mined galanite in the Dragonburn and Nomad Mountains, he informed me that there were signs that the Dragon-folk were still hiding out nearby. Talwyn, I would like you to head to the mountains to find them. If you can convince them to stand with us, they will make a truly powerful ally, which will improve our chances of success manyfold. Perhaps they can help you defend Southgate before the time comes to march to the Great Gate."

Talwyn nodded solemnly.

That would not be a simple task. The reclusive Dragon-folk had been in hiding for centuries for a reason.

Elder Berinon turned to the others. "You will all need to gather as many others to our side as possible. The more winged-folk we can convince to stand with us, the better. We will need aerial support both to counter the ainmith and to serve as a means of communications between the castle towns."

He slowly paced back and forth. "For the past three hundred years, since our kind was mercilessly hunted to near extinction, we have hidden ourselves away and ventured out of the safety of our valley only when our people were directly or indirectly threatened. Whenever we interacted with the outside, it was from the shadows, for the good of our own people and for the good of the realm of Sterrenvar. It is now time for us to step out of those shadows and make ourselves known.

"As seer champions, as our four guardians, you have prepared for this. In the morning, you will embark upon a journey that will take us outside of the safety and shelter of anonymity. However, we cannot turn our backs. Our entire island realm is under threat:

our ways of life, our cultures, our freedom, our peace, and those we care for deeply. Even though the attacks will start outside of our forest, the world is a living organism, and what affects one affects us all. Make no mistake, we will feel it.

"That our visions of these events only started coming to us recently, that none of us can see much about this foe—these things tell us that our new enemy is both immensely powerful and cunning enough to block us and leave us with little time to prepare. Keeping these things in mind will help your strength of conviction when convincing others to join with us. And they should also serve as a reminder to you all to, please, be careful. Be vigilant. Keep your guards up."

Their Elder stopped pacing and faced them again. "While you will travel separately, each with your own job to do, do not forget that you are all pieces of the whole. You each will need to complete your tasks if we are to be successful in bringing the realm through the dark times that are upon us. Keep each other up to date." With this last, he looked at Maelona meaningfully, and she nodded to him in acknowledgment.

"But what of the prophecy?" Ryia asked. "Did the prophecy not state that we will find a magical item that could save us if we lost the keystones? The Ternias—the three-in-one? I believe the wording was, 'The Ternias can save us if all else fails.' Will you send someone else to search for it while we go to the gate towns? Given its potential importance, that should be a priority, should it not?"

Berinon frowned. "Yes, the Ternias. We already have the Ternias."

"We do?" Ryia, Edun, and Talwyn all said at the same time.

"Then is it even necessary to protect the keystones?" Edun asked.

"The key words to that part of the prophecy are, 'if all else fails.'" Berinon clasped his hands behind his back, sighed, and dropped his head to his chest. He stayed like that for a moment before looking at them once again. He was deciding something, and Maelona had a good idea what that was.

She fidgeted and wiped her hands on her pants. He could soon reveal something about her she had never shared with her friends herself. How would they feel about that?

"There are only a privileged few who have heard the details of the prophecy, in its entirety," Berinon said. "You have not. The Elders of Dimia's time—and those since—kept one important detail from everyone, including the guardians, for the safety of the Ternias." Berinon met the eyes of each of the guardians. "But, let me be clear—using the Ternias will be a last resort. You must do your utmost to protect the keystones and hope that we will never have to use the Ternias."

"But why?" Edun asked. "Is it dangerous?"

"This whole situation is dangerous, my young friend. But it is most dangerous for the bearer."

"Wait. Does that mean. . ." Ryia began, not finishing her sentence. Her eyes were wide, though, and Maelona could tell that she had guessed at least part of it.

Berinon nodded. "Only one person can take the Ternias to the Great Gate. Only one person was born with what it takes to do so, and the prophecy left us clues enough to discover who that person must be."

The others stilled around Maelona, momentarily stunned into silence. Maelona let out the breath she'd been holding. Berinon had changed one minor detail.

"Waiting until now to tell you was necessary in order to keep that person safe. We could not allow any mention of it to get out. I trust you all, of course, but there are many ways someone can unintentionally reveal a secret—someone overhearing, someone talking in their sleep. We could take no chances with the Ternias. You all now need this information, but once you learn the true identity of the bearer, you must keep it to yourselves. Never mention it outside of our circle."

"But who is it?" Edun asked. "Is it someone we know?"

Berinon nodded once, then turned to look at Maelona. Soon, she was under the scrutiny of everyone in the room. She shifted in her seat and ran her palms along the legs of her pants again.

"I have foreseen that help will come to you unexpectedly on your way to see the Sorceress, Maelona," Berinon said solemnly. "I suggest you accept it. The more support and protection you have, the better."

She could practically feel the weight of everyone's gazes on her. But it was nowhere near the weight of her monumental task, her purpose, pressing down upon her shoulders.

"Maelona! Wait!" Talwyn's voice called from behind.

They had just finished the meeting and everyone had dispersed, off to prepare for leaving the next morning.

Or so Maelona had thought. Apparently, Talwyn had other ideas—not that this surprised her.

She paused and turned to let Talwyn catch up to her. The first thing her friend and fellow guardian did was wrap her arms around her.

Maelona stood stiffly for a moment before raising a hand to pat Talwyn's back.

Her friend pulled back, still gripping her shoulders, and looked into her eyes. "Why did you never tell me, Little Sister? Did you not trust me?"

Maelona shook her head. "That's not it at all. I was told not to speak of it until the time was right. Apparently, Elder Berinon decided tonight was that time." She sighed in resignation. "Logically, I knew this was going to be announced at some point. But to be honest, I was hoping someone would discover they were mistaken, and I wasn't the person the prophecy referred to after all."

Talwyn grabbed her by the hand, pulled her along, and sat her on a downed tree trunk that rested almost horizontally to the ground. Then she sat next to Maelona and put an arm around her.

"On the one hand, I wish you'd felt comfortable enough to confide in me."

"I do."

Talwyn shook her head and squeezed Maelona's shoulder. "No, you don't. You hold yourself back from everyone, even those you consider closest to you."

Maelona frowned. "I'm sorry."

"You needn't apologize. You have your reasons. And I understand Elder Berinon's reasoning in this matter. But Maelona, if there was ever a time to let me in, to let us in, this is it. Your life is in great danger. You need to allow yourself to rely on us, to count on us to do our parts. Don't be afraid to ask for help if you need it."

"I'm uncertain what you could do. We'll be far apart, since we are all heading to our own assigned gate towns."

"That is true, and I'm not sure how much we can help, either. But you need to keep in contact regularly. You are the only one of us who can reach outward. Don't be stubborn and keep everything to yourself. I will make sure I meditate and rest regularly to leave my mind open for your messages. I will pass on any information that could be important to you when you contact us. You can share anything with me. I hope you understand that. Even if it's just venting about the pressure you are under."

Maelona smiled at her friend. "You make it sound as if I'm the only one in danger here. You must convince a group of Dragon-folk to come out of hiding and join our cause. Ryia is going to Northgate, where it is likely the Dark Sorcerer has already extended his reach. And only the Universe knows what Edun will encounter between here and Westgate."

Talwyn smiled at her and cupped her cheeks in her hands. "Yes, but you are the baby among us. You will only have eighty-four years next week. We have every right to worry over you, so don't deny me the honor."

Maelona shook her head as far as Talwyn's hold would allow.

"Besides, none of us bear the Ternias." Talwyn slid her hands down to grip her biceps. "You are the person fated to stop the Dark Sorcerer if all else fails. We do not know who he is, what he knows, or what he is capable of. If he somehow learns about the prophecy or that you bear the Ternias . . ."

Maelona's heart rate sped up, and she had to concentrate to bring it back under control. She knew Talwyn was worried about her and was probably panicking a little, but Maelona already knew what rested on her shoulders and was struggling not to panic herself. Hearing Talwyn say it frankly like this did not help.

Talwyn looked down and took a deep breath. After a moment, she met Maelona's gaze again. "I don't understand why Berinon is asking you to go to Eastgate if you must be the one to carry it. Why put you in more danger like that? Why not wait until the alignment is near and send you directly to the Great Gate? He could send a champion—a guardian trainee—to Eastgate in your stead."

"It is because of the prophecy. It says—among many other things—that I will gain something I need on my journeys." She smiled at her friend. "Besides, I have an in with the Sorceress, and she is very influential. I'm sure she can help me convince all the animal-folk in the area to help us at the Great Gate."

Talwyn shoved her gently. "You joke, but it is true. It's been a long time since I've seen the Sorceress. Pass my well-wishes along to her."

"Of course."

Talwyn sighed. "Just promise me you'll look for me at the Great Gate. Promise me you'll allow Edun, Ryia, and me to help you. Don't be stubborn and do something stupid like try to sacrifice yourself to save us. Protecting the Great Gate, protecting Sterrenvar, these are our duties as well."

"But . . ."

"No, no buts." She gave Maelona a little shake. "Promise me!"

Maelona saw the familiar stubborn spark of fire in Talwyn's eyes—the one that always said there was no point in opposing her because she was determined to get what she wanted.

She sighed. "Fine. I will do as you ask, Talwyn, as long as you promise to trust in me and my abilities. Don't just jump in when I can handle it myself in some misguided attempt to protect the girl you adopted as your 'Little Sister' forty-odd years ago."

Talwyn pursed her lips and narrowed her eyes. Maelona lifted an eyebrow and pinned her with what she hoped was her own stubborn look. They sat there, staring at each other, until Talwyn finally broke. "Okay, fine. I will attempt to—"

"Talwyn."

"Alright." She held her hands up in surrender. "I promise." She stood up and brushed off her pants, then reached out a hand to help Maelona up.

"It's time for the both of us to go pack for tomorrow." Talwyn said. She turned to leave, then paused and looked back at Maelona. "Just take care of yourself. Take no unnecessary chances, okay?"

Maelona nodded. "Of course. And you as well."

They both headed in opposite directions. Maelona had only taken a few steps when Talwyn called out to her again.

"Oh, I almost forgot!"

Maelona turned to look at her.

"We won't be here next week, so I will say it now—happy day of your birth."

Maelona smiled at her fondly and waved before turning away to head down the path once again.

CHAPTER THREE

Strangers & Allies

In his wolf form, Blaez watched from the underbrush where the forest gave way to the grassy bank of a sparkling lake. It was mid-morning, the sun just high enough to warm the air. The light breeze was enough to carry the scents of the trees and the surrounding earth, but not enough to bring the scent of the person he'd been following from where she stood by the water, probably a hundred paces away.

The dark-haired, dark-eyed woman removed her pack and straps full of weapons, stripped down to her linen undergarments, and waded in.

After shadowing her for three diels, Blaez became more and more curious, wanting to learn more about her before making his presence known. And, he had to admit to himself; he was becoming strangely protective of this female trekking through the woods alone.

It made little sense when he considered it. He had watched her traveling through the forest and he had seen for himself that she was skilled at hunting and avoiding predators. . . or perhaps they were avoiding her. One thing he was certain of was that she was accustomed to taking care of herself. So why had the Sorceress sent him to meet her, and why were his protective instincts flaring?

As he looked at her now, wading deeper into the lake, he couldn't help but think that there was more to her than first meets the eye. He could clearly see the lean yet well-defined musculature along her legs, arms, and back. He had never seen a woman so well-muscled before, even though the Wolf-folk had many powerful females. This young woman looked strong, but still distinctly feminine.

The woman washed her leather clothing carefully before rinsing them and spreading them on a flat rock at the edge of the water to dry. She unwound her hair, which had been braided and twisted up elaborately so that it was tight to her head. As she undid the intricate work and shook out her hair, he realized it was longer than he'd expected, coming down almost to mid-back. Before he had enough time to truly admire it, she dove into the water.

She was submerged for some time, and when she finally reemerged and walked to the edge of the lake, she was carrying a large fish skewered on a dagger.

Strange. I hadn't noticed a dagger before she dove in. Yes, there is definitely more than meets the eye.

Blaez continued to watch her as she started a fire and cleaned and cooked the fish. The savory smell made his stomach grumble loudly, but he would wait until she slept to hunt for food for himself. Once her meal was done, she turned her clothes over on the rock and cleaned and sharpened the dagger she had used to catch and fillet her dinner. Then she tested the dryness of her clothing and, satisfied, she dressed.

Her pants were made of supple leather and were laced all the way up the sides with leather ties. Her vest was also of the same leather and laced down the center. Once dressed, she positioned two leather straps across her body. There were several small knives in each of these. She tucked her two daggers into the straps at the front of her chest. In one strap where it crossed over her lower back, she put a cylindrical object into another holder.

She was fully armed once again, but did not seem in a hurry to move. Blaez was glad. He had been shadowing her for only 2 Diels but, unfortunately, he hadn't slept for a few Diels before he found her and she hadn't rested since. Day and night, she moved at a pace that was efficient but which he suspected was almost leisurely for her, since she never appeared winded.

Because her present activities seemed to be maintenance activities, and because she hadn't slept in a couple of evenings, he suspected she would tonight. *Thank the Universe.* He was one of the stronger of his people and had excellent endurance, but it would seem he needed to sleep more often than she did.

She stayed in the area the entire day, taking care of grooming, cleaning her clothes, and maintaining her weapons. She went into the forest to gather some things as well, but she didn't go far, heading back to the little camp she had set up before twilight came.

The sun lowered on the horizon, painting the sky in reds and oranges above the tree line. The woman sat herself on the same large rock she had dried her clothing on. Looking out over the still water of the lake toward the sunset, she braided and twisted her hair again. Her expression was calm.

A lilting sound rose and surrounded him, quiet at first, but soon growing louder. After a moment, Blaez realized the woman was singing. It was not a language he was familiar with, but as she sang, her voice grew in strength and the intricate melody flowed smoothly. It had an almost hypnotic quality to it, and Blaez lay down in the brush and closed his eyes, allowing the sound to wash over him.

Sometime later, Blaez startled awake to the semi-darkness of a moonlit night. He sat up and looked towards the lake, where the moonlight traced silver paths that shifted and danced on the surface of the water. His animal sight made it rather easy to see at night, and he was certain after looking around that the female was no longer there. He was lifting his nose to scent the air when he froze at a low voice coming from behind him.

"I see you, wolf."

Blaez froze momentarily, then turned to see the young woman sitting with her back against a tree a couple of feet from him, sheltered from the moonlight by the branches above. She had her arms wrapped around her knees and was leaning slightly forward, capturing him in her keen gaze.

I guess I wasn't as stealthy as I thought I was.

"I know you've been following me."

He tilted his head in curiosity. Given how she was talking to him, she obviously knew he was a Wolf-folk and not a wild wolf. But how? Was she angry at being followed? Her neutral tone of voice gave nothing away. He stood still, barely moving but in a relaxed stance, hoping to assure her she had nothing to fear from him.

"I can guess why you are here: Alune Singlemoon sent you, right?"

Startled, his ears lifted and he tilted his head to the other side. She not only knew of the Sorceress, but she knew her name. Few people knew about the Sorceress outside of his village. There were so few sorcerers and sorceresses that their identities were carefully guarded. In the past, many were hunted down and captured—usually while they were young and hadn't yet come into their full power—by ill-intentioned people who wanted to enslave them and use them for their abilities.

The young woman smiled, amused by his reaction. "Do not be so surprised. I am a seer, after all."

A seer? Well, that explains a lot.

He'd heard rumors that there was a small community of seers not far from here, but he never imagined he would see one himself. If the stories were true, there were few of them left, and those that remained liked to keep themselves hidden.

"To be honest," she added, "that is not exactly how I know who sent you, but we'll save the full explanation for another time.

"I don't know what she told you, but I don't need a protector or an escort," she said. "I could use a partner, though. But fair warning—my journey will be quite dangerous. It is also necessary for the safety of the realm. If this is something you might be interested in, come find me when the sun rises."

At this, she stood and disappeared into the trees.

In the pale light of dawn, Blaez padded out from the brush toward a small fire, where the female was sitting, eating a breakfast of fish and tubers. The smell made his mouth water, but his hunger was secondary to his curiosity. He approached slowly and cautiously, ears up and senses alert, wary since the revelations of last night.

One concern was that, even though she didn't know him, she insinuated she'd be willing to take him on as a partner. Why?

The certainty that he was missing something crucial both worried him enough to wonder if he should leave and intrigued him enough to want to stay and learn more.

As he drew close and sat across the fire from her, he carefully took in her features, and what he found surprised him. As he had watched her from a distance this past week, and then again last night in moonlight and shadow, she looked almost plain. But from close-up in the light of early morning, he was surprised to see that her features were striking. She had dark brown hair and warm brown eyes, and her face was smooth skin and soft, feminine angles. She was beautiful, and young—although her exact age was impossible to guess without knowing more about her and her people.

How is it that I have been following her for more than a week, but these last two days have revealed more than all the previous ones combined?

Perhaps it was because that was how she'd wanted it.

Blaez watched the female as she leisurely took in his large black wolf form.

"Sit." She pointed towards the opposite side of the fire with the knife she was using to cut her food.

He did as she requested and then watched her, waiting for her next move.

She cut more food, put it on a flat rock around the size of both his hands side by side, then placed it in front of him.

The smell wafted up to tickle his nostrils, and his stomach rumbled. He hadn't eaten anything but raw game in—what was it now?—five days. But he tried to ignore it and just kept looking at her.

"It isn't poisoned, and I know you're hungry." She smirked. Yes, she definitely heard his stomach.

When he still didn't move, she sighed. "Fine. Let's get straight to the point.

"Like I said to you last night, I do not need to be protected. However, given the seriousness and the difficulty of my task, I would be grateful for another set of ears and eyes." She tapped the side of her nose. "And let's not forget about your great sense of smell in your wolf form." The corner of her mouth lifted in the slightest of smiles.

"I neither expect you nor want you to make a final decision until you know exactly what you are in for," she continued. "But since we both obviously trust the Sorceress, and we've spent the last few days watching one another, I think a sign of good faith might be in order at this point. My sign to you was when I approached you last night. Now it's your turn. Show yourself."

The female watched him with obvious curiosity as he shifted to his human form. As his body shimmered and reformed, he moved from his four paws to stand tall on his strong human legs. The change happened quickly, painlessly, as he was well-practiced at this point.

She did not look startled or awed by his change, as many who were not accustomed to animal-folk were when they saw it. Instead, she stood up as he did and, when the transformation was complete, she only had to tilt her head slightly in order to meet his gaze—she was almost as tall as he was. When their eyes met, she jolted a little, as if surprised, and he thought he saw a flash of vivid green in her brown eyes. *Must be a trick of the light.*

The young woman took him in, letting her eyes travel down over his body. She did not seem surprised or embarrassed at his nakedness, which was unusual. Usually humans, or others who always wore clothing, were uncomfortable with it. She looked at him unashamedly, but it was not a lewd look. Instead, it was as if she was assessing him.

He was a warrior of his people, and he worked hard on living up to that role. If she was looking for someone strong and capable of being her partner, he was certain she would not be disappointed. Blaez did not know what, exactly, this young woman needed a partner for, but he was certain it would become clear soon enough. Both she and the Sorceress, he now knew, were holding information back, but the Sorceress never acted without a reason.

The woman cleared her throat. Then she met his eyes and slightly bowed her head to him.

"I am Maelona Mistreaver."

He repeated her gesture and said, "Blaez."

Her mouth curved into a small smile as she said, "We should leave soon. We have a lot of travel ahead of us, and I would like to get to your village as soon as possible. But you should eat something first."

"Why would you offer to let me travel with you when I am a stranger to you?" he asked. He was truly perplexed by this. She had known he was following her, apparently, but she'd even slept twice.

She gave him a small, almost shy smile. "First, I know you've been following me for some time, but all you did was observe. If you meant me harm, surely you would have attacked by now. And if you did not mean me harm, chances are good that the Sorceress sent you to watch over me. That means she trusts you, and if she trusts you, I trust you."

"Should I be surprised that you know the distance to my village, and the Sorceress?" He asked.

"The knowledge that I am a seer should answer that for you," she replied. "In fact, that's another reason I am comfortable enough to ask you to travel with me. An Elder told me to expect you. Of course, I didn't know exactly who to expect at that time, but it's clear to me now that he meant you."

Ah. He nodded. "I know little about seers. What I have heard has mostly been rumors, and rumors are quite far from the truth more often than not."

Maelona smiled more brightly at him. "You are quite wise for one so young."

Blaez squinted at her, running his eyes down over her body before lingering on her face. "You look to be younger than I am."

She laughed. "I'm guessing the rumors you've heard did not mention how long-lived seers are, or how we age."

Blaez's brow furrowed, and he shook his head. "No, they did not."

"Not to worry. There will be plenty of time for me to teach you more about us. For now, we should get ready to head out." She considered him. "I do not suppose you have a pack hidden in the woods? Any clothes you can change into?" He shook his head.

Maelona reached for her pack and crouched down to rifle around inside. Standing, she held up a bundle of leather and let it drop open. "Here."

Was she offering him her own clothing? She was tall, but he was broader and more thickly muscled. "Are those . . .?"

"My extra pants. They should fit. They might be a little short, but there's not too much difference in our height."

"Yes, you are quite tall," he remarked.

"Not really. I'm average for a seer."

"I see." His lack of knowledge about her people embarrassed him a little. If the Sorceress wanted to be mysterious about why she was really sending him out here to meet Maelona, she could have at least taken some time to tell him about the seer people.

"Seer guardians travel a lot," Maelona explained, "so we make our clothing quite adjustable. Here, let me show you."

She lay the leather pants on the ground and kneeled beside them. He watched as she loosened the sturdy leather ties that laced up the sides of each of the legs. "Try them now."

Blaez took them and tested the feel of the pants in his hand. The leather was supple, and the pants were sturdy enough to withstand quite some wear. They were obviously made by a master of the craft. He pulled on the pants. As Maelona had predicted, though there were wide gaps where they laced on the sides, they fit well enough.

"Comfortable?" she asked.

"They are tighter than I'm accustomed to, but the leather is soft. They will do." He wiggled a little, trying to get used to the feel of them. The clothing the Wolf-folk wore in human form around the village were much lighter and looser. "I do not really need them, though," he said. "My people rarely wear clothing when we're in situations where we might have to shift back and forth."

"Yes, well, it's not something I'm used to. Not anymore, anyway. So perhaps you can humor me."

Maybe she was a little more uncomfortable with his nudity than she had seemed at first. He tilted his head and looked at her. "Not anymore? Have you spent time around animal-folk before?"

"Yes. But I will tell you about that after we meet with the Sorceress."

He nodded. "Of course," he agreed, to be polite. Internally, however, he shook his head. Maelona seemed to enjoy being mysterious, just like the Sorceress. Or maybe they were a little paranoid. The Sorceress once said to him that knowledge is power, and the right knowledge in the wrong hands can spell disaster. If Maelona knew the Sorceress, perhaps she had heard this, too.

Maelona turned to the side and leaned down to grab the flat rock with the piece of cooked fish on it.

"Here, eat this," she said. She shoved the plate toward him and he automatically lifted his hands to grab it. "I'm going to douse the fire and clean up the camp."

He squinted at her as she moved around, getting ready to leave. Unfortunately, staring at her didn't answer any of his lingering questions. He disliked feeling like the only person not in on some secret plan that involved him, so the sooner they could make it back to the village and speak with the Sorceress, the better.

Following a person was definitely a lot different from stalking prey.

With prey, you simply had to look for patterns of behavior and change your attack accordingly. When you were trying to learn about an intelligent, sentient being rather than hunting prey for food, there was only so much information this kind of surveillance could give you. The days that he'd spent watching Maelona from the bushes certainly fell far short of interacting personally, as they were doing now.

But hunting was the closest experience he'd had to this kind of thing before the Sorceress sent him out here to find Maelona. It had been his only reference point.

They had been traveling together for two days now and, in that time, Maelona had revealed much more about herself than she had during his two days of surveillance.

She was fascinating and beguiling, and he wanted to draw her out, to learn as much as he could about her and her people.

Every morning, Maelona climbed to the top of the tallest nearby tree to scan the horizon and, at first, Blaez was surprised by her balance and agility. He also felt a little surprised at the speed at which Maelona seemed capable of traveling for extended periods of time.

"You know, your speed and the way you move remind me of my people," he said one afternoon, two days after they started traveling together. "Do our people have a lot in common?" he asked. "I get the idea you know more about my people than I do about yours."

Maelona glanced at him. "You would be right," she replied. "And, yes, we have a lot in common."

Blaez waited expectantly for an explanation. At first, it seemed this would be another thing she would keep to herself. But, after a moment, she said, "My people can change our physical appearance to a degree. But since we can only make superficial changes and it is more physical than magical, we are not considered Folk."

"What do you mean?"

"We can change things like our hair color, eye color, and even skin tone. But we can do it because we have inner-sight—the ability to look within our physical selves and manipulate what we find. We can suppress some things and push others to the surface, which is how we control our coloring. We can also heal ourselves."

He looked at her with wide eyes. "Really? That is a very useful ability to have."

"Yes. If only we could share it with others."

Maelona's expression turned sad, and she suddenly seemed thoughtful. Introspective. Her statement made him even more curious, but he sensed it was not something he should ask about.

Blaez often stared at Maelona as they traveled, but he didn't always realize he was doing it until Maelona caught him watching. Then she would look over at him with a small smirk. This made him think, or worry, that she could somehow tell what was on his mind. He hoped she didn't take offense to his interest.

It might be because he hadn't had much experience with people outside of his village before, but he didn't think so. There was just something about her.

Before long, Blaez realized Maelona was a quiet person. She seemed to spend a lot of time wrapped up in her own thoughts or examining the surrounding forest. It was just her nature, it seemed. He didn't think she was being intentionally cold because, from time to time as they walked and hunted together, he would touch her or brush against her. Every time that happened, he felt a warm, tingly sensation where their skin met. He knew she felt this too, because whenever they touched, her cheeks blushed pink. She never once pulled away like someone who was unfriendly or uncomfortable would.

They'd been traveling for almost two weeks and were still two or three days out from his village when they slowed down to track small game. They moved carefully and quietly across the forest floor. When she looked over and grinned slightly, giving him that feeling like she was reading him yet again, he found himself unable to hold his curiosity in any longer.

"Tell me, Maelona, I know little about your people, but I know there is a good reason you are called seers. What is it you can do, aside from what you've already told me? I have heard you get visions. Is it the future you see? Do your visions always come to pass?"

Maelona straightened from where she was leaning forward, looking for signs of game as they walked.

"Yes, we get visions of a sort," she replied. She kept walking slowly, shifting her attention between him and the ground. "They can be of the past, present, or future. It's often easy to tell which, though sometimes time itself seems to lose all meaning. And no, our visions do not always come to pass, thankfully. If that were the case, then it would be pointless for us to intervene, to attempt to guide things in the right direction. Sometimes, though, those involved may be so intent on their goals, so focused on the actions they have decided on, that nothing could change the outcome."

"Is there more you can do?" Blaez asked. "Some years ago, I heard rumors that your people can see into the minds of others. Is there truth to this?"

"No," she responded, shaking her head. "At least, not how you mean." She sighed and glanced at him before continuing. "It is not the mind we read. Rather, it's a person's physical cues. We are so attuned to our own physical bodies that reading what lies behind others' physical reactions is easy for us. And we also hone this ability from an early age. It's a person's choice of words and their tone of voice. It's their facial expressions, the gestures they make. These things can often be subtle, but they sometimes stand out as if they were begging to be noticed."

"And me? Do you find me easy to read?"

"You have been very calm and steady. Even this unassuming way you have about you says a lot. Also, your eyes are very expressive. They have many stories to tell, and many more questions than you have given voice to.

"A person's eyes speak the loudest as to who they are on the inside," she explained. "And there you have one reason I am answering so many of your questions after only knowing you a short time."

Maelona went back to looking for tracks of any would-be prey as she walked, scanning the ground and the nearby bushes.

Blaez smiled and shook his head, figuring her change of attention was a signal that she'd had enough of talking for now.

Blaez was just turning to search on the other side of the trail when he noticed Maelona freeze.

He stopped moving, his senses suddenly on high alert. He looked at her, listening carefully at the same time to see if he could notice whatever had caught her attention.

After a moment, he said, "Did you—"

"Shh!" Maelona hissed, holding up a hand in a silencing gesture.

CHAPTER FOUR

Hunters & Hunted

The strange rasping and the rustling of something moving over dead leaves and roots was a sound Maelona was familiar with, but one she hadn't heard in many years.

She turned her head slightly towards Blaez. "Draccon," she whispered.

"Did you say dragon?" he whisper-hissed back.

She shook her head. "Drak-kon," she repeated, being careful to sound it out clearly.

"What's a draccon?"

She held up her hand. "Later." This was not the time for long explanations. The sound was getting closer and moving fast—much faster than the huge snake-like beasts usually moved. . . unless they were hunting.

She looked at Blaez and said, "Run."

She took off through the brush and trees, the sounds of Blaez's footfalls following close behind. She soon heard the sounds of two running feet switch to the rhythmic thudding of four—Blaez had shifted to his wolf form, as she expected from a Folk under threat.

Leaves and sticks crunched underfoot as they ran; tree branches whipped her exposed skin. Still, she ran on, and the rasping sound continued to follow.

She broke through the tree line into a clearing of short grasses and brush. On the other side of the clearing, there was a steep cliff-face. She ran to it and immediately climbed.

A deep, low rumble of a growl made her pause, and she suddenly noticed there were no sounds of anyone else climbing after her. She glanced down and saw Blaez standing on the ground below, back end pointed toward the cliff and hackles raised.

"What are you doing?" she yelled down at him. "Shift! Climb!"

The Wolf-folk stubbornly held his ground. Maelona sighed, then she let go with one hand and foot and turned until her body was perpendicular to the rock face. She pushed out and let her body drop, landing in a crouch a few paces from Blaez. She stood and whirled to face him.

"You don't understand, Blaez. I don't want to fight it."

Blaez's growl grew louder, his attention fixed in front of him. When she turned to look, she realized it was too late to climb now. The draccon would be upon them any second.

A loud, piercing cry sounded from up above, startling her. Maelona looked up to see a huge golden eagle diving for the draccon. The long, scaled creature veered off to the left and slithered past them.

"It isn't hunting us," she said. "It's being hunted."

The draccon was covered in dark gray scales with spines that traveled from the back of its head to a quarter of the way down its length. Its elongated, thick body came up to shoulder height. Its tail trailed way back, now just two or three paces from the tree line.

"Surely it must be too big. . ." she muttered.

The eagle swooped in with its talons extended. Despite the draccon's attempt to evade the immense bird, its head was soon in the clutches of the hunter.

The wing beats were powerful enough to send detritus from the ground flying in all directions when the eagle launched itself back into the air with its prey.

Maelona shielded her eyes with her forearm to protect them from the spray of dirt, rocks, and leaves. When she felt the wind pressure from the eagle's wings grow weak with distance, she looked up again.

The long body of the snake-like creature slid in front of them for what felt like a long time but was probably only half a minute. The draccon's body writhed as it rose and Maelona had to duck when its tail crashed into the cliff above their heads, sending a shower of rock down on them. Finally, the eagle gained enough height to lift the draccon out of range. Soon after, the giant snake went still, its body hanging loosely from the talons of the majestic bird.

Blaez made a rumbly sound next to her and shook the dirt out of his fur. He was watching the eagle intently. Maelona expected the hunter to disappear into the distance with its catch. Instead, it doubled back, then circled the clearing from high above.

"What is it doing?" She wasn't expecting an answer, of course—Blaez was unlikely to shift back until he was sure the danger was past.

As the eagle passed almost directly above them on one of its loops, it let go of the draccon. The lifeless body crashed to the ground close in front of them, shaking the earth and sending even more ground litter up at them. She looked over at the creature that now lay there in a heap.

Maelona swallowed thickly and took a few cautious steps forward. Blaez kept pace beside her, letting out low growls every now and again. When she got close enough, she saw blood pouring from deep puncture wounds in the creature's head, which had also been crushed—as evidenced by the misshapen mass of scale-covered bone that its skull had become.

Blaez's growls grew louder and more menacing, and Maelona looked up to see the eagle landing across from them, on the other side of the draccon's lifeless corpse. As it stood there staring, her suspicions were confirmed. As large as golden eagles naturally were, this one was even bigger. This was not a bird, but a Folk.

"Do you realize what you've done?" Maelona asked in a firm, almost angry tone. She took a deep, calming breath before continuing. "Do you know how rare these creatures are?"

The Eagle-folk shifted into its biped form and the tall, brown-haired, brown-eyed man dipped his head. She wasn't sure if it was meant as a greeting or an affirmation.

The man's voice was deep and smooth as he responded. "I know that. But this creature was targeting our children."

Maelona gasped. Folk that young could not shift yet. They would have looked almost human, and she had never heard of a draccon hunting a human—or a Folk in human form—before.

"Was anyone. . ." she couldn't bring herself to say it.

"Killed?" the Eagle-folk finished for her. "No. It came close but, luckily, our protectors got there in time. The child that was attacked has fractures in both arms and a couple of ribs, but she will heal."

Maelona shook her head. "I'm so sorry."

She looked back at the dead draccon and noticed several fresh nicks and scars. There were even some puncture wounds along the body, but they didn't look deep—certainly not as deep as the ones it recently received in its head, courtesy of the Golden-eagle-folk's talons.

She had heard before that a draccon's body was well-armored, and that the head was the weak spot. Apparently, the scales there were softer and more flexible to allow it to open its jaws wide enough to swallow large prey. The draccon in front of them looked large enough to swallow a mature stag whole, without needing to expand its jaws.

Beside her, Blaez shifted from his wolf back into his—once again nude—human form. "I've never seen one of these creatures before," he said. "Is it common for them to hunt Folk, or humans?"

The man shook his head. "No, it isn't."

"I've only ever heard of them hunting prey animals," Maelona added. "Though they are rare to begin with, so we don't really have a lot of information to go on."

"I'd wager the lack of human-like prey in the past is because we live in groups, rather than any deference on their part."

"Yes, they are shy creatures." She looked at the stranger. "Which begs the question of why it was near your village in the first place."

Maelona crouched down next to the creature and put a hand on its neck, just below its crushed skull and between two spikes. She got the impression of something writhing just underneath the surface—something dark and almost intangible. She closed her eyes and concentrated, and the image of the cloaked man from her dream-visions flashed in her mind.

Could the Dark Sorcerer have somehow used magic to compel this animal to attack? From what she felt and saw, it seemed likely, yet she had never heard of a sorcerer or sorceress being able to compel animals before. Well, not unless the sorcerer in question was a Folk that shared the same animal type. But there were no Draccon-folk. They simply didn't exist. So, that someone had compelled it was a very disturbing possibility.

She suddenly worried she was taking too long, so she cleared her throat and stood. Seeing inside beings other than themselves was not a seer ability, so she wouldn't tell them what she felt in case they might guess she was more than 'just' a seer. But it was something she'd have to discuss with the Sorceress.

"I'm sorry," she said. "We're being rude. This is Blaez. My name is Maelona. I'm a—"

"Seer. Yes, I know."

She narrowed her eyes at him.

"Your people are not the only ones who keep histories or track the passage of time," the man said. "We know the Great Alignment is mere months away. Our Elders asked us to monitor your village. Lately we've spotted more activity than usual. We know you aren't the only one who left. There were others that went in different directions. My people know that when the seers move, something is afoot. Your people have foreseen something, haven't you?"

Apparently, she needed to get into the habit of looking up more often, and not just at night when she was star gazing. Yes, her people knew that the Eagle-folk kept watch over the forest, so she was never overly concerned if she spotted one. But she hadn't been aware that they watched her people so closely. If they were ill-intentioned, though, she or one of the others surely would have had visions about it.

She considered him warily. "You know, you still haven't given us your name."

"My apologies. I am called Kosseth. I am a high-level scout reporting directly to Elder Moyses. It might ease your concerns to know that there are only three scouts who are aware that the Elders have decided to keep an eye on your village. The Elders are worried and figured if anyone would know if there were any threats, they would be among your people."

Maelona nodded. This fit with her mission. It gave her the opportunity to prepare them for what was to come.

"Tell your Elders that we are heading for the Wolf-folk village of Wildegrove. We should arrive there in two or three days. I have some business to attend to first, but then I will call for a meeting of the Elders and leaders from all the neighboring Folk clans. I will send for them then."

Kosseth bowed his head to her, stepped back, and shifted into his eagle form. He took a couple of steps and launched into the air, looping around and gaining some momentum before swooping down again to grab the heavy form of the draccon. He flew off to the southeast, where Maelona knew the Eagle-folk lived, the long tail of the draccon almost touching the treetops as it trailed below him. She shook her head at the sight. Kosseth must be incredibly strong.

As Maelona watched the Eagle-folk and his prey grow smaller and smaller in the distance, she pondered what she'd discovered when she touched the draccon. What did the evil intent lurking inside it mean? There were magical protections in place to keep evil beings out of the Sacred Forest, so did someone capture the beast and put a spell on it? If so, how did they capture it? Did it wander outside of the forest on its own, or was it lured?

Whatever the case—whether it was lured out and had a spell placed on it, or whether someone entered the forest to do it—it meant that someone or something evil must have successfully passed through the magical protections of the Sacred Forest, and that was a very disturbing thought.

She needed to discuss this with the Sorceress.

"Come on," she said to Blaez. We should quicken our pace.

That evening, Blaez watched Maelona as she sat, shoulders hunched, and absently stared into the fire. She ate slowly and her movements seemed mechanical; her thoughts were obviously elsewhere.

They were sharing their evening meal—a savory stew of rabbit meat and roots and tubers they dug up along the way. It was all seasoned with some herbs they found growing wild. It was delicious, but Maelona didn't seem to notice.

Blaez cleared his throat. "Would you like to share what's on your mind? I'm a good listener."

Maelona sat up straight, took a deep breath, and turned to him.

"You work closely with the Sorceress, right?"

He nodded.

"I've been thinking about what happened earlier with the draccon. I think I'll need to get her opinion on it. Has she spoken to you about them before?"

Blaez shook his head. "No. Today was the first I've heard of them. They must really be as rare as you say." Not that he'd doubted her, but he had almost 80 years behind him. He'd assumed he knew all there was to know about this forest. "Was its behavior really that unusual? Could it just have been a hunt of opportunity?"

"I haven't had a lot of first-hand experience with them myself," she said. "They are rare, burrow underground, and tend to be shy of others. They also hunt at night, as far as I know. I've seen them only twice before today. However, as children, seers are educated about all the creatures that can be found in the Sacred Forest. Everything I've learned about them suggests this was very atypical behavior." She pursed her lips, as if she was considering saying something else. In the end, she just shook her head and looked back at the fire.

They finished their meal, cleaned up, and put out the fire just as dusk was coming fully upon them. Now they sat in silence upon the low ridge where they were camping out for the night, watching the moonlight dance among the tops of the trees. The buzzing and chirping of nocturnal insects filled the sweetly scented air. It was a soothing sound, and Blaez breathed deeply and relaxed, letting go of the tensions from earlier in the day.

He looked over at Maelona and noticed she was watching him. When she realized it, her face flushed and she turned away. She cleared her throat.

"We need to get you some new pants," she muttered.

Blaez smiled. Did she blush out of embarrassment, or because she was attracted to him? He hoped it was the latter.

"I'm sorry I let your pants get ruined after you so kindly allowed me to use them."

"Chances are, they aren't ruined," she said. "The way they were made, it's likely the laces broke, but the leather panels are still intact. If we'd wanted to take the time to go look for them, they'd probably just need new laces."

"Do you want to go back for them?" he asked.

She shook her head. "No. We traveled farther than you'd probably expect when we were running. And I told Kosseth to let his Elders know we'd be sending for them in a few days. I don't want to keep them waiting any longer than necessary."

"But are you still uncomfortable. . .?"

Maelona let out a short huff of a laugh. "I'm a big girl. I'll just have to learn to deal with it, won't I? Besides, I'll be around many other Folk soon. This will be an excellent opportunity for me to get used to it again."

Blaez lay back in the grass and looked up at the stars dancing above them. "Tell me more about your people," he said.

"I suppose it's only fair, since I know much more about your people than you do about mine." Blaez turned his head to see her smiling down from where she sat next to him.

"I told you before that we read a person's physical cues," she said. "But there's actually a lot more that we do as well." She paused and picked a few blades of grass, then wove and twisted them together. She watched her hands for a minute before taking a deep breath and looking over at him.

"We also watch," she said, "and we study the people and cultures in our world. Seers are even more long-lived than your people, and that gives us plenty of time to study and learn. Usually from a distance, but sometimes joining with different groups, assimilating their ways and blending into the culture. This gives us the opportunity to learn things that outsiders would normally not be privy to."

"Doesn't that give you a kind of power and control over others? Are you not worried about some of your people being tempted to abuse such power?" he asked.

Maelona gave him a wry smile, and he could see sadness in her eyes. "We are protectors of balance and light. We do not long for power and control. It is not in our makeup. And even if there were one among us who would be tempted by such things, my people learned long ago that we are not infallible. By showing our abilities too openly in the past, people worried about that exact question. It started with the humans but spread to some magical races as well, as I'm sure you know." She glanced at him, and he nodded. "And that led to our kind being hunted down and slaughtered."

Maelona fell back so she was lying on the grass next to him, staring up at the stars. His heart beat a little faster. Seer senses weren't so good that she could hear it, were they?

"So, for the past few centuries," she continued, "we have gotten involved only when our visions have shown that the safety and security of entire peoples or our entire realm was in danger, either in the short- or long-run. And we have taken care to act from the shadows, never revealing ourselves openly—not from a desire to keep secrets, but from a need to keep the peace. Sometimes our actions can be as subtle as influencing someone to make the right decision when they otherwise may have made the wrong one. But only if, for example, they were already being manipulated to spread the seeds of dissent, like what had happened all those years ago."

Blaez looked at her, brow furrowed. "If you have such powerful visions and so much knowledge, then how is it that your people could not avoid being targeted and cut down like they were? We've all heard the stories, but I never really understood how that could have happened."

"One interesting thing about my people," she said, "is that we do not get clear visions of things that will affect us personally. We may get a sense of things that will affect us, but not one of us can see our own fates. It is our blind spot, so to speak. The Elders at the time knew there was something evil brewing, but they did not know the exact nature of the threat or how it would begin until the chain reaction had already started."

"Even if they were attacked without warning, the seers are a powerful people. So, how was it they suffered so much loss?"

Maelona sighed. "Many of the seer people believed in letting the humans make their own decisions and mistakes and not interfering. It was only after the attacks began many seers began having visions, and learning in other ways, that even though we decided not to interfere with the humans, there were others who did not have the same consideration."

She turned to look at him, her expression somewhere between concern and anger. "In fact, it was discovered that there were evil forces acting behind the scenes, fear-mongering and manipulating the humans into believing that we were a danger that needed to be destroyed. Our elders then decided that we needed to intervene, to stop these evil forces from destroying the peace of our realm."

In a much softer voice, she added, "But, by then, it was too late to stop what had been put into motion."

Blaez looked up at the night sky again. "I still don't fully understand. You seem strong and resilient, like someone who can take care of yourself. Are other seers not like you? Didn't your people fight back?" If they were all as capable as she'd shown herself to be, why did her people suffer the losses the histories spoke of?

"Like I said before," Maelona replied, "we are protectors. Mostly, our attackers were humans whose fear and insecurities were being used against them. Many seers refused to fight back against innocents who were being manipulated by evils that hid like cowards in the background. And because of who we are, what we do, we have a better understanding, respect, and appreciation than most for other cultures, as well as points of view that differ from our own."

Blaez turned to look at her and Maelona quickly looked away, but not before Blaez saw the sadness in her expression.

"We eventually found peace again," she said, "but not before many innocent lives were lost."

Blaez took a deep breath, thinking over her words. "Can it really be called peace, though," he asked softly, "if you had to hide yourselves away and deny your very existence to get it?"

CHAPTER FIVE

Speculation & Revelation

The next morning, when Blaez awoke, Maelona was no longer at their camp. He followed her scent until he broke through the underbrush on the bank of another of the small lakes that dotted the forest. This one was less than half the size of the lake where they'd first officially met.

Looking out over the water, he saw her a short distance out, floating and facing away from him. Without thinking twice, he stepped into the cool water and swam out to where she was drifting and looking up into the clear blue sky.

As he swam toward her, without moving or looking back in his direction, Maelona acknowledged his presence by asking, "So, what's your story, Blaez? Why did the Sorceress choose you to send to me?"

As he came up next to her, he relaxed onto his back so he was floating next to her. "Surely you must know the answer to that better than myself."

Maelona moved in the water until she was treading water, facing him. "I have seen you before, but usually only in flashes. I know your face, your eyes, your smile, your wolf, but that is all. Do you know what these flashes tell me? Can you guess from what I told you yesterday?"

She'd given him a lot of information to take in and consider, but he couldn't figure out which part, exactly, she was referring to. So, he shook his head and waited for her to continue.

"They tell me, Blaez, that you will be an important part of my future."

His heart skipped a beat.

Get a hold of yourself. She didn't mean it that way. It would be great if that were the case, but he shouldn't get ahead of himself.

"You will become too close to me personally for me to see more than blurred images, general feelings, and the picture of your face the first time we met. I do not yet know the nature of our connection, and I am sure by the surprise I see on your face right now that you know no more than I do."

"I know only what Alune Singlemoon has told me," Blaez responded. Belatedly, he realized he probably should not have used the Sorceress's name. But then again, Maelona had used the name before, hadn't she? So he wasn't giving anything away. It was proof, though, that he was dropping his guard around her.

"I was instructed to meet you and escort you to our village, and to provide protection along the way." He knew, though, that it was not as simple as that. Things rarely ever were with the Sorceress.

"The Sorceress always acts with a purpose," Maelona said, as if she'd heard his thoughts. "She knows very well that I know my way to the village and that I do not need protection. But since you only live in the shadowed corners of my mind, I do not yet know her reasoning."

"I work with her sometimes when she needs help with something. Maybe she believed you need my help," Blaez surmised.

"Well, she would certainly be correct if that's the case. We need all the help we can get." After a pause, she added, "You work with her, yet you aren't a sorcerer, are you?" It was more a statement than a question.

Blaez chuckled and said, "No, not at all. She helped me out when no one else would. Now, we help each other whenever we can."

Blaez watched as Maelona's expression turned sad for a moment. Then, just as quickly, it cleared again.

"I don't know if you will be keen to extend your help to me once you learn the nature of my mission. And before I can tell you that, we need to go see the Sorceress."

At that, Maelona started swimming back to shore. Blaez turned to follow her and noticed how well she swam; it looked natural for her. It suddenly made him wonder how old she was. How many years had she had to practice all the skills he'd seen her proficiency with?

And then there was her physical build. Because of the animal-folks' divergent physical nature, it was not uncommon for males and females alike to be naked or barely clad in front of one another. So he had seen plenty of examples of the female form. Still, hers stood out amongst the others he had seen, with both feminine curves and firm and developed musculature that was more defined than what he was accustomed to. She must have partaken in her fair share of hard work—or perhaps she had trained a lot.

Maybe she had trained for whatever she needed help with now. That she was holding back information about that until they reached the Sorceress. . . well, his instincts and her behavior told him it must be something significant.

Two days later, they walked silently through the forest at an almost leisurely pace, tracking prey. Maelona patted Blaez's forearm as she slowed to a stop. When Blaez looked at her, she kept focused ahead and lifted her chin to point out what had caught her attention. From her peripheral vision, she saw Blaez turn his head to follow her gaze; through the foliage and into the clearing beyond stood a magnificent stag.

Up to this point, they had hunted only small prey—enough to keep them fed, but not so much that they had to leave unused portions behind. They were less than half a day out from Wildegrove, so she would hunt the stag and bring it to share with others who lived there.

Since they were off to one side from the direction the deer was facing and slightly downwind, Maelona knew their scents would not give them away. She signaled to Blaez to hide in the undergrowth behind the stag and upwind. She crept through the underbrush, where she hoped to stay out of sight. Glancing over at Blaez, she saw him move stealthily into position. Then he shifted, and she was impressed at how quietly he could do this given where he was.

When the time was right, Maelona signaled Blaez, using the light of the sun reflecting off the blade of her dagger.

In wolf form, Blaez headed to the rear of the stag. Lifting its nose in the air, their prey startled at the earthy scent of wolf and bolted towards Maelona's hiding spot. Blaez took up the chase, and Maelona watched intently as they came closer and closer. Once it was in range, Maelona sprang forward at a dead run: At the same moment, Blaez pounced, latching onto the stag's haunches. Leaping into the air, Maelona propelled herself toward the stag's shoulders.

Blaez twisted his body so that his movement and Maelona's attack brought the animal to the ground on its side, where

Maelona quickly dispatched of it with a dagger directly through the heart.

Maelona leaned over it and said a prayer of thanks to the stag's spirit for the sacrifice it made. It would keep many people in the village fed and clothed. One thing that the seers and the Wolf-folk had in common was that they always tried to use as much of the animal as possible. Nothing was wasted. To her, that seemed the best way to honor the life that was given.

Blaez shifted back to human form and looked at her. "I have seen no one move faster or leap farther with more efficiency and grace before—not unless it was an animal or in animal form, at least. You would make a formidable ally." He smirked. "Or a fearsome opponent."

Maelona smiled up at him from where she already worked on the deer carcass. "I guess you should stay on my good side, then."

Blaez chuckled. "Yes, I probably should." His brow wrinkled, as if he was trying to figure something out. "Do your people hunt together as mine do?"

"From time to time," Maelona said. "But usually I hunt alone—mostly because the other guardians and I travel alone. It was nice to have a partner."

"I have to say, you seem very familiar with my people and our ways. And you know the way to our village. Have you spent time there?"

"I have. Years ago, in my childhood and youth."

"Why don't I remember seeing you around?"

"There are many potential answers to that. For example, you haven't asked how old I am. I may have been there and gone again before you were even born. Or maybe we were just unlucky and were never in the same place at the same time. Also, sometimes people change a lot as they age. Maybe I just look a lot different from when I was younger."

He narrowed his eyes at her. "You know which one of those scenarios is correct, don't you?"

Maelona paused what she was doing and looked up at him. She considered him for a moment, deciding how to respond. Then she shrugged her shoulder and smiled. "Maybe it's all three."

In the late afternoon of that same day, Blaez and Maelona arrived at Wildegrove with Maelona dragging the deer carcass behind her. For this purpose, she had made a sleigh of branches formed into a frame, criss-crossed and secured with vines from the forest and ropes from her pack.

From the time they'd placed the deer on the sleigh to the time they arrived at the village, Maelona had become more and more quiet and serious. This was concerning to him, since she was quiet and serious to begin with. But Blaez sensed he shouldn't push, so he left her to her thoughts, only speaking twice to ask her if he could haul the sleigh for a while. She declined both times. He had hoped she would decide to talk to him about whatever was on her mind, but she did not.

Why are you so disappointed? He asked himself. *You haven't known each other for a very long time. It's to be expected.* Yet, it saddened him to see her pull back from whatever it was they had forming between them. Had he asked too many questions? Had he pushed her too far or crossed a line somewhere?

Blaez had expected Maelona to leave the carcass with the men and women who were tasked with preparing the meat and hides from the hunts and then go directly to see the Sorceress. Instead, she stayed with the group, looking over their tools and chatting with them before she herself began taking care of the carcass.

The others had smiled at her and accepted her among them with no fuss. It was quite amazing that someone as reserved as she was could also charm others so easily. He shook his head at himself. She'd certainly charmed him easily, hadn't she, so why was he surprised?

Should he ask her to go with him now? He didn't want to push her and increase this coolness that had been between them since the hunt, so he headed off to see the Sorceress on his own. After all, it was his duty to check in with her upon their return.

Unlike the other folk in the village, Sorceress Alune Singlemoon did not live in a hut in the village. Rather, she lived in a cave whose entry-way was carved into the rocky side of an escarpment that jutted up from the forest past the northern edge of the village. This made sense, Blaez supposed, as it was more protected than the regular huts. There was also more room for the mazes of tunnels and rooms upon rooms that continued deep under the escarpment, where she practiced her arts.

He entered this cave now and found Alune sitting by the cozy fire in the reception room just past the entrance. There were chairs and benches placed around the central fire, with small tables in between for drinks and food. She was currently preparing two cups of tea.

He smiled and shook his head. How did she always seem to know?

Alune looked up expectantly and greeted him as if it were any other day and he had not just returned from a journey. She did not show any sign of surprise that he was alone.

"Sorceress Alune," Blaez said while inclining his head to her in greeting.

The Sorceress had striking amethyst eyes and violet hair, and she looked not much older than Blaez himself. But she had a motherly way about her and—despite never admitting her age—he knew she was much older than she looked.

Blaez had grown and changed so much since his boyhood, yet the Sorceress looked almost the same. Rumor said that sorcerers live an even longer lifespan than those of their own peoples, with the magic that flowed through them renewing their physical forms repeatedly. He suspected this rumor was true.

"My dear Blaez, come and have some tea with me and tell me of your journey. I take it things went smoothly?"

Blaez sat on the sturdy wooden bench in front of the fire and accepted the hot cup the Sorceress passed to him. "Yes, they did," he responded, "though our guest does not seem inclined to come greet you at the moment. We hunted on the way in and she stayed behind to process the kill."

"I expected such," the Sorceress replied, nodding solemnly. "She is going to need some time to adjust to the idea of being back here."

So, Maelona had been here before—not that he doubted her, but hearing it confirmed by a separate source made it more real, somehow.

"I don't understand why you sent me to her, Sorceress, or why you didn't tell me more about her. She seems very capable of taking care of herself and she knew her way to our village. I don't think you really sent me out there to guide and protect her. Do you not trust her?"

"I sent you, dear Blaez," the Sorceress replied in a soft, warm voice, "so you could get to know each other a little without pretense and prejudice, before you realize who you are to each other. I also sent you specifically, my friend, because she could be the key to us surviving the dark times that are to come, but only if she heals old scars and becomes whole again. You and she can help each other there. You can help her heal. It is what you are destined for.

"And besides," Alune continued, "as tough as she is, she is only one person. She cannot be everywhere at once, and she will need help if she is to succeed in her mission." In a quiet, sad voice, she added, "She will need help if she is to survive."

Blaez sat in silent thought for a moment. Then he asked, "Tell me, Sorceress, who is this woman?"

Alune turned to Blaez with a sad expression on her face. After a pause, she answered, "She is my daughter, my only child."

The words hit Blaez like a punch to the sternum. His heart beat faster and his hands shook so much that drops of tea spilled out over the edge of his cup. He quickly placed it back on the little table.

If Maelona was the Sorceress's daughter, then he could only guess how she would respond once she discovered who he was. He didn't think it would be good. Would this destroy any connection they had formed on the journey here?

"Wait," he said, "if she is your daughter, I would have seen her around the village when I was a child. Why did I not recognize her?"

"Because, knowing her, she hasn't shown her true self to anyone since she left here over forty years ago."

CHAPTER SIX

Truth & Connection

Blaez approached the hut where Maelona was staying shortly after sunrise the next morning. The sound of metal sliding along stone came from somewhere behind the small wooden structure. As Maelona came into view, he paused and watched her sharpening her dagger as she sat next to the hide of what he assumed was their stag, stretched out on a wooden frame.

Blaez respected Maelona for the strength and self-sufficiency she'd shown in the short time they had known each other. They had gained some understanding of one another and they'd begun to form a bond—as new and fragile as it was. Now that he knew who she really was, however, he hesitated to approach her.

This is not the time to be a coward. He took a deep breath and set off towards her once again.

"Good morning, Maelona," he greeted, trying to keep any nervousness out of his voice.

She looked at him with a small smile and a nod as she greeted him in return. "Blaez."

"The Sorceress wishes to confer with us this morning."

As a reply, she wiped her dagger on a soft piece of leather and stood. Then, returning the weapon to its place, she turned to face him. "Let's be off then, shall we?"

Her tone was neutral and calm, but the look in her eyes told him she was a little more anxious than she let on. Still, Blaez breathed a small sigh of relief at Maelona's willingness to address the Sorceress this morning.

She was quiet as they walked to the Sorceress's cave on the outskirts of the village. He could now guess the reasons for that, as well as for her silence. He knew it had been some time since the Sorceress had seen her daughter face to face. The Sorceress had told him once that her daughter had left just two months before he himself came into her care. That was close to forty years ago. Now, he would be the sole witness to their reunion after such a long time apart.

He suddenly felt jittery and had to wipe his damp palms on his light linen pants.

Alune stood waiting at the cave entrance as Maelona and Blaez approached. Blaez stayed back as Maelona approached her estranged mother. Maelona hesitated, but then the Sorceress held her hands out toward her. "My darling Lona," she said, using the pet name she often used when speaking about her daughter, "it has been too long."

Maelona walked into her mother's arms. They each held the other's forearms and stood forehead to forehead, nose to nose. It was a typical Wolf-folk greeting for family and those very close. Blaez was hit with a pang of longing at the sight, but also let out a breath of relief that it was going so well.

"I am so sorry that I have not come to see you in such a long time," Maelona said as she leaned back.

"I understand your reasons, my dear; do not fret. Still, I wish our reunion could have been during happier times. If you'd arrived seven Diels earlier, it would have been on the anniversary of your birth."

Blaez jolted. Seven Diels ago? That meant the day they met was the anniversary of Maelona's birth.

"I have so much to apologize for, Mother, and there is much we need to discuss." Maelona briefly glanced in Blaez's direction before looking back at her mother. "Perhaps we should speak alone for a time."

The Sorceress looked at Blaez with a warm smile and reached out her hand to him. He stepped up next to her. "My dear Lona, the three of us have much to discuss together. We each have different parts of the same story to share with one another." Blaez felt his entire body tense up.

Maelona gazed at her mother questioningly, and her mother looked back at her with a small, sad smile. "Blaez," Alune said, "is the son of Guarin Stronghunter."

Blaez watched as a myriad of emotions flitted across Maelona's usually calm face. From shock, disgust, panic, anger, and hatred, her face finally settled into a mask of sadness. She looked at her mother before looking back at Blaez. Then she turned and walked away.

In the short time he had known her, this was the first time Blaez had seen Maelona show so much obvious emotion. After a silent moment or two, Alune reached her hand out to him once more and said, "Come, Blaez. We will have some tea. Then, when we are done, you will speak with my Lona."

"Why would she ever want to speak to me again?" Blaez asked with a slow shake of his head.

"Because you are not your father, Blaez. Maelona knows that. Maybe someday you will come to accept it yourself."

An hour later, Maelona heard footsteps approaching from behind. She knew from the sound of the footfalls that it was Blaez. She wasn't surprised that he'd found her. The Sorceress had either told him where to look or he had used his keen sense of smell to track her scent. As he came close, she could hear that he was moving slowly, hesitantly, as if unsure whether to approach her.

Once the footsteps stopped, Maelona asked without turning around, "Do you know what this place is, Blaez?"

She sat cross-legged at the edge of a crater in the ground. It looked like a shallow bowl a couple of hundred meters across, with scorched earth spreading across it to the edges.

"My people call it the Crater of Sorrows," Blaez answered. "My mother and the Sorceress told me enough to know that this is the place where my father tried to harm you. I have no other details. It's like the people think it is bad luck to talk about it. I asked Alune one time to tell me more about it, but she simply said it was your story to tell. At that time, I did not know that I would ever meet you."

After a brief pause, Blaez continued, "I understand if you refuse to have me accompany you, but I really would like to help. I feel I need to help. It is my duty."

Maelona turned to look over her shoulder at Blaez, who stood a couple of paces back. She patted the ground beside her.

He approached slowly, as if he was afraid of startling a wild animal. Once he was settled, Maelona turned to look out over the crater again.

"My mother, as you now know, is a sorceress of the Wolf-folk—your people. I do not know, however, if you know my father was a sorcerer of the seer people."

"I'd heard different rumors, but I do not like to take anything as fact until I hear it from the person the news is about."

Maelona nodded and looked at him. "That is for the best." She picked up a small stone from beside her and tossed it into the crater. "Each race of Sterrenvar has the potential to produce those capable of drawing and controlling magic from the Source, but they are very rare. It usually only happens once every few generations.

"My father heard a prophecy stating that there were dark times coming. . . the dark times that are descending upon us now, in fact. He knew our realm could use all the help it could get, and he did not feel we had the luxury of waiting another generation or two to have more beings on the side of good that could control magic.

"As both a seer and a sorcerer, he had extra sensitivity to other magical beings. He knew of my mother, and he left his village to seek her out. So, you could say their pairing started as a partnership in securing our future. But they came to love each other very much and were very devoted to each other, even though they could not stay together all the time. My mother and her skills were needed here with the Wolf-folk and my father was needed with the seers. However, my father came to visit us as often as his duties allowed."

"That must have been difficult for you."

She shrugged. "It was all I knew. I visited Clearview, the village he was from, many times as well.

"But this creature you see here before you," she said, gesturing to herself, "is a product of both the Wolf-folk and the seers, and the daughter of two magically gifted beings. I result from their purposeful attempt to create another magically gifted being."

Blaez let out a surprised sound, and she looked at him. His eyebrows were lifted high on his forehead and his eyes were wide. She couldn't help but smile a little at his shocked expression. She'd felt the same way when her parents told her as well.

"There are things they could predict about what characteristics I would have, but there were other things that they could not predict since I was the product of two different races. I am not the only one ever born in such a situation, and history has shown that the offspring of two different peoples can have any combination of traits from those peoples."

Maelona turned to look more fully at Blaez, shifting her body so she was almost facing him. "Seers are long-lived. In fact, they live longer than the various animal-folk. Where your people can live for seven hundred to eight hundred years, seers usually live for a thousand years or more, barring illness or injury. Of course, you can consider the two life expectancies to be close when compared to the humans' seventy or eighty years.

"Still, this difference in life span left some questions about how I would age and mature, such as when I would enter my adolescence, if would shift, if I would have magical abilities and, if so, how powerful they would be. So, I lived my early years, until I was forty-four years old, sheltered either here or in my father's village. There were always extra protectors with us when we traveled between the two places."

"What about the magical protections that were placed around the Sacred Forest? Didn't they trust them to work?" Blaez asked.

"Those protections keep evil creatures from entering the Sacred Forest. They would not do a lot to discourage deceitful behavior if the person was already inside of its protective barriers."

Maelona looked at Blaez. His lips were pressed together, and he nodded thoughtfully.

"I was watched carefully for clues about how my development would progress, while remaining hidden and protected.

"Don't get me wrong," Maelona continued, "my parents loved me very much and ensured I had the proper education in all things both seer and Wolf-folk. They even made certain I learned basic survival and fighting skills. However, this was not enough to prepare me for the evils of the world."

"Evils such as my father," Blaez said in a somber tone. Maelona couldn't help but notice the disgust in his voice as he said the word 'father.'

Nodding and swallowing back a lump in her throat, Maelona continued. "Well, my adolescence did not begin at twenty-five or thirty years, as typically happens with animal-folk. We were not sure when it would happen, but as I passed my thirtieth year, it became a waiting game. It had been clear from an early age that I had some magical ability, but we would not know the extent until I passed that stage in my maturation.

"When I was forty-two, changes finally became apparent. My body developed into that of a young woman, and my magical abilities became stronger. I had not yet shifted at that point, and we did not know if I would."

Maelona paused and glanced at Blaez to see how he was faring. He must know where this story was headed. He didn't seem to be uncomfortable, though. He was observing her, waiting for her to continue. So she did.

"My parents warned me I would need to be careful with my use of magic and to keep my magical abilities private. Sorcerers are few, and there are many evil beings who seek to either destroy us, enslave us, or sell us to others who want us to do their bidding.

"Since we stand out because of our unusual hair and eye colors, many sorcerers prefer to stay hidden as much as possible. As my magic became more powerful, my father instructed me in how to hide the traits that would make my identity apparent once I headed out into the world. Every time he came to visit, or I went there, he had me practice the seer skill of inner-sight, changing my hair and eye color. We seers are lucky that we have this ability to hide our features. Sorcerers of other races do not."

Maelona watched Blaez's eyes run over her brown hair and pale face, stopping when he met her brown eyes. She could see the questions there, but he didn't voice them. Unlike most other creatures of Sterrenvar, sorcerers could have just about any coloring found in nature. Her mother's hair was violet and her eyes amethyst. Her own natural coloring was not the same as her mother's, but it still was not something commonly seen.

She continued to hold Blaez's gaze for a moment, knowing he was curious and wondering if she should show him. However, she'd been brown-haired and brown-eyed for so long now that the coloring stayed even while she was sleeping. While it wasn't her natural state, she had done it so long that it now felt natural to her. The very thought of showing her true self to someone now made her feel raw and exposed—almost as if she was allowing someone to see into her very soul. She wasn't ready for that yet.

Maelona looked over the crater again and continued her story. "Despite my father's training, I was young and naïve and thought myself safe here in the village. And mostly I was.

"But I started noticing that, when I was in the village, your father was often nearby, watching me. It wasn't long before I realized he was following me. At first, I thought he was assigned to watch me by my mother. She always had a couple of trusted protectors monitoring me. Then, one day in the market, I turned and saw Guarin looking at me with an expression I could only describe as. . . calculating. It was unnerving." Her voice was tight as she remembered the spike of fear she'd felt.

"I used to sneak off to practice my sorcery here in private. One day, I was sitting in the middle of this clearing," she said, nodding towards the center of the crater and remembering what it looked like back then, "practicing changing the natural hues of the surrounding wildflowers, and your father approached me from behind. He said he knew someone who would give him a substantial reward for a 'creature' like me," Maelona continued, "but that first he wanted. . ."

Maelona could not suppress the shudder that ran through her body.

Blaez reached his hand out toward her, but stopped before he made contact. She was grateful for that. She did not think she could handle it right now.

She shook her head. "I can't. . . I can't. . ."

Her throat was tight, and she felt like she could barely breathe. She was afraid she would lose control if she allowed herself to go too deeply into those memories. Already, she felt as if there was static running underneath her skin.

"It's okay, Maelona. You don't have to say anything you don't want to. Just take a deep breath."

She closed her eyes, inhaled deeply, and held it before letting it out slowly. When she felt like she was under control again, she slid down the side of the crater and walked to the center. She heard footsteps on dry dirt and knew Blaez was following. She stopped in front of a bleached white, flat, round stone that didn't seem to fit in with the brown, gray, and black dirt and rocks that surrounded it.

"What you need to know," she said, "especially if you travel with me as my mother obviously wants to happen, is that I lost control of my magic that day. In a moment of panic, I screamed. All I saw was a blinding white light, and then. . . nothing." Maelona paused for a moment and stared down at the spot of white on the ground in front of her.

"When I awoke sometime later, I was at my mother's sanctuary with her sitting beside me. She told me that my magic had responded to my extreme stress and fear by creating a powerful, outward force like an explosion. Your father was killed instantly."

She nodded to a dark patch on the ground off to the right, then glanced at Blaez, expecting to see anger, maybe sorrow, on his face. Instead, his brows were drawn down, his lips were curled on one side, and his nose was wrinkled. He looked. . . disgusted.

"I'm sorry. Maybe I shouldn't be telling you this, but I thought you should know. I know he was your father, and I—"

"Don't," he ground out through clenched teeth. "Don't you ever apologize for this. You were just a child, and your magic acted to protect you. I'm the one who is sorry. I'm sorry my father put you through that." His voice was firm with an angry edge, but his words made her realize that his disgust and anger were not aimed at her.

"Take your own advice and never apologize for your father either," she said. "You were also a child, and you had no control over your father's actions."

He paced away from her, hands on his hips, then turned and paced back again, stopping a few paces in front of her.

"My father was cruel to my mother and me at home. If I had told someone, a protector maybe. . ."

"Don't do that to yourself, Blaez. It is not your fault. There is no way you could have known what he would do."

He looked at his feet. "I sound like I'm making this about me. I don't mean to. I just hate what my father did to you. You didn't deserve it, and I wish I could have done something about it."

"But you couldn't have, and what's done is done. I wouldn't even be telling you about this, but you need to understand why I don't use my magic; you need to know there is always the potential for danger when you're near me." It was why she avoided situations that could turn emotional or volatile. She was surprised nothing had yet happened during this conversation.

Blaez shook his head. "That was years ago. I don't believe you're dangerous. Not unless you intend to be."

She let out a wry chuckle. "You haven't known me long," she said. "There's no way you could know that. Especially since I don't even know that myself."

Maelona walked back towards the edge of the crater, left of where they had been sitting earlier, and looked down at another dark spot.

She had told no one this story. She'd never even spoken it before. It was her mother who gave her the details of what happened during and after the magical explosion once she'd regained consciousness. But if there was anyone who deserved to know it—both because of his connection to the story and because of his offer to help her—it was Blaez. So she took a breath, mentally gathered her courage, and continued.

"Your father was not the only casualty that day," Maelona said in a sad, quiet voice. "My father was a seer, as you know. After I woke up at my mother's, she told me he had run into the village to find me. He'd had a dream-vision warning of Guarin's intentions. He could not see what happened to me because of our limitations on seeing ourselves and those who directly affect our lives. My father rushed here from the Valley of Sight to save me."

Maelona met Blaez's eyes when he looked up at her. She could feel tears tracking down her cheeks. When she spoke again, it was barely more than a croak. "I didn't even know he was here. He was trying to save me."

She took a deep breath, looked down, and swallowed past the lump in her throat. Then she whispered, "I killed him."

She stayed there for some time, looking down at the last place her father ever stood alive. Her tears streamed incessantly and her whole body shook. She did not know how much time passed as she stood there, lost in her anguish.

She jumped suddenly when she noticed that the rocks and sand around her had started to shake, like ground wheat being sifted in a basket. Her magic was vibrating just under her skin, reacting to her emotions.

She pulled herself out of her memories, trying to distance herself from what she'd felt. The more emotional she was, the more her magic reacted, and how could she ever live with herself if she lost control and hurt someone again? She'd barely survived the last time, and Blaez now stood just a few paces from her, waiting for her to continue her story.

She wiped her eyes. When she felt fairly confident that she could talk again without her voice shaking, she continued.

"As soon as I was strong enough and had perfected the ability to hide my features, I left for my father's village." She let out a wry laugh. "I'd just learned the hard way how important it was to not let strangers know I what I was, so I didn't want to travel until I could hide the parts of me that stood out. But it was my fault that Clearview was without its sorcerer, and I wanted to fill the hole I had caused in any way I could."

Blaez reached out and grabbed her hand, running his thumb in soothing circles on the back. "I am so sorry that happened to you, Maelona. You are not to blame. It was my father's cruel actions that brought about this tragedy—all of it.

"I want to assure you," he said forcefully, "that I am nothing like my father. I never knew exactly what happened until now, but after my father was killed, people would watch me, look at me with suspicion. I knew he'd done something unforgiveable, even if I didn't have all the details, and I didn't want anyone to think I was like him. So I vowed to be as good and as helpful as I could to anyone who needed it.

"That's one way Alune helped me after she took me in. People would go to her for help, and if there was anything I could do, she let me—from gathering herbs for medicines to helping to build or repair things."

Maelona squeezed his hand. "I have not known you long, but I already know you are not like him. I would not tell you any of this if I thought you were."

She sighed. "This has haunted me for years, and the hardest part for me to live with is what I did. I took the lives of two men, one of whom strived to be a good man, a kind man, every day of his life."

Speaking in a quiet, sad voice, she added, "I will work on my redemption all the days of *my* life."

Maelona stared into the crater for a few moments more. "I have not used magic in the presence of others since that day." In a whisper, she added, "And I don't know if I can fulfill the prophecy without it."

Maelona led Blaez back to the Sorceress's sanctuary, where the Sorceress prepared tea and a light lunch for them.

Once they'd finished their meal, her mother said, "Blaez and I will fill you in on some of what has happened here since you left." Then she nodded to Blaez.

He took a deep breath. "I already told you that my father was cruel to my mother and me. Shortly before his death, he inflicted a wound on my mother that never seemed to heal. It began to fester, but she would not get help or allow me to. After some time, it became severely infected, and she became delirious with fever. At that point, I disregarded her wishes and came to your mother for help. But it was too late.

"Sorceress Alune comforted me. She taught me about healing plants—mostly to take my mind off my grief, I suspect." The smile he gave her mother then was sad, but fond. "She eventually employed me as her assistant; I mostly search for any ingredients she needs. I still do protector duty when needed, but mostly I work with her."

"And an excellent assistant he has proven himself to be," her mother said as she smiled affectionately at Blaez.

Maelona felt a sharp pang at the clearly visible mutual regard and the bond that her mother and Blaez obviously shared. Her discontent was not aimed at them, however. After all, it was her own decision to leave, and her own excuses that kept her from coming back.

Blaez turned to smile at Maelona warmly, and some of her discomfort dissipated. "Alune understood my drive to prove to myself and others that I am more than my father's son. I yearned to ease some of the suffering and damage he left in his wake. So, when someone needed aid that I could give, she pointed me in their direction. She became like a mother to me."

Maelona could see the concern in his eyes as he said this—he held her gaze and his expression was one of pleading, like he was begging her to understand, to not be upset about this.

Maelona smiled at Blaez and responded in a soft voice, "I am glad you were there for each other, and happy she had you to keep her company and keep her safe when I could not."

Her mother stirred in her seat, looking like she wanted to say something, but she hesitated for a moment before speaking.

"Maelona, my love, I understand why you went away. No one here will judge you. Everyone has to deal with life's trials in their own way, and that was yours. It was noble, even, to want to make up your father's loss to those in his village who needed him.

"However, as a sorceress, and as your mother, I am very concerned about your refusal to use your magic. It is a part of you, my dear, and denying it is denying yourself. I want you to have as many advantages as you can, knowing what likely lies ahead for you."

Maelona had the urge to ask her mother how she could know whether she'd practiced her magic in the years she'd been away. However, even back when Maelona was a child, her mother somehow always knew as much as, or more than, the seers. But she would never reveal the why or how of the many things she knew it seemed she should not.

"And what lies ahead?" Blaez asked. His question caught her attention, and she looked at her mother, curious what her answer would be. "Maelona has spoken to me about the danger involved in her mission," Blaez continued. "She warned me I might not want to help once I knew what it was. Now, Alune, you speak of wanting Maelona to have all the advantages she can. What is it we're facing, exactly?"

"War, my dear Blaez," her mother answered. "War against a very formidable opponent and his many formidable allies. It is a long and complicated story, my friend, and you will hear all the details soon enough."

After a brief pause, Maelona said, "Don't worry, Mother. I have said I do not practice in the presence of others, but that does not mean I do not practice my magical skills at all. My goal is to not lose control of my magic. At some point, I realized that by constantly trying to suppress it, I was not controlling my power. Instead, I was allowing it to control me.

"I have many free nights when the seer in me does not need to sleep," she said. "I spend my time preparing, gathering, or making what we need, practicing my martial arts and weapons skills, and sometimes even practicing with my magic."

"I am so glad to hear that, my daughter. It will comfort me during your upcoming trials and battles to know you are well-prepared."

Maelona shifted uncomfortably in her seat. "I don't know if I'd say 'well-prepared' exactly. It's probably more accurate to say I'm not oblivious to the magic. I may not have been completely ignoring my magic, but I was hiding it from everyone around me and I wasn't practicing it as much as I should have, either."

"Perhaps you and I could practice together some evenings and nights during your visit," her mother suggested. "I'm sure I could go without sleep for a night here and there to have the privilege of working with you, doing all I can to ensure your safety."

"I would like that, Mother," Maelona replied with a warm smile. "I would like that very much."

So Much to Protect

An hour later, Maelona was sitting at a wooden table off to the side of a large open area in the town's center. Most of the pack came and went here at mealtimes, as it was customary to eat together whenever duties allowed. Apparently, that was something that had stayed the same after all this time.

Maelona watched on as Blaez used this opportunity to spread word of a meeting they planned for that night to any off-duty protectors who were present, trusting them to spread the word along as well. This meeting was just to get them to agree, hopefully, to train together and set up a schedule.

Maelona chewed a sweet, red apple from one of the many fruit trees off the southwest side of the village as she watched Blaez interact with some young from the pack. He was play-fighting with them, but Maelona recognized the bigger benefit to this type of play. Wolf-folk young did not start shifting until puberty, so this game also taught them some basic hand-to-hand techniques that could come in handy if danger came their way.

Maelona found herself a little in awe of Blaez as she thought of all the inconspicuous things he did for others, from playing with and teaching the young ones, to taking part in protector duties. And, of course, he had also helped her own mother for the last forty years, when she herself had not been in the correct frame of mind to do so. For that, she would be forever grateful.

Seeing Blaez interact so comfortably with the young and with the others in the village made it clear any negative feelings because of his parentage were long past.

Turning from Blaez, Maelona looked around at all the energetic and joyful signs of life to be found here, in the village center. Near the group of young ones play-fighting with Blaez, another group of youth played hunters and prey. Closer to the center of the common area, there were many booths set up where people could trade items and get food. Groups of young and old alike sat eating their midday meal together, talking and laughing animatedly. Some sat at tables and others sat on the grass.

At one table, a group of young had various containers of inks and different sized needles strewn around them. They were practicing inking their marks onto pieces of animal hide. Wolf-folk young learned how to ink their marks before they learned how to write. Each young would create his or her own mark, practicing it until it was just the way they wanted. It sometimes took years of practice and development of fine motor skills before they came up with what would be their official mark. They then used this mark throughout their lives to represent themselves. It was their signature and their symbol.

Maelona remembered when she first created and practiced her own mark along with other young her age, many years ago. She was light and carefree back then, her only worry being getting that mark to be just the perfect representation of herself and still have time afterwards to play with her few friends. For the first time since she left, Maelona allowed herself a moment to feel nostalgic for what she had left behind.

Just as when she had left the seer village and looked back down upon it, reality now struck her again as she looked at all this life surrounding her: the laughter, the joy, the freedom, the love. This was what they would soon fight to protect. This was what they stood to lose.

Maelona sat there in the village center, feeling the freedom, energy, and goodness all around her, and it made her that much more determined to stand up against any evil that threatened to destroy it. At that moment, she decided to take her mother up on her offer to train with her. She didn't know exactly what it entailed, but if using magic was the only way to fulfill the prophecy and save the people of the realm, then she needed to face her fear of her powers head-on.

Maelona had had dream-visions that showed children like those around her today who were pried from their families at a young age, forced to serve masters who thought themselves better and more powerful. She'd seen them mistreated and beaten, fed only what was necessary for them to remain strong enough to serve their 'masters.' She'd seen them trading in play time for the many menial tasks involved in pampering creatures who could care for themselves. Each time she remembered these visions, she felt her rage ignite—just as it did now.

The light hairs on her arms and the back of her neck stood up, and she could feel her skin tingle. Her rage fought for control and her magic threatened to surface. She trembled with the effort of holding them back and tensed her muscles to stop her body from quaking.

"Maelona!" a voice called.

Startled, she looked up to see Blaez walking toward her. He must have finished his game with the group of young. Luckily, his arrival pulled her out of her disturbing thoughts and helped calm her emotions.

She took a moment to breathe deeply and relax. She would have to be more careful. If he hadn't interrupted her silent fuming, would something have happened with her magic? She really needed to learn how to control it, so it stopped controlling her.

"Are you ready for our one-on-one practice?" He asked. She nodded to him and they headed out.

It did not take long for Blaez and Maelona to reach the clearing where the protectors came regularly to hone their skills. It was at the eastern edge of the village. As they entered the clearing, Maelona said, "Let's begin with hand-to-hand skills. We can work our way up to various weapons."

"I am a Wolf-folk," Blaez said. "I can shift into wolf form and have built in weapons. This would not be fair to you."

Maelona laughed a big, warm laugh. He wasn't certain what she found so funny, but he could not help but grin along with her. Such a laugh was a rare gift from Maelona, and he had never seen her laugh that openly with anyone but himself.

"I assure you, Blaez, that even in your wolf form, a hand-to-hand fight with me would still be fair. I do not sleep as often as you do, so I have much time during the night to devote to pursuits such as physical training. Also, I've been taught by the best martial trainer in the realm.

"When I first went to Clearview, the seer village," she said, "the elders knew I would be in much danger in the future because of who I am. Refusing to use my magic left me at a further disadvantage. So, the elders ensured I underwent stringent physical, martial arts, and weapons training so that I would be capable of protecting myself. They assigned their best fighter to teach me."

She turned to face Blaez fully. "And therefore, we are starting here, Blaez. Some of the first, yet essential, lessons Owyn taught me are: know your enemy, yet take nothing for granted; never assume you are better than your opponent; be prepared for the unexpected and be unexpected. Also, train your weaknesses so they become strengths."

He held up a hand in front of him. "Wait a moment. Did you not just proclaim it would be a fair fight between us? You've never seen me fight before. Aren't you assuming you are better than me?"

She distinctly looked like she was trying to hold back a grin. "Technically, I believe I was assuming we are at least equally matched."

He put his hands on his hips. "Fine. I guess we'll see, then."

Her smile bloomed fully, and his heart skipped a beat. "I guess we will," she said. "However, let's get back to what I was saying.

"Any opponent who knows you are Wolf-folk might assume you will depend on the strength, speed, teeth, and claws of your wolf. You need to make sure you are equally formidable in your human form to prepare for this and other eventualities. Folk are more dexterous in human form. Maybe you will be attacked while completing a task you need your human hands for. Maybe a sorcerer will lock you into your human form—"

"Is that really possible?" Blaez interrupted, fighting back a spark of panic. His wolf was a part of who he was. He would have never thought it possible for it to be locked away from him. The very idea of it filled him with a strong sense of discomfort.

Maelona replied in a soft tone. "It is not common, to be sure, but it has happened." She contemplated him for a moment, and he squirmed internally at the weight of her attention on him. "I wish to show you some of a wolf's vulnerabilities. Shift into your wolf form and attack me. I will defend first with a weapon, and then without."

Maelona walked a dozen paces away from Blaez and turned to face him. As usual, she wore her typical leather outfit with straps crisscrossing her body and weapons in various holsters in the straps. Now she reached up and behind to her lower back. When she brought her hand back around, she held what looked to be a cylinder about two feet long. Holding it in front of her in one hand, palm down, she pressed a button, and the cylinder sprung open with the rasp of metal sliding against metal, then clicked into place, forming a short staff about four feet long.

Ah, that was the weapon she'd used when fighting the demonkin.

"Shift," she said.

Blaez turned his back, removed his pants and shifted into his formidable black wolf.

"Attack me."

Blaez paused for just a moment before running towards her. As he moved, Maelona crouched down, switching her grip to the ends of the short staff. Just as Blaez jumped up to lunge at her, Maelona jumped as well, straight at him and higher than his extended claws, with the staff held horizontally in front of her. She rammed the staff into his open mouth, driving it back as far as it would go, essentially locking his jaw open. If the staff had been wooden, he could have snapped it easily. But Blaez could taste that it was some kind of metal. . . sound metal. If he were a real animal instead of an animal-folk, he was sure he would have lost some teeth.

He had barely a moment to think on this before Maelona flipped herself up and over the staff—and over his head—twisting around to face the front as she did so. She now sat astride Blaez's back. She gripped the staff firmly as she jerked her body to the side, using her body weight to throw him off balance.

As Blaez fell sideways to the ground, Maelona leaped off his back again while keeping the pressure on the staff. When they came to a stop, Blaez lay on his back on the ground, looking up at the upside-down face of Maelona, who kneeled on one knee, bending over him and pressing down on the staff. Blaez tried to twist to the side to right himself, but Maelona did not budge and he could not find any purchase. He felt like a turtle, stranded upside down on his shell. He was also drooling considerably. The staff pressing back in his mouth kept it open and made it almost impossible for him to move his tongue.

"From here, I could perform several killing blows," Maelona said, looking down at him. Then she got up and stood in front of him as he righted himself.

"That," she continued, "didn't even use all of my strength. Locking the jaws on an animal-folk has somewhat the same effect as a joint lock on people. If it is done effectively, you can control your enemy and gain the upper hand with relatively little effort.

That was an unnerving thought. Few were brave enough to get that close to a Folk's jaws, so he hadn't considered it before.

"Again," Maelona commanded. "This time I will use no weapons." With that, she stalked off away from him, retracting the staff and returning it to her holster at her back as she walked. She stopped and turned at about the same distance from him as before. Nodding to Blaez, she said, "Whenever you are ready."

Blaez paced back and forth, hoping to take her by surprise by making it harder for her to predict when he'd attack. He took off like a shot toward her, and Maelona stood still, watching him. Then, when he was about to go in for the killing strike, with fangs bared and great paws reaching for her, she dodged to the side. She grabbed a handful of the fur on his shoulder and swung herself up onto his back. She locked one arm around his neck, and with the other hand, she reached out and grabbed his jaw. Maelona quickly used the leverage on his jaw to jerk his head around, almost to the point of doing actual damage.

Maelona leaned forward, her mouth close to his ear. So Blaez heard her clearly when she said, "Crack! I just broke your neck."

Blaez stopped moving and Maelona jumped off his back, moving into his line of sight. "That might not kill a Wolf-folk, but it will put him out of commission for a while." She quirked an eyebrow. "Do you need another demonstration?"

Blaez huffed and shook his head. He would have laughed at himself if he were in human form. She was obviously right when she'd told him she didn't need a protector, and he was obviously not as good a fighter as he thought he was. Maybe training with the same group all the time had made things a little too predictable.

He was learning many uncomfortable truths lately.

"In that case, shift back to your human form and we will practice some hand-to-hand combat."

Blaez shifted as he walked away toward the edge of the clearing where he'd left his loose cotton pants.

Once he was dressed, Blaez walked back toward Maelona. "I'm ready." The words were hardly out of his mouth when Maelona threw a punch at him. He instinctively blocked the punch and offered one in return.

Maelona blocked his strike but then unexpectedly turned into his body, pushing his punching hand out to the side and turning so that her back almost touched his chest as she brought her elbow up and around behind her, striking him in the jaw. She kept turning her body until she was behind him, where she hopped back a step and then moved forward again to add more force as she punched with both fists into his kidneys.

Blaez groaned at the sudden pain, yet he knew that the amount of force she put behind it was not enough to do any permanent damage. She was pulling her punches while still ensuring he felt it.

Blaez spun around, throwing another punch at Maelona, but she blocked again and somehow grabbed his wrist, flipped it over, and pushed up on his hand, locking his wrist. Then she swung her body around again while keeping his hand pinned in hers until his elbow was locked and she was pushing him face first into the ground. Blaez had to either move where she was leading him or take the chance of having his arm broken or elbow joint damaged.

They continued this practice for some time, taking turns attacking and defending. Maelona was a patient instructor as he learned the new techniques, breaking down the movements afterwards whenever she had moved too quickly for him to really absorb what she'd done.

In the last technique of the practice session, Blaez ended up flat on his back while Maelona straddled him, pinning his legs with her feet on his thighs and pinning his arms with her own. Maelona was stronger and more muscular than most females he knew, and the dense muscle made her heavier than most, as well. Still, Blaez was certain he could throw her off him if he wanted to.

But suddenly, as he looked up at her, he found he didn't want to. Instead, his body stilled as he gazed up at her. When Maelona looked down at him and saw his expression, her own morphed from a mischievous grin into something more serious.

He was acutely aware of her lithe body pressed along his, the closeness of her lips to his own. It was as if, in that moment, something changed, sparked between them. Blaez closed his eyes as Maelona lowered her mouth toward his. He felt her breath on his lips as she slid her nose along his in an affectionate gesture.

He sensed Maelona pull back slightly, and he opened his eyes to see her looking down at him with genuine affection. Then suddenly, in his peripheral vision, he caught movement above and just to the left of Maelona's head. He turned slightly to see what it was and was awed by what he found.

He gasped. All around them where they lay, loose objects that had been on the ground—pebbles, leaves, twigs, grass—were floating in the air. Maelona turned to see what he was looking at, and she jumped up with a start. All the floating objects fell back to the earth.

Blaez could see that Maelona was upset by what had happened, and he wanted to comfort her. So, he stood and reached a hand out to her, saying, "It's okay, Maelona. It was nothing dangerous. We're fine."

"No, it is not okay," Maelona said quietly while staring down at the ground. Her hands were clenched in tight fists by her sides. "This is the reason I try not to get too close to people. I can easily lose control over my magic in emotionally charged situations. I can't help but worry that I will hurt someone else I care about."

Blaez sensed a warmth spreading through him with the realization of how important their moment was to her—how it stirred her enough for this reaction—and her implication that she cared for him. However, this new understanding was tempered by the knowledge that she was afraid of her powers—afraid of losing control.

He wished they could go back to a few moments ago, when they were close, so he could ignore the distracting movement and just stay focused on her. He regretted interrupting that moment of connection and feared she would not let them get that close again.

She looked so upset, so shaken by what had happened—he wanted to reassure her, but he didn't know how. So, he just stood looking at her, not knowing what to say and wishing she would really let him in.

Maelona turned and started walking out of the clearing. After a few steps, she hesitated. Turning to face him again, she said, "We meet with the protectors tonight. If they agree, we will start training with them tomorrow."

Chapter Eight

The Prince & the Demonkin

Early the next morning, Maelona burst into Blaez's hut, yelling, "Blaez! Wake up! We need to go—now!"

Blaez jolted upright in his bed, looking confused and alarmed. The little dull-gray light of pre-dawn that came in through the window was barely enough to illuminate his features. Even though he did not know what was happening, he still jumped up, dressed quickly, and took off after her.

She was glad he didn't hesitate because she didn't think they had much time. Visions were rarely accompanied by information that could pinpoint when, exactly, the events would take place, but from what she remembered of the sky, it was just after dawn. She couldn't be certain that the events she saw would take place today, but her instincts were screaming at her they would.

Just outside the village, Blaez shifted into wolf form, and Maelona guessed it was so he could use his heightened senses to alert him of danger. That wasn't surprising—there was no way he didn't pick up on her sense of urgency.

They ran without slowing for what felt longer than it probably actually was. When she saw a stand of trees that looked familiar, Maelona stopped running and crouched low to the ground, using the trees and thick brush to camouflage her. Blaez followed suit.

"Listen," she whispered. The sounds of fighting and swords clashing came from up ahead. Keeping low and moving silently, Maelona continued forward until she was close enough to see what was happening.

In the middle of the clearing, three creatures were attacking what appeared to be a human male. These creatures were taller and broader than the human—larger than any human, really—and each of them had skin that varied in color from light pink to a mottled red color. Their faces looked like distorted versions of human faces, like they had swollen and had been pulled out to the sides. Their noses were flat and their eyes sunken, and they had various bony protrusions that ran over their cheekbones and up over their temples, ending in horns on their foreheads. These protrusions and horns varied in size from individual to individual.

"Demonkin," Maelona whispered.

The human male fought valiantly with sword and fist, but he was outnumbered, and it was apparent that he was losing the battle. Maelona leaned close to Blaez and whispered, "Circle around to the other side of the clearing and wait for my signal to attack."

Blaez's large black wolf form disappeared from her side, moving quickly but silently. Maelona climbed up the tall, ancient tree closest to her, then used its thick branches to sneak across to the next tree, and the next one, until she was above the area where the fight was taking place. She spotted movement in the bushes where she had directed Blaez and knew he was in position.

With a fierce, wordless battle cry, Maelona jumped from an overhanging tree branch, pulling out her galanite staff and pushing the button to extend it to half-length as she moved. She landed on the shoulders of the demonkin nearest to her.

Maelona brought her staff straight down onto the crown of her target's unprotected head with her full strength, using her momentum to increase the force of the blow. She had never fought demonkin before and, though she was targeting an area typically vulnerable to any enemy, she did not know how tough these beasts were. So, she felt a sense of relief and satisfaction when she heard a sickening crunch as the demonkin's skull gave way under the impact.

When the demonkin lay lifeless in a heap, she glanced up and saw Blaez tearing into his opponent with claw and fang, all the while dodging strikes from the demonkin's dull blade. As soon as he saw an opening, he lunged for the demonkin's throat, tearing it open as he twisted his body and threw the demonkin to the ground.

Maelona ran over to the demonkin that was fighting the weakened human, grabbed the beast by the shoulder, and spun it to face her. She danced around the large creature, striking out with feet and hands whenever an opening presented itself. Though she wielded her staff, she did not rely solely on the weapon, as many would have done. Instead, she used her whole body as a weapon and the staff as just an extension and a defense.

Though large and strong, the demonkin was overcome by Maelona's agility and skill within moments. As the demonkin swung its sword in an arc towards Maelona, she blocked the strike with her staff. Continuing her block in a circular movement, she caught the demonkin's wrist with the end of the staff, disarming him. She quickly brought the staff up, end pointed at the beast's throat, braced herself, and pressed the button to extend the staff to its full length, crushing its windpipe. The demonkin grabbed at its throat with both hands, struggling to breathe, before it shuddered and dropped to the ground. Maelona quickly hopped out of the way.

She turned and saw the human on the ground, trying and failing to get up. He was obviously injured.

"Lie still," she said to him as she hurried over and kneeled next to him. "We're here to help."

Blaez padded over to her side, still in wolf form, and looked down at the young man. He was bloodied, battered, and barely conscious. Maelona looked at his face, then she looked down to where an amulet, now stained with dirt and blood, hung by a chain from his neck.

"Where did you get this?" Maelona asked the man, her voice quavering slightly.

The stranger ground out in a hoarse voice, "Eluard. . . M. . . Mis. . ." before succumbing to unconsciousness.

Maelona quickly undid a clasp at her side and swung her pack from her back to her front. "You will need your hands, Blaez," Maelona said, and he quickly shifted back to human form. She pulled out some leaves and some bandages and handed them to Blaez.

"Press the leaves against his wound here," she instructed Blaez, while pointing out a large wound in the man's chest. "Then bandage it up. Cover him to keep him warm." She pulled a thin cloak out of her pack and handed it to him. "We need to get him back to my mother as quickly as possible."

Maelona took off into the woods, hoping the leaves from the crimsonleaf tree, which had great healing properties, would be enough to keep him alive until they could get him help.

A short time later, Maelona returned with a sleigh like the one she had made to pull the deer carcass. It wouldn't be a smooth ride, but it would be easier on the young man than if she carried him that distance. She laid it down next to the man and then moved to his other side to check him out for other injuries.

"He also has a broken leg, so be careful when we move him," Maelona said. Blaez helped her move the man onto the sleigh as gently as possible, and they pulled it back the way they had come. They moved as quickly as they could without jostling him too much.

"Why were demonkin here, so close to the village?" Blaez questioned as they traveled. "Evil has never ventured inside the Sacred Forest before."

"It has," Maelona replied. "Recently, in fact. I felt it with the draccon. It was under some kind of dark influence."

"What about the magical defenses the Sorcerers of the Light placed on the forest?" Blaez asked. "First the draccon, and now this. How could these demonkin just walk right in here? What do you think this means?"

"I think it means enjoy the beauty of nature," she said darkly. "Breathe it all in. Spend time with your friends. Cherish them. But do it all in between training sessions. Because if we are not victorious in the war to come, none of this will ever be the same again."

Her frank, ominous response took Blaez aback. It was so far from what he'd come to expect from her. It was likely a good indicator of just how dire the situation could become.

"If the Dark Sorcerer has this much magical influence now, if he can breach defenses put in place by a group of the realm's most powerful sorcerers, his plans could tear us all apart—unless we stop him."

"We have not really talked about this yet," Blaez said. "What are his plans? What does he want?"

Maelona sighed. "How much has my mother taught you about the magical history of the realm? Did she tell you about the Battle of the Gate that happened around three-thousand years ago?"

The sleigh bumped over a root and the man groaned. Blaez looked at him. He was still unconscious, but his brow was furrowed.

"She gave me the basic information," he said, bringing his attention back to Maelona.

"We can't be sure," she said, "but from what we've seen, it looks like this new sorcerer plans to replicate what Azedel, the Dark Sorcerer from that time, was trying to do."

"He wants to open the Great Gate?" Blaez tried to keep the panic out of his voice, but he wasn't sure he'd fully succeeded.

Maelona nodded. "He plans to open it, let the demons cross over, then use them to bolster his army so he can take over the realm."

They walked on in heavy silence for a while, Blaez pondering what would happen if this sorcerer succeeded. There were already demonkin in the North—descendants of the demons that escaped being sent back last time, according to the histories. No one was sure how many remained, but if they added full demons to those numbers. . . well, it would mean nothing good.

"Do you think it's possible, Maelona?" he asked. "Do you think we can defeat them? The Sorcerers of the Light almost lost that time and, as far as I'm aware, we do not have as many sorcerers left."

Maelona frowned. "I don't know, Blaez. Already, it feels like a violation that they could breach our precious forest. They have surely attacked some human settlements by now as well. But the one thing I know for certain is this: I will do whatever is in my power to do in order to save our beautiful realm from the darkness. It may be flawed, but it is ours and we must protect it."

Blaez nodded, then eyed the human man with suspicion. "Speaking of protecting, we don't know this man. How do we know it's safe to bring him to Wildegrove? There are elderly and children there."

"The amulet," Maelona replied, glancing back at the unconscious form on the sleigh behind them. "He wears an amulet that is only gifted by seer Elders to trusted friends and allies of our people. It grants safe passage through seer territories and aid in times of need. I think I know who he is, thanks to the amulet and my vision, but I don't yet know his character. He also bears a resemblance to someone I once knew well. If I am right, and his father is who I think he is, then he was sent to us for a reason.

"We will bring him to the Sorceress's sanctuary and keep him away from the village once he's awake. When we leave again, we will take the north path, so we will not have to pass close to your people. He is human, and he is too young to have received the amulet

directly from my father. We will stay cautious until we know more about him."

"Your father?" Blaez questioned. He was so curious about the great man he had only heard stories about, but he didn't want to push Maelona to talk about him if she wasn't ready.

"Yes. The name he gave was my father's name. Eluard Mistreaver."

Blaez studied her face for a moment, but her expression was giving nothing away about how she felt about that. He wondered if this was a seer ability as well. He always found it hard to hide how he was feeling, though he tried often enough, but he often found it difficult to read her.

Looking down at the injured man, Blaez commented, "He would never make it as far as the seer village. It's a week's walk from here at a regular pace and it will be slower still if we have to transport an injured man. It seems we have no choice. Should we send someone to Clearview to alert them when we arrive at the sanctuary?"

He saw a flash of what looked like sadness before her expression cleared again. "If the amulet was indeed given by my father, it falls to me now to honor its promise, so there is no need to travel all the way there."

They traveled the rest of the way to the Wolf-folk village in silence, conserving their breath and their strength for transporting the stranger to the help he desperately needed.

When they were a short way out from the village, they came upon a wolf protector on sentry duty doing his rounds.

"I am glad to see you, Gawn," Blaez greeted, not needing the warrior to shift to know who he was. "We have an injured man here. He will need the skills of the Sorceress. Please, run ahead and let her know of our arrival."

The wolf nodded his head in acknowledgment and took off at a run.

When they reached the edge of the village, a crowd of townsfolk in both human and wolf form had gathered.

The Sorceress came forward to greet them and to look at their guest. "Come, quickly," she said. "Bring him to my sanctuary."

Once they arrived at the Sorceress's dwelling, they moved the injured man into one of the many rooms carved into the rock that made up her living and working spaces. Alune had a cot ready, a fire burning, and a pot steaming above the fire. There were also several vessels containing various items laid out on a table by the bedside.

As soon as the man had been placed upon the cot, the Sorceress got to work removing his clothing and checking his injuries. "Crimsonleaf," she said as she came upon the dressing Maelona had Blaez cover his chest wound with. "Good. How soon after his injuries did you place this on the wound?"

"Within a few minutes," Blaez replied. "Maelona had some in her pack. It saved us much time since I would have had to search for it." Looking over at Maelona with a small smile, he commented,

"It's hard to carry weapons and supplies when you have to shift back and forth from one form to another."

The Sorceress talked and explained as she worked, which Blaez was accustomed to. She continuously instructed him on the medicines and techniques she used as she used them. Had she done the same with Maelona when she lived here?

"I am making a compress from the crimsonleaf, boiled in water with some added herbs to help numb the pain. Once it has thickened enough, we will place it on his wounds to help them heal more quickly. But his wounds are too extensive for just external treatment.

"When he has regained consciousness and can take fluid, we will give him a tea made with plants and herbs that will help with reducing pain, fever, and swelling." Once she got to the man's leg, she looked up at Blaez and Maelona and said, "Unfortunately, if we were to treat his broken leg without the use of magic, healing it would take more time than you have to spare. So, once he can take the liquid remedy for pain, I will realign the fracture and fuse it using my magic. It will take some time to heal fully, but only a fraction of the time it would take using only non-magical methods."

Blaez knew from working with the Sorceress for years that she, like all sorcerers, channeled magic from the energies found in nature and the surrounding elements, and these magical energies came from ley lines connected to the Source. Those who could wield magic drew it into themselves and then focused it to do their bidding. It took many years of practice to learn to focus it when and where you needed it, and even more years to learn to do it quickly and efficiently. Even then, this process consumed a lot of energy. Even after centuries of practice, the more powerful feats of magic, like treating serious and life-threatening injuries, still left the Sorceress exhausted and physically drained. So they used plants and herbs for healing whenever they could.

"Don't push yourself too much, Sorceress. Take care of yourself as well."

"Don't worry, Blaez," she replied. "I'm old enough to know my limitations."

Blaez now wondered about Maelona's magic. From what she'd told him, she had essentially turned her back on it. He felt guilty for the years of practice she'd lost because of his father's evil actions and disappointed that she would not have this added strength to rely upon to protect her in the battles that would surely come.

It was up to him then, he decided, to return some of that strength and protection by always having her back.

Andrion came awake slowly, first registering the smell of various herbs and smoke from a wood fire, and then the sound of the fire crackling. The warmth emanating from a hearth warmed him pleasantly, but he quickly noticed some other, less pleasant sensations as well—a searing pain in his chest, a deep ache in his left leg, and many sore muscles.

His eyes flickered open, and he stared up at a ceiling of solid, dark gray rock. Actual hewn rock—not stones like at the castle. He turned his head to the left and saw more of the same. He was obviously in a cave of some sort, but where?

He turned his head to the right and jumped with a start when he found a person sitting next to him, rather close, looking at him intently.

"By Father's beard!" He cursed as his startled jump caused excruciating pain to shoot through his leg and chest. He groaned loudly and tried to breathe through the pain.

Once the intensity of it lessened some and his breathing slowed, he looked up again to find the person still staring at him with the same stoic expression as before, studying his features. The corner of his mouth rose in a smug smirk when he realized the person was a young woman—a rather attractive young woman with long, shiny chestnut hair and deep brown eyes.

"You are the Prince of Eastgate, are you not?" Her expression was serious and her eyes inquisitive.

His smirk fell quickly at her question. "Yes," he replied hesitantly, a little surprised by the sudden, blunt question coming from a complete stranger. How did she know who he was and where he was from?

"Yes," he said again, more firmly this time. "I am Andrion, son of Nele, King of Eastgate."

"Well, Andrion, son of Nele, I am Maelona, daughter of Eluard." She handed him a cup and said, "Here, drink this. It will help with the pain."

As the mention of Eluard's name sunk in, he remembered his mission, his days of riding in the woods alone, and his attack by demonkin. And then he remembered someone leaping from the trees to come to his aid.

"It was you, wasn't it? You jumped into the fight to help me."

"Unfortunately, not soon enough, it would seem. The demonkin stabbed you in the chest before I could get to you. You were very lucky that no vital organs were hit."

"Still, I have the feeling I wouldn't be alive now if it weren't for you."

"I can't take all the credit. I had some help." She nodded toward the opposite corner of the room.

Andrion followed her gaze and jumped again when he saw a huge black wolf. He sucked air in between his teeth. "I have to stop doing that. It hurts every time I move."

"Drink the tea," Maelona reminded him. "It will help ease the pain."

Andrion looked warily over at the large black wolf and noticed it had striking blue eyes that stood out in bright contrast against the dark color of its fur. He took a sip of his tea and made a face at the bitterness, but he didn't complain. If this tea really got rid of the pain, he would deal with the taste.

"This is Blaez," Maelona said. "He took down one of the demonkin that attacked you and helped me bring you here."

Andrion looked from the wolf back to Maelona. It was strange that she would introduce him to her pet but, then again, many people were strange when it came to their animal companions.

"Well, I am grateful for his help and yours." Though he still felt weak, he flashed her the smile that had won over many others in the past, but she just stared at him with a stoic expression.

He twitched an eyebrow flirtatiously. She narrowed her eyes and tilted her head.

"Are you sure you're in pain? One would think you'd be more concerned with your injuries than with making eyes at strangers."

Andrion's smile dropped. "Ouch. You're a tough one, aren't you?" He sighed and took another sip of his tea. "Don't be too hard on me; I'm just trying to distract myself."

"Is it working?"

"Not particularly. I don't think I've ever felt this wretched before." He lifted his free hand to his injured chest but didn't press down on it, worried he would make the pain worse.

"The tea will begin working soon."

He took a large gulp of the warm drink. "You didn't see my horse when you rescued me, did you? He ran off when the demonkin attacked."

"There was no sign of him, but that also means there were no signs that he was injured either. If you are lucky, he'll have headed back to the castle." Maelona stood up. "The Sorceress will be here shortly to tend to your leg." She turned and began walking out of the room, the enormous wolf following in her wake.

"Wait," Andrion called out to her. "You said you were the daughter of Eluard? Where is he? I need to speak to him immediately. It's a matter of some urgency."

Maelona paused but did not turn around. "My father passed back into the universe many years ago," she replied. "You will speak with me. . . once you have healed a little." With that, she continued to stride out of the room.

He stared after her for a moment before it hit him.

"Wait. Did she say sorceress?"

CHAPTER NINE

Unexpected

Maelona paced restlessly in the hearth room of the sanctuary, waiting for her mother to complete the current round of treatment for the young prince. She'd stayed calm in front of him, but now she needed to get rid of some of her nervous energy.

Blaez was still in wolf form, and she could feel his eyes on her as she moved. He made a grumbly sound from his place near the door, and it sounded like a question.

She looked at him. "Why are you still in wolf form?"

He shifted back to his biped form and turned to the little alcove carved into the rock next to the door to grab a pair of pants. Most Wolf-folk huts all had shelves or baskets near the entrances for storing light linen pants and tunics for when they shifted back and forth. Here, in her mother's sanctuary, the shelves were etched out of the rock.

She'd never thought about it when she lived here as a child, but she suddenly wondered if this place was shaped with magic. She decided to ask her mother about it sometime. The sanctuary was extensive, with hallways and rooms wandering far underneath the escarpment. Then there were all the alcoves, nooks and crannies, and hiding spots carved out of the rock itself. If it all had been hewn by hand, it would have taken a very, very long time, and would have been physically taxing for anyone working on it.

"People are themselves more around animals," Blaez said, drawing her attention back to him. He was now wearing pants, but his thick, muscular chest was still on display. Maelona's eyes dropped, staring. She quickly realized what she was doing and looked him in the eye again.

"So, you're testing him, then?" she asked.

He shrugged. "I don't know if I would call it that," he said. "I just want to see what he's like when he's not on his best behavior for his rescuer and a sorceress. Both of whom are attractive women."

She quirked a brow at him.

He shrugged one shoulder and tilted his head. "He seems the type of man that would note that and adjust his behavior accordingly."

She nodded. He was right. Andrion was the Prince of Eastgate and he would be expected to follow rules of etiquette and social protocols.

"He must know about animal-folk, though," she said. "He is a prince and is likely educated on all the goings on in Sterrenvar."

Blaez looked at her with an eyebrow raised. "I've traveled to the human towns many times. I get stares because of my size sometimes, but no one seems to suspect I'm not human. If it isn't something they are accustomed to, they don't seem to think of the possibility."

"Okay, I understand what you're saying. Staying in your wolf form from time to time is probably the best and fastest way to get to know him. I'm not really comfortable with it—it feels too much like deception—but we really don't have any time to waste."

She walked over to a chair and sat down. "Today's events have interfered with our plans. We only came to an agreement with the protectors and set the training schedule last night. It's short notice and I don't want to lose training time, but I need to speak with my mother. Perhaps you can train with the protectors without me tonight. Please pass on my apologies and let them know I will join the training session tomorrow.

Blaez nodded. "Okay, I will do that." He glanced at the door. "It's just about time to meet them, so I will head out now."

"Thanks, Blaez."

Maelona watched Blaez leave, then her mind drifted to recent events. What did these encounters with the draccon and the demonkin mean?. Actually, she had a good idea, but she was reluctant to admit it, even to herself.

"The Prince is doing as well as expected given the circumstances," her mother said as she strolled through the door to the back tunnels.

Maelona nodded absently. "Hmm? Oh, good."

Her mother sat down on the chair across from her and sighed. "Tell me what's on your mind, my Lona."

Maelona couldn't help the grin that formed when she heard her mother's nickname for her. But it quickly fell away as she leaned forward towards her mother.

"I haven't told you this yet, but a couple of days before we arrived here, we came across a draccon."

"A draccon?" her mother asked in surprise. "Oh my, how lucky you were. I can't recall how long it's been since I've heard so much as a mention of a sighting. I'd worried they'd all died out or left the forest."

She took a deep breath. "Mother, I think it was compelled."

Her mother sat up straighter and her eyebrows rose. "Compelled? Really? What makes you think so?"

"The draccon was pursued by an Eagle-folk, who hunted it and killed it."

Her mother gasped, and Maelona nodded in understanding.

"When I questioned the Eagle-folk about why he would kill it, he told me that the beast had been targeting children in their clan. Children who aren't old enough to shift yet.

The Sorceress put a hand over her mouth in horror. "Was anyone harmed?"

"There was only one, from what I heard, but she had fractures in both arms and a couple of her ribs were cracked."

Her mother shook her head. "I know they're rare, so we don't hear much about them, but I have never heard of a draccon attacking humans or Folk in human form."

"I haven't either, so that made me suspicious. I got this idea to try something I'd never done before. You know how we seers can see inside ourselves and trace the elements in our bodies?"

Her mother nodded.

"I wondered if it would be possible to use a little of my magic as a bridge of sorts, so I could use my inner-sight to see inside the draccon."

"Did it work?"

"Yes, to an extent. Since the creature was dead, the traces were faint, but I felt something dark and evil crackling underneath the surface."

Her mother's eyes went wide. "How could that be possible?"

"I don't know," Maelona said, shaking her head. "But all the signs point to that being the case. And if it's true it was compelled, then that means someone either had to lure it out to put a spell on it and then send it back, or they had to cross into the Sacred

Forest to do it." She blew out a frustrated breath and ran a hand through her hair. "Either way, the magical protections should have prevented anyone or anything with evil intent from crossing the borders of the forest. And then today, with the prince—those demonkin were attacking him far inside the forest."

Maelona reached across and grabbed her mother's hand. "Either the magical protections are failing, or the Dark Sorcerer has found some way to circumvent them."

"He can get to the Great Gate."

Maelona nodded and repeated, "Yes, he can get to the Great Gate. That's one of our protections down. Now the only things standing between him and opening the portal there are the keystones."

Her mother tipped her head forward and looked up at her from under her lashes. "That isn't the only thing," she said.

Maelona stood so quickly that the wooden chair she'd been sitting on squealed against the smooth stone of the floor. She paced back and forth quickly, unable to calm the panic that started to rise within her.

"Mother, what am I going to do? I am not ready for this. Can I really be the person the prophecy meant if I'm too cowardly to use my magic?"

"You are not a coward, Maelona."

The force of her mother's voice, which verged on anger, surprised Maelona so much that she jumped in her seat. Then she shook her head and shared her concerns.

"They've already figured out how to get past the protective spells, which means they can enter the forest and just walk right up to the Great Gate whenever they want. If they get past our defenses at the gate towns, they will destroy the keystones so they can access the magic at the source."

"I know you and your friends will not allow that to happen."

"But what if it does? How am I supposed to stand up to a Dark Sorcerer when I've been afraid of my magic for most of my life? I've been so naïve!"

Her Mother stood and grabbed her forearm, halting her attempt to wear a path in the floor. "Maelona, breathe. Relax."

Her mother's gaze captured her own, and Maelona matched her breaths until her panic lessened.

"I believe in you, my Lona," her mother said in a quiet but firm voice. Then a mischievous little smile lifted the corners of her lips.

"But if you're really upset about not being able to use your magic, follow me."

Maelona followed her mother down tunnels that twisted and turned far underneath the escarpment. She walked on her toes, hardly making a sound—she had never been allowed back here as a child and coming here now felt strangely like she was doing something forbidden.

Her mother turned and smiled at her over her shoulder, undoubtedly amused by the way her grown daughter still snuck around like she was breaking the rules just by being back here.

The way was lit by a magical orb of lavender light that floated just above and in front of her mother, advancing as she did. It was barely bright enough to cast dull shadows, but it was plenty for them to see by.

They continued until they hit what looked like a dead end. Her mother placed her hand in the center of the narrow wall and the section under and around her hand glowed purple. A crack formed in the stone, traveling up one side, across the top, and down the other side. The now-visible door then slid slightly back and to the side, allowing them entrance. As soon as they were both inside, the door slid shut behind them and torches lit around the room. The familiar scent of herbs hit her—her mother carried this scent on her clothing all the time, but it was stronger here.

Maelona knew her mother had secret rooms within her stone sanctuary, but she had never been allowed inside any of the ones past certain markings on the stone walls. Her mother had told her they were too dangerous. Now, she spun around slowly, taking in the shelves that lined the walls, filled with vessels of many shapes and sizes that no doubt housed herbs, plants, and anything else her mother might need.

"Is this your store room for elements with magical applications?"

Sorcerers and sorceresses could channel magic that originated from the Source through their bodies and then reshape and redirect it the way they wanted. Sometimes, though, for more difficult acts of magic, different plants, objects, or elements could provide focus and a boost of energy.

"It is," her mother said as she looked through some simple woven baskets on a shelf. "I don't bother to hide my medicinal ingredients so well."

She pulled something out of one basket then continued to look through others. She pulled a second object out, then a third, before going to the small circular table in the center of the room, where she laid them out for Maelona to see.

There was a large, semi-translucent yellow gemstone, a large gold nugget, and a chunk of some other metal she couldn't identify. If she survived the coming war, perhaps she'd get Aleyn to teach her to recognize all the known metals.

Maelona looked at her mother questioningly.

"What is your favorite weapon? The one you are most likely to pull out and carry into battle?"

Maelona reached behind her, pulled the retractable staff out of its holder, and placed it on the table next to the other objects. Her mother picked it up and examined it, turning it over in her hands. She pushed the button near the center until it quickly slid open, then further, then retracted.

"As you might guess," her mother said, "with the Great Alignment coming again soon, I've been thinking a lot about the

Source of magic, the ley lines, and the keystones, and one day, an idea came to me."

She placed the staff on the table again, picked up the gemstone in one hand and the metal nuggets in the other. She placed her hands, so she was holding the two chunks of metal on the staff towards one end, and the gemstone so it was just touching the tip of the same end. Alune closed her eyes and soon a purple light emanated from her hands, infusing the objects in them and the staff they were touching.

Sweat formed on Maelona's brow and her heart picked up speed as she watched her mother magically modify her favorite weapon—the one Aleyn just recently gave to her for her day of birth, after carefully crafting it with his own hands. Would it still work the same way when her mother was done? Would it still be retractable? *Just what, exactly, is she doing to my staff?*

Before she had a chance to really panic, her mother was done. She held it up in front of Maelona. Instead of her practical, plain gray, galanite staff, there was an ornate and bejeweled... scepter? Wand? At least, that's what it looked like fully retracted like this.

"I'm sorry, I had to change how it works, but just a little," her mother said.

Maelona could suddenly see her mother's fatigue in the slope of her shoulders and the circles under her eyes that hadn't been there before. Performing this magic on her staff when she'd also been treating their guest's injuries regularly must be draining. She pushed the center button and, instead of expanding on both ends like before, it expanded out on the side that didn't have a large yellow gemstone attached.

"That's lovely, Mother, but don't you think a bejeweled staff is a bit out of place on a battlefield? What if I break it, or lose the gemstone?"

Her mother shook her head. "It may look decorative, but it is magically imbued. It would take an incredible force to break it now. Also, it is more practical than you realize. You can use it to help you control your magic."

Maelona's heart thumped and her eyes grew wide. "What do you mean?" She could hear the note of cautious hope in her own voice.

"Why do you fear using your magic, Maelona?" Her mother's expression was clear and nonjudgmental. There was even a slight smile on her lips.

"Because I lose control of it when I become highly emotional."

"And what happens when you lose control?"

"Mother. . ."

"My dear, I know this is difficult for you, but humor me and answer the question, please."

Maelona nodded and took a deep, calming breath. "Well, when it happened the first time, it just exploded out of me. From the look of the crater afterwards, it went out in a circle with me at the center."

"Have there been other times?"

She nodded again. "Yes. There have been other times, but none so bad as the first. When I have disturbing dream-visions, sometimes I wake up and everything around me is floating in the air."

Her mother nodded knowingly. "Your magic was unfocused at those times. This will help you focus it."

Maelona looked from the short staff to her mother quizzically. "How?"

The Sorceress reached out and took one of Maelona's hands and placed the staff in it. "Since you are a guardian of Sterrenvar—a keystone guardian—let me explain it in a way you'll understand.

"Imagine that you are the source of magic." Her mother placed a hand on Maelona's chest, just below her collarbone. "Your staff is a ley line, and the gemstone at the end is a keystone. What is it the keystones do, Maelona?"

"They store excess magic and let it out slowly, so that there is never too much magical power flowing through. The keystones will restrict the flow of magic to where there won't be enough for dark sorcerers to use in truly destructive ways. Well, until the Great Alignment gives it a brief magical boost."

"Right. So when you pull magic from your surroundings into you, it is like when the magic flows back into the Source. You channel that magical energy and send it out through your ley line." She ran her hand along the newly decorated staff. "Then, you gather it in the keystone," she said, tapping the gemstone at the end, "and you store it there until you need it. When you are ready to use it, concentrate. Let out only as much as you need in the moment."

"But how do I know how much I will need?"

"You will feel it, of course, and it will get easier to judge the more you practice."

Her mother said it so matter-of-factly, yet it still felt like an impossible task.

The Sorceress turned and went to a shelf that contained several empty glass jars and vials. She chose a jar and then put it on the table.

"I want you to pick up this jar and put it back on the shelf—without breaking it."

She looked at her mother incredulously. "Do you know how long it's been since I purposely used my magic for intricate tasks?"

Her mother reached out and squeezed her free hand. "It does not matter," she said. "I will talk you through it the first time." She let go of Maelona's hand and moved to the opposite side of the table, far out of the path the jar would have to take, thankfully. "Now, close your eyes and breathe deeply."

Maelona did as asked. As her mother gave her instructions, she concentrated on visualizing everything she said.

"You are the Source of magic: Feel the magic flow back into you, up through your feet, into your torso, into your shoulders, along your arms and hands. Now send it into your ley line, your staff, and let it gather in the gemstone."

Maelona felt the prickle of magical energy along the path her mother described. It was like the tingle of electricity in the air before a storm.

Her mother paused for a moment before asking, "Is it there?"

Maelona nodded.

"Are you ready?"

She nodded again.

"Open your eyes."

Maelona opened her eyes and focused on the jar.

"Imagine what you want to do with the jar—where you want it to go. When you are ready, channel some of your magic from the gemstone to the jar, telling it what to do."

Maelona figured the first step would be to pick the jar up, so she concentrated, and. . . the jar flew straight up into the air at full speed toward the high rock ceiling. She sucked in a breath and froze, and the jar froze at the same time—stopping just before it could shatter against the ceiling.

"Pause, Maelona, and breathe," her mother said. "Get yourself calm and centered again. You are very powerful, my dear. That's why you've had trouble controlling the magic. Concentrate on creating just a little pinhole in the gemstone for the magic to trickle through. Control how much magic you are putting into your task. Then try again."

Maelona nodded and took a couple of calming breaths. She concentrated on the jar where it still hung in the air and focused on sending just a fraction of the magic to carry the jar back to its place on the shelf. It went slowly, and the jar was a little wobbly at times, but she did it.

When it was safely back where it belonged, she lowered her staff and looked over at her mother. She couldn't stop the wide smile that broke out. She only just controlled her excitement enough to keep herself from bouncing around the room.

Her mother laughed and moved directly in front of her. "I haven't seen you smile like that since you were a child. I love to see you looking so happy. You should smile more often."

Maelona reined in her emotions until there was only a slight grin left. "Who knew I could still be so childish at my age?"

Her mother squeezed her arm. "We all should keep our childlike wonder until the very moment we pass back into the Universe."

"Thank you, Mother, for this." She lifted the staff. "I feel positive about learning to control my magic for the first time in a long time."

Her mother's smile dropped, and she looked at Maelona seriously.

"What? What is it?" Maelona asked.

"I have a theory about why you've had such difficulty learning to control your magic—why you're so powerful." Maelona froze, waiting for her mother to continue.

"All sorcerers and sorceresses are conduits for magic. We can channel magic from the Source, store it within ourselves, and reshape it to do our bidding. Just as you can."

Maelona nodded.

"What else can you tell me about your magic, Maelona? When you use your inner-sight, what do you see inside of you besides what I just described?"

"Do you mean how our cells generate magic as well?"

Her mother nodded, but the press of her lips and the way she looked down at the floor made Maelona feel it was a knowing nod, not a response to her question.

"Not 'our' cells," her mother said. "I've suspected this about you since I carried you inside my body. I could always feel magic there, even when I wasn't channeling. Perhaps if I'd mentioned it earlier, we could have gotten you past your fear of losing control sooner."

"Wait. What are you saying?"

"I'm saying that most of us do not generate our own magic. In fact, in all of our recorded history, Dimia was the first and, until you, the only."

"What?"

Her mother nodded. "Most sorcerers and sorceresses only have access to the magical power available in and around the ley lines, and the magic that seeps out into nature. But you are not limited in this way.

"You are only the second recorded sorceress to both channel magic and generate your own."

CHAPTER TEN

Trust & Uncertainty

Soon after Andrion awoke the next morning, Maelona and the Sorceress entered and came over to sit at his bedside. The wolf—Blaez, if he remembered correctly—trotted in behind them and went to the same corner he had sat in last time.

"Is it morning already?" Andrion asked, looking around. There was no way of telling in this cave-room that he could see.

The Sorceress nodded and handed him a cup; no doubt it was more of the remedies she'd been giving him since he first woke up here. "How are you feeling this morning, Prince Andrion?" she asked.

"I am feeling much better thanks to you, Sorceress," he replied. "There is hardly any pain anymore. Thank you for all of your care. You must not have gotten much rest yourself."

"Do not worry about me. I did not lose any sleep. My kind does not need as much sleep as yours does."

Andrion wondered if she meant her 'kind' as in sorcerers, or if there was something more to the comment. He'd heard rumors about the people who lived in the Sacred Forest, but he wasn't sure how much was true. As he didn't know the etiquette involved in such things and whether it would be rude to ask, he kept his question to himself. For now.

"We had hoped to give you a little more time to heal before speaking with you," the Sorceress said, "but we received some information during the night that leads us to believe we may not have much time."

Andrion carefully placed his cup on the small bed-side table and attempted to sit up straighter in the bed, but he winced as pain shot through him. Alune grabbed a couple of pillows and gently used them to prop him up.

"First, why don't we start with you telling us why you are here?" Maelona said.

"My father knew your father years ago," Andrion began.

She nodded. "Yes. I knew your father as well."

Andrion gazed at her questioningly. He knew his father was just a boy when he met Eluard. His father had told him he traveled into the Sacred Forest with his own father, Andrion's grandfather. He had never gone back to that village since, as far as Andrion knew. So, it confused him how this girl, who looked younger than he did himself, could have known his father. She looked as if she may be in her early twenties compared to his twenty-six years.

Then again, his father traveled in secret from time to time, so it may have been possible that he'd traveled back here.

He was still groggy with sleep and his head hurt when he tried to think through the fog, so he let it go and continued with his account.

"I don't know how much you know about Eastgate, but legend passed down from generation to generation says that the town is built upon something powerful, something that we are tasked to protect. The exact nature of what that is has been kept secret, passed down from king to king. Each king would tell their oldest sons once they thought they were ready."

Andrion let out a short, humorless laugh. "He doesn't think I'm ready yet, even though he apparently thinks I'm ready to send to the Sacred Forest alone to search for Eluard Mistreaver. He didn't provide me with a map or any other details; he simply told me what direction to travel in and said Eluard or his people would find me. Turns out he was right," he said, smiling at Maelona. "Too bad it wasn't just a little sooner." He rubbed his hand over his bandaged chest with a wince.

"But I digress. For the past couple of months, our outer defenses have been under attack. There seems to be no rhyme or reason to the timing of the attacks, or to the areas being attacked. My father believes they are testing us, looking for weaknesses in our defenses. Then, three weeks ago, a guard turned up dead inside the castle walls. It seems almost inconceivable that such a thing could happen. My father's theory is that our enemies somehow got close enough to one of our trusted inner circle to sway them to their cause.

"It was at this point that my father sent me to Eluard to ask for help in ferreting out the traitor. He says that what we are protecting is too important to leave to chance."

Maelona nodded. "He was right to send you to us."

"But that's not all." Andrion took a deep breath before continuing. "The day before I left, my father started feeling under the weather. It's not like him. He never gets sick. Yet he was pale, weak, and sweating enough that my sister and I noticed. He tried to play it off as nothing serious, but I'm worried that maybe whoever killed that guard has gotten too close to my father as well."

Maelona nodded. "That is possible."

"I tried to convince him to let me put off this journey so I could look out for him," Andrion said, "but he insisted he was fine; that my sister could look after him. He also said that if someone was getting close enough to harm him without us noticing, then my journey was now more important than ever."

The others had been silent as he told his tale. He looked up to see the Sorceress watching him attentively, clearly interested in his story. Maelona was sitting back in her chair, looking at him with a curious expression on her face, and the wolf was staring at him from the corner, as always. That icy gaze gave him the shivers.

Finally, he looked back at Maelona and said, "My father was convinced that Eluard would help. Do you know anyone who can help us now?"

"Yes. We will help you," Maelona said solemnly, gesturing to her wolf.

There were still many details to iron out, but her answer allowed Andrion to breathe a little easier.

Maelona leaned forward in her chair and looked at the young, sandy-haired prince. She tried to give him a little smile. Blaez had pointed out earlier that she'd probably intimidated Andrion yesterday with all the staring and the serious expressions. Blaez had seemed amused at the thought, but she decided she would try to be a little friendlier today.

"You said your father does not think you are ready yet," she said, "yet he sent you to my father, knowing you would, undoubtedly, learn the truth."

Maelona watched Andrion's facial reactions as she spoke. His surprised expression quickly changed to a small, warm smile. His father's opinion obviously meant a lot to him.

"Did King Nele tell you anything at all about my father, other than his name, and that you could find him in the forest?"

"Just that he is a good man who can be trusted, and that he helps to protect the same thing that we protect."

Maelona nodded and said, "My father was a seer. I am a seer."

She watched as Andrion's eyes grew wide and his expression distrustful. She was, unfortunately, well acquainted with that look. It was amazing, really, how long the rumors about her people carried on. She knew that was the demonkin's doing.

"Do you think your father is a good man, Andrion?" she asked quietly. She knew his father fairly well, so she had a good idea what his answer would be.

"He is the best," Andrion replied.

"Do you trust him?"

"Of course," he said. "I would trust him with my life."

"And your father trusts us. So, throw away the things you think you know about seers, the things you learned from rumors and whispered stories. Believe in your father now and open your mind to learn about us yourself."

"Did you just read my mind?" Andrion asked warily.

Maelona laughed and shook her head. "Of course not. We don't read minds. We can do many things, but we cannot do that."

"Then how. . ."

"What you were thinking was easy to read in your expression. Though we cannot read minds, one thing we can do is See—the future, the past, the present," Maelona continued. "Though our abilities in that regard have also been exaggerated."

Andrion looked at the Sorceress, whose calm, always pleasant expression gave nothing away. "Are you. . .?"

"I am the only seer within many day's walk," Maelona answered for her mother.

"Last night I had a dream-vision. In it, I saw who was behind the targeted attacks on Eastgate. Well, not actually who was behind it. He has been very careful to guard his identity. Rather, I saw who he sent to do the attacking."

"Who?" Andrion asked warily.

"Demonkin."

"Demonkin?" Andrion exclaimed while trying to get up. He winced in pain, and Alune stood to place a hand on his shoulder and gently push him back into a semi-reclining position.

"If you can't stay still, we will end this conversation now," her mother said.

Andrion groaned. "Yeah, okay. I keep forgetting until I move and the pain hits."

"I see it's a surprise to you that there were demonkin near Eastgate," Maelona said, "but it's actually quite possible that the demonkin that attacked you in the forest followed you from there."

Andrion's eyebrows shot up. "Really?"

Maelona nodded. "Some demonkin can use illusion to disguise themselves. After what you've told us, I'm wondering if it might be demonkin who are responsible for your guard's death, and possibly your father's illness."

"What? Shouldn't we be heading out there right away, then?"

"Not while you're in this condition," Sorceress Alune said. "You'll just slow everyone down."

Andrion gritted his teeth but had to admit—at least to himself—that she was right.

"A bigger surprise is that they were inside the Sacred Forest," Maelona said. "That shouldn't be possible. You have the amulet that allows you entry with no negative effects, but I doubt there is a being in the forest who would help a demonkin get past the magical protections. I don't think there are many who could."

"It is a very concerning development," Alune said. "I will have to put the word out in the forest for everyone to stay alert."

"That's not all," Maelona said. "There will be a full-scale attack upon Eastgate soon."

Andrion tensed up, but at least he stayed reclined this time.

"What? Could you tell when?" he asked.

"I could tell enough to know that we have some time, so don't worry. We'll get you healed as soon as possible—but that means you need to rest and do everything the Sorceress tells you to do."

"I know you'll want to get back as soon as you can," the Sorceress said. "However, you must wait a few days before you can go anywhere. My magic can heal you much faster than you would heal on your own, but it will still take a little time. Your chest wound is almost fully healed; thankfully, nothing vital was hit. Your leg, however—it was broken in several places, and bone protruded through your skin in one area." Andrion made a face at the description.

"I must use my magic on it for a short time," Alune explained, "and then wait a while before I can do it again. If I rush it, it may not heal correctly. It should not take more than a few days, assuming you cooperate and do as I tell you between treatments."

Andrion nodded. "Fine. I will do whatever it takes to get back as soon as I can. Eastgate, and my father's life, depend on it."

CHAPTER ELEVEN

Messages & Spies

Blaez met Maelona in the clearing again later that evening, just prior to the appointed meeting time with the rest of the village protectors.

"Maelona," he said in a soft but earnest voice as he approached her, "I believe it's clear that I would be thrilled if we were to become more than friends—more than partners and allies in times of battle. You are the most amazing woman I have had the honor of knowing, and I would be proud to belong to you, to share my life with you."

She stood stiffly in front of him, not moving at all. Was she holding her breath as well?

He knew they hadn't known each other long and it might cause her to panic hearing this from him so soon, but there were things he just needed her to know.

"However, I understand your feelings about getting close to people, and your worries and fears. I want nothing that happens between us to become a source of worry for you. Through the good and the bad, I will be whatever you need me to be. I am not going anywhere; I will be here to fight by your side."

Her expression had relaxed by the time he finished speaking. She was just opening her mouth to respond when they were interrupted by the sound of voices. The protectors were arriving.

Blaez cleared his throat and stepped back from Maelona. Hopefully, he would learn what she wanted to say later. For now, she didn't know any of these people—at least; he didn't think she did—so once they gathered around, he began introductions.

"This is Gawn, who you may remember from when we arrived with the prince. He was on patrol. Gawn is the Lead protector."

Gawn nodded to Maelona. "I look a little different at the moment, so you may not recognize me." He smiled at her, then dipped his head in greeting. "I am honored to meet you formally, Maelona."

Maelona nodded in return.

"This is Tangi," Blaez continued while gesturing to the man with reddish-brown hair who had entered with Gawn. "He is Gawn's second in command." Maelona nodded to him in greeting. "Next to Tangi is Imyne. She is third in command of the protectors."

Blaez introduced each of the other protectors as they entered the clearing behind their leaders. "These are Droyn and Rauf," he said, "Masota and Aanor, two of our female protectors, Ademar and his twin, Aymon and, finally, Cade."

As this last, tall, broad-shouldered protector was introduced, he nodded to Maelona with a smile.

"Our final two protectors are still out on patrol. They are Amfrid, who is Ademar and Aymon's younger brother, and Renny, who is the other female of our group."

With the introductions complete, Maelona smiled and said, "That is a lot of unfamiliar names all at once, so please forgive me if I take some time to get them all straight.

"I thank you all for coming here this evening. To get straight to the point, war is on the horizon. As difficult as it may be to believe, it is possible that this war may make it here, inside the Sacred Forest."

Murmurs and expressions of disbelief spread throughout the group. Maelona paused, continuing once they were quiet.

"We will need as many allies as we can get to keep that from happening," Maelona added.

"How do you know this?" Droyn, their youngest protector, asked.

"The injured man we carried into the village, we rescued him from an attack by three demonkin," Blaez said.

"Inside the Sacred Forest," Maelona added.

Someone gasped, and Droyn said, "That's not possible."

"I assure you, it is," said Blaez. "I was there, and I was left with the disgusting taste of demonkin blood in my mouth to remind me it did, in fact, happen." He frowned and wrinkled his nose as he remembered the bitter, almost rotten tang of the demonkin's blood. That was one big downside to fighting in wolf form—it was almost impossible to not get blood in your mouth.

After a few more expressions of alarm and doubt, Maelona said, "We don't have the luxury of time to convince you of what we know to be true. The Sorceress is planning a meeting with the elders and lead protectors from your closest neighboring villages. You are all welcome to attend. In fact, I would ask that you please do. Time is not on our side, unfortunately, and you will hear everything during the meeting, anyway. Until then, I ask that you please trust us." She gestured between herself and Blaez. "And trust your sorceress."

Blaez knew it would be that last request that would have the greatest impact, especially for the younger and more impatient protectors. Although she didn't use magic for large feats regularly, it was common knowledge in the village that the Sorceress's vast sanctuary under the escarpment was not all naturally formed caves and caverns. Much of it was hewn by Alune herself using her magic and was magically reinforced. Someone with that much power could easily abuse it and use it for their own personal gain. But Sorceress Alune only used it to help and protect.

"For now, we should discuss what we can do to protect ourselves and the people against this new threat," Maelona said.

Gawn took a step forward and said, "Of course. That is our job as protectors. And I, for one, look forward to benefitting from your advice and experience."

Gawn was a good, reasonable man, so Blaez hadn't really been worried they would not receive his support. However, he was glad Gawn had made that statement in front of the group. There would be less resistance from others if the lead protector was open to working together. And, as Maelona had pointed out, they didn't have the time to deal with any disagreements or conflict. Not if they wanted their village, their people, to be ready for what was to come.

"I would like the protectors, and even the pack hunters and youth, to train with us starting tomorrow. The youth may find themselves pulled into the fight or they may have to protect the village. They need to know how to defend themselves. I would ask that you, as the pack's protectors, form a plan to train and prepare them for what may come to pass.

"We only have a few more days before Prince Andrion can travel again," Maelona continued. "Blaez and I will leave for Eastgate with him. But in the meantime, I would like to leave your people with skills and knowledge that they can practice, hone, and pass on after we are gone."

Droyn, who hovered close to Gawn, interrupted with a light scoff. "Gawn has almost four-hundred years of experience. What makes you more qualified than he to teach us or lead us?"

"Hush, insolent pup!" said Imyne. "Do you not know to whom you speak?"

Before he could respond, a calm, resonant voice answered from the other side of the clearing as a tall, broad-shouldered man walked steadily toward them. It was Daue, their pack leader.

"You, my young pup," he began, "are addressing Maelona Mistreaver, daughter of our sorceress, Alune Singlemoon, and Eluard Mistreaver, who was a sorcerer, healer, and leader among the seers. You may be too young to recognize the meaning of this yourself, but let me assure you that what she lacks in age, she more than makes up for in knowledge and ability."

"Daue." Maelona bowed her head to the elder and chief. They obviously knew one another, and Blaez wondered if it was just since her recent arrival a few days ago or if they'd known one another when she lived here as a child.

"Thank you for coming," Maelona said. "I do not mind young Droyn's doubts and questions. After all, I prefer for my actions to speak louder than my parentage, and he has, as yet, nothing to place his faith in."

"Well said, Maelona," Daue responded. "Yet I expect those who serve our people to show respect to others."

"As do I," Gawn added, looking Droyn in the eye. "It is very short-sighted to judge a being based on appearances," he told

Droyn. "I hope this is not a mistake you will make in the heat of battle."

Blaez eyed Droyn, wondering how he took the correction by his elders. The youth glanced at the ground with an embarrassed expression, but soon turned his attention back to Gawn. He did not even look at Maelona. Blaez assumed Droyn held no ill will toward Maelona because of the reprimand. As far as Blaez knew, Gawn was not officially a mentor to anyone, but perhaps he would suggest it to him. Droyn obviously looked up to the Lead protector.

Looking back at Maelona, Gawn said, "Please continue, Maelona."

The next hour was spent discussing the training that would take place beginning the next morning. They also worked out a patrol schedule so that all the protectors could benefit without leaving the village with any gaps in its defenses.

When the talks had concluded for the evening, they headed out. Maelona turned to Blaez and said, hesitantly, "I have a favor to ask of you."

"Anything," Blaez replied. And he meant it. He doubted she could ever ask him for something he would not be willing to give.

"I need to do something that will leave me vulnerable. It will need to happen over the course of a night, and I need someone I trust to stand guard. I would like for this to take place tonight, but I realize it's short notice, so I will understand if you cannot. If you agree to help me, but you need a day or two. . ."

"No, it's fine," Blaez interjected. "I have already discussed it with Alune and the others, and we all agreed that what you and I have ahead of us is more important than any other job right now. My only concern is to support you in whatever you need." He was quite happy to have been assigned that task, as it was something his instincts were already pressing him to do.

"Good," Maelona replied, nodding her head. "That is good. Meet me at my hut at twilight. We will head out from there."

It was only a couple of hours later when Blaez approached Maelona's dwelling. He noticed another animal hide stretched out on a frame of sticks and branches, in the same way that she had prepared the hide when they first arrived. A few feet away, in a patch of dwindling sunlight, Maelona stood removing lengths of dried meat from a tripod of sticks attached by rope at the top. It had switches running between the legs on which the meat had been hanging.

He walked up behind her, unable to hold back his smile. "You're preparing for the long journey ahead, I see."

"Yes, and don't worry; I am preparing plenty for you as well." She turned and smiled back at him as she put the last of the dried meat into a leather pouch.

It always struck him like a blow when she smiled her full smile at him like that. Around others, she was quiet, her smile just a slight curve of her lips. It didn't make her seem unfriendly. Instead, he understood she was serious and responsible, and she preferred to watch and listen. And when she spoke, her words were of import.

So, it made him feel special that she seemed to save her big smiles and playful banter for him, like they shared a special bond. He knew, at least, that she was becoming quite special to him, and he could only hope he had the same effect on her.

Maelona took her pouch of dried meat and placed it inside a small shed made of mid-sized, interlocking logs and a thatch roof. He figured she must have constructed the structure herself, since it hadn't been there the first time he came here to see her.

Maelona's weapons had been laid on a cloth on top of a table near where she'd been sharpening her dagger the very first time he'd come here to find her. As she put all the weapons back in their places, his attention was drawn to something he'd noticed when they were with the protectors earlier.

"You changed your staff?" he asked.

"What?" She glanced up at him, then back to the staff currently in her hand. "Oh, no. It's the same staff. My mother decided to. . . decorate it a little." She smiled.

"I see."

When she was done, she turned to him and asked, "Are you ready?"

Blaez gestured in front of himself and said, "Lead the way."

They turned and headed out into the woods to the west of the village. As they left, the sun lowering over the horizon looked as though it was peeking over the trees and reaching back up to paint the sky orange in its wake. Songs from the few birds who were not yet sleeping carried around them, lifting the spirits and adding to the sense of peace and tranquility.

They walked in silence at first, with Blaez following Maelona's lead. Then, after a while, Maelona asked, "So whose hut is it they assigned me, anyway? I hope I didn't leave anyone without a home."

"No," Blaez replied. "It belonged to a young pack hunter, so it's fitting since you are quite a hunter yourself." He smiled over at Maelona. "He mated a few months ago, and they needed a bigger living space since they wish to start a family."

Blaez noticed Maelona's expression change suddenly to sadness. "What is it, Maelona?"

"It just hits me now and then," she replied, "especially when I think of children and families, how much we have at stake—how much everything will change if we fail."

"Have you foreseen what may happen?"

"I have seen a few possibilities, yes. If we are successful, the way the realm's people interact with each other will be strengthened," she said. "But if we do not stop this Dark Sorcerer—" Her voice grew tight until she was choked by her emotion.

Blaez reached out and took her hand. Giving it a light squeeze, he said, "Well, we'll just have to make sure we don't fail, won't we? We will stop him before he can activate the Great Gate."

Maelona gave him a small nod, and they continued on. Blaez did not let go of her hand as they walked. He tried to tell himself that it was only to give her support, but if he was being honest with himself, he knew it was more than that as well.

The silence continued as they walked, and Blaez decided this was a good time to ask a question he had been curious about since shortly after he learned Maelona was the Sorceress's daughter. "Can you take wolf form, Maelona?" She turned to look at him with a serious expression he could not read, and suddenly he worried he shouldn't have asked.

"I hope you are not offended by the question," he added, "but I have wondered about it often. You are half Wolf-folk and your parents were both formidable beings within their peoples. I know you have powerful seer abilities, so I wondered if you have any of the Folk abilities as well."

Maelona looked back at the path. After a moment, she said, "Yes, I can shift. I haven't tried it in years, though. Shifting happens through magic, which means my mind links it with danger. I had only shifted twice before the events that led me to leave the pack, so I'm not very experienced with it."

She looked at him and smiled, and he felt a warmth growing in his chest. "I hope that one day, I will feel comfortable enough to share my wolf with you."

They continued in relative silence for another half an hour, walking close enough to each other that Blaez could feel the warmth of her body. He did not even care that he didn't know exactly where she was leading him. He was just happy to be spending this time with her, walking together in the moonlight under a star-filled sky.

It was strange, really. Over the years, there had been a couple of young women who had shown interested in him, and he appreciated their interest. However, he could not return it. He'd even wondered if there was something wrong with him, and that was why he didn't get romantic stirrings. But now that he'd met Maelona, he couldn't help but feel he'd just been waiting for her.

Blaez glanced over at Maelona many times as they walked, taking in how her eyes reflected the silver light when she glanced up at the sky, and how shadow and light played across her features. *She is quite a magnificent creature.*

Finally, Maelona stopped beside a grassy field at the bank of a river. "We are here," she said as she turned to face him. "Now, it's time for me to explain what will happen and what I require of you."

Blaez nodded at her in encouragement, as she seemed a little nervous.

"I need to send a message out to the other seer champions and to our Elder. Through a dream-vision."

His brows rose in surprise. "Your people can do such a thing?" The abilities he had known of previously already seemed to make the seers unfairly gifted, and now there was this. But he quickly reminded himself that the Wolf-folk and the seers would stand side-by-side through whatever came their way, so he should be glad for their gifts.

Maelona shook her head. "Actually, this is not common among our people. Having the ability to see things is much simpler than causing things to be seen. For the former, one must simply be open and let the energy and visions flow in. We are mere vessels through which information passes."

Ah. It made sense, then, that they received visions as they slept, when the mind was open and unguarded.

"Sending specific messages out to others and gaining specific information in return, however, requires intense focus and concentration, and uses up a lot of energy. Usually, one only hears of the most skilled Elders being capable of such things and, even then, it doesn't happen often. There are those who believe that the fact that I can do this at such a young age is because of my parentage. There are others who believe it is because of my magic—not that there are many people who know about that."

"What do you think?" he asked.

She shrugged. "I believe it's related to both.

"Still," Maelona continued, "this is not a simple task for me. If I don't want it to only happen spontaneously, under times of great stress, then I need to focus on performing the task by essentially shutting out the outside world. Because of that, I'm left vulnerable. I could lock myself up in my hut, but the task is easier for me out in the open. Under a clear, moonlit night like tonight is even better. And the other worry is that I need to be uninterrupted until I wake on my own."

"Is it dangerous if you're interrupted?"

"Only to myself. I don't have personal experience, thankfully. But there have been a couple of occasions recorded in our histories, and. . . well, I'll just say that it is not good to be jarred out of that state. It is difficult for the mind to adjust."

Blaez nodded. "I understand. I will ensure nothing approaches."

"Good," Maelona responded. "Thank you." She walked a few paces away and lay down on her back so that she was partially obscured by the grass. Blaez watched her carefully, curious about this process but also concerned for her well-being. He hoped it didn't put too much strain on her.

Maelona lay still, her feet and hands stretched out from her body. She closed her eyes and breathed deeply. The only sounds Blaez could hear were her deep, steady breaths and the wind sighing through the grass.

He was alert to any movement or sound around him, even when his gaze was repeatedly drawn to Maelona. The temperature of the surrounding area seemed to rise a couple of degrees as he watched on. After a few moments, the air seemed to charge with energy, and a low, pale green and gold-colored light seemed to emanate out from Maelona and head off in every direction, fading away in the distance.

Blaez was mesmerized by the sight at first, but concern for her had him focusing back on her face to watch for any signs of stress. Her expression was relaxed, peaceful, and. . . vulnerable, just as she said she would be.

Suddenly, he felt like he wasn't doing enough, so he removed his clothes, folded them, and laid them at the foot of a tree. He shifted to wolf form so he could take advantage of his heightened senses and patrolled the area, all the while ensuring he stayed close enough to reach Maelona quickly should any trouble come around.

He moved slowly and stepped carefully—he wanted to be as silent as possible so that any noises that didn't belong would stand out. He traced a perimeter around Maelona at a distance where he could still see her, but far enough out that he could stop anything that got too close. It was during his tenth loop around that he noticed that the hoots, chatters, buzzes, and screams of the nocturnal creatures all fell silent. They had quieted when he and Maelona first arrived as well, but they'd gone back to their routine warnings and mating calls once they'd realized there was no threat.

Obviously, something had alarmed them again, so Blaez stilled, listening intently for anything that sounded out of place. Before long, he heard a twig snap, then the rustling of movement in the underbrush somewhere off to his right.

He glanced toward the sound and back at Maelona. Judging it to be close enough to still hear and, hopefully, see her, as silently as possible, he headed off to investigate.

Hidden by the tall grass, Blaez crept toward the suspicious sounds. He had a hunch that they'd been followed, and whoever or whatever was approaching was getting closer bit by bit, pausing from time to time.

Once Blaez pinpointed the dense bushes the intruder was hiding behind, he circled around, closing in slowly and silently until he could just make out the shape of what appeared to be another wolf. He sniffed the air, the familiar scent confirming his suspicions and telling him exactly which wolf it was.

When he was close enough, Blaez pounced, colliding roughly with the smaller wolf and knocking him out of the bush and onto the grass at the edge of the clearing. The wolf yelped, then snarled and tried to fight Blaez off. He didn't want the noise to disturb Maelona, so he quickly went for the intruder's throat and pinned him on his back on the ground. He closed his jaw just hard enough to send a message.

It only took a moment for the small, gray wolf to realize the position it was in and stop struggling. Once it was still, Blaez opened his mouth and lifted away, but then he pressed a large forepaw against its windpipe instead. He shifted, keeping his hand clamped hard enough to make it difficult for the stalker to breathe.

"What do you think you're doing, Droyn?" Blaez growled. He briefly squeezed his hand a little tighter in warning before letting go of the younger wolf and moving back a couple of steps. "Shift," he commanded.

Droyn was smart enough to do as he was told, shifting and looking up at Blaez warily before he slowly stood to face him.

"Well?" Blaez asked.

"I wasn't doing anything wrong," Droyn said, rubbing his throat.

Blaez took a deep breath and glanced in Maelona's direction to make sure the scuffle hadn't pulled her out of her vision—or her vision making, rather. He grabbed Droyn by the back of the neck and led him a little farther away. He didn't want Droyn close enough to see what Maelona was doing, and he didn't want to disturb her if he ended up losing his temper and raising his voice.

Blaez released Droyn, paced ahead a little, then turned to face the boy.

"I'm going to pretend you're smart enough to not insult my intelligence by claiming you didn't follow our scents out here, and I'm going to give you one chance—and only one—to explain yourself."

Droyn pursed his lips and narrowed his eyes and, for a moment, Blaez was certain he was going to say something stupid. But then the boy reluctantly said, "Fine. Yes, I was following her, okay? You heard what Daue said—she's part seer. How can you all trust her? I just wanted to see what she was up to, make sure she wasn't doing anything to put the village in danger."

"Aren't you too young to hold such strong prejudices?" Instead of answering, Droyn just glared at him.

"Fine. Then let me ask you, is that the only thing Daue said? Because I seem to recall him saying a few other things as well." Blaez shook his head. "You must have noticed my scent as well. Surely you knew I was here with her."

"Well, there are rumors that say seers can get inside people's heads. How do I know she hasn't messed with yours?"

Blaez glanced in Maelona's direction again, then back at Droyn. "First, do not believe rumors. They are outright lies at the worst, and exaggerations of the truth at best." He wasn't about to tell Droyn what Maelona was doing right now. That would only convince Droyn he was right, but as he now understood it, Maelona could only get into the heads of the other seers. He could confirm with her again later, but, either way, he knew she wasn't "messing" with anyone in the way Droyn was suggesting.

"Next," Blaez continued, "you do not need to trust Maelona. You need to trust Daue, the Chief of our pack. You need to trust me, your senior. And you need to trust Gawn, your lead protector."

Droyn had continued to wear his defiance on his face until Blaez mentioned Gawn. Not surprising, given how Droyn practically worshipped the man.

"We all trust the Sorceress, and she trusts her daughter. You also trust the Sorceress, do you not?"

Droyn didn't answer, but at least he looked as if he was thinking things over, finally.

"You need to think about how our leaders and decision-makers view Maelona. How they trust her." Blaez stepped closer to Droyn and lowered his face to look him in the eye. In a low voice, he said, "How do you think the Sorceress would react if she knew you mistrusted her only daughter and sneakily followed her around? How do you think Daue and Gawn would react if they knew you were openly doubting their decisions and defying them?"

"W-well," Droyn said sheepishly, "I'm not really defying them. I'm just, you know, monitoring the newcomer. Trying to make sure she wasn't causing any problems, you know?"

"No one asked you to do that though, did they? You are stepping far outside of your duties, are you not?"

"I don't understand how you all can trust her so easily, given what I've heard about seers all my life."

Blaez sighed, put his hands on his hips, and looked up at the sky, silently asking the Universe to grant him patience. How many times would the boy need to hear the same thing before it finally sank in? Shaking his head, he looked at Droyn again.

"Use your brain." Blaez tapped his index finger against Droyn's forehead. "Have you ever thought about how easy it is to spread rumors and misinformation? All it takes is one person with malicious intent who is good at fabricating lies, and someone naïve enough to believe those lies and repeat them to others. What if someone fabricated a story about you? Like. . . I don't know. . . like you are having relations with the Chief's bond-mate or something of the sort. Now imagine the trouble it could cause you if that rumor spread around and people believed it without question."

Droyn squinted his eyes into slits and side-eyed Blaez. "Are you. . . are you threatening me?"

Blaez scoffed. "Do not be an imbecile. I'm not threatening you. I'm simply trying to explain so you can understand."

Droyn relaxed a little and nodded. "Okay. I get it. But that's why I'm out here—I'm just trying to discover the truth for myself."

"Following people around, seeing things you might not understand and do not have a context for, is only going to give you an incomplete picture. Also, people have a right to keep some things close."

He shook his head and put his hands on his hips. "Maelona asked me, a village protector and assistant to the Sorceress, to accompany her, so she isn't hiding anything. But what she is doing is personal enough that she neither needs nor wants an audience. The least you can do is respect that. And if you find you cannot because you do not know her well enough, then you can respect your chief, your lead protector, your sorceress, and me. Trust that we will always do what we think is best for our people."

"But—"

"No. That is enough, Droyn. You have distracted me from my purpose here for long enough. You need to leave now. And I will check for your scent later to make sure you went straight back to the village. Do you understand?"

Droyn looked away and muttered, "Fine, yes, I understand."

The boy was only just old enough to join the ranks of the protectors. Times like this were evidence of his youth and inexperience. Blaez had only been a protector for about thirty-seven years himself—not a long time by the group's standards. But he liked to think he'd learned a thing or two along the way.

Once he was certain that Droyn was leaving and heading in the right direction, Blaez shifted back to his wolf and continued his patrol of the area. He continued right until dawn, when Maelona finally awoke.

Blaez guessed she had been actually sleeping for at least part of that time because, not long after Droyn left, the pale green light had dissipated. Yet, Maelona still looked weary as she stood up.

Blaez quickly shifted back and donned his pants and tunic. "Are you okay?" he asked her as he approached.

"Yes, I'm fine." Despite her words, her low, slow speech and her drooping lids told him how tired she was.

"Are you sure?"

She simply nodded in response.

He brushed back some hair that had fallen over her forehead and noticed the worry lines there. He burned to know what happened and if her message was sent and received, but he wouldn't push her if she didn't want to share. So, instead, he took her hand again and led her back the way they had come the night before.

Unfortunately, tired or not, there was much they had to accomplish today. One thing was to inform Daue and Gawn about Droyn's appearance last night. He hoped the boy would not cause any more trouble.

Blaez glanced at Maelona, wondering if he should tell her. But, as his eyes traced the signs of fatigue clearly visible on her face, he decided it could wait until later.

CHAPTER TWELVE

Fights & Fire-Circles

Maelona eyed Blaez, Daue, Gawn, and Droyn with suspicion where they stood speaking together at the far end of the clearing.

At first, Blaez had looked upset, standing with his weight on one leg and his hands on his hips. Droyn had seemed agitated, speaking with his chin up and his hands waving around animatedly. Now, however, the boy had his gaze locked on the ground as Gawn said something to him.

They had each glanced at her at several points in their conversation, and she was certain they were talking about her. Perhaps she would ask Blaez about it later.

She and Blaez had eaten breakfast in her small hut after returning from her dream-vision message projection this morning. Afterwards, they came straight here to practice with the group. Blaez had called Daue, Gawn, and Droyn off to talk, while she and two others waited for everyone else to arrive.

Maelona nodded at the others as they arrived, while also monitoring Blaez's group for clues about what they were discussing. Once everyone who was expected was present, the group casually sauntered back over—which made her even more suspicious—and Blaez came to stand at her side.

"Thank you all for coming," Maelona said. "I have already shown Blaez certain vulnerabilities and limitations that you may have in wolf form."

"I feel like we should be insulted," Droyn muttered under his breath.

"I assure you; I intend no insult. It is a sensible part of training to recognize one's strengths and weaknesses. We must learn to work with them and, when necessary, around them."

Droyn looked at her with wide eyes, and his cheeks flushed in embarrassment. Then, chin down and looking from underneath his lashes, he glanced surreptitiously at Blaez, then Daue, the picture of a child worried about being caught for doing something naughty. He obviously hadn't expected anyone to hear him.

"Because of a wolf's natural limitations," Maelona continued, "and because you are already adept at fighting in wolf form, I would like to focus on fighting in your human forms. I am not saying your wolves' abilities cannot be used to your benefit. They certainly can. However, you should not depend solely on your wolf. Be unpredictable and be ready to use whatever advantages you have."

She walked back and forth in front of them as she spoke, assuring their attention was on her.

"Your wolf form may overpower many of the realm's creatures, but certainly not all. You cannot depend on brute strength, claws, and teeth all the time. If your opponent outmaneuvers you, or if you need to keep an opponent alive, these things will not help you. During these times, you will need to use your intellect."

She scanned the group and saw they were nodding in agreement.

"You may not have as much power behind you in your bipedal form, but you will have more weapons, both lethal and non-lethal. Instead of a great paw with claws, you now have fingers and knuckles." Using Blaez as her partner but not making contact, she demonstrated fingers to the eyes, spear-hand to the throat, thumbs to the eyes, and a finger-joint strike to the throat. "You have hammer fist, back fist, knife-hand strikes, wrist strikes, elbow strikes, shoulders, knee, shin, top of the foot, ball of the foot, knife-edge of the foot, heel of the foot, instep." She smiled at them. "I'm sure you get the idea.

"You have these weapons at your disposal, so use them. If your arms are trapped, head-butt. If your upper body is occupied with blocking, strike out with the knee or foot. If your opponent is larger or stronger than you are in human form, then use his size against him. If he is running toward you, sword in the air, wait until he is almost in range to strike, then step off the line, striking to the side of the knee or back of the neck or head as he moves past."

"These things all sound great, Maelona," Ademar said, "but this is not how we are accustomed to fighting. Do you really think we can become proficient enough to use these strategies in time?"

"Mostly," she responded, "the trick is to not overthink things. Don't tense up or panic. Just let your body relax and react naturally."

Imyne said, "For us, in a conflict, reacting naturally would usually mean reacting in wolf form."

"And that is why you must practice as much as you can in the time you have. You will need to repeat the movements as often as you can so that your body will learn what to do and will do it automatically. You are all warriors. You will adapt quickly."

"Maybe you just want us in human form because you can't defeat us in wolf form," Droyn said.

Exclamations rang out as many of the protectors admonished Droyn, but Maelona raised her hand. "It's fine."

She looked at Droyn, unable to keep a small smirk from lifting the corner of her mouth. The boy was certainly stubborn—not to mention distrustful. "Let's just get rid of any doubt right from the start, shall we?"

There were many things she was not confident about in her life, such as using her magic. However, for melee fighting, she knew her skills were strong. After all, Owyn Axedrifter—a legendary warrior among her people, and the father of her fellow seer champion, Edun—had trained and mentored her for years.

Sweeping her gaze over the group to take them all in, she said, "shift."

"Who, me?" Droyn pointed a finger to his chest and glanced around at the others.

"All of you."

Daue and Gawn looked as though they wanted to argue, but Maelona stood firm and looked at them calmly, waiting.

After a moment, Gawn walked to the edge of the clearing and removed his clothing. The others soon followed his lead. They all shifted and approached her.

"I want you to attack me as you would any enemy—as a pack. But remember, warriors are not the same as prey. They will not run from you. You will need to confront them and, in this case, me, head on."

Again, Gawn led the way, this time in wolf form. Maelona stayed in place, but turned a slow circle as they surrounded her. She watched their faces and their bodies for any sign of intent to attack. As she suspected he might, since the young protector seemed to think he had something to prove, Droyn was the first to charge toward her.

Maelona waited until the last moment before moving. She jumped diagonally forward, off his line of attack, and grabbed his fur as he passed. She used it to launch herself onto his back, as she had done before with Blaez. This time, however, they were in a pack, and another wolf lunged at her.

Grabbing the fur on Droyn's side, she swung herself down at the last moment, and the other wolf's jaw clamped on Droyn's back, where she had just been sitting. Droyn yelped, but Maelona guessed he was more surprised than hurt. Since this was their first practice, they wouldn't be attacking full force.

Wrapping her legs around Droyn's torso, she used his fur in her hands to reposition herself underneath him. With one hand, she then pulled her retracted staff from its holder at her back. She pressed its plain end to his chest above her, then she let herself drop. She continued to put pressure on it as he continued forward, so that it traveled in a vertical line from his chest to his stomach. As soon as he cleared her, she rolled over and stood up.

"If that had been my knife, your innards would now be—"

Another wolf tackled her from behind, cutting her off. It knocked her to the ground but, as she fell, she turned to land on her back—forcing the air out of her lungs so the impact wouldn't knock the wind out of her—and pushed the button to extend her staff. As the great wolf snapped at her, she shoved the staff horizontally into his mouth, locking his jaw open. Then, grabbing one of her daggers, she drew the hilt across his throat.

"I just slit your throat," she said, loud enough to be heard over the growls and heavy breathing.

They continued like this—the wolves attacking, Maelona defending and counter-attacking—until she had demonstrated a killing or maiming blow on each. Sometimes they took turns attacking, and sometimes two or more attacked at the same time. Afterward, they all stood in place or paced slowly as they caught their breath.

"Questions?" Maelona asked, panting.

Snorts and head shakes were the response, so she said, "Then, please, shift back."

Once the wolves were in human form and clothed again, Maelona addressed the group.

"Blaez and I will leave for Eastgate as soon as the prince is strong enough to travel, so we will use all the time we have this afternoon practicing some techniques. We will meet again tomorrow for as much time as we can spare. While we're traveling, Blaez and I will have to match our pace to Prince Andrion," she said, gesturing between herself and Blaez. Humans were not as fast as seers or animal-folk, and this human will still be feeling the effects of his injuries. "Since it will not take as much time for you to travel there, that leaves you a few days after our departure to practice what you learn before you leave.

"Today, you will start with partners. Blaez and I will demonstrate first, since we have practiced some together before now, and you will watch. You will then take turns trying the techniques with your partner while I move amongst you to adjust as needed."

"Right," Gawn said, clapping his hands together. "Let's get to it. Time is not our friend in this."

The darkening sky was striped with oranges and pinks as Maelona and Blaez walked to the fire circle, just outside the Sorceress's sanctuary.

"What we know is that the Dark Sorcerer is very powerful, and he commands an army of large, powerful brutes, some of whom have magic of their own. If he opens the Great Gate and adds full demons to his ranks . . ." She shook her head and took a deep breath. "Well, I'll just say it would be best if we stop him before that can happen."

Maelona was glad she'd returned to her hut for a brief nap after practice with the protectors. The sleep she'd had the night before was the first in a few days, which was common for her. However, it hadn't been restful, and she needed to be clear-headed tonight.

Blaez had come to her hut to wake her when it was time to head out for the meeting. When she'd first awoken, she was groggy, her mind still in the replay of the disturbing message she'd received the night before, which had come back to her as a dream. Luckily, the fresh air and conversation as they headed to the fire-circle helped clear her head.

As they walked, she and Blaez discussed the preparations they would need to undertake for their coming journey.

"As a Wolf-folk, I won't be able to carry much in the way of provisions." Blaez said. "If I need to shift, I will have to abandon anything I take."

Maelona smiled, remembering his pants abandoned in the woods after the encounter with the draccon.

"And that may be even more true than you know," Maelona said. "After tonight's meeting, I would like you to always stay in wolf form when we are around outsiders, including the Prince, unless I ask otherwise."

Blaez's brows shot up. "I'm surprised you are asking, considering you questioned me on it when I stayed in wolf form to visit the prince's sick room."

"I was thinking about what you said," she explained, "about how people tend to not take care with their words in front of animals, but they would if they knew the animal was a Folk. I would like to use this advantage until we get to know Andrion better. I will ensure that you and I will have regular time to ourselves when you can shift back so we can strategize. Humans have to sleep more than Folk or seers, so it should not be difficult."

Blaez gave her a pleased smile that momentarily took her breath away. She looked away in embarrassment as her cheeks heated. She used her inner-sight to get rid of the redness of her face and took a deep breath to calm herself.

There was no way she could deny her growing regard for him, but heightened emotional reactions still made her nervous. She was already failing at keeping her feelings to herself—she knew she smiled and laughed more around him without consciously allowing herself to do so. She was especially worried about allowing herself to get close to him physically.

The way her mother changed her staff provided some measure of relief, at least. She'd just have to practice controlling her magic with it as often as she could. And maybe, someday, she wouldn't have to worry about accidentally hurting the people around her.

"It never hurts to have the element of surprise and some tricks on your side," Blaez added in agreement, bringing her attention back to what they'd been talking about.

"We're here. We can talk again later," Blaez announced.

Maelona looked around. They were near the entrance to the Sorceress's sanctuary, but the large fire circle was a little further on, past a large boulder and a copse of trees that mostly hid it from view from where they stood.

"Wait, you don't need to take wolf form for the meeting," she said.

Blaez shook his head. "If I'm going to pretend to be a regular wolf to get the prince to relax and show his true self, then I'd rather not take a chance of him recognizing any similarities to my human form."

Maelona nodded. She understood what he meant. Blaez's eyes were standout. They'd attracted her attention more strongly than anything else when she'd met him, so others would certainly notice them too.

Keeping to the shadows, Blaez removed his loose pants and put them in the rock alcove. He shifted and padded up beside her. Maelona ran her hand through the fur between his ears. He pushed his head into her hand in response.

Realizing what she had done, she sucked in a breath and quickly pulled her hand away. People didn't just relax their speech around animals, it seemed, but their actions as well and, evidently, she was not immune.

They went to take their places next to her mother and Prince Andrion.

All around the fire circle, Elders and protectors from their own village, as well as those from other villages within a few days' travel, talked quietly and solemnly. Everyone was in human form for ease of communication, except for a few protectors who were keeping watch on the periphery, mostly hidden just inside the tree line. When the last of the expected guests arrived, her mother, the great Wolf-folk sorceress, Alune Singlemoon, welcomed everyone and made introductions around the circle.

As she listened, Maelona lifted her face to the sky and looked up at the myriad of bright stars shining above them. She wondered how much closer the planets Chephus and Aragus were to aligning with the moon than they were when she'd left Clearview. What would Huet see when he gazed through his telescope this night?

"Our shared histories tell us that our world was created to be in balance," her mother began. "Light and darkness, youth and agedness, beauty and ugliness, goodness and evil. There are those species that were created to be evil, such as the demonkin. There are others who are created to be good, such as some animal-folk, including the Dragon-folk, who are rumored to be very rigid in their views of right and wrong. There are also species that are neither good nor evil, who tend to do things for the furthering of their own people, or of themselves."

Maelona felt a tapping on her forearm and looked to her left. Behind Alune, Prince Andrion was leaning toward her, wide-eyed. "Animal-folk are real?" he whispered-hissed. "There are really Dragon-folk?" Maelona put a finger to her lips to silence him and pointed to Alune.

His questions were a reminder that tonight was the first time Prince Andrion had been out of bed and moving about. He hadn't explored and didn't yet realize he was in a Wolf-folk village. How would he react once he found out?

"Of course," her mother continued, "as all beings are free to make their own choices, there are exceptions to this. There are histories, for example, of a demonkin who went out of his way to try to help some travelers in need, despite the disregard this earned him in his own clan."

Maelona lifted her brows in surprise. She hadn't heard that story before. It was the only positive thing she'd ever heard anyone say about demonkin.

"Because of these shared histories, the incident during the Great Alignment three-thousand years ago is common knowledge. All the magic Folk of the realm, and perhaps some humans as well, know that a dark sorcerer opened the Great Gate to bring demons across so he could build an army to take over the realm."

The murmur of voices rose from those seated around the fire. Many in attendance were also aware that this was an alignment year, and now they were being called to a meeting where the Sorceress was reminding everyone what had happened last time. It was sure to arouse suspicions.

Her mother nodded, as if she knew—and was confirming—what they were thinking. "Another Great Alignment is upon us. It will happen in less than five moon-cycles from now."

The voices sounded again, this time louder, and Maelona picked up the hint of panic in some of them.

Her mother waited patiently, eyes scanning the crowd, until everyone quieted again. "Exactly like last time, there is a dark sorcerer who hopes to use the magical surge of energy caused by the alignment to open the Great Gate and bring demons across to bolster his army. And he already has the demonkin on his side. From what Maelona and her peers have Seen," she said, gesturing lightly to her, "this new dark sorcerer wishes to subjugate the realm, kill or enslave any who stand against him, and name himself Emperor."

When Alune paused, Andrion spoke up. "The castle town of Eastgate, where my father, King Nele, rules, has recently been under attack. So far, it has just been small scale, as if they are testing our defenses. When I came here into the Sacred Forest, I was followed and attacked by what I now know were demonkin."

Several gasps and expressions of concern rang out around the fire-circle.

"You told me it's likely that demonkin are behind the attacks on the town as well. What I want to know now is what this history lesson has to do with the recent goings-on at Eastgate? And how do we even know if it does have to do with the goings-on at Eastgate? Could it just be coincidence?"

The prince's expression was more earnest than Maelona had seen it, although he'd been injured and in pain the whole time he'd been here. He wore a furrowed brow and a deep frown which clearly signaled his concern.

Her mother turned to look at her and nodded, passing the question on to her.

She took a deep breath and stood.

"As some of you already know," Maelona said, "I have come here from the seer village of Clearview."

At this there were mumblings, and even a couple of gasps, from some guests from outside Wildegrove. Seers were considered an almost extinct race that rarely showed themselves, even among the magical beings of the realm. And with good reason.

She looked pointedly at the crowd, pausing from time to time to meet others' eyes. "Three-hundred years ago, rumors—falsehoods—were spread about the seers that had the

humans, and some folk, thinking we were evil manipulators."
Several gazes dropped to the ground, and some glanced around at others.

"We have learned that, ironically, these rumors were themselves manipulations, fabrications concocted by the true villains. These lies were spread by minions of this new dark sorcerer, an attempt to keep us divided as part of his long-term plans."

"But why?" A female voice asked from the crowd. "And how could they have had that much influence? It's not like humans would invite demonkin to drink with them."

"The answer to the why," Maelona said, "is simple. We are stronger together than we are divided. The how—well, that's a little more disconcerting."

She paused and took a breath. "We've learned that there were two kinds of demons that were brought over last time. And some from each of those groups were stranded here afterward. As they bred with humans over the years, this led to some of the resulting demonkin having the ability to alter their appearance."

More gasps and exclamations sounded. She nodded. "Some demonkin disguised themselves as humans, infiltrated the human villages, and started the rumors that were meant to drive a wedge between us. And they succeeded."

She took a deep breath and pushed all of her conviction and determination into her next words. "But, hopefully, that ends now."

Maelona scanned the crowd again and was glad to see that several guests were nodding in agreement.

"But you can't be entirely certain that what happened three-thousand years ago is linked to what is happening now, can you? And, in particular, to what is happening at Eastgate?" Andrion asked.

Maelona turned to look at the prince, who was leaning forward in his seat to better meet her gaze. "The answer to that has to do with the protections that were put in place after the last Great Alignment." She looked back at the crowd.

"As you all know, after the last alignment, magical protections were placed around the forest to keep evil out. Because of recent events," she glanced at Andrion, "we now believe those have been compromised."

People once again spoke to one another in agitated voices, no doubt linking it to what the prince had said about demonkin following him into the forest. They would know what that meant for themselves and for access to the Great Gate.

"One other set of protections had been put in place as well." The voices quieted some and the guests' attention returned to her. "I'm sure that some of you are already aware," she said, glancing at the Elders present, "that keystones were placed at the axes of the ley lines to limit access to the power of the Source."

The Elders nodded, as did some protectors. She turned to look at the prince again. "There are four keystones: directly north, east, south, and west of the Source, which lies almost at the exact center of our small island continent. Keeps were built over and around the keystones to protect them, castles were built around the keeps, and these eventually expanded into castle towns."

"So Eastgate. . ."

"Is protecting a keystone," she finished for Andrion, who seemed unable to at the moment. He was looking a little overwhelmed, with his mouth agape and eyes staring off, wide, into the mid-distance. "With the keystones intact, the Dark Sorcerer may not be able to access enough power to open the Great Gate, even during the alignment. But without them. . ." She didn't need to finish the statement for everyone to understand the implications.

"So, all the gate towns will be targets," Andrion said.

"Yes."

She turned to face the gathered crowd. "Therefore, we've called you together tonight. My people's visions have shown us possibilities for what is coming. We will all need to work together if we are to defeat this sorcerer and his demonkin army. I stand before you tonight to ask you—no, to beg you—to please stand with us against the Dark Sorcerer and his demonkin army. No one group of us stands a chance against him alone."

She tried to hide her anxiety as she looked over the gathered crowd, trying to gauge their feelings, to see if they understood the importance of what she was telling them. Some people looked doubtful, some looked worried, and some wore expressions of determination. But she was happy to see everyone's eyes trained on her, listening intently to her words.

"They will attack the gate towns first, and we will need your support there. The Dark Sorcerer will send his forces to the Great Gate thereafter, whether or not he succeeds at destroying the keystones. And this is where we will most need to gather together, to stand against him as one. We have Seen that he has a secondary plan for if the keystones remain intact but, as yet, we have not been able to ascertain exactly what that is.

CHAPTER THIRTEEN

Predictions & Plans

Maelona was surprised when Chief Daue stood and addressed the group.

"As Maelona has explained to me before," he began, glancing in her direction, "people have free will and decisions can be changed. The future is never set in stone, and so the seers' visions can only tell us so much. However, they can provide us with information on past and current actions, intentions, and many other things that would be invaluable for us to know as we prepare for the dark times to come."

"How do we know she can be trusted?" Hadrian questioned. "How do we know she is not working with the evil forces, trying to lure us in and make us vulnerable? How can we be certain her entire story isn't a fabrication? After all, we have no proof of what she claims she Sees."

"I realize that some people still live with the unfounded fear and suspicion that had been tacked to the seer name many years ago," Daue said. "But you should remember that the same suspicion and fear was turned on the animal-folk after the seers disappeared. Maybe not to the same extent—we weren't hunted down the same way. But we felt the need to move into the Sacred Forest for its protection. That's why the younger generation of humans thinks of us as myth."

Daue strode out from where he was standing behind the crowd and stopped next to Maelona. When he spoke again, he was no longer just addressing Hadrian, but all those present.

"If I were a betting man, I would wager all that I have that Maelona is correct—that this divide between our peoples was created with a purpose; a rift intended to weaken the strength we have when we band together. The information the seers can provide could mean the difference between success and failure, victory and defeat. And I, for one, will take the gift of their friendship and support with grace and gratitude, as will my pack."

Her mother then stepped forward and stood at her side again. She was now flanked by the Wildegrove Wolf-folk chief and their powerful sorceress. Their show of support and respect touched her deeply, and it was no insignificant gesture on their parts. No doubt the others would be more likely to accept the news she carried as true because of it.

"Maelona is not just a seer," her mother said. "She is also my daughter." Maelona sucked in a breath at the unexpected announcement, then had to swallow past the lump of emotion that formed in her throat. After forty years apart, hearing her mother claim her as her own family before, so many like this hit her harder than she expected.

By the expressions on some guests' faces, Maelona could tell this hadn't been known to many of them.

"She is as much Wolf-folk as she is seer," her mother continued. "She has nothing to gain by trying to trick anyone. The news she has brought to us is shocking and unpleasant, yes. But that does not mean we can afford to call it fabrication and pretend it isn't fact. Refusal to accept it will not make it less true—it will only make us vulnerable and unprepared."

"It would make us easy targets," Daue added.

"I know what many of you think of the seer people," Maelona said in a calm voice that hid the emotions churning inside her. "But let me inform you of our truth.

"At the very core of our belief system is the knowledge that we were created for a purpose. That we were given the advantages we have for a reason. We were created to protect Sterrenvar and all the people in it. Otherwise, why would our visions always point us to where we are needed most? To where evil and danger threaten good people?"

She paused and looked around. She could not gauge how those present were leaning, but she had their attention.

"There was a time when all the people of the realm mingled together and co-existed peacefully. Then this evil force began lurking behind the scenes, fear-mongering, twisting truths into ugly lies and causing rifts between us.

"But I want you all to think about something," she said, her voice intense. "Do you really believe that the seer people, with all our advantages, could have been slaughtered by humans and demonkin if we had fought back?" She swept her gaze around, brow lifted in challenge.

"My people trusted too much that the humans would make the right choice. Then, when it became clear that they chose wrongly, many seers still saw the humans as victims who were being manipulated and used as tools by those who wished to eradicate us. But make no mistake: we have learned from our past, and we will defend ourselves if such a thing was to happen again."

"At least your people learned you are not all powerful," called an unfamiliar voice from the crowd.

"We never said we were," Maelona said. "We never pretended to be anything other than what we are."

She shook her head. "Human lives are short; thus, their collective memories are short. So, to a degree, they can be forgiven for forgetting who we are. The real disappointment came when the longer-lived, magical races of the realm believed the evil whispers as well.

"You know us. At least, you knew us. You should have known better." She was now shaking from holding back her emotions: her anger, disappointment, and even fear of what was to come.

Her mother reached her arm around her and squeezed her shoulder in support.

"When it comes to our visions, we see what the Universe sends us, and it only gifts us visions of where darkness and evil threaten. The Universe shows us where we are needed most. And right now, it needs us to bring Sterrenvar's peoples together to stand strong against what is perhaps the most powerful Dark Sorcerer our land has ever known."

There was a pause, during which everything around the fire circle was still and the only sound was the crackling and popping of the embers. Her palms were sweaty and muscles tense as she waited for a response, a reaction, anything.

"So, enlighten us, seer," Hadrian said after a moment, his haughty tone causing Blaez to growl from his spot behind her, "if this sorcerer and his army are so powerful, will us joining you in the fight really be enough to stop him?"

She nodded. "An alliance is definitely necessary for our success. However, we actually have three things on our side." She took a deep breath. "The two others are the keystones and…the Ternias."

Maelona did not know how to explain the Ternias. She only knew she would have to practice controlling her magic every moment she could if she had any hope of succeeding in what she was meant to do.

She didn't even know *what* she was meant to do, exactly. The prophecy wasn't specific about that, so she assumed she wouldn't know until the time was right. In the meantime, all she could do was practice and hope she made the right decisions.

"Might I ask," Moyses, the Golden Eagle-folk Elder, said in a deep and rumbling voice, "for some clarification here? You are concerned with protecting the keystones and the Great Gate, yet you have also said that only a powerful sorcerer could access the power of the hub. How certain are you that this Dark Sorcerer you speak of is powerful enough?"

Maelona breathed a sigh of relief that she didn't immediately have to give more information about the Ternias. However, she still hesitated for a moment, deciding how much information to give.

"For the past couple of years, my people and myself have had visions of what is coming, as well as visions of what is going on elsewhere in the present. These visions have become more frequent and more insistent over the past couple of months. However, we have yet to receive a clear image of who is behind what is happening. Our information comes from those following his orders, who never even get to see his face. Only an immensely powerful sorcerer would have the ability to hide themselves from our visions like this."

Maelona and her mother looked at each other in silent understanding of the implications. Then Alune continued. "We may not know for certain who is behind everything. We may not have solid proof it is a dark sorcerer, but the seers' visions or, rather, the holes in their visions, strongly suggest this to be so."

"Furthermore," Maelona said, "our astronomers have been watching and tracking the stars. We know that in approximately four and a half moon-cycles the planets Chephus and Aragus will once again align with the moon as they did three millennia ago, and the power at the Source will once again be vulnerable. And only a powerful sorcerer could use this advantage—to access the source of magic otherwise would be to risk death."

The rumblings of concerned voices filled the air until Moyses's voice spoke up above the crowd, asking, "Do you believe the keystones will be enough to stop this sorcerer from opening the gate?" All fell silent to hear the response.

"Honestly," Maelona replied, "until we know more about who the Dark Sorcerer is, we cannot say for certain. We believe they will be enough, but if even one of us four should falter, if even one keystone falls..." She looked at the ground and shook her head.

"What would we do," Droyn asked, "if one of you should fail in protecting the keystones, or the keystones should fail to work as hoped?"

Maelona was surprised that Droyn had asked a question, but was pleased to see he was taking this seriously, and the note of antagonism was now absent from his voice.

"The answer to your question will also answer Hadrian's previous question," Maelona said.

"About a millennium after The Battle of the Gate, a powerful seer sorceress named Dimia helped direct our peoples, alongside the Elders of the time. Dimia had visions of this battle we will soon be facing. She prophesied the coming of a powerful magical. . . artifact into our possession. Dimia referred to it as the Ternias.

"Alone, this article would not be likely to stop the Dark Sorcerer and his forces. However, if we can gather enough of the realm's people to oppose this army of evil, the Ternias could give us the edge we need to stop them from opening the gate and allowing the demons to invade our realm."

Alune looked at Maelona with concern before turning to address the group again. "There is much danger involved with the use of the Ternias, however, so we plan to use it only as an absolute last resort." She spoke these last few words with force, a resolute expression on her face.

Maelona frowned at her mother, confused. It had always been expected that the Ternias would be called into play, but, apparently, Alune was now having second thoughts.

"How do we locate this Ternias and how is it used?" Moyses asked. "My kind has unrivaled sight, even at great distances, and our gift of flight helps us to travel much faster than most. May the Golden Eagle-folk offer assistance?"

"My thanks to you, Moyses," Alune replied. "We will most assuredly need your help in the coming months, and I thank you for your kind offer. Luckily," she continued, "the Ternias was located some years back and is in our possession as we speak. We will need all the help we can get in the battles to come, yet only one can carry the Ternias to the Great Gate and wielding it in battle. And that is my daughter, Maelona."

Once again, murmuring arose between those seated around the circle.

"No offense meant to your daughter, Sorceress," Hadrian said, "but Maelona is still young. Are you sure she is the best choice to take on such an important task?"

"Maelona has been working with our protectors and trainees," Gawn said. "Most of us are quite experienced fighters, yet none of us could take her down. In a brief time, she has taught us many skills that I am certain will be highly useful in the battles to come. I can assure you, Hadrian, and any other among you who may doubt her capability—" he swept a pointed finger around the circle, "—that what she may lack in age compared to many of our fighters, she makes up for in martial arts skill, tactical knowledge, intuition, and wisdom. My protectors and I would be proud to follow her into battle."

Shouts of agreement rang out from the village's protectors. Suddenly, Maelona choked up. She lifted a hand and pressed it to her chest and covertly took a deep breath to calm her emotions. Looking at those gathered around the circle, she could tell that many of those who had not previously known her were affected by this show of faith and loyalty. She herself was very touched by Gawn's words, and she hoped she could live up to them.

"Thank you very much for your words of support, my dear Gawn," said the Sorceress. Turning to Hadrian and the others once again, she added, "However any of you feel about this 'choice,' please know that there truly is no choice. Maelona is the only one who can bear the Ternias. And, once again, I truly hope it will not get to that point."

"Why?" Hadrian asked. "Why must it be her?"

"Because this was what the prophecy foretold. When she passed into adolescence, it became clear from the wording that she is the one to whom it refers."

Not to mention the fact that I was intentionally brought into being to fit the prophecy. The sudden obtrusive thought was edged with bitterness and Maelona quickly pushed it away, as she always did. There was no point in dwelling on it, after all.

Maelona could tell from the looks on some of their faces that not everyone present was pleased with her mother's response. Of course, they would want to know more. But she also knew that no one would press the Sorceress and chance offending her.

"So tell us, Maelona," Moyses said, "what is your plan? What do you need us to do?"

Maelona nodded and relief flooded her at his willingness to offer his support.

"As I mentioned, most of what we've been able to See comes from his demonkin. We are acting on the assumption that there are things he will keep to himself until the last possible moment to keep us from learning about them. But we have come up with a plan based on what we know.

"We know they will attempt to destroy the keystones first, so the three other seer guardians and I are heading to our gate towns. We hope to recruit some help along the way."

"That would be you," her mother said to the crowd.

Maelona nodded. "I will need about two dozen Folk to stand with me and the King's forces at Eastgate. The Dark Sorcerer has to divide his numbers to send some to each gate town. So, I believe two dozen will be enough to hold them off and protect the keystone."

"You believe?" Droyn said. "What if you're wrong?"

"Then that would make the rest of the plan even more important. We are almost certain he has a backup plan for if he cannot destroy the keystones. His likely course of action will be to have all his forces regroup with him after they attack the gate towns. So, I am asking for two dozen warriors to go to Eastgate to help protect the keystone and the people there, but we believe the biggest battle will take place at the Great Gate near the time of the Great Alignment."

"Do you know when, exactly, that will be?" Daue asked.

She nodded. "We mentioned earlier that we have about four and a half moon-cycles. According to our astronomers' predictions, the alignment will occur on the twentieth diel of the second moon-cycle. I hope you can have your warriors train everyone capable of fighting in the unlikely chance that the fighting makes it to your villages. And they will also need to practice and prepare for the battle at the Great Gate, if you agree to meet us there by the eighteenth diel, at the latest. To keep him from opening that portal to the demon realm, we'll need all the help we can get."

"You have our support," Moyses said. "We will send three of our best fliers to Eastgate to meet you. I would send more, but we are still on alert for any other stray draccon that might attack."

She nodded. "I understand, thank you."

"We will prepare as best we can to send more to the Great Gate before the alignment."

"Of course, she has our support," Daue announced.

Hadrian was looking at the ground, lips pressed together and brow furrowed. Then he looked up at Maelona and said, "I need to discuss this with my people."

She kept her expression neutral. "Of course. Do what you need to do," she said. Inside, she screamed that the entire realm—all the kingdoms, all the different communities and peoples—would be lost, enslaved and subjugated to an evil tyrant, if they failed to stop the Dark Sorcerer. But she couldn't force them to act. Hopefully, they would come to the right decision on their own.

CHAPTER FOURTEEN

Gifts & Guidance

The next morning, Blaez arose early to prepare for the journey ahead. Like most animal-folk, he preferred to travel light. He had a pack he could wear in human form, but because his wolf was larger and broader, with thick fur added to that, he would have to carry it in his mouth in wolf form.

This was an issue he should address by making a pack with longer, more adjustable straps, but he did not think he had time to do so at the moment. He hadn't traveled enough as a wolf before to have thought of trying to find a better solution, and no one from the village ever carried anything with them when they went out hunting, since they always hunted in wolf form.

He had just gathered a few items together and laid them out on his bed when he heard a knock.

"Enter," he called, and he turned to see Maelona in the doorway. Always happy to see her, he smiled.

"Maelona," he greeted as he nodded to her. "I wasn't sure I would see you before this afternoon's practice, since you have your own preparations to make."

"I do," Maelona replied. "However, I have brought some things that may help you with your packing."

She took a bundle of folded, softened leather out of her pack and laid it on the bed. Then she picked up each piece, one at a time, and explained it to him.

"This is a pair of pants similar to the ones I gave you on the way here. I don't remember if I mentioned it, but the reason they lace up on the outside of each leg is because this is useful for size changes in time of feast or famine." Blaez took the pants from her and ran his thumbs over the soft brown leather in his hands.

"The extra benefit to you is that the leather of the pants is supple yet strong, and I have reinforced the eyelets, so they are stronger than in the pants I'd loaned you. If you must suddenly switch to your wolf form, the laces should break first, leaving the pants themselves intact." With a smile, she added, "I put extra laces in the pack."

Blaez wondered about this pack she mentioned, but before he could ask, Maelona held up another article of clothing. "This vest is like mine as well. It is laced in the front, again with the benefit of being able to tighten or loosen it as needed, within reason. Obviously, I could not don your vest and expect it to fit." Again, she smiled at Blaez, but he had no words at that moment.

She continued, "Unlike my own, your vest has laces between the shoulders and chest, next to the arm openings, as well. This way, it won't be shredded at the shoulders and sides with a quick shift." Smiling at him again, she added, "I put many extra laces in the pack." Blaez loved the look of mirth that shone on her face and couldn't hold back a smile of his own. But again, Maelona continued before he could comment.

"Then there is the pack itself. It is constructed similarly to my own," she said, while gesturing to the pack on her back. To demonstrate, she quickly unfastened the waist strap and swung it around to her front, where she could easily access the contents. "You should try it."

Blaez stood there, overwhelmed by her gifts and not knowing how to respond. This pack. . . it was almost as if she had read his mind. Of course, he believed her when she'd said she couldn't do that, but she'd obviously taken the time to think of him and anticipate his needs. He stayed frozen in place, at a loss for words, until Maelona took the pack, reached up, and slid the chest strap over his head. He ducked a little to aid her. Then she reached around him with both hands to grab the waist strap.

They both paused as they realized how close together this maneuver had brought them. It was almost as if she was embracing him. Blaez's heart pounded in his chest. She was so close... so close that her natural scent—like the forest after a rainfall—was all he could smell.

Maelona did not tense up, as he expected her to do like the last time they'd found themselves unintentionally pressed together. She slowly pulled back to fasten the waist strap. Blaez noticed her inhaling deeply as she moved, as if she was breathing in his scent as well. He shivered.

Once the strap was secured, Maelona looked up into Blaez's eyes, raising her hand to cup his cheek. His breath froze and his heart picked up even more speed at the feel of her warm hand on his face. It was not a soft hand. It was the strong and calloused hand of one who worked and fought hard. Yet somehow, her touch was still warm and feminine. He felt hope welling inside him, but he knew Maelona had to lead, that she had to be ready.

"I have been practicing while everyone is sleeping," Maelona said softly as she held his gaze. "Well, almost everyone. My mother believes that I need to accept it as part of myself and let it flow freely. She wants me to channel it instead of trying to repress it." Her gaze turned earnest as she continued, "I want to try, but you must understand that I have been focusing on controlling my emotions and my magic for a very long time. This will be an ongoing process for me. Already, though, I have felt more open and carefree with you than I have with anyone else in many years."

She held his eyes with her own, clearly trying to get him to understand something important. And he did. She was not just referring to her sorcery practice. He had to allow things to progress slowly. It was up to Maelona to dictate the pace.

He nodded and said, "I will give you whatever you need from me, my Lona. You need never doubt me." With these words of reassurance, Maelona pulled him to her to kiss him softly, then pulled back slightly to look at him again.

Something sparked in her eyes, as if the brief contact had awakened something inside her. He felt it too. The spark quickly spread, threatening to turn into an inferno. Maelona pulled him to her again, this time bringing him in for a deeper kiss, which he returned with equal passion.

Blaez sensed she was beginning to fully let go when she pressed her form up against his own. As their tongues met in an intricate dance, all the hair on Blaez's body stood on end, like it did when the air was filled with an electrical charge before a storm. It pulled them out of the moment, but unlike that day in the meadow, Maelona did not jump back suddenly in surprise. Instead, she pulled back unhurriedly, reluctantly, and the static electricity gently dissipated as she did so.

Maelona cleared her throat and looked down at the floor. After a moment, she whispered, "We had better get back to the task at hand." She took a deep breath and blew it out slowly. Then she continued with her instructions in the same matter-of-fact fashion as before, as if she hadn't even stopped.

"This pack is easily adjustable and easy to remove. I have added twice the length to the straps than I would have normally used to accommodate your additional size when you shift."

Blaez's gaze moved back and forth from her face to her hands in rapt attention as she showed how to adjust the straps and clasps so the pack would fit both his human and wolf forms.

When Maelona finished the demonstration, she stepped back and looked at Blaez uncertainly, almost nervously. "What do you think? Will it work for you?" she asked. "I know I asked you to stay in wolf form as much as possible, but there will be times when you will go in human form as well. You will need to have clothing with you, as the human villages are not accepting of nudity as the animal-folk are. Although, I am sure the human women would enjoy the spectacle," she added with a smirk. Then she looked at him expectantly.

Blaez could not immediately find his voice, even after Maelona's attempt at lightening the moment. Not wanting her to worry, however, he leaned in and kissed her softly. He was a little overwhelmed—happy, of course, but overwhelmed with physical and emotional sensation. He may have longed for it since shortly after they met, but this was the first time that Maelona had laid her hands on him outside of sparring. And it was definitely the first time she had kissed him.

More than that, however, he was touched by her gifts, made with her own hands, with his specific needs in mind.

"These gifts for me are what you have been working on this whole time with the tanning of the deer hides, are they not?" His voice was rough with emotion.

Maelona gave one slow nod of her head. "Actually, I did not have time to tan my own properly and have them be supple enough, so I traded mine for some leather that was ready at the tannery in the village."

"The time you must have put in, not to mention the thought and labor involved in creating items of such practicality and craftsmanship. . ."

Maelona shrugged and responded, "Back in Clearview, family and close friends customarily employ their best skills to create useful gifts for those who set out on dangerous journeys. In fact, the more useful and well thought-out the gift, the higher the esteem. That is how I came to possess the weapons I currently carry, in fact."

"Oh, yes?" Blaez teased. "And who made your gifts? Should I be worried?"

Maelona let out a quick burst of laughter. "Not at all," she said. "I have no brother, but Aleyn is the closest one can come when there is no blood relation."

Blaez studied the items again in awe. "I would normally pay dearly at the marketplace to buy such items, but they wouldn't be so carefully thought out. How is it that our own artisans haven't thought of these designs?"

"They have not had the need, really," Maelona said. "After all, for the last few centuries, the Folk, like the seers and most of the other magical beings in the Sacred Forest, have limited any contact with those living outside our beloved forest. And when we do make our way into their towns and villages, it's always in human form."

Blaez nodded. "True."

"You, however, will visit villages and towns with me as well as traveling in the forest, so you will need such things. I want you to be prepared. We seers and, in particular, the seer guardians, wear clothing made this way because it is very useful to us. While slipping in and out of villages and towns gathering information and watching for signs of trouble, we often have to alter our appearance, and we sometimes need to change quickly.

"Remember also," Maelona said, "that seers do not sleep as often as Wolf-folk. Working with my hands has helped me feel calm and focused while everyone else sleeps, and this is the result."

Blaez knew she was trying to downplay the significance of the effort she had put into this gift for the sake of remaining humble, so he let it go, simply saying, "Well, I thank you for your thoughtful gifts. They are truly appreciated." Then he leaned down to kiss her cheek.

As he pulled back and gazed at her, he marveled at how natural this now felt. It was as if something shifted between them today, like they'd stepped past some barrier. It made him excited for what was to come—for how things would progress now that Maelona seemed to be opening up to him.

Maelona smiled and tilted her head toward the door. "Come on. The protectors are waiting for us. You can thank me by allowing me to use you as a demonstration target."

"You wanted to see me, Sorceress?" Blaez said.

He had not long arrived back at his hut after practice with the protectors when Rauf had knocked on his door.

"Sorry to bother you," Rauf had said. "I was on patrol and passed by the Sorceress's sanctuary. She asked me to come by to let you know she wishes to see you."

Alune rarely sent for him this late in the evening unless someone was ill or injured, so Blaez had headed out right away. The Sorceress was already waiting outside for him when he arrived.

"Yes," she replied. "I would like to speak with you, but not out here. Follow me."

Blaez followed Alune through the twists and turns of the tunnels that made up her sanctuary. He'd always suspected this area had been magically hewn: the smooth stone of the walls and ceiling, the intricately carved images and unfamiliar words, all made it impossible to be anything but. Especially since Sorceress Alune had done it all herself. Even so, the way the tunnels meandered and split seemed almost random, like a natural cave system might. Though he'd been working with the Sorceress for forty years, he doubted he'd be able to map even the areas he'd been allowed access to, and they were just a fraction of the whole.

He'd asked the Sorceress once if it was naturally confusing, or if she'd spelled it to make it seem more confusing than it was. As she often liked to do, Alune answered without really answering. "I call it my sanctuary, do I not?" she'd said. "It couldn't be my safe space if it was easily accessible by all, now, could it?"

She led him to a passageway near the back of the sanctuary, far underneath the escarpment. When they stopped, Alune pressed her hand against the wall and her hand, as well as the section she was touching, lit with a dull, purple light until a door appeared. The door slid back and to the side, and Alune motioned him inside.

Blaez glanced around and realized he recognized the space. They were in one of her smaller rooms for creating potions and remedies. The length of one wall was filled with a bookcase that held bottles with various ingredients and several books. A small round table with a couple of wooden chairs was placed in the center of the space. The smell of a mix of different herbs added to the faint scent of smoke from the small, unlit hearth and permeated the air.

"I'm guessing that what you would like to discuss with me is of some importance, if you are taking me here to talk," he commented.

"I like this room," Alune said lightly, shrugging, "and sometimes I just feel like sitting in here to think. But, in this case, you are right. Let's take a seat before we begin."

Once they were sitting comfortably inside with a small, crackling fire to warm them—a magic spell the Sorceress had set up years ago safely dissipating the smoke—the Sorceress finally turned to address him.

"My dear Blaez," she began, "you may have figured out by now that, over the years, I have been preparing you to partner with my daughter through the dark times that are now upon us. I did not want to leave her to deal with everything alone, and there is no one else I would trust. Of course, at first, while I knew of the prophecy, I didn't yet know the exact nature of what was coming. No one did. Now I would like to explain to you why and tell you why I have chosen you."

Blaez already had a sense of her motivations, but he was still eager to learn the details.

"Maelona knows and understands the importance of her mission. There are still many uncertainties, but one thing we know is that her success or failure will determine the future of Sterrenvar. She is so young in Folk and seer years, and even more so in the years of a sorceress, yet the fate of so many rests upon her shoulders."

Alune frowned, her expression solemn and a little sad. "My daughter is special, Blaez. She is three things at once: a seer, a Wolf-folk, and a sorceress. She was born of two magical beings who were both powerful in their own right. I believe she has taken the best traits from each of us, although that may just be the pride of a mother speaking." She smiled and glanced up at Blaez.

Blaez smiled back and nodded. He wholeheartedly agreed, but he was hardly any more objective than Alune was.

"Though she has the best parts of her father and I, she is unique." She paused and took a deep breath. "Years ago, I explained to you we sorcerers harness magical energy, draw it into ourselves from the natural world around us, where it has spread out from the Source, and then refocus it where we need it. The strongest among us do not have to capture it—magic is drawn to us and we are, for lack of a better description, natural conduits for it." She caught his gaze, her expression intense.

Blaez nodded. "I remember."

"Maelona does not only draw and harness magic, Blaez," she continued emphatically, leaning forward towards him. "Maelona is magic. It is a part of her, just as surely as her heart and her head are. She is made up of cells and molecules that radiate and produce their own magic."

It took a moment for Blaez to make sense of Alune's words. When he finally comprehended, he gave a start, and his eyes widened in surprise. "What?"

"I may not be a seer, but I am a sorceress who has been around for a very long time. I am also Lona's mother," Alune continued. "I carried her in my body. I could sense her magic. I can sense it still. I do not know if you are aware, Blaez, but Maelona has allowed me to work with her in private recently. She only agrees to work with me when most others are sleeping or at home in the evenings. Even then, she still fears she may inadvertently hurt someone."

Blaez nodded. He had been around Maelona enough to know how important it was to her not to put anyone else at risk.

"When I work with her, Blaez," Alune continued, her words coming faster and her eyes alight with excitement, "I can see her magic radiating out from her like an aura, touching the trees, the earth, the animals—anything that is close to her. I can feel her power, and when we practice together, I can see and feel her magic coiling back inside of her as she focuses on having it do her bidding."

The Sorceress paused for a moment.

"You may not know this, Blaez," she continued, "but this type of magic is extremely rare. Dimia was the only other sorceress I've heard of whose power emanated from within, and that was more than a millennium ago."

"Dimia. . . the sorceress who gave the prophecy, right?"

"Yes." Alune scooted forward to the edge of her chair. "What this means, Blaez, is that Maelona's magical abilities are limited only by her own mind and imagination. Her magic is powerful, but it cannot be used to its full potential until she learns to forgive herself—to trust in herself and her power again. She must accept the magic as part of herself.

"Your job, dear Blaez, is to support her, to encourage her, to be her strength when her own wavers, throughout her physical and emotional journeys to come.

"When I first saw you at my door all those years ago, I knew it was fated. You were both linked by a common history. A very tragic history, yes, but it has affected both of you in similar ways. You are both trying to heal from tragic circumstances that neither of you had any say in or control over."

Blaez shifted uncomfortably. He could do without the reminders. He still found it unbelievable that Maelona was willing to partner with him, given those events. He was grateful for that, but he longed for a time when the past stayed in the past.

"You, more than anyone else, can help her let go of the past and accept herself as she is, magic and all. When she releases some control of her emotions, she will access more of her magic. I can see she has already started to open up with you. This is good. . . very good. But she will only reach her full potential, Blaez, when she lets her magic flow naturally.

"She has only recently learned that her magic differs from most other sorcerers'. I gave her a way to focus her power, but once she gets past the fear, she will not need it."

If Maelona only recently learned that her magic is different, then that meant that the Sorceress only told her recently. Blaez wasn't sure how he felt about something so important being kept from her for so long, but it wasn't his place to say anything.

"I'm surprised that you say you've felt I can help her since I first showed up in front of you. Why did you think I would be the best one to help her?" Blaez asked. "Yes, we are linked, but not in a happy or positive way."

"This is why you are perhaps the only one who can truly help her." Alune said. "You have both allowed yourselves to be molded by the same events. You have both been carrying guilt that was never really yours to bear." In a softer tone, she added, "You both, deep down inside, do not feel you are deserving of others' esteem, or of anyone's love."

He allowed her words to sink in. He wanted to be angry at what she was saying. He wanted to deny it. However, he could not.

When Alune spoke again, she said, "Because of your shared experiences, your shared understanding, you can heal each other."

Alune took a deep breath and released it slowly.

"I am not telling you this, Blaez, to put more pressure on you. I am telling you so I can ask you, as both a mother and as a Sorceress of the Light, to please be patient with her and remain supportive through the trials to come. Do not give up on her. I know you care for her, so it should not be too much of a difficulty for you to give her what she needs in order to become her full and true self."

Blaez could not speak right away. He was touched by the fact that she trusted him and believed in him this much. He swallowed past the lump of emotion in his throat, then leaned forward to meet Alune's eyes. "You are our pack's sorceress and my dear friend," he said. "I would do anything for you. In this case, however, you need ask nothing of me. Your daughter already has my devotion, and it will not waver."

Alune's smile spread across her face. She gave one sharp nod and said, "Good. Then it is as I have hoped.

"Go now, Blaez," Alune told him. "You have a long journey ahead of you that begins in the morning."

Blaez turned to leave, but hesitated for a moment. He turned back to Alune and took her hand. "I do not know how long it will be before we see each other again. I will miss you, my dear friend and mentor."

Alune tipped her head forward and looked up at him intently. "I will see you at the Great Gate."

She placed her other hand on top so that his was cupped in both of hers. Then she gave him the customary Wolf-folk prayer for those embarking upon long journeys.

"May the moon shine luck and protection down upon you, until fate crosses our paths again."

Farewells & Journeys

Early the next morning, Maelona and wolf-Blaez made their way to the Sorceress's sanctuary for the last time.

Andrion was already sitting outside by the fire circle, awaiting their arrival. Maelona gave him a nod, then went inside to speak with her mother. Blaez remained outside with Andrion.

"I am glad you came to see me before beginning your journey, my daughter," Alune said as Maelona entered the hearth room. "Sit and speak with me a little before you leave."

As she sat across from her mother, Alune handed her a cup of tea. Maelona did not fail to notice that the tea had already been prepared the way she liked it. The warmth of affection filled her chest, swiftly followed by the sadness of having to leave again so soon. For such a brief visit, it had been remarkably healing. She shouldn't have waited so long to return.

"Are you sure you don't have some seer in you too, Mother?" Maelona asked, smiling.

"Maybe I keep tea ready at all times, just so it looks like I know when someone's coming." She laughed. "But really, I didn't think you would leave without saying goodbye on your way through."

"How are you feeling this morning, my dear?" Alune asked.

"To be honest," Maelona replied, "I am feeling. . . uncertain. Nervous. I feel ill prepared to take on this task. However, the danger is upon us, and there is no more time to prepare."

After a pause, she continued, "You and the other Elders and sorcerers expect me to put an end to this danger that looms over us finally. Yet I know I am still young, and I am not as practiced in my magic as I should be."

Looking into her mother's eyes, she voiced her fears. "What if I cannot complete the task that has been set out for me? What if I am not strong enough?"

Alune took a deep breath and reached out to take Maelona's hand, giving it a reassuring squeeze.

"Over the years," she began, "I have vacillated many times between certainty that your father and I made the right choice for the future of the realm, and regret that I have placed such a burden on the shoulders of an innocent who wasn't given any choice—and my daughter at that. Yet I have never doubted that you could handle the path that has been set before you."

Alune leaned towards Maelona. "You are strong, Lona. So strong! And you are good to your very core. I have known this about you since you were a child, gently correcting the other children when they would steal another's toy or were cruel to one another. But you must come to accept, my beloved daughter, that you are never alone. You have people in your life who care for you and who would like nothing more than to support you in any way they can. You just have to let them.

"You cannot continue to hold people at arm's length, Maelona. You need to let them in. You must let go of your fear that you may hurt those you let close to you. Stop blaming yourself."

"But it was my fault." Maelona's voice shook as she spoke—her hands had already started shaking at her mother's words. She felt the familiar prickle of electricity run underneath her skin, and she closed her eyes and breathed deeply until she calmed. Her mother must have noticed, because it wasn't until Maelona had her emotions under control that she spoke again.

"No, my dear. It was Guarin Stronghunter's fault. I have said these words to you before, but it's time for you to believe them." Her mother squeezed her hand once more, as if to emphasize her words. "The chain of events that happened that day was set off by his choices, his actions. You and your magic. . . well, you just responded to what was happening. It was an automatic defense when faced with danger. Your magic is not a bad thing, Maelona.

It was just trying to protect you. . . you were just trying to protect yourself."

They were both quiet for a moment as Maelona sat, absorbing her mother's words. She wanted to say something, to tell her mother how much it meant that she believed in her; to let her know how much she loved her and how much she regretted staying away for so long. But she didn't think she'd be able to speak past the lump in her throat.

Her mother stroked the back of her hand and looked her in the eye with the warmest gaze Maelona had ever received, and Maelona knew she understood. Then Alune stood and helped Maelona to her feet. "Enough with this topic," she said. "It needs to be left in the past. Now we must think about the present and the future of the realm. Go! I will see you again at the Great Gate."

Andrion sat waiting on a rock next to the now unlit fire circle while Maelona was inside saying her goodbyes to her mother. He absently drew designs in the ash with a stick, eager to leave and get home to his family. He had already been away too long, and concern for his father's well-being ate at him.

"By Father's beard!" Andrion exclaimed, hand to his heart. "How long has he been there?

Suddenly feeling the hair on the back of his neck stand up, he looked to his left, only to find the black wolf staring at him unblinkingly.

The gaze from those icy blue eyes seemed to bore a hole in him, and he shivered. He put the stick down—the wolf didn't expect him to throw it for him, did it?—and tried to distract himself by double-checking his pack, which sat at his feet. Once he was satisfied he hadn't forgotten anything he looked up again, only to find the wolf staring at him still.

He turned as he heard Maelona approach. "Finally!" he said. "Your wolf is giving me the shivers."

"Blaez."

"What?"

"His name is Blaez."

"Right. Sure. But something like Ice might be more fitting, what with the color of his eyes and the icy stare. Why does he constantly look at me like that, anyway? Does he stare at everyone so intently?"

Maelona walked past Andrion toward Blaez with her hand outstretched. The creature rose and padded over to meet her. "Animals can be peculiar like that," she replied with a smirk as she stroked the fur on its head. "He is just trying to figure you out; to get a feel for who you are. The novelty will wear off once he gets to know you."

"He is quite a large wolf. I have never seen one as large before—not that I've seen many, mind you. Is he a particular subspecies of wolf that grows to a greater size than most?"

"Maybe," Maelona answered. "Though it is difficult to say for certain. He just started following me one day."

Her mouth quirked up at the corner and he eyed her suspiciously. Why did he feel like she meant something more than the words indicated?

She scratched the top of the wolf's head, adding affectionately, "However, he has become invaluable to me since then."

"Is that a pack he is carrying?" Andrion asked curiously. "It looks much like your own."

"Yes," Maelona answered with a nod. "Like I said, he is invaluable. Carrying things is just one of his many uses."

The wolf let out a whiny huff, and Maelona laughed. Andrion felt like he was left on the outside of an inside joke, but he did not know what it was. Andrion was usually the person making those types of jests with others—most often, his sister. Having someone do it to him felt kind of strange.

Bah! What nonsense was he thinking? How could a person have an inside joke with a wild animal? But at least Maelona seemed to be in a jovial mood, which was an improvement from the seriousness he'd usually seen from her up to that point.

He shook his head at himself. Perhaps he'd been cooped up in the cave too long if he was imagining wordless conversations between people and animals.

They started out on the north path that went up and over the escarpment that the Sorceress's sanctuary was built under. It was slow going over the steepest parts since his injured leg was still stiff. He wouldn't gripe about that, though. It was quite phenomenal how quickly and how well it had healed.

As for Maelona, she was patient and didn't complain about his pace, thankfully.

"I can see how having such a beast would be useful for a woman who travels alone," he said, nodding at the wolf. . . er, Blaez. Still looking forward, Maelona raised her brows and shook her head slightly, but otherwise did not respond. How did her mood switch back to serious so quickly? Was it what he said?

He tried again.

"We haven't had the opportunity to really converse or get to know one another during my stay here, what with the meetings and preparations, and me being confined to bed while I healed," Andrion said. "It's too bad, really. I could have used some company." He flashed Maelona his most charming smile.

"I am sure the Sorceress provided good company," Maelona said. "There are many who travel long distances just to speak with her. She is very well-respected for her wisdom and insight."

"Oh, without doubt," Andrion agreed, nodding. "I enjoyed my conversations with your mother. It's interesting, though, that I only learned she was your mother at the fire-circle, wouldn't you say?"

He glanced at Maelona, suddenly realizing how tall and well-muscled she was now that he was walking beside her. . . and not distracted by pain.

Maelona gave a little shrug with one shoulder. "It hadn't come up previously, I guess."

"Right. Well, during my brief stay, she gave me much to think about. Like you, however, she was often drawn away on business."

"I am not a very social being, anyway. I usually prefer to be on my own," Maelona said. "I probably would have bored you with my lack of social skills. And aside from that," she added, "you came to us for help, and help we shall provide. While your injuries have kept us from returning to your father as soon as you would have liked, the time you have taken to heal has given us the advantage of being able to better prepare. . . and not just for King Nele and Eastgate, but for what may follow as well."

He thought back to what had been revealed during the fire circle. A gateway to a demon realm and a mad dark sorcerer who wanted to be lord of the entire realm of Sterrenvar. He shook his head.

His father barely ever had time to himself, and Andrion had often thought that being in charge of one kingdom was a lot for one man to handle—what with all its citizens, and everything that had to be done to keep things running effectively and peacefully. And this madman wanted to control all four kingdoms, plus all the self-ruling peoples who occupied the Sacred Forest? The man was truly crazy.

"I really appreciate what you are doing for my father and our kingdom," he said to Maelona. "I just hope we get there before it's too late to stop what's been going on."

Andrion immediately realized how that sounded, so he added, "Do not misunderstand. I am truly grateful for your help and I'm looking forward to the opportunity to get to know you better during our travels." He leaned his head forward and to the side to catch Maelona's gaze, and a growl immediately sounded from off to her right.

"Yes, I am sure our journey will be quite educational for you," Maelona replied. "I hope you take the lessons to heart."

Andrion pursed his lips and squinted at her, wondering why that sounded almost like a threat. She must not have meant it that way, right?

They walked on in silence for some time on the narrow path. The forest was dense here, with trees encroaching all around. This route must not be well-used. Did that mean the people who lived in the nearby village rarely left, or just that they rarely came this way?

Andrion's gaze regularly traveled from the path ahead of him—he did not want to stumble and re-injure himself, after all—to the woods. The sun was high enough to send filtered beams down through the canopy. It was lovely; he had to admit. Still, he could easily imagine how much different it would seem in the darkness of night, with those immense trees looming tall and threatening all around. He shivered—he needed to distract himself from the gloomy thought.

"You say this Dark Sorcerer wants to subjugate the realm," he said, "and everyone at the meeting seemed shocked that demonkin followed me into the forest. Then there are the attacks on Eastgate. So, you think this sorcerer has already begun his plans for taking over the realm, then?"

"Oh, I'm certain he has. I'd wager his plans have been progressing in the background for years, even. The real worry is that the demonkin made it this far, into the Sacred Forest no less, and we hadn't foreseen it. I am going to have to try harder."

"I thought you said you don't get to choose the visions you get?"

"Not normally, no. However, I have a few advantages the others do not. I just usually choose not to use them."

By her expression—lips pursed and nose slightly scrunched up—whatever she intended to do must be distasteful to her.

"I don't suppose you'd care to share what you mean, would you?" he asked.

"No, I would not. At least, not yet."

They walked on in this manner for the rest of the day. Andrion tried to impress Maelona with his charm and conversational skills to get her to open up some. However, she remained impassive. But he counted one small victory for himself: By the time the sun had started to lower itself onto the horizon many hours later, Blaez had stopped growling at him regularly.

Without warning, Maelona suddenly headed off the path and walked into the forest. Andrion hurried to keep up.

"Is it wise to wander off the path?" Andrion inquired.

"It's wiser than setting up camp in the middle of the path."

"Right. Good point. So, I guess we're camping then."

When she reached a small clearing in the trees, she turned in a circle to take in her surroundings. Andrion followed her gaze to see what she was looking at.

Ah. The area was perfect for providing shelter. They were ringed by trees, and the overhanging branches above opened just enough in the center to give a glimpse of the clear sky.

"We will camp here for the night," Maelona said.

"Good," Andrion replied, shaking out his sore leg. Aside from the stiffness when climbing the steep path over the escarpment, it had felt good as new when they set out that morning. However, walking all day with very few breaks was apparently pushing it. He wouldn't complain, though—the sooner they got back to Eastgate, the better.

"I'm famished. I hope we will have something other than the berries and unleavened bread we've been eating all day. Did you pack any meat during your preparations, by chance?" he asked. "My father's cooks always pack dried meats for us when we head out on a journey."

"I did," Maelona answered, "but that is for when other food sources run scarce."

"Well, that's a disappointment. I was looking forward to something substantial."

"You really are not much of a woodsman, are you, Prince?" Maelona said. She looked at him and spoke with the slightest touch of exasperation, but also humor, in her voice.

Ha! Was he finally breaking through, even just a little?

"Well, to be honest," he responded, unable to hide his grin, "I am the Prince of Eastgate. When I was a child, there were often threats to the royal family and, in particular, to the heir. So, my mother kept me fairly sheltered, and I rarely left the city walls. My father tried to fight her on this, saying the future king should be prepared for anything. My mother, however, liked to dote, and she could be quite spirited when crossed. So, her will won out most of the time." He chuckled at this. "She passed away when I was 15, so my father got a little tougher with me after that."

"I am sorry for your loss," Maelona replied in a soft tone.

Andrion nodded his thanks to her. "I received some training, of course: sword fighting, archery, knife throwing, hand to hand fighting, basic survival skills. I practice fighting skills regularly, but I haven't had much opportunity to practice survival skills."

"Has your father never taken you out hunting?" Maelona asked.

"Well, yes, but as I said, there were always threats, so we were always surrounded by our men... men who seemed to want to stay on our good side by doing much of the work for me."

Maelona chuckled and shook her head. "You will get your meat, Prince, do not fear. Lesson number one in basic survival—which I have been trying to show to you all day—is that, inside the forest, nature shall provide." She lifted her hands to gesture around her. "Do you remember which berries I showed you are safe to eat, or have you forgotten already?"

Andrion shifted uncomfortably on his feet. "I think I may be able to recall them."

"You had better be sure, because if you are caught in the forest alone and eat the wrong berries, they could make you very sick. Certain ones could even kill you."

"Well, if I'd known you were giving me a lesson in survival—"

Maelona laughed. "It may be best for you to assume that everything you see or experience is a lesson. If you pay close enough attention, you will find there is always something new to learn. But then, when I was your age, I wasn't mindful enough of certain things either."

Andrion squinted at her. Despite her height—she was slightly taller than he was—he was sure she must be younger than him. At least, that was what her features suggested. But this was not the first time she'd made such a comment. She must be older than she looked. He wouldn't ask, though. His mother had taught him all about how dangerous it could be to ask a lady her age.

"Now, search around the area for dead wood for the fire and I will go forage for our supper." Maelona headed into the trees, Blaez following closely behind her.

An hour later, Andrion had a good pile of branches and dead wood, which he was carefully stacking in a small fire pit he had fashioned from stones. He was determined to show Maelona that he was not completely inept and could be a useful companion.

He had to admit to himself, however, that he enjoyed poking at her by pretending to be even less skilled and more spoiled than he actually was. He was sure that her experiences had made her much more skilled and knowledgeable than he was. Even so, he was not completely useless. So, he placed some wood in the fire pit, being careful to leave space for the air to flow through, and carefully arranged dry moss for tinder underneath.

He had just started the fire with the flint and steel he always carried in his pack when he heard movement behind him, and he turned to find Maelona walking toward the fire carrying a large bird.

"I see you've had a successful hunt."

"I have indeed."

"Is that a flightless bird?"

"It is not."

"But you're not carrying a bow and arrow."

"Well spotted," she replied. "However, I do have these." She took a throwing knife out of her chest strap and spun it in her hand before returning it to its place.

"Hmm," he replied with an arched brow. He watched Maelona set the bird down on a large rock a few feet from the campfire.

She turned to him and said, "Now you will learn how to clean and prepare a meal that has been freshly caught."

"This is exactly the kind of thing someone would do for me back at Eastgate," Andrion responded, lips pressed together in mock disgust.

"And it is exactly the kind of thing you need to be prepared to do for yourself," Maelona said. "You are the future King and Guardian of Eastgate. You may not always have a party of men with you, and you need to learn how to rely on yourself if need be."

"I can rely on myself just fine," Andrion said in a fake irritated tone. Then he jumped as he heard a loud snort from behind him.

Turning around, he noticed Blaez sitting just this side of the tree line.

Maelona couldn't help it; she burst out laughing. Blaez looked as if he was rolling his eyes and shaking his head over by the side of the clearing, and it made her laugh even more.

She had been aware that Andrion had been exaggerating, playing up the part of a spoiled, inept prince most likely to lighten the tension between them. There was no way her old friend Nele would leave his heir completely untrained and unprepared, however. There was too much at stake. She was as sure of that as she was that Andrion lacked real-world experience. No doubt that's what King Nele hoped his son would gain when sending him to her father. There was also no doubt that her father would have given him as much experience as he could, so it was up to her now to do the same.

Of course, the young man was, in fact, a spoiled prince to some degree, but she at least had to admire him for playing up his own weaknesses to make her feel more comfortable around him.

Maelona had known before leaving the village that she would not give in to Andrion's attempts to charm her, at least not in the way he seemed to hope. After all, he was barely more than a child in many ways, and the son of an old friend.

And he seemed to consider himself a bit of a charmer, which she supposed was useful for ruling a kingdom and leading soldiers. She hoped it worked better on the citizens he tried it on than her. . . as long as he was using it for the right reasons, of course.

"Alright then, Prince, show me what you can do to make this catch edible," she said, and Andrion set about cleaning and preparing the bird for the fire. He actually proved to be more competent than she'd expected.

Meanwhile, Maelona set a flat stone over the fire and sliced some roots and tubers they had dug up earlier in the day. She then placed these on the hot stone to cook. Every once in a while, she would check Andrion's progress and give him some pointers.

"Isn't this nice?" Andrion mused at one point.

"What?" Maelona asked.

"Just you and I, preparing a meal together. Such an image of domestic happiness and comfort." He let out a dramatic, happy sigh. "Does it stir longings in you, as it does for me?"

Her own sigh was more of the exasperated sort. "First, you live in a castle, so I don't imagine this is the kind of domestic happiness you are accustomed to seeing. Don't you have cooks and servants?"

"I have friends in town," he said, chin lifted and an eye-brow raised. "I see things."

"Second, it isn't just you and I," she said, gesturing to Blaez with the knife in her hand. As if to back her up, Blaez padded over and sat at her side.

"I don't think pets can really be considered chaperones," Andrion muttered.

Blaez's low growl rumbled in response.

"And last, you are a baby when one considers the number of years I have behind me compared to you."

"Okay, what exactly do you mean?" He narrowed his eyes at her. "This is not the first time you've mentioned being older than me, yet you look younger. Also, the others at the fire circle kept mentioning how young you are. So, you can't be older than I am, and if you are, it can't be by much."

"Let's just say I first met your father when he was a child."

Andrion considered that for a moment. Then his eyes widened.

"What?" he said. "You jest."

She shook her head.

"How is that possible?"

"Do they not teach anything about Sterrenvar's magical races in Eastgate?"

"A little, but I have to admit that I haven't always been the best student."

"These are things you really should know if you're going to be King of Eastgate one day. You really need to pay more attention to your lessons."

She glanced at the prince and saw he was looking at her with his brows raised expectantly.

She sighed. "Fine, I will tell you more about it, but another time. For now, focus on cooking the fowl before it burns."

A little later, when they had mostly finished their meal, Maelona sat leaning against Blaez, feeding him bits of what was left of the meat. "Shouldn't we be saving that for our next meal?" Andrion asked.

"Don't worry, I have already put some inside a pouch along with some herbs that will help it remain edible a little longer than normal. If we happen upon some more of these herbs during our travels, I will point them out to you. They can be invaluable on long journeys."

"What do you do in the winter when there are no herbs growing?"

"It's never winter in the Sacred Forest. Nevertheless, we dry a lot of our herbs so we can always have them on hand."

"What? What do you mean, never winter?" Andrion's eyebrows lifted almost to his hairline and his eyes were wide.

"The Source and the ley lines you heard about at the meeting? Well, the forest is right on top of all that. It's magical. It does rain regularly, but I don't think it's as often as it does outside of the forest."

"Why doesn't everyone live in here, then?"

"There are many reasons, but one of the largest is that there are magical protections keeping others out." She pointed at his chest. "Your amulet allowed you to pass without noticing, but you could not just walk in here otherwise."

"And that's why everyone was so concerned about the demonkin in the forest, right?"

She nodded. "Yes. It should not have been possible."

Andrion stretched and yawned.

"It's late," Maelona said, "and we still have much traveling ahead of us tomorrow. You should get some rest."

Andrion grinned and looked at Maelona. "There is a chill in the air tonight. Perhaps we should share body warmth."

"You needn't worry about me," Maelona replied, smirking and leaning into Blaez. "I have my own fur blanket. But you could perhaps lay on the other side of him. I'm sure he wouldn't mind."

Andrion looked at Blaez, who emitted a low, menacing growl. "I think I'll pass," he said. "Come to think of it, I have a thin blanket in my pack that should work just fine."

Maelona shook her head and tried to hold back a smile. She should probably be stressing the seriousness of what's to come upon him instead of encouraging his behavior. But then again, she may as well let him have some harmless fun while he still could.

After all, things were bound to change once they left the safety of the Sacred Forest.

CHAPTER SIXTEEN

Starlight & Confessions

A tugging sensation on the fur of his shoulder pulled Blaez from sleep.

He lifted his head to see Maelona incline her head towards the forest, then walk silently in the direction she'd indicated. He glanced over at Andrion, who was lightly snoring, then he rose and followed Maelona through the trees. Before long, they ended up at the top of a little grassy hill, where Maelona sat and looked up at the clear night sky.

Lingering behind so he could shift, Blaez shrugged off his pack and dressed in his pants before coming to sit beside Maelona. He loved this new pack that she had made for him. It was so very convenient to carry his things with him, no matter what form he was in. And, of course, he was perhaps more pleased than he should have been that she made it with her own hands for him.

Maelona turned to look at him, giving him a small smile before gazing up at the stars again. "It's a clear night tonight," she said. "The stars are bright."

Blaez glanced up at the sky. Its dark fabric was indeed pierced with billions of tiny pinpricks of light. But he doubted she was really just stargazing. He looked back at her. She was frowning slightly and her brows were pinched close.

"Tell me, my Lona," Blaez said, her mother's nickname for her slipping out easily, "what is on your mind?"

She took a deep breath and let it out slowly. "I keep watching the stars, wondering how much closer Chephus and Aragus are to aligning with the moon. It's silly, really, I know. Huet, our astronomer, uses a very large telescope to watch the skies, and he has many tools to help him calculate and predict events. There is no way I can see all the little movements simply looking at them like this."

"You're feeling anxious, aren't you?"

She laughed lightly, the sound somewhere between wry and amused. "I am always anxious."

"What can I do to help you?"

She turned her head and smiled at him. "You are doing it right now."

He nodded in understanding. She just needed someone to be there for support; someone to listen.

After a quiet moment, Maelona spoke again. "Lately, I've been thinking about what a person's true nature is made of. How much our parentage forms who we are as opposed to our experiences? And then, how much fate influences our paths as opposed to our own desires?"

"Those are pretty complex questions." He frowned. He had wondered about that before, given the past. Hopefully, blood didn't have as much influence as other factors, given who his father was.

"For instance," she continued, "Andrion shares his father's hair and eye color, and even mirrors his effortless charm. Yet his father was already more worldly and intuitive when I first met him many years ago and, back then, he was much younger than Andrion is now, by human standards.

"Then there is you." She nudged him lightly with her elbow. "I was truly surprised when my mother told me who your father was, though I had already spent some time with you by then. I am not surprised very often."

She looked at him and smiled again. "You are a wonder to me, Blaez. I could see nothing but good in your eyes when we met. I could see your desire to help and protect. Never once have I thought that you deserved to do your father's penance, yet you happily take it upon yourself to ease as much of the pain he left behind as possible."

He raised his eyebrows. "What are you basing that on? Since we arrived back here, I've been focused solely on preparing for the coming battle."

"I hear things," she said. One side of her mouth lifted in a smirk.

Reaching across to take Maelona's hand in his, Blaez responded, "Well, when it comes to one's nature, I believe each of the elements you mentioned has some part to play. More than that, however, I believe it is the choices we make that have the final say, as you yourself once said. We can choose to be happy, to lead a good life. We can decide on the person we want to be, and then make a thousand small choices each day to keep us on our path."

His mother had taught him that. She'd repeated it often, especially after his father had his violent episodes.

"I was lucky I had my mother," Blaez said after a brief pause. "She was patient and kind. When I was very young, I thought she was weak for putting up with my father. Over time, however, I've come to realize that she had her own kind of quiet strength. She never gave in or cowered to him. When he would lose his temper with me, she would step in and draw his attention away from me. Sometimes she could calm him, but more often than not, it meant she suffered his wrath in my place. She never became violent herself. She didn't even raise her voice. She showed me that there is always a better way; that there is always a choice."

He looked at Maelona, who met his eyes with a soft gaze. "You are very lucky to have had such a positive influence in your life. Not every young one is so lucky. I wish I could have met her."

"From having spent years working with your mother, I would venture to say you are one of the lucky ones yourself. I have seen her love and devotion to you—even in your absence, she was always thinking of you and speaking of you."

Maelona's smile brightened her face as she responded, "I was lucky to have both of my parents." Then her smile dropped and her expression turned serious. "You know, there was a brief period when I doubted my parents' love for me."

Blaez's eyebrows lifted in surprise.

"Back when I first discovered I'd been conceived with a purpose in mind, I questioned whether they truly loved me or if I was just a tool, a means to an end. But they have proven their love for me repeatedly over the years, with my father even giving the ultimate sacrifice to protect me from harm. And now, as you may have noticed at the fire-circle, my mother has shown her reluctance to allow me to continue on the very path I was born for."

The Sorceress believed Maelona was the only one who could carry and wield the Ternias, but Blaez did not know why or how. Now he wondered about the nature of her task and the amount of danger involved. So, he asked, "What exactly is this path you were born for?"

Maelona frowned. "To be honest, I don't know what I'm supposed to do exactly, but I assume it will require me to confront the Dark Sorcerer at the Great Gate. Beyond that, I'm hoping it will become clear when the time is right."

"I don't suppose the Ternias is something you can use from a safe distance, is it?"

Maelona tilted her head and looked at him. Her brows were once again pulled together. She looked confused about something. "I don't think so, but I won't be certain until I'm there."

They were quiet again for a few moments. This time, the silence felt heavier than before.

"You spoke about choices," Maelona said, her voice soft. "These days, I feel as though all my choices are between doing what would make me happy and doing what is right. But in reality, there are no choices—there are just the many things I'm responsible for. I don't really have the freedom to choose whatever I want."

She looked at him, her expression earnest. "I like you, Blaez. I am attracted to you."

His breath caught, and hope bloomed in his chest.

"You may not know this about seers, but physical attraction is rare. We usually only feel this way towards the person we are meant to be with. It's one reason there are so few of us." She shrugged. "It could be, of course, that I'm more like the Wolf-folk in this. But I can't help but feel that it's possible that you and I were meant for one another."

The little spark of hope inside him grew larger and hotter. But he knew she had more to say, so he reined in his emotions as best he could.

She chuffed out a short, humorless laugh. "Yet I also can't help but feel that making the choice for us to be together would be selfish of me. Dangerous times are upon us, and my personal mission is perilous." Her gaze briefly dropped to his lips before she met his eyes again. She whispered, "Would it be fair of me to get involved with you that way if it meant you might have to suffer the pain of loss so soon?"

The very idea of losing her caused a shot of pain to pierce his heart. His hand lifted automatically to rub his sternum. She had so many reasons to be hesitant toward letting things bloom between them. It was brave of her to put her feelings out there for him to see.

He was determined to be brave as well.

"You may be a seer," he said, giving her an affectionate smile, "but you yourself have said that things can always change. We may never truly know what the future will bring until it is our present. So, I choose to live for what I know to be right in this moment. I choose to be yours."

With those words, Blaez slowly leaned forward and pressed his lips to hers in a soft kiss.

Andrion squinted up at the top of the tall, ancient tree through breaks in the foliage to where Maelona was currently perched on a branch he worried would not hold her weight.

Of course, it was difficult to tell how thick or strong that branch was from here, but they got thinner and shorter as they progressed to the top, which would imply they were weaker as well.

This was their fourth morning waking in the woods since leaving the Sorceress's sanctuary. Each of those days, until today, Maelona scaled trees in the early morning. It was brighter at that time than it was now, shortly after twilight, so he worried she would not see well enough to maneuver without slipping.

A whimpering sound came from off to his left, and Andrion looked over at Blaez, Maelona's ever-faithful wolf companion, who was also watching her balance in the treetop high above.

"Do not fret, wolf. She's climbed every day since we headed out, so she must be accustomed to it." Andrion said. Only, he'd never seen her climb when it was this dark before. "She'll be okay." *Right?* He used a calm tone when he spoke—he didn't need the fierce animal to be any more agitated than he was now, with Maelona high in a tree and Blaez clearly unhappy that he could not follow.

"What's she looking for, anyway?"

When Maelona finally climbed down—much faster and more nimbly than he could have, even during his childhood tree-climbing phase—she seemed tense. She went to her wolf's side and stroked the fur on his ear before giving it a bit of a tug. "It's time," she said.

Andrion wasn't sure what she was talking about, but that she continued to look at the wolf instead of at him felt like a bad sign. Was she angry? Was she about to suggest they part ways?

He did what he always liked to do in tense situations—make a joke. "Time for what? You aren't going to allow him to make a meal of me now, are you?"

Maelona looked at him with a serious expression and Andrion let his smile drop. She walked over to a fallen tree and sat down. He sat down beside her.

"There are things within your kingdom and within our forest that you would not normally be privy to, Andrion," Maelona said, "until you were officially sworn in as King of Eastgate. Given the current situation in the realm, however, there are things you need to know now."

"What, you mean there's more than what I learned at the meeting at the fire-circle?"

Maelona nodded solemnly. "But before I tell you, I ask you to remember that, at the moment, we have the element of surprise on our side. We need to keep it. Always remember that not everyone is what or who they seem."

This warning made Andrion think about the situation with his father and who could have gotten close enough to him to harm him, and how. It had often been on his mind since what he'd learned at the fire circle. As annoyed as he was that his father had been keeping so much from him, he would wish no ill to befall him. Before he had time to dwell on this in any detail, however, Maelona spoke.

"Blaez."

Andrion looked at her in confusion for just a moment before movement off to her right caught his attention. Eyes and mouth opened wide, he watched on as the great black wolf shimmered, contracted, and re-formed before him. It stood on its hind legs until it was upright and, even more surprising, human. *Well, not really human*, he mused. *Definitely Wolf-folk.*

The man lifted his head as he stood to his full height, and Andrion found himself looking at the same ice-blue eyes that had stared at him so often, making him feel almost paranoid over the past couple of weeks. The man before him was tall, broad, and well-muscled—more so than any of the men at the castle, including their toughest warriors.

Now that he knew that the wolf, or Blaez rather, was a Folk, he could see the differences between a man and a Folk in human form. Of course, he knew that at least some guests at the fire circle had been animal-folk as well, but most of them had been sitting and he'd had a lot on his mind, so he didn't note the differences.

Blaez was much larger than any of the guards at the castle, both in height and musculature, with an intensity about him that was intimidating. Yet Andrion also realized that Blaez could still pass as a very large human male if one was not expecting a Folk.

"Well then," Andrion began hesitantly, "this explains a lot." With a mischievous grin in Maelona's direction, he added, "Now I understand why you've been so unaffected by my charms."

"Yes," Blaez retorted in a deep, rumbling voice. "I am sure it has nothing to do with how annoying and arrogant you are."

"Ouch!" Andrion quipped, mock-flinching. "Who would have expected such sharp sarcasm from a man who sounds like he is growling when he speaks?" Then he added, "The eyes still give me the shivers, by the way. Would you please be so kind as to point those things elsewhere?"

"Women do not seem to mind them," Blaez responded, quirking one eyebrow. "Usually, they want a closer look."

Maelona chuckled and shook her head. "You two can duel to prove who is the better once the war is over. Right now, though, I need you both focused."

Blaez dressed in a pair of pants he pulled from the—apparently adjustable—backpack he'd been wearing, then took a seat on the opposite side of Maelona. He sat so close to her, in fact, that they were touching arm-to-arm. Then he narrowed his eyes at Andrion.

He grinned at Blaez's possessive actions. Then he shook his head.

"I'm still trying to decide if I should be offended that you kept this from me all this time. From the very first time we met at the sanctuary until now, did it never cross your mind to tell me the truth? Were you having fun, playing me like that?"

"We didn't do it to play tricks on you or to mock you," Maelona said. "The fact was, we'd only just met you, we didn't know you, and we didn't have much time to spare to decide if you could be trusted."

"Again, trying to decide if I should be offended over here."

"You cannot tell me you trust us completely after such a short time," Blaez said.

Andrion nodded. "You have a point. Especially after this. But why is it a secret that you're a Folk? I've been convinced animal-folk are real since the fire circle. It's not like I still believed they're extinct, or only exist in fairy tales." The question was directed to Blaez, but it was Maelona who answered.

"It's not that it was a secret," she said. "But we've found that people are less guarded and more genuine around animals, for the most part."

Andrion thought about the many times Maelona had headed off to search for food while Blaez stayed behind with him. Was this why? So the man could judge his actions and, thus, decide if he was trustworthy? Because that's what it sounded like Maelona was saying.

"Are you surprised that Blaez is a folk, Andrion? That he and the wolf you've been spending time with are the same?"

"Well, to be honest, yes," Andrion answered. "Logically, I know that there are animal-folk because it was clear from the discussion at the fire-circle that many of the people there were Folk."

"All," Maelona corrected. "They were all Folk."

"All?" Andrion surprised himself when his voice came out a little higher than usual, so he cleared it. "Even the Sorceress?" Maelona nodded.

Once the initial shock had passed, he said, "That reminds me. I should thank you for the warning." He made sure the sarcasm was clear in his tone. "It wasn't easy to focus on the important details discussed while I was reeling from the revelation that a species I thought had died out long ago—or at least whose numbers must be dwindling—still exists in fairly large numbers. But knowing that and seeing the evidence with my own eyes are two different things." He looked pointedly at Blaez before turning back to Maelona.

"I didn't think seers still existed either until I met you and you told me who and what you are."

Maelona nodded. "It is not by accident that humans believe that the animal-folk, and the seers, all but disappeared from the world long ago.

"When the seer people were almost wiped out about three hundred years ago, we were hunted by those who feared our abilities, such as humans, and even the Folk and other magical beings. The evil that had crept in behind the scenes planted the belief that we were almost omniscient and that we played with people's lives. But this is far from the truth."

"So, what is the truth, then?"

"As I mentioned before, it is extremely rare that any seer can choose what they see, and at what point in time. When we have our dream-visions, they seem to be random, but they usually point us to where danger lies. It is like the universe itself sends us where we are most needed.

"However, the idea that we could see anything about anyone, then change our appearance to sneak in unobserved and manipulate people, was a very frightening idea for most, and these rumors spread like wildfire."

Andrion really wanted to ask her if the seers—if she—could really change their appearance. He wanted to ask her to demonstrate. But he didn't want to interrupt.

"We were hunted down in cold blood," Maelona continued, "with most seers refusing to fight those who were being manipulated by an evil hand. Many seers died, and some others were captured by those who wished to use us against their enemies. The rest went into hiding here in the Sacred Forest.

"When the dust settled, however, many humans and other non-magical beings now looked at the animal-folk—to those who were magical in any way—with paranoia and suspicion, even though humans far outnumbered the rest. In the end, ironically, many of the magical races that had helped hunt us then ended up here in the Sacred Forest with us." Maelona chuckled. "Lucky for them, the seers knew and understood what had happened, and did not blame them."

"If there are so many magical beings here, so close to human habitation, why are there not more sightings? Why don't we know more about you?" Andrion asked.

"Those are excellent questions," Maelona replied. "And they are tied to the reason the battle is headed our way. Do you remember what the Sorceress said about the magical ley lines, and the magical energy they contain?"

"I do," Andrion replied.

"Well, where better for a large group of magical beings to hide but within a significant source of magical power? The Sorcerers of the Light had used the power of the ley lines to create magical defenses around the forest millennia ago, effectively shielding us from the outside world. Of course, other beings do travel here from time to time. Tell me, Andrion, how did you feel when you entered the forest?"

Andrion paused in thought for a moment before answering, "Well, I felt a little uneasy. I might have turned around again if my father had not tasked me with venturing here to find Eluard Mistreaver."

"That sense of unease," Maelona said, "turns to dread that unimaginable horrors await you in the forest, and the more darkness a being holds inside of them, the stronger that feeling gets. The uneasiness you felt was to be expected. Everyone holds at least a little darkness inside, after all. But you had the amulet, so it would not have been strong in any case. What is surprising is that the demonkin who pursued you were not paralyzed with fear. I can only guess that they carried something that could neutralize that part of the magical protection, which is something else to be concerned about."

Andrion fingered his amulet, trying to recall if he'd seen anything similar on the demonkin.

"As for why there haven't been more sightings," she continued, "there have been many more than you would suspect. How would you know, for example, if a traveler passing through your town was truly human or not?"

He thought about this for a moment. Even if he'd come across someone as large as Blaez, he'd have just assumed it was a tall human who regularly took part in physically demanding work. "Well, now that you ask, I suppose I would not know."

"The reason I am telling you all of this now," Maelona said, "is that in about a day and a half, we will leave the protection of the Sacred Forest. And once we pass the tree line, you need to be prepared for anything. Demonkin can be easy to spot, of course, being physically very different from us. But as I mentioned at the fire-circle, there are some demonkin who can hide their appearance."

"Like the seers and the animal-folk," Andrion observed.

"Well, yes and no," Maelona responded. "Yes, we can all change our appearance to some degree, but with Folk and seers, it is as much physical as magical. The Folks' bodies really change from man to animal and back again. Seers physically manipulate factors present in our bodies to change our outward appearance, like hair and eye color, so we really physically change as well. With the demonkin," she continued, "it's all an illusion. If you get close enough to touch one, for example, it is possible to notice that what you feel may not be the same as what you see. Demonkin can make themselves look like anyone, so if you have doubts about a person, you can use this as a test."

"So, I only have to get close enough to touch one, is what you're saying."

Maelona frowned and shrugged apologetically.

Andrion sighed. "Sure, no problem. Sounds easy.

"Well, all of this information certainly answers several questions I was left with after the meeting. So, I have to ask, why are you explaining this now?" Andrion said. "Why didn't you explain it all at the meeting?"

"Everyone else at the fire circle already had most of this information," Blaez said.

"Yes," Maelona agreed. "Plus," she added, "you did not need to know this information then, but you do now."

"And why is that?" Andrion asked with a cautious tone.

"Because, as I watched from the trees," Maelona answered, "I could see firelight just outside the forest. This could be campfires of those sent to watch the forest. After all, I am certain that you did not disappear into the forest, with three demonkin disappearing behind you, without being noticed."

"Well, this is great news," Andrion said sarcastically.

"I am afraid it's not the worst," Maelona replied.

Blaez looked at her with concern. "What is it?" he asked.

Looking at him, she responded, "There were fires further on, as well. Into the farmsteads. I fear they are invading the farmland and building their numbers before attacking the city."

"What do we do?" Andrion asked, alarmed. Those people in the farmsteads might be outside of the limits of Eastgate, but they were still under his father's protection. They were still under his protection.

"Well, for now, I suggest we get some rest. We will need our strength," Maelona responded. Then she turned to look at Blaez. "I will need to sleep tonight," she said meaningfully, and Blaez nodded.

Andrion looked at them with narrowed eyes. He knew Maelona did not need to sleep as often as humans did, but the way she'd announced that to Blaez seemed kind of suspicious. As much as they'd told him so far—and his mind was almost reeling with it all—he could guess there were even more secrets still.

CHAPTER SEVENTEEN

Plan of Attack

A myriad of colors danced above the treetops as the sun rose the next morning. Maelona had started a small fire to cook a simple breakfast of leftover fowl and roots for herself, Blaez, and Andrion. The sky was just light enough that the fire would not be visible from a distance. The men had not stirred yet, and she used the stillness of the early morning to help focus her disordered thoughts.

After she had sent out her message to the other seers the night before, Maelona had fallen asleep. As soon as she stopped guiding her own thoughts, visions flickered in—messages from the others—and she was now quietly contemplating what they meant.

At first, when she'd been in the state between purposely sending messages and falling asleep, a vision came in from Edun in the west. She saw an arrow tinged with green. She knew this was a warning, something she had to look out for. Immediately following that, an image had flitted in from Talwyn in the south, showing battle. But it was not a battle at Southgate. She knew this because, in the vision, she saw Blaez being attacked from all sides by demonkin. Unfortunately, the vision ended before she could see the outcome. This must be something Talwyn had seen in a vision of her own. A warning—another danger Maelona had to watch out for.

Talwyn had seen what she herself could not since she was too close to Blaez, and her friend had sent her a message to help her prepare and, hopefully counter, what the vision had shown. Just thinking about what she saw made her heart pound and sweat bead on her brow. She tried to shake off the details of the vision because, if she thought too much about it, she could never focus on what needed to be done.

After the sending and receiving of messages had finished, Maelona had forced herself to clear her mind so she could fall asleep. When she finally did, she had visions of the figure in a dark cloak. His face was hidden inside the cowl, as it always was. He was in a cavern of some sort, and eerie sounds of hissing and stone scraping over stone echoed throughout. She could also hear a name being whispered over and over. She had listened intently, trying to make it out, and just as she had started to get it, she awoke and it was lost to her.

Maelona was certain that the dark figure from her dream was the same sorcerer behind the quest to take over Sterrenvar and enslave the people. No other seer or sorcerer had seen this evil being in what seemed to be his own environment before, and she wondered why she was seeing it now. Was he becoming weaker, perhaps overtaxing himself, or was she becoming stronger?

Maelona knew that each time she took a step closer to opening up to others and, in particular, to Blaez, her magic flowed through her a little more freely. When she let go of her tight control of her emotions, she also let go of some of her control over her magic, hence allowing it to flow more naturally through her. Even her budding comradery with Andrion added to this feeling.

This would have frightened her in the past. But with her Mother's training and the changes to her staff, she felt confident that she would soon master how to channel that energy and focus it on what she intended to do.

For the first time in a long time, she felt hopeful that she could free her emotions. She wanted to truly allow others in, so she wouldn't have to feel alone in the world. Of course, the fear of possibly experiencing more pain and loss in the future still lingered. Yet, she knew everyone had to face this fear at some point in their lives. Perhaps she was finally ready to take that chance.

Maybe she could finally have a meaningful relationship with a man she cared deeply for. As close as she was to Aleyn, she had never let him in the way she had with Blaez. There were parts of herself she had always kept guarded. She now felt hopeful that she would be ready when the time came to face her fears and her foes. And she knew she would no longer be fighting her battles alone.

Maelona suddenly felt lighter, freer, as she realized that her self-acceptance would open many more options for dealing with what was to come. She now understood what she needed to do.

A rustling sound next to her indicated Blaez was waking. Rousing himself, he moved over to where she sat. Then he reached his hand out and stroked his thumb along her cheek. "Good morning, my love," he said. "How was your sleep?"

"Oddly, both informative and confusing at the same time," Maelona replied with a small smile as she gazed up at him.

Blaez was always interested in what she was thinking. It was written on his face even now that he was tempted to ask for more details. However, he was always patient with her, giving her time to sort through things herself before she shared, and she figured he would do the same now.

He proved her right when, instead of asking questions, he simply said, "I am going to make my way back to the brook we passed to collect some water. I believe I'll also take a swim to refresh myself while I am there."

Maelona simply nodded to him with a smile before once again becoming engrossed in her thoughts.

A short time later, Andrion awoke as well. "Mmm, something smells good," he said. He made his way over to the fire, which was mostly embers by now, and partook of the small meal Maelona had prepared.

"This is pretty good for not being prepared by castle chefs," he said with a wink. He looked around. "So where is Blaez?"

"He went to the brook to collect water and wash up," she replied.

"Now that we are alone," Andrion said, "I would like to ask you about something that's been on my mind since I found out that your wolf is really a Wolf-folk."

"Go ahead," Maelona said with an encouraging nod.

"I have to ask you, Maelona—you are a seer and Blaez is a Folk. My people are human. As far as my people know, your kinds had gone the way of legend. And when you are spoken about, there is still an undercurrent of fear and superstition."

He paused and took a deep breath before continuing. "I saw the attitude of some others at the meeting once it became known that you are a seer, and that was from another magical race. Do you really believe all our peoples can work together?"

Evidently, Andrion held serious doubts. His flippant façade was stripped away for once, and Maelona could see apprehension in his face and body language. She could hear it in his voice. And she understood his reservations.

Her eyes met his as she answered. "I do not just believe it can happen, Andrion. I know it must happen."

From their dream-visions, she and the other seers knew there were a few possibilities, but she did not want to leave Andrion any room for doubt, so she kept this to herself.

"Not one of the many and varied races in the realm can take on the evil that threatens us by itself and hope to be victorious," she said. "Not only are we facing a Dark Sorcerer with powerful magical abilities, but our visions have shown he has the support of the demonkin, the snowbeasts, and the human tribes that live in the northern mountain range. Now, with recent revelations, I fear he is bringing his followers into the conflict both sooner and further south than we expected. We will all need to stand together to resist being used as servants, slaves, and fodder for the evil beings who wish to subdue us.

"You and I, Andrion," she continued emphatically, "are leaders amongst our people. It is our responsibility, our duty, to bring our people together to protect the realm.

"It shouldn't prove too difficult," she added with a wry smile. "Nothing brings people together more readily than having to face a common enemy. And watching the three of us work together will provide an excellent example to our peoples. Anything less could lead to failure."

The sun was high in the sky when Maelona, Blaez, and Andrion cautiously approached the edge of the Sacred Forest. The trees were less abundant here—the vast spread of mostly flat farmlands, with just the occasional swell and fall, was becoming more visible. They would soon lose the cover the forest provided them with.

She and Blaez had been watching for signs of anything passing here that did not belong. A couple of hours earlier they had come across the telltale freshly broken saplings and bushes and tracks too large to be human. However, she knew they weren't Folk either.

Maelona took a careful look, noting that while the footprints were like human, or Folk in human form, they were also broader and thicker at the heel.

"Demonkin," she said.

They veered off the main path, staying hidden in the trees as best they could. They moved along the perimeter of the forest in the direction Maelona had seen the nearest fire coming from two nights ago. This was the place where the neighboring farmland brushed up against the Sacred Forest.

Peering through the trees, Maelona and Blaez, with their heightened eyesight, could make out the burned-out husk of a barn. A short way beyond that was the dwelling of those who farmed the land. From here it looked intact, but Maelona knew from her visions that the demonkin who had been hunting Andrion were still nearby. Only three had pursued him into the forest, but there were others who had followed, but stayed behind.

"I have a plan," Maelona said. "There are demonkin inside that dwelling, and we need to draw them out. Since they were sent here to hunt down the Prince of Eastgate, I think Andrion should approach from the front, walking down the path as if he were returning from his trip and on his way home. Blaez and I will approach from the back, in wolf form, so we do not attract attention."

Blaez's eyebrows shot up in surprise at this suggestion, and a huge smile spread across his face.

As for Andrion, he looked confused for a moment before asking, "You mean Blaez will be in wolf form, right?"

"No," Maelona clarified. "I mean, we will both be in wolf form."

"Wait, are you telling me that seers can shift too?" Andrion asked in surprise. "I thought you said you could only change hair color and the like."

"Seers can't usually change to animal form, no," Maelona answered. "However, I am only half seer. My father was seer, but my mother, the Sorceress, is Wolf-folk."

"So, you are saying you have the abilities of a seer *and* of a Wolf-folk?"

"Yes. Though I have not shifted in over forty years." She prayed to the Universe that she still *could* shift. She squeezed her hands into fists to stop them from shaking.

"Over forty years!" Andrion exclaimed. "Forty years? Just how old are you? You look like you can't have over twenty-five years, at most! I really thought you were just trying to throw me off when you said you knew my father as a child."

"I am not nearly as old as most of the others you met at the Sorceress's sanctuary; I assure you. I am, in fact, considered to be barely into adulthood by most in that group, as you may recall."

Andrion puffed out a big breath before putting his hands on his hips and walking a small circle. "Okay, from now on, only tell me what I need to know. I do not need to be passing out in shock as we're about to take on a bunch of demonkin."

Maelona could not help but chuckle at Andrion's antics.

"Andrion, walk back to the path in the forest, then follow it out toward the dwelling. Blaez and I will shift and approach from the back. Since they are not looking out for animals but are rather watching for you, we should be able to go unnoticed. Once you draw them out, we will check out the area for any other demonkin so we will not be taken by surprise before heading to join you. We will also need to check for any survivors." *Please let there be survivors.* "But let's neutralize the danger first."

She pursed her lips and took in Andrion. He was mostly healed from his recent injuries, but he did still limped some by the end of each day's travel. "Walk slowly," she told him. "With any luck, we'll be able to sneak in to free any captives, then get the demonkin's attention again before they make it to you."

A little more subdued than before, Andrion nodded to Maelona before turning and heading back the way they had come.

"Andrion!" Maelona called before he was out of earshot. He paused and turned to look at her. "In case we get tied up, do you think you can handle a demonkin or two on your own?"

"Of course I can! I am the Prince of Eastgate," he called back with a smile.

"Don't plant your feet," she advised. "Keep moving. Demonkin are not agile. Use that to your benefit."

Andrion's smile softened, and he nodded to her again before turning and continuing on his way.

Maelona then turned her attention back to Blaez. He was looking at her with his brows raised and a small smile tugging at the corners of his lips.

"What? His father is an old friend. He would never forgive me if I didn't bring his son back in one piece."

Blaez's smile grew, but stayed soft and warm. He reached out and stroked her hair. "Of course," he said.

Maelona took a deep breath and let it out slowly. She met Blaez's gaze.

"It has been a very long time since I last shifted, Blaez, and I have never tried to hide my true coloring in wolf form. This may take me a moment."

She quickly undressed and placed her clothing in her pack. "My pack is expandable like yours, but I did not make it with shifting in mind. I hope it holds up." She secured it back into place and tugged on the clasps to loosen the straps.

Maelona squeezed and relaxed her sweaty hands. She turned towards Blaez and looked into his eyes; she wanted to read his reaction. When his calm, warm gaze locked on hers, it immediately anchored her. She could see the acceptance and support there, and her agitation lessened.

Let's hope it stays that way.

She took a deep breath, steeled herself, and shifted.

She heard the whoosh of breath as Blaez inhaled sharply. His eyes no longer met hers: Instead, they perused her wolf form with an expression of awe.

It was strange, looking up at him from this angle. It was stranger still to feel four paws on the ground instead of standing upright.

Assuming her natural coloring hadn't changed since the last time she'd allowed it to show—many years ago—she could guess what he was seeing. The brown eyes he would have been accustomed to would now be a bright green—gemlike like her mother's, but where her mother's eyes were amethysts, hers were emeralds. The common chestnut brown of her hair would now be a dark, forest green.

Reading his expression, Maelona was glad it seemed to be one of admiration and not one of shock or dislike.

"Beautiful," Blaez whispered. He reached out and caressed the soft fur on the back of her ear just once before pulling back again.

She couldn't show herself in front of humans or demonkin in her natural colors. They would know immediately that she was a sorceress. Only those strong with magic could have any coloring that could be found in nature—in other words, only sorcerers and sorceresses. That's why she was lucky to be a seer as well. So many sorcerers and sorceresses were hunted down in the past because their natural coloring gave them away. Most of the time, they kept themselves hidden for this very reason. At least her inner-sight allowed her to show more common coloring. And, ever since what had happened all those years ago with Guarin Stronghunter, she'd always hidden her true colors.

She didn't think she'd be brave enough to show Blaez even now if not for the fact that she was too out of practice to focus on both shifting and hiding her natural looks simultaneously.

Maelona took another deep breath and concentrated on changing her eyes to a yellow-green and her fur to gray and white with a little tan blended in, just like any true gray wolf.

She looked up at Blaez expectantly. She knew she'd been successful with her transformation when Blaez gave her a nod and a smile.

"Perfect," he said, his voice warm with affection.

He then stepped back, removed his pack, disrobed, and put his clothes inside the pack. He put the pack back on and loosened the straps, then shifted into his beautiful black wolf to join her.

It was time to hunt some demonkin.

CHAPTER EIGHTEEN

Subduing the Captors

Maelona and Blaez crept up to the old stone cottage from the rear.

Sniffing the air, Maelona caught a now-familiar scent; It was the same earthy smell with a sour edge that she'd smelled the day she and Blaez rescued the prince. The directions the scents came from indicated at least two demonkin, as well as a couple of humans.

As Blaez scanned the perimeter, Maelona stood on her hind legs to peek in through the nearest window. On the inside, the main living area was one big room. There was one doorway off to the right and, judging from the size of the dwelling on the outside,

Maelona guessed it was a small bedroom. From her vantage point, two demonkin, and who she assumed to be a mother and son, were visible.

The human boy looked to be in his early- to mid-teens, based on what she knew of human aging. He was as tall as the woman and a little gangly, as if he hadn't quite grown into his limbs yet. He had the tanned skin of someone who worked outside every day, but it was otherwise smooth and unblemished—youthful in appearance.

Maelona glanced to her left to see Blaez disappearing around the corner, but her attention was quickly pulled back inside by the deep, gravelly rasp that was particular to most demonkin. "Well, look here," it said. "Looks like our prey is walking right into our hands."

With that, the large, ugly demonkin strode out of the cottage, leaving the door open so that Andrion, who had just left the cover of the forest, was now visible from Maelona's vantage point. He looked like he was just out for a leisurely stroll and, after what he'd been through at the hands of demonkin, Maelona had to admire his poise.

Maelona immediately shifted back into her human form, since she did not want to alarm the humans. And, she could admit to herself, she also didn't feel comfortable in her wolf form yet.

She quickly dressed in her clothing, securing all her weapons in their proper places. By the time she was ready, the first demonkin was far enough away for her to sneak around to the front of the building and quietly make her way inside.

She entered noiselessly, and since the second demonkin was busy goading the humans, it did not notice her enter.

"Thrak there is going to destroy your prince," the large, ugly beast the color of bedrock said to his captives. "Then when the Emperor signals that the time is right, we are going to lay siege to the city. Once it is ours, all the people of Eastgate will be our slaves. If you show your worth to me now, I may keep you as servants of my household, maybe even as my own personal pets."

So this Dark Sorcerer was already calling himself an emperor, was he? The arrogance of it disgusted her. With no more delay, she stepped into the open doorway.

"It is ironic that you are talking to your prisoners about worth," Maelona cut in from behind the demonkin, "when you yourself are so worthless."

The demonkin jumped up with a start and turned to face Maelona. She knew she needed to get it outside, away from the humans and into an area where she had more room to maneuver. She pulled her long dagger from its sheath with one hand and she turned her other hand palm up. With a taunting smirk on her lips, she beckoned to the demonkin and stepped back out through the doorway. As expected, the demonkin followed her.

This demonkin was as tall as Blaez in his human form, but wider and more stoutly built. Its arms and legs were probably half again as thick as Blaez's well-muscled ones. This type of demonkin had skin that was various shades of gray to black and was just about as tough as the rock it looked like. Maelona was stronger and heavier than a human woman her size would be, as seer muscles were denser. However, she knew that in a fight with such a creature, she was unlikely to overpower it. The best plan of attack would be to outmaneuver and outsmart it.

She backed away from the door a few more feet, then stood her ground as the demonkin came for her. She stood completely still until the demonkin was just in striking distance, then, as its hand stretched out towards her in a punch, she dodged, pushing its punching arm to the side at the elbow. From there she stepped backward and then forward in a three-hundred-and-sixty-degree turn until she was behind it. She dropped to one knee and struck out with her dagger across the back of its leg, severing the hamstring with one stroke.

However, demonkin themselves were as tough as their hide, so it stayed on its feet, even with only one fully functioning leg. It dragged itself around to face her again, but before the beast even made it all the way around, she struck it with a vicious sidekick: Swinging her back leg forward and around so it was parallel to the ground, her knee close to her chest, she then pushed her leg out with all her might as she let out an angry yell. The heel of her foot contacted the demonkin's sternum and kept on pushing at a high velocity.

The demonkin was sent stumbling backwards a couple of meters, curling in on itself as all the air was forced from its lungs.

Maelona ran forward into striking distance again, spun so her back was to the demonkin, and looked over her shoulder before bringing her knee up and pushing her foot back, connecting with a powerful back kick to the demonkin's face.

Before the demonkin even hit the ground, Maelona spotted movement off to one side. Looking to her right, she saw another demonkin running towards her from the cottage. There must have been another in the room with the closed door.

Before Maelona had time to react, however, a great black form flew by her. Blaez, in wolf form, jumped onto the back of her downed demonkin, which had twisted itself over onto its hands and knees, and pushed against the beast as he launched himself towards the newcomer.

Trusting Blaez to take care of himself, she turned her attention back to her opponent, who was now face down in the dirt from the force of Blaez leaping from its back. Maelona nudged it with her foot until it rolled onto its back. "Sit up," she ordered, holding the point of her sword to its throat.

The demonkin slowly brought itself to a sitting position. Maelona grabbed its tunic at the shoulder to help it move faster. As they moved, Blaez, still in wolf form, pulled the other demonkin's limp form forward by the throat. Its neck was bloodied and mangled, and its head was hanging at an unnatural angle; clearly, the neck had been broken. Blaez dropped the body in direct sight of the other demonkin.

Maelona held her sword at the ready, just in case the creature got any ideas. "Who sent you here?" she demanded. "Who is behind this invasion?" Any information beyond what she'd learned from her unclear visions could be helpful. If she was lucky, maybe she could discover how they'd breached the magical protections of the Sacred Forest.

"That is no concern of yours," the demonkin replied, lip curling in a sneer.

Maelona pressed her blade against the carotid artery at the side of its neck until she drew surface blood. "Does it concern me now?"

The demonkin answered without really giving her any new information. "The Emperor," he replied.

"And who, exactly, is this emperor?"

"You will find out soon enough. When he comes, he will rain destruction down upon all who try to resist him."

The demonkin continued to regard her with an icy stare. Maelona shook her head and tsked.

"And I suppose he promised you a share of his riches? Perhaps a castle and females and whatever other luxuries you desire?" The demonkin did not respond but continued to glare at her.

Maelona slowly paced back and forth in front of the demonkin, shaking her head as if she felt sorry for it. "I am sorry to have to tell you this, but you are the first evil minions I have come across in some time. You are the creatures relegated to the front lines. Do you know what this means?"

She stopped pacing and turned to face the creature. When the demonkin did not respond, she continued. "This means you are fodder to your emperor. Completely expendable. I could end you right now and he would not even blink." The demonkin tried to appear unaffected, but the way its Adam's apple moved in a deep swallow and his eyes blinked rapidly, told her it was trying to appear braver than it actually was.

She turned and paced again. "But you are lucky today. I am feeling generous. So, if you would like to share some information about your leader, perhaps I might let you li—"

The last word was not even complete when the movement of a blade flashed in her peripheral vision. It sliced through the demonkin's neck and its head went rolling to the ground at her feet.

Maelona had heard human footsteps approaching and had expected that it would be one of the hostages, or maybe Andrion catching up, so she hadn't paid much attention.

What she hadn't expected when she looked up, however, was a bloody, dirty, emaciated man grasping a dripping sword he looked like he could not possibly have the strength to wield.

While Maelona had first made her way inside to confront the demonkin and free the humans, Blaez had followed the scent of human blood and sweat until he found himself in a root cellar. There, he found a man hanging by ropes that were attached to the ceiling beams and tied around his wrists. The man's feet were only just touching the ground by the tips of his toes, and Blaez could only imagine the difficulty of his position when he couldn't stand like that any longer and was forced to rest.

The single demonkin present was preoccupied with picking out its next implement of torture when Blaez had arrived on silent paws.

When the beast finally noticed another presence there with them, it just looked at Blaez, clearly confused why a wolf suddenly appeared. Blaez used this hesitation to his advantage, quickly dispatching of the demonkin before switching to his human form so he could free the man from his restraints.

The man looked gaunt, as if he'd been starved for the last few days, and he was covered in cuts; some shallow and some deeper. His face was a bloodied mess—his left eye was almost swollen shut and his nose was crooked—and his torso was covered in black, purple, green, and yellow bruises from beatings that obviously began days ago and continued on until. . . well, until just now.

As beat up and weak as the human man looked, as soon as Blaez had freed him from his restraints, he somehow dragged his damaged body up from the root cellar, grabbing a sword from the demonkin's corpse along the way.

Blaez followed him up the steps. Then, looking towards where Maelona was fighting another demonkin, he saw a third emerge through the doorway of the cottage. He took off running, shifting back to his wolf mid-stride. Using Maelona's now downed opponent as a springboard, he launched himself at the demonkin in the doorway. His jaws landed unerringly around his intended target—the demonkin's throat. Blaez felt bones crunch and flesh tear as he shook his wolf's great head, and when the body went limp, he brought it over and dropped it next to Maelona. He hoped it could be used as incentive to get the demonkin she was now questioning to talk.

Noticing movement behind Maelona's captive, Blaez looked up to see the man he had rescued come up behind the demonkin that was now sitting on the ground in front of Maelona. When Blaez realized what the man was doing, he hesitated, thinking the man had earned his right to retribution. Then it was too late for him to change to human form to warn Maelona. The demonkin's victim brought the sword up and across with much more force than Blaez would have expected from him, given his physical state.

Blood spattered all around as the sword cut through the demonkin's neck, splashing onto Maelona's clothes and boots. She didn't even flinch at the bloody mess, which led Blaez to wonder just how much battle she had seen in the forty years since she first left the Wolf Folk village.

Finally, after expending the last of his energy beheading one of his tormentors, the man's strength failed him; he faltered, and then he fell unconscious to the ground.

CHAPTER NINETEEN

Innocent Victims

Still gaping from the unexpected, unbelievable end to her interrogation, Maelona heard Andrion's footsteps approach from the left, and the woman's footsteps from the right. The woman dropped to her knees next to the unconscious man and wept.

The sight brought Maelona back to her senses; she turned to Blaez, who was still in wolf form, and said, "Crimsonleaf." Blaez gave her a quick nod and took off back around the house.

Maelona moved around the body of the demonkin and kneeled next to the injured man. Looking at who she assumed was his wife, she said in a soft voice, "Let me help him." The woman paused and looked Maelona in the eye for a quick moment before nodding her consent.

"Here, let me help you," Andrion said. But he had barely taken a step forward when Maelona scooped the man into her arms as if he were a small child and carried him into the house. Andrion stood frozen for a moment, but soon followed behind her.

It was only a couple of moments later when Blaez entered, in human form and fully dressed, carrying both his and Maelona's packs. "That was fast," Andrion commented.

Maelona accepted her pack from Blaez and reached inside for her pouch of dried leaves from the crimsonleaf tree.

"I found the man restrained in the root cellar," Blaez said. "and I freed him. I wouldn't have guessed he could behead a demonkin in his state. I'm surprised he even had the strength to move."

Maelona nodded her agreement. "The human spirit is strong," she said. "There is no denying that."

She turned to Andrion. "I need you to start a fire for me, then boil some water." Then she turned her attention back to the woman. "What is your name?" she asked, her voice soft with compassion.

"Edelinne," the woman responded.

"And your husband?"

"Dafydd." She nodded towards the youth, who now sat by the hearth, "My son is named Lancelin."

Maelona looked at Lancelin and noticed he was covered in bruises and scratches. She felt a flash of rage at the thought of what the demonkin had done to this family. She pushed it aside for the moment, however, so she could focus on caring for Dafydd.

"Well, Edelinne, your husband will be fine. He has suffered some trauma, and he looks to be dehydrated and malnourished, but he is in no immediate danger. We cannot stay for long, unfortunately, so I will teach you how to care for him and, if you follow my instructions, he will be fine."

"Thank you," Edelinne responded. Her responses were brief and clipped, and she shivered noticeably. Maelona worried she was in a state of shock and hoped that giving her a task to complete would help her come around.

Maelona emptied the contents of the pouch into her hand. Showing it to Edelinne, she said, "This is the leaf of the crimsonleaf tree. It is a wonder of nature. It can heal almost any injury or illness from the inside and from the outside. I will show you how to prepare it. This will help speed Dafydd's recovery."

Edelinne nodded and listened intently as Maelona explained how to prepare the compresses to place on his external injuries, then how to prepare the tea.

"As soon as he is conscious and able, have him drink as much as he will take," Maelona instructed.

Maelona explained her actions, step-by-step, to Edelinne as she worked. Still, she worried about this family, alone out here with their nearest neighbor so far away. There would be no time to instruct them on how to protect themselves. But there was one piece of information she could give them.

"If you need more crimsonleaf, you can find it in the Sacred Forest."

"In th. . . the forest?" Edelinne asked nervously.

"Yes," Maelona answered. "You need not fear the forest. It is only dangerous to any evil beings that enter, despite what you may have heard. The crimsonleaf tree is a very tall tree, with dark green leaves all over except at the very top. It is capped with dark red leaves. Both the green and the red leaves have healing properties, though the red are stronger." Edelinne nodded her understanding.

"Also," Maelona continued, "I believe no more demonkin will make it back this far, but if they do, take your family and head into the forest. There are those in the forest who are always willing to help someone in need. If they question you, tell them Maelona Mistreaver sent you." Maelona knew that, after the meeting with the Elders, word of what was happening would have spread to all those who lived in the Sacred Forest by now.

Edelinne was looking at her with a mix of disbelief and fear, so Maelona went to her pack and reached into a small pocket near the bottom. She removed an amulet similar to the one Andrion had been wearing when she and Blaez found him. Before she moved it into Edelinne's line of sight, however, she clasped her hands around it for a moment. A pale green glow shone briefly, visible where her hands came together. Then she turned to Edelinne and placed the amulet around her neck.

"Wear this," she told Edelinne, "and my people will know who sent you." Amulets were usually given sparingly by the seer Elders to trusted friends, but given the current circumstances in the realm, Maelona had taken a few with her, just in case. Maelona looked Edelinne in the eye and added, "Trust me." Edelinne must have been satisfied with what she saw in Maelona, as her shoulders relaxed and she nodded her agreement.

Maelona monitored Edelinne while they prepared the medicine and waited for it to be ready. Now, Edelinne no longer seemed like she was in shock. The human woman had shown genuine interest in learning how to heal, limited though the time allowed it to be. She also began talking more animatedly with Maelona, explaining how they had become captive to the demonkin.

"Lancelin had been working the small field between the cottage and the road," Edelinne told Maelona, "and noticed Prince Andrion as he passed through. Of course, we did not know at the time that he was the Prince, but Lancelin told us he was dressed as if he were someone of importance. Lancelin noticed as well that three demonkin followed Prince Andrion down the path and into the forest not too long afterwards. When he came inside that day, he told us about what he had seen. Then, a couple of days later, these three new demonkin arrived, barged into our home, and demanded to be provided with food and shelter while they waited for the others to return."

Edelinne had started to shake a little again but, before Maelona could do anything, her son moved to sit next to her and hold her hand.

"Dafydd had tried to fight them off, and was beaten for his efforts, right in front of us." Edelinne's eyes began to tear up as she recounted this part of the story. "Lancelin tried to jump in at one point. I tried to hold him back, but he was determined to help his father. The demonkin just tossed him aside as if he was a sack of feathers." Edelinne shook her head and swallowed back a sob.

"Dafydd fought valiantly and held his own for a while. In the end, though, the three demonkin overpowered him. They beat him until he was barely holding onto consciousness, then one of the demonkin dragged him outside. My son and I did not see him again until today. We did not know if he was alive or dead."

Edelinne was shaking again by the time she was done with her story. Maelona placed her hand on Edelinne's back and rubbed small circles to help soothe her. Then she told Edelinne, "You are safe now."

A couple of hours after they began, the medicines were administered and Maelona had given Edelinne instructions on how often to change the compresses and administer the tea. She also had Edelinne and Lancelin drink some of the tea as well.

When she was satisfied they had done all they could for now, Maelona donned her pack and headed out the front door, where Andrion and Blaez were standing guard after disposing of the demonkin bodies. Lancelin followed her outside and stood facing her.

"I want to thank you for helping my family," he said. "I was so scared. We hadn't seen father in three days, and I thought the demonkin were going to eat us or carry us off to be slaves."

"You are very welcome," Maelona said warmly. "I am glad you are all okay." Her eyes scanned the youth's face with concern. "It was very brave of you to help your father," she said. "Place some compresses on your injuries as well. It will help them heal faster."

Maelona looked at Lancelin thoughtfully for a moment. She swung her pack around to the front and again reached into the small pocket. She took out another amulet. This time, she didn't try to hide it as she held the amulet between her cupped palms and closed her eyes. Rays of pale forest-green light peeked out from where her hands came together once again. When it was done, she opened her eyes and looked at Lancelin.

"I want you to wear this at all times," she said as she placed the amulet around his neck. "It will keep you safe." Placing her hand on his shoulder, she met his eyes and added, "Stay close to your parents until the coming dark times have passed. When you are ready, come find me and I will teach you how to protect yourself and your family."

Lancelin looked at her, eyes wide in awe. "Are you a sorceress?" he asked.

"Wait. you know about sorceresses?" Andrion asked Lancelin, eyebrows raised in surprise.

"Well, I never thought they were real before, but what else can explain what she did with the amulet?"

Maelona chuckled. He was a smart boy. "I am a sorceress, yes. But that part must not be mentioned to anyone else, you understand?"

He nodded once at her in response, seemingly at a loss for words.

"If you ever find yourself in times of darkness and fear your strength has failed you, think back to what your father did here today: that amount of power should not have been physically possible in his condition." She pointed to the boy's chest. "That kind of strength and bravery comes from deep inside, in your spirit, your soul, where no one can steal it from you."

The boy's eyes glistened with emotion. "I understand. Thank you."

Turning to look over her shoulder at Edelinne, Maelona said, "Don't forget, you will always have friends in the Sacred Forest if you are willing to accept them." Then she nodded to Blaez and Andrion, and they headed off down the path to the road.

Once they were out of earshot of the humans, Andrion asked Maelona, "What was that thing you did with the glowing green light?"

"Protection spell," Maelona replied.

"Really? Why didn't your father think to put one of those on the amulet he gave my father?" he asked. "It could have saved me from some pain and suffering, not to mention healing time, when I was attacked by those three demonkin."

"Maybe Eluard foresaw you needed some tough love to help you become a man," Blaez said, deadpan.

"If I need some tough love to help me become a man," Andrion retorted, "maybe Maelona here should be the one to give it to me." He waggled his eyebrows at Blaez, and Blaez growled at him in return.

Maelona shook her head and sped up her pace to walk on ahead of them. She still heard Andrion, however, when he asked Blaez, "How do you do that growly thing when you're in human form, anyway?"

Maelona was glad they could still jest and aggravate each other in such a lighthearted manner. As for her, she could feel a burning anger simmering hot and low inside her at what they'd found here today.

She worried it wouldn't take many more situations such as this for her mother to get her wish—the weak hold she had on her emotions would snap, and only the Universe knew what would happen then.

Maelona, Blaez, and Andrion kept walking until the moon shone brightly overhead.

Blaez kept glancing over at her, brows furrowed and lips pressed together in a frown. She let him be for a while, hoping he would get around to saying whatever was on his mind in his own time. When it seemed like that wasn't going to happen, she finally gave in.

"What is it? Why do you keep looking at me like that?"

He looked down and rubbed the back of his neck. Then, meeting her gaze again, he said, "I don't want to seem like I'm doubting you, or that I don't trust you, but I'm just curious why you gave those humans so much information about the forest."

"I was curious about that as well," Andrion said. "Don't you have all those protections to keep everyone out? Isn't there a chance that other humans will flock there if they discover they can enter by just ignoring the fear response, and that there are trees in there filled with leaves that can heal just about anything?"

Maelona nodded slowly. "Yes, that is possible. In fact, I'm hoping that will be the case."

"Really?" Andrion said at the same time Blaez made a surprised sound.

She nodded. "How can we ask the humans to trust us enough to stand with us against a powerful dark sorcerer and the formidable army he commands, yet give them none of our trust in return?"

"Hmm," Blaez said in a tone that suggested he understood. She glanced at Andrion, who was nodding his understanding as well.

"Besides, Sterrenvar had been a divided realm for long enough. I'm hoping our new alliances will bring us closer together. And, although it isn't the only possible future my visions have shown, the one I strive for is where all the peoples of Sterrenvar interact with one another; where they learn and enjoy taking part in each other's ways of life."

Blaez chuckled. "That paints a pleasant picture."

"It does indeed," Andrion agreed.

After that, they walked on in silence for a while longer. Maelona and Blaez had rested just the night before and they would not rest again this night. Andrion, however, was human. He tried to insist that he was fine to keep going through the night. However, Maelona had seen the scenarios they might encounter and needed him to be at his best. She did not want to worry him with possibilities, however, so to make him feel a little better about giving in and sleeping, she convinced him she had some matters to attend to.

"Get some rest, Andrion," she said once they entered a wooded area. "I need to clean and sharpen my weapons, and this will be an excellent opportunity to do so. In fact, hand me your weapons and I will clean and sharpen them as well."

This was true, to a degree. While her weapons were still in good condition, she didn't know when she would have a chance to take care of them again and she liked them to be in top condition for a battle. So, she figured this may be the best opportunity she would have before the storm that was to come.

She and Blaez moved a short distance from where Andrion lay sleeping off to the side of a small clearing in the trees. They were close enough to hear if any wild animal or enemy came upon him as he slept, but far enough that the sounds of metal against metal and stone would not wake him.

They set about their tasks in companionable silence. Maelona could feel Blaez's eyes on her from time to time, but it was a while before she was ready to speak.

"If you shift from wolf to human during battle, grab the first weapon that since you won't be able to carry one in wolf form." She knew she was repeating something he likely already knew, but she couldn't help herself.

"I will," he responded.

She looked down to continue sharpening her blade. A short time later, she said, "Maybe we should have Andrion practice with us more. He plants his feet too much. He is so much smaller than some of the beasts we will be battling. He can't count on strength to get him through what's coming."

Blaez got up from the stump he had been sitting on, turned to Maelona, and held out his hand to her. When she hesitated, he said, "Come." With that, she laid down the dagger she'd been sharpening and took his hand. He led her over to a patch of grass, where they both lay down on their backs, gazing up at the stars. It reminded her of another night not so long ago, though it already felt like a lifetime ago.

Blaez reached across to grasp Maelona's hand in his. He took a deep breath in, inhaling the fresh scent of the clean air. Maelona did the same. Then Blaez spoke.

"I know and understand how useful, life-saving even, seers' visions can be. But at times like tonight, I can see how they can be a curse as well." He turned his head to look at her as he continued.

"You can't do this to yourself, my Lona. I don't know what you have seen, but you yourself have said that the future is always shifting."

"There are things that shift, but also things that will stay the same," she said. "Sometimes I wish I could see things I can't." And sometimes she wished she hadn't seen things she had.

"It does no good for you to spend all of your time worrying about what may come and being blind to what you have in the present," Blaez said. She could see his worry for her on his face, furrowing his brow.

Shaking her head, she said, "I understand that, Blaez. Logically, I understand. But I've been having a difficult time staying rational and neutral, as I have always been in the past. Sometimes it seems as though, now that I am allowing myself to feel my emotions, I feel too much. Now that I have allowed you and Andrion in, especially you, I feel like I have so much more to lose."

"You need to trust us to take care of ourselves."

"I do Blaez," Maelona insisted. "Honestly, I do. But it's been a long time since I've dealt with my emotions. It's been a long time since I have done anything more than deny them, locking them away deep inside. It's been a long time since I let anyone in, and now I fear the possibility of losing what I've gained." She took a deep breath before adding, "It just feels a little overwhelming."

Looking at him, she said, "Don't worry. I will learn to moderate my emotions, but it may take some time." *I just hope I can learn to do it before I need to use my magic.*

CHAPTER TWENTY

Damage & Disaster

The early morning was dark and gloomy when the trio packed up their camp and headed out the next morning. It was the first poor weather Maelona had experienced in a very long time. The climate in the Sacred Forest was magically enhanced since it was directly over the Source and its major ley lines, so, while it did rain there sometimes, it never felt oppressive like this.

The sky was heavy with low-hanging gray clouds and a misty rain fell lightly, just enough to dampen everything and add a slight chill to the air. It weighed her down, made her feel boxed in, even though logic told her that was not the case.

The three companions were quiet as they traveled, which Maelona knew was normal for Blaez, but it was not what she'd come to expect from Andrion. She glanced over at him. He was staring straight ahead, frowning, gaze far off and wrinkles between his eyebrows.

"Is there something on your mind this morning, Andrion?" she asked.

The prince looked at her, his expression unsure at first, as if he didn't know if he should say anything or not. Then he sighed and looked forward again.

"I keep thinking that it's my fault that the demonkin attacked that family," he said. "The beasts wouldn't have been there if they hadn't been following me."

Maelona huffed out a humorless laugh. "You know, my mother and I recently had a discussion about guilt and fault concerning something that happened in the past. Do you want to know the conclusion we came to?"

"Please."

"We cannot blame ourselves for the actions of others," she said, briefly squeezing his shoulder. She was surprised that she actually meant those words after so many years of blaming herself for things outside of her control. The realization was liberating, and she felt lighter than she had in a long time.

"Everyone has choices. The Dark Sorcerer sent the demonkin after you. The demonkin chose to follow his orders. They chose to hold that family captive and torture them. Then you chose to help Blaez and I fight back against them and free Edelinne, Dafydd, and Lancelin. You made the right choices. It was those beasts who made the wrong ones."

Blaez, who was walking to her other side, reached out and grabbed her fingers with his, tightening just slightly before dropping his hand to his side again.

Yes, this was a lesson all three of them needed to learn. Hearing it and agreeing with the sentiment was one thing, but believing it and allowing yourself to let go proved to be a little more difficult. At least, that's how it was for her.

"I don't think it would have mattered anyway," she said.

"What do you mean?" Blaez asked.

"When I was surveying from the tree before we left the forest, I saw some fires, and they didn't all seem to be along the same path. I doubt it was only the demonkin following Andrion who are responsible." She pursed her lips and took a calming breath. "From what I've seen in visions, I get the feeling this is one of the Dark Sorcerer's early tactics."

"What, attacking farms?" Andrion asked. "Why?"

She looked at him. "Surely you must have studied strategy with your father. Can you not think of any reason for it?"

"Are you thinking it's intimidation? Trying to beat them down?"

"In part, yes. It's still four moon-cycles or so away, and the humans aren't aware of it yet, but the Dark Sorcerer plans to begin his bid to take over Sterrenvar once he opens the gate and builds his demon army. He likely intends to show them what will happen to those who resist. But there is another reason as well."

Andrion looked at her, brows drawn in confusion.

"Who supplies most foodstuffs to Eastgate?" she asked. "Where will its citizens and soldiers get their supplies when the Battle of the Gate begins? What will happen to Eastgate's forces without these resources?"

Andrion's eyes went wide, but he didn't say anything. From his serious expression and furrowed brow, Maelona guessed he was thinking about the implications of what she'd just told him.

They were quiet and contemplative as they continued towards Eastgate, heads bent against the light precipitation that continued to fall. A couple of hours out from where they had camped for the night, they saw smoke rising lazily in the air. It seemed to come from just past the next rise.

Soon, they crested the hill, and what they saw on the other side twisted Maelona's stomach and caused a wrenching pain somewhere deep inside her. She placed a hand on her chest and pressed down, hoping to ease it somehow.

"By the Universe," she whispered.

Blaez and Andrion stopped short on either side of her. The destruction that lay only a few meters in front of them was near incomprehensible. The burned-out husk of a farmer's cottage stood as the backdrop to a pile of charred remains—what was left of three people, from what she could see. One of them—the smallest—was face down, an arm extended out in front as if they'd attempted to crawl away.

Blaez sucked in a sharp breath.

"Universe help us," Andrion said. "They were. . ."

"Burned alive," Maelona finished, choking out the words he could not say.

Smoke billowed around them as the wind gusted through, carrying a putrid, nauseatingly sweet stench with it.

"I have never smelled burning human flesh before." Andrion placed a hand over his mouth and nose.

"It's a smell I will not soon forget," Blaez said, his face twisted in disgust and anger.

"How could anyone do such a thing to innocent people?"

"You would be surprised what some would do for power and wealth," Maelona said, her voice cracking. She might expect this kind of cruelty from demonkin after all she had Seen, but that didn't make it much easier to witness it first-hand.

Every time she thought she'd seen the worse in others, something else would come along to surpass it. While she knew the motivations that could be behind such actions, she never truly understood it, or how living, sentient beings could bring themselves to do such things to others.

Part of the reason her extendible staff was her preferred weapon was because it was effective in disarming and disabling the enemy without having to kill to do so. . . most of the time.

"Do you think their attackers are still here?" Andrion asked.

"Could it have been the same demonkin that attacked the other humans?" Blaez said.

"It's not likely it was the same group of demonkin," Maelona said, "unless they traveled back and forth between the two places. The fires here are still smoldering, and the demonkin were waiting at the other farmstead for days."

"Right," Andrion said. "And I'd guess the fires would be much bigger still if it wasn't for the light rain falling today."

When they'd arrived, their attention had been drawn straight to the corpses. Now, Maelona looked around. The closest building was the stone cottage, which was still standing, but whose thatch roof and interior furnishings had been destroyed by the fire.

"It looks like they grew crops and raised livestock." Maelona pointed to the barn that lay a short distance past the cottage, next to a paddock that held several cows and sheep. A smaller paddock off to the left of that housed what looked to be two sturdy workhorses. She was surprised that they were still there—they were the type of animal she guessed would be of use to raiding demonkin.

"Let's split up and search for survivors," Maelona suggested.

"I will shift and see what I can sniff out," Blaez said.

"Good idea." She turned to Andrion. "You can start with the cottage. Check carefully, as long as it's safe to do so. It looks bleak, but there is always the possibility that people may have tried to hide. I don't want to take a chance that someone is unconscious and trapped somewhere."

"Understood," Andrion said with a nod.

"I will check the barn."

Blaez quickly shifted and lifted his nose high, scenting the air. Then he moved toward the victims, sniffing at the ground.

Andrion strode off toward the cottage. Maelona took a deep breath, set her shoulders, then stepped forward with brisk, purposeful strides toward the barn. She had a bad feeling about that seemingly innocent structure. It loomed ominously, growing ever larger as she quietly approached.

She paused and listened just outside, but did not hear a sound. As soon as she stepped through the rickety wooden door, she smelled it—the pungent, metallic, almost rust-like scent of blood. Although it was the last thing she wanted to do, she lifted her head and inhaled, trying to pinpoint where it was coming from. Once she turned in the right direction, she saw a trail of blood, like someone or something had been dragged along the dirt and hay floor and out through a back door. The trail began at a half-door to a stall: Maelona walked slowly ahead and peered inside.

The floor of the stall was covered in blood-soaked hay. She crouched down, grabbed a few pieces, lifted it to her nose, and sniffed.

"Pig's blood." She let out a tremendous sigh of relief and stood up. Luckily, her inner-sight allowed her to process even the most subtle differences in blood, allowing her to determine if it was human, Folk, seer, or animal. If it was something she had smelled before, she could even tell what kind of animal.

The demonkin had probably slaughtered the farm's stock of pigs and made off with them. They were smaller and easier to handle than cows.

She turned around to check out the rest of the barn, and she froze. Across from her, hidden from where she'd first entered by farming equipment, was a boy—younger even than Lancelin had been—pinned to the far wall by a pitchfork through the chest.

She clenched her teeth against the urge to scream, to cry. Anger and a thirst for revenge threatened to rise and take over. She wanted to hurt whoever was responsible for this. She squeezed her fists tight, took a deep breath, and held it. It took everything she had not to explode with fury and sorrow, and her body trembled and shook with the strain of controlling it.

"Maelona—"

"Stay back!" she shouted.

"What. . ."

Maelona could feel the electric force tingling under her skin, making the tiny hairs on her arms stand up. All round her, she could hear the rustling of hay; the creaking of boards that threatened to pull away from whatever they were secured to.

From her peripheral vision, she saw Andrion take a step toward her from the doorway. A moment later, Blaez's huge black wolf lunged at him—it grabbed him by the back of his doublet and pulled him outside.

She closed her eyes and stood there, breathing deeply and focusing only on the rise and fall of her breaths, until the shaking stopped and her fists relaxed and opened. Only then did she feel calm enough to leave the barn.

Outside, Blaez was once again in human form and dressed, standing a few meters away and watching the door with Prince Andrion standing beside him.

"What did you find?" she asked.

"There were no signs of anyone else in the cottage," Andrion said. He gazed at her, tilting his head, but not uttering the questions he clearly wanted to ask. Blaez must have warned him against it.

"I followed the scents of two demonkin back through the cornfield, almost to the other side," Blaez said. "In there, the path of trampled crops widened enough to serve as a main road to the castle town. It looks as though many of them passed not too far from here, and a few of them were sent in to look for supplies."

Maelona nodded absently. "Okay. Let's build a proper pyre for the victims and then get out of here."

They did as she suggested with barely another word. They collected the driest wood they could find—much of it came from the stalls and equipment inside the barn—and piled it together in a clear area where a fire would not easily spread, especially with the light rain that continued to fall. Next, they gathered the bodies and laid them carefully on top.

By the time they were done, the rain had stopped, even though the sky was still cloud-covered, and the air was still humid. They lit the pyre in a few spots, then watched on as it went up. Maelona spoke a few seer prayers to send them on their way back into the Universe.

When they were once again on the road to Eastgate, Maelona blurted, "I have a confession to make."

"Okaaay," Andrion said, drawing out the word.

Blaez said nothing, but he turned to look at her, giving her his full attention.

"I love fighting," she said. "Especially hand to hand." She felt like she was confessing to some horrible sin.

"And is this a bad thing?" Andrion asked.

"It is not the seer way," she answered. "We learn to fight because we are Protectors of the Light. Protectors of the Realm and all that is innocent and good in it. We learn to be very skilled at what we do because it is our duty. Fighting and killing others, even when they are evil beings who harm the innocent, is not something to be done lightly. These are actions seen as sometimes necessary, but always regrettable."

She let out a small laugh as a memory came to her. "My trainer, Owyn Axedrifter, used to get annoyed with me for smiling while we sparred. He would say, 'Fighting is a serious matter, Maelona!'" she said, deepening her voice to imitate him. "But it's not the killing or harming of others I enjoy. It's the beauty and artistry behind the fight. It's watching your opponent for subtle hints of what they will do next, and the feeling of accomplishment you get when you are victorious because you anticipated correctly. It's how the two combatants move together, back and forth, as they attack and defend and counter-attack. It's almost like a dance. It is exhilarating."

"That is a beautiful image," Blaez commented.

Maelona glanced over at him. "It was never the killing or harming of others that I enjoyed," she continued, her voice steel.

"However, when I find those responsible for these atrocities, I will thoroughly enjoy making them pay."

The closer Maelona, Blaez and Andrion got to Eastgate, the more populated with cottages the area became. Yet there was no human life to be found.

They came across many other burned-out shells as they went forward. However, there were intact homes that seemed abandoned as well.

"Where are all the people?" Andrion asked. "The number of bodies we've seen is only a small portion of our population. Of course, that's a good thing, though it would be better if there were none. But where is everyone?" He continuously scanned the area, shoulders high and tense, and brows drawn together.

"It's possible the inhabitants were captured or fled," Blaez answered.

As they approached the castle town of Eastgate, they veered off the main road and into the woods.

"We need to keep the element of surprise as much as possible," Maelona explained, "and take in the state of things in the town before heading to the castle."

When they were close to the tree line, they crouched low to the ground and looked out onto the town, scanning for any hidden dangers.

As with the other homes they'd passed, smoke and ash rose into the air and swirled all around, but they could detect no movement otherwise. Houses were nothing but ruins and rubble on the ground. The corpses of several companion animals lay strewn in the street. Straight ahead, the marketplace was in the same sad state. Fires still crackled and burned, and what wasn't burning smoldered. The acrid scent of smoke—from burned wood and other scorched things she did not want to identify—permeated the air.

"Where is everyone?" Andrion asked. His voice was pitched higher than usual and laced with tension. "Where are the demonkin? The town is a mess, but the castle does not seem to have been breached."

"The demonkin are hiding behind that ridge," Maelona answered, lifting her chin to indicate the hill line to the north-west of the castle. She had seen many of these sights in her dream-visions, though there was still much that fluctuated in her more recent ones.

Maelona took in the sight before her for a time and then turned to look at Andrion. "Is there another way into the castle, Andrion? A secret way? Preferably one that is hard to detect?"

"Yes," he answered. "Follow me."

The castle town extended in a circle all around the castle proper, and the area beyond the town was mostly wooded. Andrion led Maelona and Blaez through the woods and around to the side of the castle. He stopped in front of what appeared to be a rock sitting in front of a small hill. Moving behind the rock, he pushed aside a curtain of moss and vines and said, "Through here."

Instead of entering the hidden tunnel, Maelona turned to look at Blaez. As if he read her mind, he said, "The others should be here by now. I will shift and head off to meet with them."

"Tell them to stay hidden in the forest until after the battle begins," Maelona said. "I want them to watch the perimeter of the castle and to stay behind the enemy, if possible. I am hoping we can take the demonkin army by surprise.

"I don't think they'll be expecting a seer and animal-folk to be fighting alongside the humans. Not with our history. This should give us an advantage. We will draw them in, letting them think they have gained the upper hand. Then, when Gawn thinks enough of the demonkin force is on the battlefield, the Folk will come in behind the enemy, leaving them no means of escape."

"Agreed," Blaez responded. He turned to leave.

"Wait," Maelona said, grabbing Blaez's arm. He turned to face her again.

"When you know the others are ready, come back here to this tunnel and find me inside the castle. I will need you by my side."

Blaez smiled affectionately at her, reaching to cup her cheek in his large hand. "Until then, stay safe, my love," he said. He dipped his head to give her a brief, chaste kiss.

"And you as well," she responded, placing her own hand over his briefly. Then Blaez turned and ran back the way they had come. A moment later, they heard a wolf howl, followed by an answering howl.

"Good." Maelona commented. "They're here."

When she turned to face Andrion, he gestured to the tunnel and said, "Let's go."

"We're not going that way," Maelona said, her voice immediately harder. "I just wanted Blaez to know the way. We are going through the town."

"What?" Andrion's eyes went wide with alarm. "Why in the Universe would you want to do that? We'll be completely exposed out there. You may as well paint targets on our backs. And I really don't think that Blaez—"

"We need to check for survivors," she said, cutting him off. She was well aware of how Blaez would feel about her decision, but he would likely respect it, anyway. "And I think the demonkin will stay hidden, for the most part. They have pulled back to wait for reinforcements."

"How could you possibly know tha—" Andrion started. "Oh, never mind."

Maelona pulled her staff from its holder on her lower back and pushed the button to extend it to its full length. She held it in her hand and thought about what she wanted to do. She concentrated, sending her magic into the stone and setting it aglow in a golden-yellow light. Then she sent that power out to surround them.

"What in the. . .?" Andrion said. She looked over to see him staring at the stone while smoothing down his hair, which was now standing on end.

"Let's go," she said.

They headed through the town in the castle's direction. As they walked, they saw several dead, comprising the good people of Eastgate and their enemies, the demonkin.

"I thought it was said at the fire circle that there were others working with the Dark Sorcerer. Snowbeasts and the like," Andrion remarked. There was the slightest tremble to his voice, like he was trying to hold himself together and almost succeeding. "Why are we only seeing demonkin?"

"They are doing as we are," she replied. "Hiding their numbers, trying to take us by surprise. Also, they will save their strongest forces to take the Great Gate, which is why we asked Moyses and Hadrian to meet us there with their warriors."

"Lucky we have you then," he said. "It's hard to take a seer by surprise, I would imagine."

Maelona didn't respond this time. She was too focused on controlling her tension and anger; on channeling her magic where she wanted it. The closer they got to the castle and the more bodies they passed, the harder it got.

Andrion glanced over at her, eyes flashing and his jaw tight. She'd never seen him with such a hard expression before.

"You know, I'm angrier than I've ever been. It's like this pressure building inside of me that can only be released by making these wretched beasts pay for every single life they've taken. Still, you. . . it's like I can physically feel your anger radiating off of you. How am I feeling that, Maelona?" Not a moment after that, he glanced behind them, stiffened, and yelled, "Watch out!"

He needn't have worried. The physical sensation that he said he'd felt was more than just her anger or his imagination.

When the arrow now heading straight at Maelona's back got within a few feet of her, she could sense it. Her magic slowed the projectile almost to a stop and disintegrated it, from the tip out to the end.

Maelona didn't even flinch. She had surrounded them with an invisible magical shield and was not concerned with retaliating at the moment. The demonkin would have their reckoning; she would make sure of it. For now, she was fully consumed by the anger and anguish that had her knuckles turning white where she gripped her staff, and with the fight to keep control of her magic in the face of such powerful emotions.

Andrion gaped at her in shock. "Is there something you've neglected to tell me, my friend?" he asked. When Maelona didn't answer—couldn't answer; not yet—he added, "Remind me to not get on your bad side."

A couple of minutes later, Maelona spoke quietly, angrily, not knowing if she was talking to Andrion, to herself, or to the Universe. "So much life lost," she said. "And for what? For one man's greed and his quest for power."

"Is that all that motivates him? Wealth and power? Is that really all he wants?" He shook his head. "I guess that shouldn't surprise me, should it? It's not like evil needs a reason to inflict pain on others."

His question distracted her, and she closed her eyes and took a deep breath. She pressed her lips together and tried to piece together the flashes she'd Seen. "This sorcerer is so careful to not allow us to read him. But I have been having these strange dream-visions about a boy, and his mother locked in chains. I don't know for certain if it's related, but if it is, it could mean there's something from his past that pushes him. He may be looking for some kind of revenge."

The words struck her as soon as they were out of her mouth, and a wry laugh escaped her.

"What is it?" Andrion asked.

She shook her head. "Oh, nothing really. It just seems that, no matter who we are, there's no escaping our pasts."

By now they had reached the gatehouse, and they paused as the bridge descended and the portcullis opened. When they entered, the two guards at the gate bowed to Andrion, saying, "Your Highness," in unison.

Andrion nodded at them regally but clasped the shoulder of the nearest guard, like one would when greeting a friend. "Fernbrace Saurdew. It's good to see you again."

"And you as well."

As they walked through the outer bailey and looked around, Andrion let out a sigh of relief from beside her. "Oh, thank the Universe," he said. "Most of the citizens are safe inside our walls, it would seem."

Maelona dropped her magical shield and looked around. The outer bailey was set up as a temporary camp, and even had some merchants selling food. She let out her own sigh of relief at the welcomed sight.

They had just walked through the gate to the inner bailey when they heard a feminine voice say, "Welcome home, Brother."

At the sound of her voice, Maelona turned to look at Andrion's sister, who looked a couple of years younger than him. The Princess was a stunning young woman with hazel eyes and dark auburn hair that tumbled in waves to mid-back.

Without giving Andrion a chance to respond, Maelona stepped forward. Some of the anger from just moments before lifted as she took in her good friend's only daughter. It was nice to meet the family he'd built for himself finally.

"You are Sephare, daughter of Nele, King of Eastgate."

Sephare gave her a small smile and a nod. "I am. And who might you be?"

"I am Maelona Mistreaver, daughter of Eluard Mistreaver, who was a friend of your father's."

"Yes, I know who he is. Father has spoken of him often." Then, with a sense of urgency, she grabbed Maelona's hand in both of hers and said, "Come, I will take you to him."

The three of them headed to the staircase at a hurried pace, but when they reached the bottom, Maelona paused, dropping her hand from the Princess's grasp, and turned toward a darkened hallway to their right.

"What are you doing?" Andrion asked her. Before she could respond, a figure emerged and walked towards them.

Maelona smiled and nodded her greeting. "Blaez," she said, reaching her hand out to grasp his for a moment.

"Well, that was quick," Andrion commented.

"Yes, it seems I can move much faster when I don't have to pace myself to match a sluggish human."

Ignoring the men, Sephare said to Maelona, "Father has been waiting for you. Actually, he's been waiting for Eluard, but I am sure he'll be glad you are here." In a worried tone, she added, "He has not been well."

As they reached the door to the King's chambers, they passed a guard who was posted outside. Maelona cut a sideways glance, looking over the guard quickly before entering the room.

They all paused and waited just inside the doorway. Maelona turned to make sure it was firmly shut and locked.

"He's been very weak," Sephare said, sending a concerned look in the King's direction. "He has lost a lot of weight and has been sleeping for longer and longer periods. Let me just tell him you are here."

As Sephare walked away, Maelona removed her braid to leave her hair loose along her back.

Sephare approached her father's bed quietly. Shaking his shoulder gently, she said, "Father, you have a visitor."

"Who is it?" he asked in a weak, raspy voice.

Before Sephare could answer him, Maelona responded, "It's me, old friend." As she walked toward the King's bed, she allowed her hair to return to its natural color, eliciting gasps from Andrion and Sephare.

Chapter Twenty-One

Unveiling the Illusions

Maelona hadn't shown her true colors since she was a child—to most people. But she'd first met Nele before she had perfected changing her hair and eye color, so she figured he'd more easily recognize her this way.

Her natural coloring made her feel awkward. It announced loud and clear that she was a sorceress and caused people to stare. She much preferred how the seers usually dealt with visiting human villages or dealing with non-magical folk—changing their coloring, accents, and behaviors to match whatever group they were temporarily a part of, usually for information-gathering to ensure that all was well in the realm.

Once she reached the King's bedside, Maelona smiled down at him. Smiling back, he said, "Maelona Mistreaver! You are a sight for sore, old eyes. How long has it been? Forty, fifty years?" King Nele's voice was raspy, not as clear or as strong as it once was.

"Something like that," she replied.

"Well, it would seem that you have aged much better than I have," he quipped.

Maelona laughed lightly at that. Still smiling, she said, "Your daughter tells me you haven't been feeling well."

"No, not for a month or two, though it has gotten worse of late."

"Well, let me take a look at you, old man."

"I may look old, but let's not forget that you have a few years on me, my friend."

"That I do," she responded. She gently placed her hands on his cheeks and pulled his lower eyelids down with her thumbs. Next, she looked at his mouth and lips. Finally, she took his hands in hers and examined his nails. Then, turning to the others, she said, "Come closer, everyone."

They all gathered around the bed and looked at Maelona expectantly.

"King Nele has been poisoned," she said in a quiet voice. Andrion and Sephare gasped at this news. Then Maelona added, "It looks like this poisoning has been going on over a period of time. A few months, probably."

"But how is that possible?" Sephare asked. "My father is always guarded. His Royal Guard has been with him for decades, and he always tastes my father's food and drink first."

"Well, the answer to the how," Maelona responded, "probably has much to do with the fact that the guard outside the door is not human. He is demonkin."

There were sharp intakes of breaths from all around at this news. Maelona shushed them, not knowing just how good the beast's hearing was.

Then Sephare asked, "We've had a demonkin on our staff for decades? How is that possible?"

Maelona shook her head. "It's more likely that it killed your real guard so it could take his place."

"I'm going to kill it!" Sephare practically growled out. "I'm going to tear him apart with my bare hands!"

"Let's wait on that a bit," Maelona responded calmly. "I may be able to use the creature to gather some more information."

"Okay, let's get back to the important stuff," Andrion said impatiently. "Is Father going to be okay?"

Maelona gave him a warm, compassionate smile. "Yes, he will be. I can help him, but we have no time to waste." Turning to address the King she added, "What I have seen in my visions would suggest that the attack will happen within the next couple of days. Possibly even as early as tomorrow." Looking back at the others, she said, "We need him to get well before then."

"Maybe we should just have him sit this one out," Andrion suggested softly.

Maelona could hear the worry in his tone, so she gave him a small smile of understanding as she replied, "I'm afraid that won't be possible, Andrion. We seers consider ourselves to be guardians of the realm, but I also have a more specific task, as does your father. We are the Guardians of Eastgate, tasked with protecting the keystone."

Looking back at the others, she explained, "Guardianships are passed down from parent to child for humans. They are sometimes passed the same way for seers, but not always. Children are more rare for us, so we do it a little differently if we need to.

"Our fathers protected Eastgate when King Nele and I were young, but with their passing, the honor and the responsibility falls to us. Actually, I insisted on taking my father's place, though they made me train for several years before allowing it. They appointed another seer champion until I was ready."

Taking off her pack, she dug around for a moment before pulling out a pouch. She looked at the hearth and noticed the fire was low. "Andrion, could you stoke the fire, please? We need it hot." He nodded and set to work.

Maelona continued, "Sephare, you will need to heat some water." Sephare moved to grab the pitcher of water on the table near her father's bed. "Wait," Maelona said. Taking the pitcher, she smelled the water, then poured a small amount into a cup and tasted it. "The water is fine," she announced. "It must have been the food that was poisoned."

She handed the pitcher of water to Sephare, who then poured it into a small pot and placed it over the fire Andrion had brought back to life.

"The crimsonleaf tea will help you heal, but it will take too long. So, I will try to help it along," she said.

Maelona had never attempted what she was going to try now, and she was nervous. Though she tried to hide it, her hands shook slightly. This would be her first time trying this, and this was her good friend, who also happened to be a King and a Keystone Guardian. She needed to get this right the first time around.

Blaez, who'd been guarding the door, walked over, stood close to her, and said, "I will prepare the crimsonleaf leaf for the tea." He placed his hands over hers where she held the pouch. He squeezed her hand gently and his gaze met hers unwaveringly. He gave her a small, almost imperceptible nod. She took a deep breath and, suddenly, she was feeling much calmer.

"Just wait a moment first," she said. She placed a hand on Blaez's forearm and turned to King Nele. "This is Blaez Stronghunter. He is accompanying me to help me with my mission. He is from the Wildegrove Wolf-folk clan."

When the King pushed himself up to sit, Maelona put a hand on his shoulder. "I just wanted you to know who he is and that you can trust him. Don't try to move. You can speak and get to know one another once you are feeling better."

After King Nele had drunk most of a cup of crimsonleaf tea, Maelona pulled a stool over next to his bed, near his head. "I'm going to boost the healing properties of the crimsonleaf tea," she explained. That wasn't exactly all she was going to do, but he didn't need the details. "It's been a long time since I have tried anything like this, but I'll do my best to make it quick and pain free." *Actually*, she thought, *I have never tried anything exactly like this*. She would not tell her patient, though. She needed him to be calm, for both their sakes.

Many years ago, before she left the Wolf-folk to take her father's place with the seers, her mother had tried to teach her some healing spells. She hadn't gotten very far, but she was a seer and a sorceress, and once she had committed herself to the seer ways, she learned how to focus her abilities inward. Her father had taught her how to manipulate the elements within her body to change hair and eye color, and it hadn't taken her long with the seers to figure out how to use this ability for healing as well.

Her instincts now told her she could use her magic like a bridge to enable her to focus her inner-sight into the body of another. Seers could use this ability to not only see their own illnesses but also to heal many of them. She hoped to be able to use it to help heal Nele in much the same way.

"I trust you, Maelona," the King said, smiling at her weakly. "I have faith in you."

Maelona placed one hand on King Nele's forehead and another on his abdomen and, closing her eyes, she focused her mind inward. She could see inside her own physical form. She saw all the molecules of matter, and she felt her life force. Then she called upon her magic: It flowed through her body like a warming, tingling static charge as it slowly responded to her will. It traveled up through her arms and into her hands, where she pushed it forth to flow between her own body and Nele's. She followed its path as her inner-sight traveled through his physical form until she found the molecules of the chemical used to poison the King. When she was certain she had isolated all the toxin, she then used her mind and her magic to obliterate it into nothingness.

Now that she had gotten rid of the toxin from his body, it was time to help the tea circulate and heal the damage that had been done to his body. Satisfied that she had done everything she could, Maelona opened her eyes and the pale green light of her magic faded from sight. She looked down at Nele and, surprised, she muttered, "It would seem I'm better at that than I thought."

Sephare and Andrion came forward to check on their father. "What did you do?" Sephare asked. Her eyes were wide with disbelief.

"I healed him," Maelona answered simply, not knowing what else to say.

"But he looks even better than he did before," Sephare said. "He looks ten or fifteen years younger than he did before he took ill."

Maelona shook her head. "I'm uncertain, but I can only assume that the magic I sent through his body had the same effect on him as it does on sorcerers," Maelona explained. "It is our magic that causes sorcerers to age more slowly than others because it renews our cells as it flows through us. But it could have been the boosted crimsonleaf as well. I would love to study these effects to learn more, but we don't have time right now."

"But your mother healed my leg," Andrion said, "and I still look the same."

Maelona shook her head as she tried to puzzle it out. "Maybe it's because she had localized her magic to your injuries, whereas I had to spread mine throughout your father's body to find and destroy all the molecules of the toxin. Or maybe it's because my magic differs from hers."

"Perhaps that is something you can study once all the danger is past," Blaez said. "In the meantime, it would probably be best to not mention this to anyone outside of this room." She nodded in agreement. If word got out that this kind of effect was possible, it could cause chaos.

Honestly, she'd spent so long ignoring her magic that she was sure everything she did with it was going to be a learning experience. She really should not have waited until the realm was in such danger to explore it, especially since practice could have built up her endurance, so she wouldn't feel as fatigued as she did right now. It was too late to change that, however. She would just have to learn to trust her intuition and her instincts.

King Nele swung his legs over the bed and stood to his full height. "It is a lovely side-effect," he said, watching his hands as he squeezed and relaxed them. "However, we should save the 'whys' for another time. We have some strategizing to do."

Leaning toward Maelona, Andrion whispered, "A couple of decades from now, I'll be asking you to do that for me." Maelona couldn't help but grin.

"First things first," Nele continued, looking at Maelona, "we have a demonkin posing as my Royal Guard. We need to find out if it's the only one to have infiltrated the castle. Most importantly, we need to find out if the keystone has been tampered with. The creature has been loose out there while I have been incapacitated in here."

Maelona nodded her agreement at the same time as Sephare asked, "How are we going to do that?"

"Just like this," Nele said, striding to the door and swinging it open. Maelona quickly switched her coloring back to her customary browns.

The guard turned to look at the King, then took a step back in surprise. "My l...lord! H...how...?" he stammered.

"Step inside my chamber and we will tell you all about it," the King said. He moved to the side to allow the imposter to enter. Once he was inside, the King locked the door again, then stood in front of it, blocking any potential attempt at escape. Maelona couldn't help but smile at Nele—her old friend had apparently not lost his boldness with age.

The guard looked from the King to the others before saying, "What is this about?"

"I have some questions for you," the King said. "And if you value your life, you will answer them truthfully. First, I want you to tell me what you did with Drest."

"What are you talking about? I am Drest," the demonkin answered with a confused look on its face. If Maelona was not naturally skilled at detecting falsehoods in others, she might have been convinced it was being genuine.

The King pulled a dagger from underneath his sleeping robes.

"Did you have that dagger on you in your sickbed?" Andrion asked.

Nele shrugged. "Being King is a dangerous profession, as you can see. You would do well to remember that." He focused on the demonkin again.

"I will ask you again," he said, pressing the tip of the dagger against the false guard's throat and pushing him up against the wall. "Where. Is. Drest?"

"I don't know what you're talking about, My Lord," the demonkin replied in a shaky, seemingly innocent voice. Maelona was impressed—he was hanging on to his charade well.

The King sighed and shook his head. Moving the dagger away from the impostor's throat just long enough to gesture towards Maelona, he said, "You see my friend over there? She will be able to tell me without a shadow of a doubt whether you are lying or telling the truth."

The demonkin looked at Maelona, and she watched its eyes widen in realization. "How can you trust one such as her?" it spat. "Her race is tricky and deceitful! I am horrified to know that any survived!"

"Hmm," Maelona said. "That does not sound like something a human would say." Perhaps she shouldn't have been so impressed after all. "I'd be surprised that a human we didn't reveal ourselves to directly would even believe we still exist, let alone guess what King Nele meant. After all, human lives are so brief, they have a difficult time remembering beyond one or two of their short generations."

Maelona stepped forward and, looking into the demonkin's eyes, she asked, "Shall I let them see what I see?"

Without giving it a moment to respond, she raised her hand and placed it against the pretender's chest. Her magical touch dissolved the illusion it had wrapped around itself, shattering the image of the guard and, in its place, leaving the disturbing reality of what lay underneath.

The demonkin's shape was roughly that of a large human, but that was where the similarities ended. Its skin was mottled red and pink, the way a human's would look while recovering from severe burns. Its facial structure looked distorted, almost skeletal, and it had small horns all along its cheekbones that became larger and larger as they continued past its temples.

Letting go of the charade, the demonkin's demeanor suddenly changed from one of a nervous and confused guard to an angry and spiteful monster. "Do to me what you will, I will tell you nothing!" the demonkin spat.

"Make no mistake," Maelona calmly said, "you will tell me everything you know. You can either choose to do it the easy way and answer our questions, or you can do it the hard way, where I pull the answers from you. And I can promise you, that will not be pleasant for you."

"You have no power over me," the demonkin declared. "Soon you will all be crushed under our feet!"

"Okay," Maelona said with a sigh. "The hard way it is. So be it."

She placed her hand against its forehead, and the demonkin suddenly stood still as if it were being pinned against the wall. Her hand glowed with a low, white and green light that soon became brighter and brighter. After what felt like a long time, Maelona pulled her hand away and the body of the demonkin fell to the ground in a lifeless lump.

"Is it dead?" Sephare asked.

"No," Maelona replied, "but I can guarantee that it won't be doing much more than drooling for a while."

"Isn't that a little harsh?" Andrion asked, wincing.

"Well, I dislike taking life unnecessarily, but I also didn't want to take the chance of it escaping and tampering with the keystone while we are distracted with battle. I can undo the effects if the need arises."

"Speaking of battle," Nele interjected, "let's stick to our first priorities. What did you learn, Maelona? Is Drest. . .?"

Maelona shook her head slowly. Her throat felt tight, and she swallowed past a lump.

King Nele looked stricken for a moment. Sephare grabbed hold of his forearm in a show of support. Then, in a rough voice, Nele said, "There will be time to mourn later. We need to focus on dealing with the current threats."

"I will begin with the things we need to take care of immediately," Maelona responded. "First, he was not the only demonkin placed in the castle. There are three others. There is one taking the place of a cook in the kitchen. Its job was to administer the poison in low doses over time to keep you weak and under control." The King made an unhappy sound at this, but otherwise did not interrupt.

"The guard here," she continued, while gesturing to the unconscious form on the ground, "was to keep tabs on you and make sure you consumed your poisoned food. And the final two demonkin were tasked with compromising the keystone. Should they fail, they would have the weak and pliable King show them the way. . . or so they thought."

"Were they successful?" the King asked, alarm evident in his tone.

"As of their last check-in with your friend here, no, they were not," she answered. "But I suggest that our first order of business be finding the imposters and taking them out of the picture." King Nele nodded his agreement, and Maelona continued, "Blaez and I will take care of them. It shouldn't take us long. They don't know they've been discovered, so they shouldn't be difficult to catch off guard."

"Agreed," Nele said. "Meet us back here afterward and you can tell us anything else you learn. If we are lucky, maybe you will discover something that will give us the upper hand in the coming battle."

Maelona signaled Blaez and headed for the door.

As she and Blaez left the room, Maelona could hear Sephare saying, "I didn't know seers had those kinds of abilities."

"Normally, they don't," King Nele replied. The warmth and affection in his voice was clear as he continued, "But Maelona. . . she is special."

Hunting the Enemy

In the corridor just outside the castle's large kitchen, Maelona stumbled; she reached out to steady herself against the wall, then relaxed against it to rest for a moment.

Drawing on her magic so much in one day was like flexing muscles she had never used. She was lightheaded and even a little physically sore all over. She would have healed the soreness with her inner-sight, but using her powers got her into this position, and it would only make things worse right now.

Blaez stepped up next to her, wrapping a large hand around her upper arm to help steady her.

"You're exhausted, Maelona. You should rest for a while before we continue."

She shook her head. "These demonkin have been left to run freely through the castle for too long. I will rest when we are done."

Blaez's eyebrows furrowed, his lips pressed tight, and he shook his head. She appreciated his concern, but her work for the day was not finished, so she would have to push through the fatigue.

Maelona walked into the main kitchen and found what she was looking for right away. It amazed her that the humans milling about didn't notice anything different about a person they worked with regularly. Did they not notice any changes in habits or mannerisms? Did they never accidentally brush up against or touch one another while working within this limited space? Demonkins' illusions were just that—illusions. They were visual, not physical.

Then again, humans—most beings, actually—were good at passing off unusual things as coincidence or as products of their imaginations.

In this case, a tall, broad, demonkin male was disguised as the short, plump, female cook. She looked around the room to see if the other demonkin were there, but all she saw was a couple of kitchen workers. She approached the demonkin.

"Are you the head cook?" Maelona asked.

"Yes, I am," it replied, perfectly mimicking a human woman's voice. It must have watched the original for some time to get it right. "How can I help you?"

"I am a friend of King Nele. I brought some special herbs to put in his meals to help him feel better." Maelona held a closed hand out to the fake cook, who looked down to see what she had. Maelona touched her other hand to the back of the poser's head and its body stiffened before it went unconscious. She lowered the limp form slowly to the ground.

There were alarmed gasps from the other kitchen staff as the illusion dissolved and they realized they had been working with a demonkin.

Maelona swayed a little where she stood—locking away the creature's consciousness took more effort than when she'd done the same with the guard earlier, probably because of her lack of practice with her magic. It was like she was just starting to exercise and needed to build up stamina.

Blaez stepped forward and held her by the elbow, steadying her for the second time that day. She looked at him and gave him a grateful smile, but the smile dropped when she noticed how worried he looked.

Turning back to the humans, she said, "My name is Maelona. This is Blaez. We truly are friends of the King and we're here to help. There are two other demonkin wandering about and I do not want to alert them we're on to them and are searching for them. So, if you can keep this quiet for the time being, it would be much appreciated."

The staff nodded their heads in understanding.

"Do you have somewhere to hide the body until we get back to bring it to the dungeon?"

"Is it dead?" one of the staff asked.

"No, just unconscious," Maelona said.

"What do we do if it wakes up?"

"It won't."

"We have a large pantry back here," a man said. "We can hide it in here."

"Thank you." She stepped forward to help the man carry the demonkin, but Blaez reached out and grabbed her shoulder to stop her.

"Let me."

She nodded and stepped back.

Once the demonkin was safely hidden, Maelona looked at the group of human kitchen staff and said, "We are truly grateful for your help. We'll be back soon to collect the demonkin."

She turned to leave the kitchen, but Blaez stepped directly in front of her, blocking the door. She looked at him with narrowed eyes; his jaw was set and his eyes were steely. He leaned around her to address the closest kitchen worker.

"Might I bother you to boil some water for tea?"

"Oh, that is no trouble at all," the woman said. "Please come and sit." She gestured to a long wooden table at the other end of the kitchen—it was probably where the staff themselves sat to eat. Blaez wrapped an arm around Maelona's waist and led her over, pulling out a chair for her with his free hand.

Once she was sitting, she sighed and, for the first time, noticed just how warm and delicious smelling the room was. The kitchen worker brought two cups and placed them on the table. Blaez nodded to her in thanks and the woman's cheeks flushed before she hurried away. Her reaction to Blaez did not surprise Maelona in the least. He was a very handsome man.

"Blaez—" she began.

"No, Maelona. If you won't take a proper rest, the least you can do is allow me to make you a crimsonleaf and verve thistle tea. I do not want you to face the other demonkin weakened as you are. What if you fainted from exhaustion in the middle of an attack?" His voice was tight with concern, his body tense. His desire to care for her in this way made her smile, and she nodded.

Since she couldn't heal from her overuse of magic using magic, or even her inner-sight, weakened as she was, what Blaez suggested was the best option.

"Okay, Blaez. Let's have some tea."

He looked in his pack, which was now sitting on his lap, and rooted around. He pulled out the familiar pouch of crimsonleaf and a small wooden box. When he opened the box, she recognized the familiar dried plant and its scent right away. She hadn't carried verve thistle herself in a long time, but she knew her mother always kept stores of the energy-giving plant. So, it should not surprise her that Blaez carried some.

"But we will leave as soon as we are done," she said.

He looked up at her with a serious expression, and she worried he would try to argue. But then, one corner of his mouth lifted in a small, crooked smile. He huffed out a little chuckle, shook his head, then looked back to his tea preparation.

"Fine. But you must be careful and not take any unnecessary chances."

As soon as she finished the last sip of her bitter, yet refreshing tea, Maelona stood up and left the kitchen, Blaez following her closely. She was already feeling the positive effects of the restorative tea—she was much more clear-headed and steady on her feet than before.

They walked in silence, branching off twice until they were in a smaller, less obvious, and less used hallway. They followed it to its end, where there was a sturdy wooden door reinforced with metal bracing. Maelona studied the area, running her hands lightly over the door and the surrounding walls.

"Are there any signs of tampering?" Blaez asked.

"Yes," she said. "It's magical, but demonkin magic is very limited and very specific. The Dark Sorcerer must have given them something to help them get through." Could whatever he'd used to allow them to enter the forest have worked here as well? "Let's hope that we aren't too late."

Maelona wasn't sure what could destroy a magical keystone, but if the Dark Sorcerer sent his demonkin here, he must have some ideas.

She ran her hands over the stones of the wall surrounding the door again, this time pressing the ones that would unlock it.

The door swung open, revealing stairs that should disappear into darkness just a short way down. However, the torch that sat in a sconce just to the left of the door was lit, illuminating the path down into the keep.

Maelona glanced at Blaez meaningfully. "Be cautious. They may still be down here." Blaez nodded to her and they started down the stairs.

Maelona was taught how the keep was configured when she first was named Guardian of Eastgate. The staircase spiraled around the outer circumference of the keep, which had been dug down to fifty feet underground. It was as if a stone tube encircled a stone tube, and between the two was a widely spiraling staircase.

When they reached the bottom, the steps led into a corridor that widened some from the stairwell. Maelona explained the layout in a hushed voice.

"The keep is not more than a few hundred feet wide, and it was designed like a labyrinth. Now that we're on the bottom level, we can walk all around the tunnel, and we will find several doors. Each of these doors has narrow stone paths that lead in, with twists, turns, branches, and dead ends. We are not looking for the keystone, however. We are looking for the demonkin that are searching for it.

"This is where your wolf's nose comes in. There are two more demonkin, we know. We are looking for fresh scents to let us know they are down here. If they are, they will probably have split up to search faster. If they have, then we should split up as well."

"Do you think that is wise?" Blaez asked. "What if something happens?"

A mental image of Blaez being attacked by a demonkin flashed through her mind, and she knew he was probably worried about the same thing for her. So, she considered his question for a moment.

"How about this: As soon as we've each dispatched the demonkin we're tracking, we drag it out here. Then, if the other is not back yet, we can go looking in case they—one of us—needs aid."

"Agreed. Are you ready to shift again, Maelona?"

"I think so," she answered. "I will admit, I am a little nervous. I should have shifted more often to practice with the heightened senses, but there is no time to worry about that now."

They both stripped out of their clothing and placed it in their packs.

"Wait," Maelona said, putting her hand on Blaez's arm. "Do you have rope in your pack?"

"I do," Blaez said, nodding.

"Good. Try not to kill the demonkin if you don't have to. I know that will be harder for you in wolf form, but if you can manage it without endangering yourself, then keep him alive. If you're the first one out, make sure you tie it up securely before you look for me."

Blaez tilted his head as he looked at her. "Why do you want to keep them alive?" he asked.

Maelona debated whether to tell him all of her reasoning or just part of it. However, she was not comfortable keeping things from him—it might damage the connection that continued to build between them.

"The reason that will count most for everyone else is that we can question them afterwards and see what they can tell us. I can read what is in their minds like I did with the fake guard, sure. But if there are any humans here who are suspicious of strangers or seers, then it will be best if the King and his men can witness firsthand what the demonkin have to say.

"If I'm being completely honest, though, I don't like killing anyone or anything if it can be avoided. There has been, is, and will be enough senseless killing in the realm without me contributing to it."

Blaez looked at her with a warm smile. "That makes sense." He moved close to place a soft kiss on her lips.

"That being said, though," she added when he broke the kiss, "if it comes down to you or it, make sure it's you who comes back in one piece."

He nodded and took a step back. "The same goes for you."

Maelona watched as his form shimmered and changed into his beautiful black wolf.

"Find the doors, Blaez, then I will open them and shift."

Blaez sniffed along the passageway as Maelona followed him. He checked each of the doors before coming back to one he had checked a moment before. He yipped and looked from the door to Maelona. Then he walked a couple of doors over and yipped again. Maelona opened the doors he indicated and watched Blaez disappear inside one. She shifted to her natural, green-tipped wolf, took a moment to change to gray wolf coloring, then entered the other door.

It was dark inside the tunnels but, in wolf form, she could easily make out shapes. Soon, she realized she didn't need to rely on her sight, anyway. She could hear every minor scuffle of rodents and bugs, smell every scent from the stale odor of the dank earth under her feet to the smells of the small critters scurrying about.

She noticed one other scent as well. It was both foreign and familiar to her, and neither pleasant nor unpleasant. It was earthy, yet different from the other earthy smells around her. It was like it was lightly scented with an unfamiliar spice.

This was the smell she was looking for. She had caught a much more subtle hint of it back when she'd been fighting the demonkin in the forest, and again at the farmstead. When she came to a choice of three tunnels, she followed the scent to the left. She followed it again as it took a tunnel to the right. Finally, she saw a flicker of light around a corner not far ahead and heard an aggravated, gravelly voice.

"Curse the human who made this cursed maze!"

Maelona peeked around the corner to see that the demonkin male had come up against a dead end.

She stepped back and silently shifted back to her regular form. Rather than taking the time to re-dress, she did as the demonkin did and created the illusion of clothing around herself. As unpracticed as she was, she still seemed to know intuitively how to use her magic. She just had to think of what she wanted and will it to happen. Once she was ready, she stepped fully into the light of the demonkin's torch.

It was facing away from her, feeling along the wall. It placed its torch in a sconce and tried to use the hilt of its dagger to knock in stones in the wall. "There's got to be an easier way through this place," it muttered to itself.

"That won't work," Maelona said.

The demonkin startled at the unexpected sound of her voice and turned around with its dagger at the ready.

"All the walls in here are magically reinforced," Maelona continued. "There is only one way through."

"Who are you?" the demonkin demanded.

"I'm an apparition," Maelona said. "A ghost." She smiled at the beast and took a step closer. The demonkin looked like it wasn't sure what it should do in this situation.

"What do you want?" it asked as Maelona moved slowly toward it.

"Don't move!" it said, pointing its dagger toward her.

She raised her hands palm out in front of her. "I'm unarmed she said," still inching slowly forward.

It narrowed its eyes at her. "What do you want?" it asked again.

"Your consciousness," she replied, reaching for it, hoping to touch its head before it realized what was happening.

No such luck.

The creature lunged forward, aiming its dagger at her heart. She slid to the side and performed a palm block to its elbow, hard enough to throw it off balance a little. As it stumbled forward, Maelona grabbed the back of its tunic with both hands and brought her knee up as she pushed the beast down, kneeing him in the chest. It grunted as she made contact and would likely have fallen forward if she hadn't quickly grabbed its collar with one hand while touching the back of its head with the other.

Its full weight jerked her down a little as it went unconscious, but she rebalanced before it hit the floor. She quickly crouched in front of it, positioning its body across her shoulders and holding one of its wrists in front of her to secure him in place.

This feat would normally be easy for her, despite its size, because of the dense muscles she inherited from her seer father. However, because of the fatigue she was left with from today's magic usage, it made her grunt a little with the effort. She carried the limp, unconscious form out through the tunnel.

Blaez was already in the outer corridor. He was sitting calmly, in wolf form, in front of a hog-tied demonkin who was growling threateningly. The demonkin watched Blaez warily until he spotted Maelona carrying its comrade's body out through the doorway.

"What did you do to him?" The demonkin barked. Blaez growled a warning, but Maelona continued forward, unfazed. She laid the unconscious form next to its associate and then turned to face Blaez's prisoner.

"Let me show you," she said. Then, without further warning, she placed her hand on its head and repeated the process of locking away its consciousness.

She reached out to Blaez and gently stroked his fur before saying, "Come on. Let's get dressed and get our prisoners to the dungeon. The King and the others will be waiting for us."

Maelona watched as Blaez shifted back to his human form. Just as she was about to turn to get her clothing out of her pack, he spoke.

"Maelona?"

"Yes?" She turned back to face him.

"Are you sure they are unconscious? Oblivious to anything around them?" He looked up and down the corridor, as far as the curved walls allowed them to see.

"Most certainly," she replied.

"Then come here," he said, holding his hand out to her. When she took it, he said, "This may not be the best time, or the ideal setting, but I don't know if I'll get another opportunity before the battle."

"Opportunity for what?"

"To let you know how much you've come to mean to me. I'm not trying to be pessimistic, or to suggest I don't believe the battle will have a good outcome for us. But it seems like a fitting time to share this with you."

Maelona felt the "just in case" implied there.

He pulled her tight to him. Maelona gasped as she felt her body press against his firm, taut form for the very first time.

"I was so worried about you earlier," he whispered in her ear, making her shiver.

Seers mated for life, seeming to never have the urge to become physical until they met the one who was right for them. She knew this, and in her attempt to remain distant and in control of herself, she had always ensured there was some physical distance between herself and Blaez, even when they kissed. The exception, of course, was when they'd practiced fighting and it could not be helped.

At this moment, however, Maelona knew he was the right one for her, because her desire to get even closer to Blaez just about consumed her. It felt like every molecule of her being was begging her to let go of her tight control.

As Blaez stared down at her, she met his gaze and was pulled in by the beautiful blue depths of his eyes. Right now, they shone with desire, longing, and love.

Maelona's heart pounded in her chest. She could feel Blaez's heart doing the same against her. He ran his hands along her back, taking his time as if he were savoring something he had desired for a long time. His fingers trembled against her. Finally, he dropped his mouth to hers in a searing kiss.

Maelona could feel her magic rising to the surface, swirling around them and whipping her hair to the side. Blaez's hands stroked down her back and up again, as if he wanted to touch as much of her as possible without crossing a line. Her magic encompassed them like a cocoon, shielding them from the outside world.

"You feel even better against me than I imagined," Blaez whispered against her mouth. Then he trailed kisses along her jawline and down her neck. Maelona tipped her head back and whispered his name.

Blaez took a deep breath, enveloped her in a tight embrace, and buried his face in the crook of her neck. He stayed like this for a moment, his whole body shaking against hers even as his breathing and heart rate slowed.

Maelona dipped her forehead to his shoulder as well and took some deep breaths to calm herself. Her magic slowed its spinning motion around them and slowly withdrew back inside her. When everything calmed, they both lifted their heads to look at one another.

Blaez cupped Maelona's cheek, placed another soft, quick kiss on her lips, and stepped back. He reached down to Maelona's pack and took out her clothing. He re-dressed her slowly, reverently, one item at a time. As he worked, his fingers brushed and lingered from time to time, causing Maelona to shiver.

Once she was fully clothed again in more than just an illusion, Blaez dressed himself quickly.

"Come," she said, smiling at him lovingly, "before someone comes looking for us."

CHAPTER TWENTY-THREE

Strategies & Preparations

Before heading back to update the others, Maelona and Blaez carried the captured demonkin to the dungeon and had them locked up. It might have been more than necessary considering the creatures were unconscious, but they couldn't think of a better place to put them. They dropped off the two from the keep first before going back for the one in the kitchen.

As Maelona had predicted, the others were waiting for them in the King's chambers when she and Blaez rejoined them a couple of hours after they first left to search for the demonkin.

"It's about time!" Andrion exclaimed. "I was about to send a guard to search for you."

"You sound like a worried mother hen," Sephare said to her brother.

"Well, better to be a worried mother hen than to wait too long and end up with dead friends."

"Hmm, I can see your point," Sephare said. "It took you so long to find some friends who don't get annoyed with your antics, it would be devastating to lose them so soon."

"Oh, we get annoyed with his antics," Blaez said. "But Maelona insists I not shift to my wolf and eat him."

Andrion's eyes widened. "Do wolves eat human flesh?"

"Not usually," Blaez responded, quirking his brow at Andrion. "But exceptions can be made."

"Oh, lovely!" Andrion exclaimed. "It's like I now have two siblings to put up with."

Sephare laughed and Maelona smiled at them, feeling quite pleased with that comparison.

"My father is in his study. He'll want to see you right away, if you're up for it," Andrion said.

"Of course," Maelona replied. The King's chambers comprised a sitting room, the bedchamber, and a study, that Maelona knew of. They were all located next to one another.

Andrion knocked lightly on the study door.

"Enter," the King Nele called.

The King stood and smiled when he saw Maelona and Blaez.

"Welcome back. Come sit and we can discuss what you've found."

As they entered, Maelona looked around. The walls were covered in intricately woven tapestries with images that depicted war scenes and one that showed a family tree. There were also true-to-life paintings of Nele, his late Queen, Andrion, and Sephare.

They all sat in chairs arranged in a line in front of the King's large, wooden desk with ornately carved legs. Maelona smiled when she noticed a colorful stone weighing down the bottom edge of a parchment roll. The stone looked suspiciously like the ones she and Nele had placed outside the door to Talwyn's hut when he visited Clearview as a child. She was willing to wager that was exactly where it came from.

"These are two leaders of the Eastgate Guard, Thim and Hervi," he said, gesturing to the men on either side of him.

The King and his men had not been wasting time while Maelona and Blaez had been out hunting demonkin. There were maps spread out across the wide surface of the desk. At first glance, Maelona could see maps that laid out the areas within the castle walls, from Eastgate to the lands that bordered the Sacred Forest, and a larger one of the whole of the Island of Sterrenvar.

"First, please tell us what you know," King Nele said.

Maelona filled them in on where they had found the demonkin and how they had dealt with them.

"I learned little new information from them," she said after the brief update. "I did not spend as much time viewing their memories as I did with the false Royal Guard. I thought it might be more effective, all things considered, if you or your men questioned them." Maelona didn't doubt the King would know exactly what she meant.

"What I learned, however, confirmed that the Dark Sorcerer has been taking pains to not let anyone, not even his closest warriors, know all the details of his plans, unless they absolutely need to. The demonkin seem to believe this is because he doesn't trust anyone and doesn't want to take the chance of the information getting out."

"And what do you think?"

"I believe he is doing this because it is a lot easier to guard just his own thoughts. It would be too difficult, even impossible, to guard or block the thoughts of more than himself. If this is the case, he must believe there are still seers alive today. At the very least, he must suspect there may be, since he has taken pains to block our dream-visions. So, he would want to lower the chances of us finding out his plans in any way that he can."

The King, sitting back in his chair, nodded thoughtfully.

"There also seems to be an interesting rumor circulating the lower ranks of the elite demonkin army." Maelona continued, "They are saying the Dark Sorcerer has a back-up plan in case they cannot destroy the keystones. It hasn't come from official channels, though, so the demonkin I read are uncertain if there is any truth to the rumor. However, I have had inklings of this in visions as well, so we should be cautious and assume he does."

"And what does it mean for us if he does?" Andrion asked.

"It means we will have to defend the Great Gate, even if we are successful at the Gate towns," Maelona said. "He will still need to use it to get demons across from the demon realm. We should be cautious and thorough and assume he has come up with another way to access the power of the Source if the keystones remain intact."

"If he has another way, why is he even bothering to attack the Gate towns at all?" Hervi asked.

"If I were to put myself in the enemy's shoes," King Nele said, "I could see a couple of likely reasons. His back-up plan may be even more difficult to achieve or not as certain to work. But also, by attacking the Gate towns, there will be fewer human soldiers to stand against them at the Great Gate."

"Couldn't the same be said for his forces, though? He'll lose some of his own soldiers as well," Sephare said.

"If he opens the Great Gate and gets some demons across before we can stop him, he could replace those numbers quickly," Blaez said.

"He may be also cocky enough to assume he will come out on top either way," King Nele said.

"You may be right," Maelona said, "as I doubt anyone, including the Dark Sorcerer, will expect you to have Folk as backup."

"And seers," Andrion added.

"What else can you tell us?" the King asked.

"At this moment, I can tell you what I foresee to be the greatest chance for success, with minimal casualties. Just know that there are many players in this game. Events can always change from what we expect. So be prepared and don't take anything for granted."

She looked at each person and after they each nodded their understanding and agreement, Maelona continued by gesturing to the map once again. "We have to go out to meet them. If they get too close to the outer wall, the resulting chaos will make it too easy for an illusion-disguised demonkin to slip through and sneak its way to the keep."

"I doubt they would have any more luck getting in than our guests in the dungeon had," Captain Hervi said.

"That may be true," Maelona said, "but they got closer than I am comfortable with, and this Dark Sorcerer is cunning. We should take nothing for granted."

"Is their army made up mostly of demonkin?" Captain Thim asked.

"Yes," Maelona replied. "But from what I have seen, the Dark Sorcerer likes to keep his strongest followers close, sending out his armies made up of the weaker among the demonkin—those with less magical power—to be fodder for the battles at the four Gate towns. Some of these demonkin can project visions into the minds of humans to confuse, mislead, and torment their targets.

"He has also included a few demonkin who can change their appearance, such as your friend the false guard and your other three guests. They are to disguise themselves and attempt to sneak past undetected while we are distracted with the battle. Their sole aim is to locate and destroy the keystone."

Turning to the King, she said, "It will be essential for you to stay close to the keystone at all times, My Lord."

King Nele tipped his head forward and raised his eyebrows as he met her gaze. "Excuse me?"

The King set his jaw in a stubborn expression that Maelona recognized from earlier times; it was the same one he would get as a youth when he had set his mind on something.

"I am the King. I should be on the front lines with my soldiers," he said in a commanding tone.

"You are the Guardian of the Keystone," Maelona replied. "It is your place to be in the keep, close to the stone. You are our last line of defense should any slip past us."

"You are a Guardian as well," Nele retorted.

"Yes, but you and I both know that my particular skills and abilities would be of better use out there," Maelona answered, gesturing toward the window. "I can see past their illusions and, hopefully, stop any imposters from sneaking through."

The King pressed his lips together in a hard line and narrowed his eyes at Maelona. She hoped he would see that this was the best option—she did not want an argument or any ill feelings between them.

"Are you saying *my* skills are of no use out there?" King Nele said, his eyes still narrowed in her direction.

Maelona shook her head. "Of course I'm not." The man knew better than that. He was just being argumentative, so she ignored the question, hoping to deflect it with what she was going to say next.

"Sephare should be positioned at the keep with you. More than one demonkin may make it through."

"Wait. Wait a minute," Andrion interrupted. "Are you suggesting that my baby sister stand with my father at the keep, which is the primary target for these beasts?"

"Yes, of course. Why not?" Maelona asked with just a hint of a smile.

"Well, first, she's my baby sister. . ."

"I am not a child, Andrion!" Sephare interjected.

". . . and second," Andrion continued, as if Sephare hadn't even spoken, "she has only been in combat training for a year and a half. She is not ready."

Maelona looked at Sephare and back to Andrion, and smiled wider. "It is true, Andrion, that Sephare has only been training for a year and a half. However, you seem to forget that, in that time, she has been training for hours upon hours each day.

"Also, there is one other important thing that neither you nor your sister know," Maelona continued, looking at King Nele with a conspiratorial grin. "Sephare's trainer is a seer who has lived over seven hundred years, and he was my trainer. His name is Owyn

Axedrifter, father to a fellow seer champion, and the best fighter the seer people have seen in a millennium."

Sephare gaped and turned to face King Nele. "Father?"

"Yes, it is true," he said. "Just before you started your training, Owyn came to me. He explained who he was and that the seers knew there was a battle coming. He insisted you needed to be prepared."

"Just for the record," he added, smiling warmly at his daughter, "I agreed, and I am very proud of how hard you have worked and how exceptional you have become."

Sephare took her father's hand and returned his smile with one of her own.

Andrion just stared at them, mouth agape and seemingly at a loss for words.

Captain Thim spoke up, saying, "I thank you for the knowledge and advantages you have given us. Most of the people here at Eastgate and the surrounding lands would have never believed this kind of alliance would be possible. We all know the histories. We would have never believed you would stand with us after what our kind did to yours. I, personally, am grateful to you for this," he added, his sincerity clear in his voice, "and I know our people are as well."

"What most people do not know, Captain, is that each gate is always assigned two Guardians," Maelona explained. "The King of the gate town guards the keystone itself, and the second, always a seer, watches from the outside for any insidious dangers unseen to most. Therefore, it is my duty to be here for your people in times of danger."

"Well, duty or not, I thank you," Thim said with a nod to her.

"As do I," agreed the King. "Is there anything else we should know?"

"Yes. Their numbers are not great, as they don't expect you to have any backup. However, they have reinforcements on the way. They will arrive after the battle begins," Maelona said.

"What reinforcements?" Andrion asked suspiciously.

"Snowbeasts," Maelona replied.

The more seasoned in the group sucked in sharp breaths. Sephare and Andrion, however, who were the youngest of the group, just looked at each other in confusion.

"What is a snowbeast?" Sephare asked.

"Unpleasant," Maelona quipped.

Blaez smiled at her. She couldn't blame him for his amusement. She did not joke often. It made her feel a little uncomfortable.

"The main thing to remember about snowbeasts," Maelona continued, "is to not stay directly in front of them for long. They have an icy breath that can freeze a human solid in seconds. And from what I hear, they like to step on their victims afterwards, effectively shattering them."

"Okay. Stay away from snowbeasts," Andrion said, his mouth set in a grim line. "Noted."

After a silent pause, King Nele addressed the group with a soft voice full of unspoken concern for his family and his people. "It is late, and we will need our strength. I suggest we all turn in for the evening and begin preparations first thing in the morning."

"We will make sure our soldiers know what we are up against," Thim said. Nele gave a nod of approval.

Maelona was certain that they wished, as she did, that there was more time to prepare.

With some goodbyes and goodnights, they all shuffled out of the room and into their chambers. As tired as she was, however, Maelona doubted sleep would come easily tonight, knowing the enemy waited just over the ridge.

By early afternoon the next day, most of the defenses were in place and the Eastgate soldiers were working on setting up the offensive weaponry. Maelona stood on the allure of the outer wall, scanning the area for any sign she would recognize from her visions. It was sunny and dry, and a light breeze blew wisps of loose hair around her face. The only thing that obscured her view from here to the trees was the curve of the ridge in the mid-distance off to the north-west.

She had been standing there, virtually unmoving, for some time already when she heard Blaez approach.

"The preparations seem to be going well," he commented.

"Yes."

"Your brow is furrowed with worry, Maelona. Please share with me what's on your mind. Do we not have a good chance of standing up against the sorcerer's army?"

"We stand a chance of winning the day," she answered. "The trick is to keep the horde from breaching the castle while minimizing casualties."

"Is that what you are worried about? Our friends being wounded, or worse?"

Maelona kept her gaze focused unwaveringly on the ridge as she responded. "You know, I used to think it was a blessing that we seers cannot see our own futures, or the futures of those whose lives are, or will be, tightly entwined with our own. I always thought that it saved us from needlessly worrying or living our lives in fear of our visions coming to pass. I believed this kind of knowledge would lead us to turn our visions into self-fulfilling prophecies.

"But now," she continued, "Now I wish I could see. The most difficult part of opening up and allowing others in is the fear of losing those you love." She paused and turned to look at Blaez over her shoulder. "I fear for the safety of my friends, yes. But, most of all, I fear losing you."

Blaez moved behind Maelona, wrapping his arms around her as she returned her gaze forward. "You know," he said softly, his mouth close to her ear, "you seers are the only beings in the realm with this ability. I have learned from your mother that sorcerers have ways of discovering the future as well, but that what they see is not as clear. As for the rest of us, we live with uncertainty of the future every moment of every day."

He brushed his lips gently along her neck before continuing. "If we always worry about what horrors await us along life's path, we wouldn't be able to live in the present. We would be frozen. . . paralyzed. Do not let your worries paralyze you, Maelona. Trust that I can take care of myself."

Blaez stayed behind Maelona as she stood quietly, contemplating his words. He stayed there while the hours passed and she stood watch. He kept his arms wrapped around her, cocooning her with his warmth and support.

Maelona closed her eyes and attempted to imprint that feeling in her memory; she hoped more than anything that it would stay with her all throughout the coming battle.

CHAPTER TWENTY-FOUR

The Battle at Eastgate

It was mid-morning the next day when Maelona finally spotted the movement she'd been waiting for, just over the ridge in the distance.

"It's time," she said. Blaez, standing a dozen feet to her left, threw his head back and let out a howl as a sign to the other Wolf-folk. They wouldn't move in until the enemy was already on the field, but this was a signal to them to get ready.

As they descended from the allure, Maelona and Blaez were met at the foot of the steps by Andrion and King Nele.

"So, I see you can do more than growl like a wolf in your human form," Andrion said. "That was a pretty impressive howl. I made a sound like that once when a horse accidentally kicked me in the—"

"Do you not realize we are about to go into battle?" Blaez interrupted. "Are you never serious?"

"I try not to be."

Maelona shook her head at the two men. They clearly dealt with stressful situations in entirely different manners. But their banter helped her to relax some, so she would not complain.

The residents of the town of Eastgate, who had fled to safety at the castle, had been moved to the inner bailey in anticipation of today's battle. Now, the King turned to address his soldiers, who had gathered in the outer bailey.

King Nele was one man standing tall and regal before hundreds of his soldiers, but his voice boomed for all to hear.

"Mighty men and women of the Eastgate army, remember what you have been taught," he began. "Our enemies are not human, but demonkin. They are large and strong, but we are quick and smart. They fight for greed and power; we fight for freedom and peace. They fight to subjugate the people of Sterrenvar; we fight to protect them.

"When you are standing out there on the field of battle today, use your strengths and find the enemy's weaknesses. Keep yourselves moving, especially when the snowbeasts arrive. Do not make yourselves targets. Stay calm; do not let them into your heads. Believe what you know to be true. Also, do not lose heart when the beasts come. Remember, once the enemy is on the field, our backup will arrive."

Maelona understood her old friend, and she knew his brief speech was a reminder to them; a way to let them know that, though their enemies were formidable, they were not undefeatable. But most of all, she knew it was his understated way to show his concern for his people, while also showing his trust in them.

War had a way of bringing about the most complicated emotions.

However, King Nele's speech was also a reminder that they were not alone. The Wolf-folk and the three Eagle-folk who'd been sent would be waiting for their moment to attack.

Maelona had worried that it would be difficult to get the Folk and the humans to cooperate and trust in one another, given their volatile history. However, Nele's men seemed to trust in him and his judgement, and they did not question it when he told them they were now allies. She was quite impressed by Nele and what he had built here at Eastgate, and she sent a silent prayer out to the Universe that it would remain standing, if not unscathed, at the end of the coming battle.

A dozen archers ran by and up to the allure as Maelona, Blaez, and Andrion moved forward to join the two dozen men and women that made up the King's guard. Directly behind them stood two-hundred Eastgate soldiers. Another two dozen local men and women took position inside the gate of the outer bailey, ready to fight off any demonkin who might make it through.

When King Nele was satisfied that everyone was in place, he turned to look at Maelona. He did not need to say a word; she could see the struggle in his eyes.

"It is time for you to head to the keep," Maelona told him. "Sephare should be in position by now. Do you want her to stand guard over the enemy's primary target without support?"

The King shook his head, smiling wryly. "I don't remember you being this underhanded before."

"We've never had so much on the line before."

"Well, that is true," he said. "Fine, I will go. Send for me if you need me."

She squeezed his shoulder. "Trust in your captains and their men," she said. "They are loyal and well-trained."

King Nele looked to the right and nodded his head. Maelona followed his gaze with her own until it landed on Andrion. "Look out for him," the King said. "He is barely more than a boy."

"I don't think he'd appreciate that comment," she laughed, "but of course I will. Now, get going."

Finally, the King nodded and headed off, back inside the castle walls to take his place guarding the keep.

Maelona, Andrion, and captains Hervi and Thim positioned the men in ranks a few hundred meters out from the castle gate. Soon, the enemy forces became visible over the ridge, heading toward them at a steady pace. The Eastgate ranks held their places unwaveringly, hoping to draw the enemy within range of the archers. As if they'd expected this strategy, the demonkin stopped just past the estimated distance.

After a short stand-off, Maelona tried to goad them into attacking first. Through her visions, she had learned many things about the demonkin. For one, women weren't held in high regard, so she figured it had to irk the demonkin who seemed to be the leader that he was facing a woman right now. The way he glared at her seemed to support this theory.

She rotated her sword in her hand, then brought it in an arc above her head before slicing it diagonally through the air in front of her. She held the demonkin captain's gaze and gave him a mocking smile as she did so.

This was a quite blatant threat amongst their kind, and the demonkin captain was receiving it from a woman, no less! Raising his sword in the air, he roared with rage and charged forward, exactly as Maelona had hoped he would, with his troops following on his heels.

The army of Eastgate stood firm as the demonkin came barreling toward them. Once they were in range of the archers, Maelona raised her hand in the air. The row of foot soldiers kneeled with their shields lifted diagonally, bottoms touching the earth at their feet, and tops tilted over their heads to protect them. Then, she brought her arm forward, and the archers let loose a volley of arrows from the top of the outer wall.

The demonkin had a line of archers as well and let loose a volley of their own. The Eastgate soldiers were protected by their tight shield formation, so there was little in the way of damage to them.

On the other side, several demonkin—who seemed poorly armed and armored—dropped all around their captain, and yet he charged toward Maelona with a single-minded focus. After the arrows had passed overhead, the few soldiers with mounts who were lined up at the back took off, jumping over the line of soldiers crouched at the front and galloping toward the enemy with sword and pike at the ready. As soon as the horses were clear, the crouching soldiers stood and ran forward to meet the demonkin army, letting loose their wordless battle cries.

Maelona let out a menacing cry of her own as she charged forward to meet the enemy captain. She wanted to keep the beast off balance, so she ducked in and out amongst the enemy, taunting him with her presence and taking down the closest target before disappearing again.

Movement from the tree line across the field caught her attention, and she saw the wolves charge in from the rear. The demonkin didn't even notice they were there until Gawn's group of protectors had taken down a handful of enemy soldiers.

As she made her way forward, Maelona made sure to always be aware of where Blaez was, glancing over at him from time to time. He was a sight to behold. He would attack in wolf form, take down his target, change to human form as he leaped, roll to his feet, and grab a weapon as he did so. Maelona was glad to see that he took what she had taught him to heart with such exuberance.

At one point, Maelona and Blaez kept eye contact for too long. A demonkin rushed up behind him. He turned to the sound, but he didn't even have time to position himself to defend.

Maelona grabbed a throwing knife from the holster on her chest strap and threw it with force. The blade whizzed past Blaez's ear and planted itself right between the demonkin's eyes. Blaez turned back to look at her and she nodded to him before she turned to face another enemy.

She tried to scan the periphery as often as she could. After a time, she noticed huge, lumbering forms rising over the ridge.

"Brace yourselves!" she yelled. "The beasts are coming."

The people of Eastgate paused for just a second as three enormous beasts with matted white fur dulled by the elements came thundering toward them. They were dog-like in form, with longer legs in front than in back, which made them taller at the shoulder than at the rump. They were twice as tall as a human man and at least twice as long as a large horse, and they were an intimidating sight as they charged into the fray.

"Smelly demon turds!" Andrion suddenly exclaimed from just behind Maelona's right shoulder. "What are those?"

"Smelly demon turds?" Maelona asked, looking at him with her brow raised. "Did you just make that up?"

"Yes."

"Did you just blurt out the most ridiculous thing you could think of off the top of your head?"

"Maybe. Now, back to my original question. What *are* those things? They're. . . very, very big!"

"Those, my friend, are the snowbeasts I told you about," Maelona replied with a sinister smile. "And the earth will shake when they hit the ground." She spun her sword in her hand as she spoke.

"You really do enjoy fighting a little too much, don't you?" Andrion gave her a sideways glance, looking at her as if she were crazy.

"Go back and protect the castle gate, Andrion," she said, remembering the King's request. "You must not allow even a single demonkin to enter while we are distracted by the beasts."

Then she was no longer paying attention to him. "Move!" she bellowed as she ran forward to aid an Eastgate soldier who was now within range of the beast's ice breath. Without pausing in her run, Maelona whipped out a throwing knife, sending it unerringly into the side of the beast's neck. This did not slow the beast down, but its attention shifted off its intended target. It whipped its head in her direction, leaving a path of ice and frozen vegetation as it did so.

A piercing screech sounded from above and she looked up to see that the promised three Eagle-folk had arrived. They started dive-bombing the two snowbeasts at the rear, distracting them.

They targeted the eyes—an excellent strategy against these beasts, but she hoped they remembered to stay away from their mouths.

The snowbeast in the front was still advancing in her direction, getting perilously close to the Eastgate soldiers. Luckily, its icy breath didn't travel too far, but it was large and moved quickly for its size. Now, it was opening its mouth again, prepared to blast a group of Eastgate soldiers that was now attacking it.

Maelona swung her head left, then right, taking in the battle all around her. The soldiers of Eastgate were holding their own, as were Blaez, Gawn, and the other Wolf-folk protectors who had run into the fray once the snowbeasts appeared. However, the two other huge, menacing beasts were almost upon them. The Eagle-folk were slowing them down, but they stubbornly kept advancing. She knew they would not refrain from destroying her people even if there were demonkin among them.

Fortunately, some Wolf-folk were now close enough to hear Maelona as she called to them.

"Gawn! Ademar! Imyne!" When they looked in her direction, she pointed to the closest beast and yelled, "Get it to open its mouth!"

The wolves each gave one sharp nod and went running towards the snowbeast. *Fire! I need fire!* Maelona thought frantically, looking all around her as she ran. *If only it were nighttime and torches were lit.* Then, suddenly, she could feel a prickling of electricity under her skin, and she remembered what her mother had said to her about embracing who she was.

She tucked the dagger in her hand back into her belt and let go of her control completely, thinking; *I don't need fire; I am fire!* With this thought, her skin heated to such an intense degree that an approaching demonkin jolted back at the feel of it. Then, holding out her hand, palm up, Maelona focused some energy into the shape and size of a large stone. Only, instead of stone, it was made of bright green flames.

She turned to track where Gawn and Ademar were, and spotted Ademar's wolf approaching the closest snowbeast from the rear. He jumped up and latched his teeth onto the tendon of the beast's hind leg. The beast then did two things at once: it flicked back the paw Ademar was attached to, sending him flying, and it opened its mouth in a roar of pain.

Maelona quickly took advantage of this opening and threw her ball of fire as hard as she could. Her aim was true, and the fireball went straight into the beast's open maw. The snowbeast closed its mouth, its throat working as if it were swallowing, and then it let out another roar of pain. It crashed to the ground in a cloud of dust, its momentum carrying its now lifeless body forward a few lengths before finally stopping. It shook violently for a few moments, then stilled in death.

Once she was satisfied that it was no longer a threat, Maelona looked for Ademar to ensure he was okay. However, she had only gone a few steps before fast-approaching, pounding footfalls sounded from behind. She whipped around to face the second beast that was now charging at her. It had already opened its mouth to breathe its ice breath in her direction; with no time to think, she could only react. Her instincts took over, and she held her hands up in front of her, palms out, sending white-hot flames to meet the snowbeast's breath. She watched as the flames hit the ice only a couple of paces in front of her.

She concentrated on sending her power into the beast—to stop it dead in its tracks. Crackling channels of flashing, emerald-green electricity suddenly seemed to flow up through the ice and toward the beast. This electrical energy charged out in front of her fire, which chased the electricity up the icy path created by the beast's breath until they both entered the beast's body.

The creature did not just shudder and fall to the ground dead as the other one had. This time, when the electricity and fire entered the snowbeast's body, it exploded into the air, pieces of its flesh obliterating into ash as fragments fell back to the earth.

Before the smoke had even cleared from the exploding snowbeast, Maelona searched the scene again for the other one. Before she could locate it, however, the smoke did clear, and she saw a sight she had been praying would not come to pass.

It was not a dream-vision that she had received herself. No, she was too close to Blaez for that. Rather, it was information that had been passed along to her from Talwyn, her fellow seer champion, the last time she had Blaez guard her while she slept in the woods.

"No. No, no no no."

Blaez was engaged in a fight in human form, blocking blows from a demonkin's sword. While he focused on defending the onslaught from two demonkin, yet another figure moved up behind him. It was the demonkin captain who had glared at her across the field at the start of the battle.

Too far away to reach him in time, Maelona could do nothing but watch as the captain's blade pierced Blaez's back and jutted out through his abdomen.

The demonkin barely had time to remove its blade before Maelona was on top of it. It raised its small shield as she started pummeling it with the hilt of the dagger she'd pulled out again as she ran. She continued strike after strike after strike, her dagger upon his wooden shield, until it cracked and he finally fell to the ground, dropping the broken pieces in front of him.

The two other demonkin attempted to come to their captain's aid. But Maelona was so enraged that her power was radiating from her body. When the demonkin approached within a few feet of her, they screamed in agony before slowly dissolving into dust.

No one else dared approach her.

Maelona flipped the captain over onto its back, straddled its body, and continued her assault bare-handed until the demonkin was a bruised and bloodied mess laying in the dirt.

"Maelona!" Andrion was calling to her. The urgency in his voice snapped her out of her rage and she pulled back, panting. She looked at her bloodied hand, then wiped it on the demonkin captain's tunic before standing.

Then she turned and went to Blaez.

Andrion was already there tending to him, and upon her approach he looked up to meet her gaze. With watery eyes and sorrow clear on his face, he shook his head at her.

Maelona dropped to her knees next to Blaez and placed her hands on his bloodied abdomen. She felt as though she could hardly breathe through the agony that constricted her chest. She could not bear the thought of living her life without him.

Throwing back her head, she screamed wordlessly. The force of her sorrow and anguish was so strong that her magic exploded out of her body in a shockwave.

But this time, it was not like what had happened with her father and Guarin Stronghunter. This time, she could feel every single life force her magic touched. She could feel the light and the dark. And as her power surged outwards, she left all the light standing and obliterated all the dark.

Then, suddenly, her power was sucked back into her in a rush as she felt something unexpected.

She felt...hope. She felt a tiny flicker of life where she had thought there was none.

"He is still alive," she whispered. Then, louder, "He is still alive!" And she knew what she had to do.

She knew he was close to passing back into the Universe, and she didn't have much time. She needed to expose him inside and out. She placed one hand under Blaez's neck at the base of his skull and lifted, tilting his head until his mouth and throat opened. Moving her hand to his forehead, she placed her other hand on his wound and leaned down, covering his mouth with her own.

CHAPTER TWENTY-FIVE

The Prince's Fight

During the battle, while Maelona and Blaez were fighting at the frontline, Andrion had returned to the castle gate as Maelona had commanded. And he was glad he did.

A group of demonkin had broken through their defenses and reached the barbican. He rushed over to help the group of Eastgate soldiers who were fighting back five demonkin. As soon as he arrived, he engaged a stone-colored demonkin.

One of his Eastgate soldiers, Jodoca, even closer to the portcullis than he was, was engaged with both a stone-colored demonkin and a mottled-red colored demonkin. Andrion knew what this color difference signified, thanks to the information that Maelona had given them. He knew he needed to get over to Jodoca to help her. However, he had to take care of his own opponent before he could do that.

He fought sword to sword against his foe. The demonkin was lumbering and a little clumsy, but it was strong. Andrion knew from experience that if he let even one blow touch him, it could spell disaster. He deflected a blow by bringing his sword across to strike from the outside. He continued to push his opponent's sword across the front of its body until the demonkin was off balance. As the demonkin stumbled, it bent forward, allowing Andrion to see another demonkin running towards him.

Andrion swept his sword along the back of the thighs of the demonkin in front of him, effectively hamstringing him. When this first demonkin dropped to its knees, Andrion leaped onto its back and jumped into the air. He raised his sword above his head, blade pointed down, intending to skewer his new opponent swiftly so he could get to Jodoca. The demonkin reacted by aiming its sword up towards Andrion, who could do nothing but twist his now-airborne body to avoid his enemy's blade.

Andrion avoided being run through, but only just. The demonkin's blade grazed his side, but Andrion kept his focus through the sudden flare of pain. Though his strike wasn't as true as intended, he still drove his blade down through the side of his enemy's neck. As Andrion hit the ground hard, so did the now lifeless body of his opponent.

The breath had been knocked from Andrion's body when he hit the ground. He'd hardly had time to recover, however, when he noticed that his first, now crippled, opponent had grabbed a pike from a nearby corpse. The demonkin was trying to position its now uncooperative body so he could run Andrion through. Before it could, Andrion grabbed a dagger from his boot and threw it full-force at the demonkin, hitting it in the throat. The demonkin made disgusting gurgling noises until it finally lay still.

Andrion pulled himself up from the ground and looked over to where Jodoca had been standing. Her body now lay on the ground, along with the body of the gray demonkin. The mottled-red skinned demonkin was standing over Jodoca's body, pulling its blade from her chest. Andrion's own chest twisted and constricted with pain at the sight. He was too late. *I've failed her,* he thought.

Andrion had no time to dwell on his sorrow. As he watched, some sort of mist rose off the demonkin's body. As it got thicker, it wrapped around the demonkin's form. It changed color and solidified until Andrion was now looking at Jodoca's likeness. The demonkin then walked toward the barbican with a purposeful stride.

Andrion suddenly felt a white-hot rage rise inside of him. This beast who had just killed Jodoca, his father's loyal soldier, now dared to wear her likeness! He looked around for a weapon he could use. A couple of feet to his left, he spotted a demonkin corpse holding a bow. *Perfect.* Andrion hurried to the body, grabbed the bow and an arrow from the nearby quiver. He nocked the arrow, drew it back and aimed. Then he yelled, "Hey, ugly!" and let the arrow fly.

The demonkin, disguised as Jodoca, paused mid-stride and turned its head in Andrion's direction. Andrion watched as his arrow hit its mark, piercing the demonkin's left eye. The demonkin, still looking at Andrion with its one good eye, took a couple of steps forward. Then, its illusion flickered and died just before it dropped to the ground dead.

Andrion lowered his hands to his sides and stood for a moment in disbelief. He looked around himself at the three opponents he'd just taken down.

Oh… my… I can't believe I did that!

Andrion was considered an expert marksman in archery and knife-throwing in the training field, but he'd never had to use these skills in battle before today. He would have never thought that practice on a target, as extensive as his father had ensured it was, could translate to the stress of a battlefield. As he had gotten better and better, he had started working with moving targets. Sometimes he would be on horseback, targeting stationary objects. Sometimes the targets were mounted on horses. Sometimes, both he and his target would be mounted.

Still, as skilled as he had become, he had been told repeatedly that actual battle would be nothing like targeting inanimate objects. And really, it was not. He didn't know if it was skill or luck, but either way, he was grateful for his victories—for surviving—today.

Suddenly, he wondered if Maelona's father had put a protection spell on his amulet after all.

The area he stood in was now relatively quiet. Andrion shook himself from his reverie and turned to locate his friends. He turned just in time to see a snowbeast explode and incinerate right before his eyes. Maelona was standing close to this scene, and now she was scanning the area, looking for something.

Andrion's eyes traveled across the landscape to the right of her. Suddenly, his eyes stopped on Blaez, who was surrounded by demonkin. Andrion watched on as another demonkin crept up behind Blaez while he was distracted. Seeing what the demonkin intended to do, Andrion took off in their direction, yelling to both Blaez and Maelona as he went. They were far enough away that, with the sounds of battle going on between their positions, he doubted they could hear them.

But he had to try.

Andrion was crouched on the opposite side of Blaez from Maelona. He had seen his Wolf-folk friend run through and had watched on as sorrow and devastation washed over Maelona's features. He had felt her anguish as her magic passed through him.

Yet now, somehow, she emanated hope.

At first, as Maelona leaned down and put her lips on Blaez, Andrion thought she was kissing him in a last farewell of sorts. When he noticed a pale, iridescent green glow coming from underneath Maelona's hand and then from around their joined mouths, he realized what she was doing.

With the hand that was touching his wound, Maelona was attempting to heal Blaez's external wound, while at the same time trying to heal him from the inside by breathing her magic into him. Andrion had seen her cure Dafydd and his father, but was she powerful enough to bring someone back from the very brink of death?

Mere moments later, he sucked in an amazed breath as Blaez's eyelids fluttered. Soon, his friend opened his eyes and whispered, "Maelona."

Maelona looked down at Blaez and burst into tears. She leaned down to give him another gentle kiss before she dropped her head to his chest and quietly sobbed.

Overcome with relief, Andrion flopped back from his crouch to sit on the ground. Elbow on his bent knee, he dropped his head to his forearm and took a deep breath. Oh, thank the Universe.

Even though he understood what had happened and that there was magic involved, he couldn't help but feel that he had just witnessed the impossible, and he was awed. Above all else, he was grateful for fate bringing these two people into his life, and for sparing their lives this day.

When he first met Maelona and as he had gotten to know her, Andrion had hoped there could be more between them. Yet, he was not disappointed at how things turned out. He saw the deep connection that Maelona and Blaez shared, and he saw the enduring friendship between Maelona and his own father had—and he understood the difference. He had become fond of Maelona and, yes, even Blaez, in the short time they'd known each other. He hoped they would all remain lifelong friends, as Maelona and his father had.

Once Maelona had calmed considerably, Andrion stood and offered her his hand. "Come, Maelona," he said. "Let's go find our friend here a pleasant room with a soft bed and start a fire for him." Maelona reached up to take his hand, giving him a grateful smile. As she stood, Andrion glanced up, and then he froze.

All around them, over the entire field of battle, every last one of the demonkin was gone. Only scorched, black earth remained to mark where they once had stood. Yet most of Eastgate's soldiers were still standing.

"Umm, maybe you should have done that at the *beginning* of the battle," Andrion said when Maelona turned to see what he was looking at.

"I didn't know I *could* do that at the beginning of the battle," she returned with a small smile, leaning heavily against him.

"Come on, let's get you both inside. You deserve a nice, long rest."

CHAPTER TWENTY-SIX

The Aftermath

Blaez awoke slowly, looking up at the wood-beamed stone ceiling of his assigned room in the castle. He turned his head to the side and looked around. The bed chamber he was in was nicely appointed, with wall tapestries and a hearth where a low fire burned. Judging by the angle of the sunlight that filtered in through the window, it was around midday.

He was surprised to find himself alone. The night before, had awoken in the dark, only to find Maelona sleeping next to him, clinging to him like she would never let go. The feel of her in his arms and her familiar scent were comforting enough that he immediately fell asleep again. The very memory warmed him inside and made him smile. But where was she now?

Just then, the door creaked open and Maelona entered, carrying a tray of food.

"You're awake," she said, smiling. "I brought you some lunch. You need to keep up your strength so you can fully recuperate."

"Thank you, my heart," Blaez said, sitting up slowly and carefully and taking the tray from her. He noticed her hands were shaking a little.

"What about you, Maelona? How are you?"

She smiled warmly, but it didn't cover the signs of fatigue clear on her face. She still had dark smudges under her eyes and her eyelids drooped a little. Just the fact that she wasn't using her inner-sight to cover it up spoke to how she was feeling.

"I'm fine. Just tired. I'll be back to normal with a little more rest, so don't worry about me. Just worry about getting well. It was you who almost died." She nodded to his plate. "Eat something."

He took a bite of meat and nearly groaned at how good it was. He hadn't realized how hungry he was.

"I'm sorry I had to leave you this morning." She sat on the bed beside his legs and put a hand on his knee. "I had to check on things."

"Will you give me an update?" he asked.

"Well," she began slowly, "when I thought you were—"

Maelona's voice cracked, and she took a deep breath. When she spoke again, her voice was tight. "I thought the demonkin captain

had killed you," she said, shuddering. "My magic responded similarly to the way it had at the Crater of Sorrows. Except, this time, I could distinguish the dark souls from the light, and only the dark ones were destroyed. All the demonkin were destroyed, save one."

Puzzled, he tipped his head to the side and looked at her. "Really? One survived? Why do you think that is?"

Her lips came together in a tight line and her brow furrowed. "I remember what happened, and what I felt. If it was passed over, that could only mean there is more light in it than darkness."

"Is that possible?"

"Do you remember what my mother said about how there are always exceptions, how there are always those who defy the nature of their kind?"

"I do," Blaez replied, nodding.

"Well, it seems we've found one of those exceptions." She gave him a small smile. "The King's Guard insisted on placing it in the dungeon until we know for sure where it stands. But, if it doesn't have evil intentions like the rest of the demonkin troops, then why it is here? How is it different from the others? I am going to speak with it a little later."

"I'm going with you," Blaez said.

"Oh no, you are not!" Maelona replied. "I could repair some of the sword's damage with my magic, but not all. You still need to rest and recover."

"You are not going to go talk to a demonkin alone, are you?" The thought of her in a small space with a rogue demonkin and no other support made his muscles tense. It may have survived when its evil brethren had perished, but Blaez was not about to trust the creature based on that alone. What's to say it didn't have a change of heart when it saw all its fellow demonkin soldiers perish around him?

"It is imprisoned. Chained to the wall. The guards are not taking any chances. However, I will take Andrion with me if it helps you relax some."

"I appreciate that," Blaez said. "However, I hope you will consider waiting a day or two until I am strong enough to accompany you. If our situations were reversed, would you want me to go into such a situation without you?"

Maelona smiled, shook her head, and scooted forward until she was close enough to place a gentle kiss on his lips. "Okay. I will give your request some consideration."

"Thank you," Blaez said. "What other news do you have to report?"

"Ademar was injured when a snowbeast threw him. He was stunned momentarily, and while he was down, a demonkin approached him with its sword raised, intending to finish him. . ."

"No!" Blaez breathed, anticipating what she would say next.

But Maelona shook her head. "Ademar was not killed. Droyn saved him."

"Droyn?"

"Yes," she nodded, but her expression was solemn, and he was hit with a sense of dread.

"When Droyn saw Ademar was down and in danger of being killed, he charged at the demonkin. The demonkin was startled and turned toward Droyn with its weapon raised." There was a quiver in her voice when she added, "It struck him straight through the heart."

"No! Droyn. . . he was so young!" Blaez raised a hand to his chest, pressing in to ease the sudden pain.

"He was a hero, Blaez," Maelona replied. Her voice was low, but firm. "Yes, the demonkin sealed Droyn's fate, but Droyn ripped its throat out on his way down. Droyn fell as a hero, Blaez. He saved Ademar's life, and he fought until his very last breath."

Blaez dropped his head to his chest and sent up a silent prayer for the safe passage of the young protector's soul. Awash in sorrow, he needed a moment before he could speak.

"Who else?" he asked.

"Renny was seriously injured," she said, referring to the young female protector. "She was brought to one of Eastgate's healers.

"The King lost three of his soldiers, and Thim was also seriously injured. He was treated by the healers and is doing much better now."

"I am glad to hear he will be okay."

"There were many other injuries as well," she added, "but nothing else life-threatening. Overall, we were extremely lucky."

Blaez took Maelona by the hands, then dipped his head to encourage her to meet his gaze. "And how about you, my heart? How are you feeling about everything that happened? I know you hate to take lives—"

"It's true," she interrupted, "that I hate to take life unnecessarily. And, believe me, I've thought about what happened a lot, analyzing what I felt. But in this case, I felt their life forces before they died. There was no remorse in them and, for most of them, if they had lived, they might have killed many more innocent people."

"I'm guessing," Blaez said as he stroked the back of her hands soothingly with his thumbs, "that you are having some trouble coming to terms with all this death, anyway."

With a small, sad smile, she responded, "You know me well. I hate knowing that I am capable of such destruction. No one being should hold that kind of power."

Blaez wanted to remind her she was capable of great healing as well. He wanted to tell her that the universe gifted her with this power for a reason. However, she changed the subject, and he lost his chance.

"There is one more thing, but I am not yet sure what to make of it," she said. "It was Andrion who went deep into the keep to inform Sephare and the King that the battle was over. They apparently had seen no sign of demonkin or any other sort of trouble while they were down there during the battle."

"Well, that is a positive thing, is it not?" Blaez inquired.

"Yes, of course it is," Maelona agreed. "But this morning I awoke early to this nagging sense of worry. I couldn't shake the feeling that something was wrong. So, I went down to the keep to check on the keystone." She stared ahead, and Blaez was sure that whatever she was seeing was not in this room.

"When I placed my hand on the stone, I was flooded with feelings: fear, anger, pain. At the same time, I was hit with many random, disjointed images, and I am sure none of these were my own."

"What kind of images?" he asked.

"Honestly, I'm not sure. I think there was a flash of someone digging in the ground. And there was some kind of transparent box. Then there were all of those emotions."

"Was it a vision?"

"I think so, but I've never had a vision while I was fully awake before."

Blaez considered that for a moment. "Back at the meeting with the Elders before we left my village, you said something about the keystones stemming the flow of magic from the source, did you not?"

Maelona's eyes lit up. "Of course! You're right. Each keystone has a direct link to the source by ley line, and it's at the keystones that the magical power is regulated. Maybe I was linked to someone else who was touching a keystone or a ley line. If so, it was not anyone I know. Or it may be possible that I was given enough of a boost of power to have a waking vision."

"Do you have any idea what it was about?"

"I've been thinking about that. Since it is linked to the keystone, I suspect it might have something to do with the Dark Sorcerer's 'Plan B' that we learned about."

"Okay," Blaez said slowly, pondering her words. "That adds another, unknown complication to the mix. But I think all we can do at this point is to hope that the other seer guardians were successful in protecting their keystones, as we were here. I suggest we continue with the plan as discussed; we march on to the Great Gate, meeting the other seers and animal-folk there as intended. But we also plan for the possibility that the Dark Sorcerer and his followers will wait there for us with some unpleasant surprise."

Maelona nodded. "I do not see any other choice."

They remained lost in thought for a few more moments before Maelona spoke again.

"There will be a ceremony on the field of battle tonight at dusk to honor the fallen." Her voice had cracked on those last words, and she pressed a hand to her chest. "Do you feel strong enough to attend?"

"I would attend even if I had to crawl there," Blaez responded. "However, thanks to you, that won't be necessary. I am feeling much better than I should, considering I was almost dead yesterday afternoon. I am lucky I can attend as one of the living." He squeezed her hand gently.

Maelona looked down at their entwined fingers. In a quiet voice, with just a bit of a waver, she admitted, "I was so scared, Blaez. I thought I had lost you."

"I am here, my heart. Thanks to you. And I promise to do my best to be here for you for as long as the Universe allows."

The evening sun was low, almost touching the horizon, when Maelona walked out onto the field in front of the castle with Blaez at her side. They watched as several Eastgate citizens and soldiers worked together to put the finishing touches on the wooden structures built for the funeral fires. Soon after the pyres were complete, the bodies of the fallen—wrapped in fine cloth that was painstakingly decorated with messages of love and respect—were brought out and placed on top.

This sunset, which painted the sky in a beautiful array of pinks and fiery oranges, was a fitting backdrop for a last farewell.

As the sun continued to set and the sky grew darker, Maelona and Blaez were joined by the Wolf-folk protectors who had aided in the Battle of Eastgate. The humans had been trickling out slowly, but a large group of them arrived together once it was dark enough to light the fires. Many of them greeted the Folk who had come to their aid and gave the Wolf-folk their condolences for their lost brother.

Maelona looked around and realized that most, if not all, Eastgate citizens had come out to pay their respects.

King Nele, Maelona, Blaez, Gawn, Andrion, and Sephare lined up in a row. Hervi handed them unlit torches and kept one for himself. The King lit his first, then touched his flame to Maelona's torch. They did this down the line until they were all alight, then they went to their preassigned places around the pyres to wait for the signal from the King.

The King nodded to Maelona and, holding her torch low in front of her, she sang an ancient seer prayer-song that was still sung to this day for departed loved ones. No other in the group understood the ancient language, but Maelona hoped they could feel the sentiments of love, loss, and surrender.

These brave souls were now giving themselves over, sending their energy out into the Universe. The seers saw death as a time of loss for the loved ones left behind, but also as a time of celebration for the departed as they moved on to serve a greater purpose. And this was what the prayer-song was all about.

Once Maelona's song ended, Gawn, as first in command of the Wolf-folk protectors, sang a Wolf-folk prayer-song. The other Wolf-folk present, including Maelona, joined in as he sang:

> Every evening as the moon shines bright,
> Breaking its way through the dark of the night,
> We will sound our sorrow and remembrance.

> Every morning as the sun rises high,
> Bringing its warmth and its light to the sky,

We remember, the Universe holds your essence.

We are not alone; your spirit is always near,
Touching us all though we remain here:
Your people celebrate your transcendence.

Following the prayer-songs, all those present stood in complete silence, showing their respect to their departed loved-ones. After a few moments, the King turned to address the crowd.

"According to custom, once the pyres are lit, we will spend the next day in silence in memory of our fallen. Before we do that, though, I have some things to say.

"Friends and family," he began, gesturing around him. "Brave Droyn of the Wolf-folk, and valiant Varden, Jodoca, and Tobyn of Eastgate all believed that our freedom was important enough to fight for. To die for. They understood that by failing to act now, we increase the chance of losing our freedom, our future, to the forces who wish to subjugate us.

"With all their hearts and souls, these brave men and women believed in the righteousness and justice of our cause. They were determined to not stand by and become victims. They chose instead to be heroes, doing whatever they had in their power to do to stand against our foes.

"Do not doubt for a moment, my people, that the battle we saw here was only the beginning. We have won the day, but the largest battle is yet to be fought. Will we remain here at Eastgate and allow others to fight a war that will ultimately decide the fate of Sterrenvar and all who live in it? I think not."

Maelona wished there was some way to show them what she had seen in visions. No one could doubt the importance of stopping the Dark Sorcerer after seeing them.

"Maelona Mistreaver, the Wolf-folk protectors here in our presence today, and my son and daughter will leave Eastgate a few days from now to march toward the Great Gate. They will be met there by seer champions, Folk warriors representing the various clans, and human warriors from the other gate towns and beyond. I must stay here with several Royal Guard to keep watch over our keystone until the last possible moment. It is my purpose and my responsibility to do so, even as I hope to join you on the fields of battle."

"I ask that every soldier willing to fight—everyone who values our realm and our way of life—meet in the outer bailey at sunrise the day after tomorrow once our Day of Silence is over. I ask that you plan and prepare for the coming fight. I ask that you march to the Great Gate with the intention of winning the day. I ask—no, I beg—for you to fight for our freedom and our future."

Many people shouted their support from within the crowd of people. Many others stayed silent but nodded their heads.

If they left the day after tomorrow, if they didn't run into too many demonkin causing trouble on the way, they should get to the Great Gate with plenty of time to set up a perimeter of defense around the Great Gate. There were still almost four moon-cycles until the Great Alignment, after all.

"I ask you, my people, to fight valiantly, with all your hearts and souls," he said, lifting his hand to cover his heart, "never once allowing yourself to forget what is on the line."

Pausing in his speech to turn and look at the pyres, he added, "I ask you, my friends, to fight as Droyn, Varden, Jodoca, and Tobyn have done. We cannot let their sacrifices be in vain. We WILL not let the darkness swallow the light!"

With this last, he touched his torch to the nearest wooden structure and Maelona and their fellow torch holders did the same. All the people stood watch as funeral pyres went up in flame and the bodies of their friends turned to ash and were carried on the wind back into the universe.

CHAPTER TWENTY-SEVEN

The Ternias

Maelona's hands shook as she entered Blaez's room in the castle around suppertime the night before their planned departure. She found him sitting in a large, upholstered chair in front of the small fireplace.

The day of silence began with the lighting of the pyres the previous evening, so the time of quiet reflection and thanks had only just passed. She'd waited until now to execute her plan so they could talk properly.

Right after the funeral ceremony, Maelona had insisted that Blaez spend more time resting in order to heal from his wounds before they left so that the stress of travel would not worsen his condition. She'd regularly been giving him crimsonleaf tea to help speed his recovery, and she hoped it was enough, because she doubted there'd be any way to convince him to stay behind. Just like Andrion had had no hope of convincing her to stay behind to heal longer when he'd tried. She'd made crimsonleaf tea for herself every time she made it for Blaez in order to make the Price feel a little better about it.

Tonight, Blaez appeared deep in thought, watching the embers flicker in the fire. He was so engrossed that he did not turn to look at her until the door thudded shut behind her.

Her heart beat faster than normal and her hands shook slightly as he focused his attention on her while she walked toward him. Would he see the items she carried and figure out her plan before she could explain it to him?

He watched her still as she placed the tray on the table next to the bed before coming over to stand close to him by the fireside.

Before she spoke, however, Blaez looked up at her, catching her gaze as he stood.

"Why must it be you to carry the Ternias to the Great Gate?" he blurted. "Is there no one else who could take on that task? Carrying it will make you a target for the Dark Sorcerer."

"We don't know if he is even aware of its existence."

"I think we should work on the assumption that he does."

"And who else would you have take my place, Blaez?" she asked softly, patiently. "Whose life should I place below my own?"

"Mine!" he answered vehemently. "I will carry it for you! I just—I cannot bear the thought of anything happening to you."

Maelona smiled sadly at Blaez before taking him by the hand. "Come," she said, leading him over to the tray she had brought in.

As upset as he was, it took Blaez a moment to focus on the items on the table before him, and when he did, his eyes went wide, and she knew he recognized them.

From a very young age, every Wolf-folk in their village was tasked with creating a mark, a symbol that would represent them. She'd remembered how important it was to them when she'd watched the young ones working on them back in Wildegrove. For most, much trial and error and many revisions occurred before they finally created a mark that they felt truly represented themselves.

They practiced making their mark, over and over again, until they got it just right. They used animal skins to practice placing their marks on, using items such as the ones Maelona had laid out on the tray: several small bowls with different dyes made from plants and insects; a couple of different sizes of hollow needles made of metal or bone to pick up and place the dyes; and a very strong and pure alcohol to cleanse the skin and needles with.

Sometimes Wolf-folk used their marks as a kind of signature. Sometimes they scratched it on stones or in the bark of trees to mark territory or to announce that they had passed by. But there was one main, very important reason Wolf-folk young were taught how to do this and made to practice it until they had it just right; they would one day permanently ink their mark on their chosen mate as a sign of their love and respect for one another, and of the partnership they were entering, for life.

Blaez's gaze met Maelona's for a moment before he looked down at her clothing. His eyes went wide briefly and then started to glisten.

Instead of wearing the practical leather clothes of a warrior that she was used to wearing, she now wore a long flowing green robe—the robe of the mating ceremony. She had never actually seen one before since Folk mating ceremonies were always just between the lovers. But, as with the mark, they were taught all about it as children.

When Blaez had been injured and unconscious, but recovering, Maelona had gone to Sephare to tell her about her idea, and to ask where she could find the proper materials. Sephare had offered the use of her seamstress as well, but Maelona wanted to make the robe herself, given the meaning and significance of this ceremony. The hardest part was remembering all the details from the few drawings she had seen as a child, but she was fairly certain she'd gotten it right.

Blaez looked into Maelona's eyes, his gaze searching her own.

"Before you say anything or give your answer," she said, "I have some things to say, and something important to tell you."

He nodded once, slowly. She could tell he was trying his best to stay calm. His eyes looked red and glassy and, when she reached down to take his hand, it was clenched into a fist, likely to keep it from shaking. She hoped this was a good reaction, but she would know for certain soon. She took a deep breath.

"I was drawn to you from the very start, Blaez, as much as I tried to deny it. I have never felt the desire to open up to someone so quickly. It soon became clear to me I would not be able to hold you at a distance, as I do with everyone else. I tried hard, though, because I knew the nature of the threat coming our way and I feared for the future. What would it mean, for example, if I failed to learn to control my power? How would I feel if I let you in and something happened to you, or if I accidentally hurt you? Would it make me lose control if it did? Most importantly, how would you feel if something were to happen to me?"

Blaez opened his mouth to respond, but Maelona held up her hand to stop him. "Please, let me finish everything I have to say first."

"Okay. Please go on."

"Even after I realized I was fighting a losing battle by trying to keep some distance between us," she continued, "I feared giving in completely, because of the things I know and what they could mean for my future. But after almost losing you," she said, swallowing back her emotion, "I realized something.

"I realized that none of us knows for certain what the future will bring. And, as you yourself have pointed out to me, we can't let our fears keep us from living in the present. In that moment, when I thought you were gone from me forever, I was in anguish. I mourned the time and the closeness we lost because of my worries and fears. And then when I realized you were still living, I vowed to myself that I would open up to you and place my feelings fully before you. I vowed I would tell you the one thing that makes me most worry about the future. I promised myself that I would put it all out there and let you decide."

"Please, Maelona," Blaez begged, "please tell me what this thing is that you think would make me turn away from my feelings for you."

Maelona looked down at her feet and swallowed nervously. Then she took a deep breath, gathered her courage, and lifted her head to look Blaez in the eye.

"The reason no one else can be given my task—the reason it must be me—is that I am. . ." Maelona hesitated for a moment. "I am fated for this, Blaez. Sorceress Dimia, who foresaw what is happening right now, who foresaw the Ternias. . . she foresaw my birth. She foresaw my role in this part of our history. I worry about our future together, Blaez, because I know I am meant to stop the evil forces at the Great Gate, but I do not know if I am meant to survive it."

"That's why you should let me carry The Ternias. You are more valuable than I am."

"No, you don't understand." She sighed. "I'm sorry for not telling you this more clearly and directly before. I just couldn't bear to say the words. But Blaez, I am not just carrying the Ternias. I am the Ternias."

Blaez froze. He stared at Maelona with wide, unblinking eyes, but she doubted he was aware of anything outside of what she had just told him. She stood there quietly, expectantly, anxiously awaiting his response.

Finally, his stiff posture loosened, and he grabbed both of Maelona's hands. He said, "Since we never know how much time we have, let's not waste one more moment of it."

With that, he removed his vest and headed to the bed, where he propped up some pillows so he could sit semi-reclined against the wall.

Maelona pulled the table close so she could reach what she needed as she worked, then she climbed onto the bed and kneeled, straddling his thighs with her own. Her heart sped up, and his body trembled beneath her.

She prepared a needle with ink and brought it close to his chest, but she paused before making contact.

"Are you sure, Blaez? This is permanent, and I do not want you to regret this decision, ever."

Blaez wrapped his warm hand around hers—the one that held the needle. Looking deep into her eyes, he gently pressed her hand down until she felt the tip of the needle make contact with his skin.

"I am certain, my heart. There is nothing I wish for more than to be yours."

She smiled at him and blinked back tears. It wouldn't do to mark someone permanently when your eyes were hazy, so she took a breath and waited for the urge to cry to pass. Once she felt calmer, she leaned forward again and began to work.

She inked her mark slowly and painstakingly, taking her time as she lovingly placed it on the left side of his chest, close to his heart.

When she was done, Blaez picked her up and turned her over so that he was now above her. His fingers lightly brushed her skin as he lowered the top of her robe just enough to work, sending a shiver down her spine. Just as Maelona had done, he took his time as he carefully placed his mark on her, leaving her with an overwhelming sense of joy and pride once it was complete.

These marks in ink upon their skin might fade over their long lifetimes, but they would never fully disappear, and they would remain forever etched on their hearts.

Maelona gently guided Blaez up and back as she rose to her knees to face him on the bed. Their bodies pressed close together, leaving only enough space between them for her to place her hand over her mark on his chest, and he on hers, before then reciting the simple words that were customary for a Wolf-folk mating.

"I am yours," Maelona said,

"And I am yours," Blaez returned.

And then, just a breath before their lips came together in a passionate, loving kiss filled with promises of things to come, they recited the final words together.

"We shall never be alone."

Next in the A Trial of Kingdoms Series

A Tribe of Dragons and Dreamers: A Trial of Kingdoms Book 2

She's a seer with trust issues. But her terrifying visions will force her to put faith in a fearless creature.

Talwyn would rather be lonely than endure another tragic loss. With disturbing visions of a dark legion closing in, the Seer fears any friendship is doomed to end in heartbreak. But unless she can persuade a reclusive tribe of dragon shifters to help her safeguard the magical power source, there might not be anyone left to love...

Hoping to win over one of their winged leaders, Talwyn joins his guard in fending off demon raiders from their mountain fortress. But despite a growing bond with the handsome dragon shifter, she fears she'll have to step onto a hopeless battlefield alone.

Can Talwyn secure the dragons' aid before a ruthless warmonger enslaves her realm?

A Tribe of Dragons and Dreamers is the second book in the gripping *A Trial of Kingdoms* epic fantasy series. If you like fearless warriors, breathtaking landscapes, and impossible odds, then you'll love Sherry Leclerc's captivating tale.

Read *A Tribe of Dragons and Dreamers* to join the front lines of a supernatural battle today!

Glossary of Terminology

Aragus: One of the two planets that line up with the moon at intervals to cause The Great Alignment

Azedel: An evil and powerful sorcerer who discovered how to use the power at the hub of the ley lines to create a magical gate that would allow demons from another realm to pass over into the realm of Sterrenvar

Axes: Points where two ley lines join, resulting in increased magical power

Chephus: One of the two planets that line up with the moon at intervals to cause The Great Alignment

Crimsonleaf leaf: Healing leaf

Crimsonleaf tree: A very tall tree with green leaves over most of the foliage and capped with dark red leaves at the top. All its leaves have healing properties, but the red ones are more potent.

Dragonburn Mountains: A mountain range to the south of the Sacred Forest and outside of the magical ley lines

Demonkin: Descendants of demons that bred with humans who lived to the north of the realm

Demons: Evil beings originally from another realm that were brought through the Great Gate by Azedel to help form his army and subjugate the land

Dream-visions: True visions of the past or present, and true or possible visions of the future that the seers receive as they sleep, when their minds are most open to the messages of the universe

Sacred Forest: A large, dense forest range found within the magical ley lines at the center of the realm of Sterrenvar, and home to most of the magical races of Sterrenvar.

Galanite: A very strong and light metal found beneath the Dragonburn Mountains; very useful for fabricating armor and weaponry

Gates (Gate Towns): Eastgate, Westgate, Southgate, Northgate were fortresses built atop the keystones to protect them. They eventually developed into castle towns.

Great Gate: The gate formed from magically imbued, large, rectangular, and upright stones placed in a circular pattern (similar to Stonehenge) on top of the hub of the ley lines. This gate stabilizes the power at the hub, allowing a portal to be opened between realms, but can only be used during the Great Alignment. Azedel created the Great Gate with the intention of freeing demons to cross over and form his army, which he would then use to subjugate the realm of Sterrenvar and all its people.

Guardians: Those assigned the responsibility of protecting the realm and/or the keystones

Hub: The center of the diamond shape of the ley lines at which point more lines from the four axes join to result in markedly increased magical power (see also, The Source)

Inner-sight: The ability to see into one's physical self and manipulate the elements present there in order to heal or change appearance

Keystone: One of four stones imbued with magical properties meant to act as a deterrent and obstacle to anyone hoping to misuse the power of the ley lines. The keystones are intended to have a dampening effect on the amount of magical power flowing to the hub and, therefore, the Great Gate.

Ley lines: Invisible lines of magic that join at four points (axes), forming roughly the shape of a diamond. More of these lines travel from the axes to the center (the hub).

Protectors: Those assigned the responsibility of protecting their villages, towns, and people

Seers: A race of people of the realm of Sterrenvar who have the gift of Sight, with images of the past, present, and future coming to them in dream-visions. They are also capable of seeing into their own physical selves, an ability referred to as inner-sight.

Sight: (capitalized) The ability to receive images of the past, present, or future during dream-visions

Seer champions: Seer warriors trained with the possibility of eventually becoming guardians of the four Gates and their keystones. Until that time, the provide support for the guardians when needed.

Folk: Beings that can shift between human and animal form at will. More human than animal, their spirits and physical forms contain elements of both. They share a strong kinship with the true animal they share form with.

Snowbeast: A large animal that lives mostly in the northern mountain range of Sterrenvar called the Pilcier Peaks. It has matted white fur, and is similar in shape to a hyena, with its front legs slightly longer than the back, thus making the shoulders taller than the rump. On an average snowbeast, its body is as broad as a human male laying horizontal and it is twice as tall as the average human male. The snowbeast has an icy breath that can freeze a man solid in seconds. Rumor has it that they have been known to stomp their victims after freezing them, thereby shattering them.

Sterrenvar: The name of the realm in which this story is set

Thanks for Reading!

I hope you enjoyed
A Realm of Seers and Shifters.

If you would be kind enough to leave a review
on Amazon or wherever you purchased the book,
it would help make a big difference to how this
book is represented in the algorithms. The better
represented it is, the easier it will be for other readers
to find it.

A huge thank you in advance!

Also By Sherry Leclerc

A Trial of Kingdoms:

A Realm of Seers and Shifters (Book 1)

Demons and Damsels (Book 1.5 - *A Trial of Kingdoms* novelette)

A Tribe of Dragons and Dreamers (Book 2) July 2023

Book 3 TBA

Book 4 TBA

The Guardians of Sterrenvar (*A Trial of Kingdoms* short story

collection) - **FREE to newsletter subscribers**

Dragon Flightmasters:

Shendahli (Book 1) September 2023

Ori (Book 2) TBA

Rixtan (Book 3) TBA

Rafe (Book 4) TBA

About the Author

Sherry Leclerc is a Fictionary certified StoryCoach editor, Fictionary content creator, certified copyeditor, educator, and independent author of fantasy and sci-fi books. She also writes sci-fi romance under a pen name and has planned a series of nonfiction books with helpful information on writing and editing.

She is the owner/operator of Ternias Publishing & Editorial Services, through which she offers various editorial services and writing and publishing advice. She also has a YouTube vlog focused on providing information on writing, editing, and author tools and resources to new and aspiring writers.

Sherry happily resides in a chaotic household in Sydney, Nova Scotia with her husband, two sons, dog, cat, and two birds.

If you wish to keep up to date on new releases, promotions, and giveaways, please subscribe to my newsletter by checking out the sign-up form on my website.

You Can Reach the Author at:

Website: https://sherryleclerc.com/

Facebook: https://www.facebook.com/SherryLeclercAuthor/

Twitter:

https://twitter.com/sleclercauthor

Instagram:

https://www.instagram.com/sherryleclercauthor/

TikTok: https://www.tiktok.com/@sherryleclercauthor